SMOKE
AND
EMBERS

Also by John Lawton

SMOKE
AND
EMBERS

AN INSPECTOR TROY NOVEL

JOHN
LAWTON

Atlantic Monthly Press
New York

FIRST EDITION

Published simultaneously in Canada
Printed in the United States of America

This book was set in 11.25-pt. Warnock Pro by Alpha Design & Composition of Pittsfield, NH.

First Grove Atlantic hardcover edition: May 2025

Library of Congress Cataloging-in-Publication data is available for this title.

ISBN 978-0-8021-6489-6
eISBN 978-0-8021-6490-2

Atlantic Monthly Press
an imprint of Grove Atlantic
154 West 14th Street
New York, NY 10011

Distributed by Publishers Group West

groveatlantic.com

25 26 27 28   10 9 8 7 6 5 4 3 2 1

for

Sue Freathy

Disguise is the face we wear. There is no such thing as natural anymore. Everything is a disguise. The point is . . . is the disguise to restrict or pursue freedom? *Larvatus prodeo.*

Jerzy Kosinski, 1989

One must always avoid being a nobody.

Primo Levi, *The Truce*, 1963

§

Prologue

Do you often have the dream? Or should I ask, do you ever have the dream? The one in which you are you, you as you are now, but the house is not the one you live in, the room is not the one you live in, but the one before and the one before that and the one before that and so on, until the infinity of infancy is reached and the room becomes the world, the only one you have ever known—a regression scarcely short of the womb.

If there is a guardian angel of our dreams then that angel knows that Fabian had that dream, von Niegutt too—not at the same time, of course, but it was the same dream. Two men, much the same age, half a continent and a few years apart, dreaming of the same room. Time after time.

Troy

§1

Brompton, London

February 23, 1950

Brompton Cemetery was full of dead toffs. Just now Troy was standing next to a live one—John Ernest Stanhope Fitzclarence Ormond-Brack, umpteenth Marquess of Fermanagh, eligible bachelor, man-about-town, and total piss artist. They stood, as they had done this day every year since 1946, at the grave of Johnny's elder sister, Lady Diana Brack. It was her birthday. Neither man was sure how old she would be turning until they read the dates on the stone. Forty. And they would forget again by the next time. Neither man had brought flowers.

A few years ago they had reached an unspoken agreement not to mention the fact that Troy had killed Diana. At about the same time, they had reached a spoken agreement to the effect that the previous umpteenth Marquess, Johnny's father, had been, in the words of the incumbent, "an utter fucking gobshite."

They stood a few moments in silence.

Johnny Fermanagh, like nature, abhorred a vacuum and usually filled a silence.

"Got time for a quick one, Freddie?"

"It's nine o'clock in the morning."

"Call it a nightcap then, almost my bedtime."

"A copper's working day, Johnny. I'm picking Jack Wildeve up at his flat in less than ten minutes."

"Might one ask . . . a body?"

"A body on the beach, to be precise."

"Really? The body on the beach? Sounds like a book by one of those popular lady crime writers. Marjorie or Gladys somebody-or-other."

"I have to go. The beach in question is St Leonard's."

"St Leonard's? In February? Sooner you than me."

Troy hoped that one day Johnny might forget about Diana's birthday and leave him to the silence he wanted. To the expiation and contemplation he deemed necessary. He thought of Oscar Wilde, *The Ballad of Reading Gaol*: "Yet each man kills the thing he loves . . . the brave man does it with a sword, the coward with a kiss." Or was it the other way around? No matter. He'd killed Diana with a gun, not a sword, a gun he'd bought off a spiv in Soho. He wasn't brave, nor was he a coward—but he had most certainly killed the thing he loved.

"How about this evening?" Johnny drew Troy back from reverie.

"What about this evening?"

"There's a huge election-night do at Claridge's, and at the Savoy, and I reckon at half the hotels in Mayfair."

"Think where I should be tonight, Johnny. Just for a moment, think."

So often, Johnny didn't.

"Of course. Your brother . . . I wasn't . . . Does he . . . does he reckon he'll lose?"

"I don't know. I've done my damndest to avoid him during the whole campaign."

§2

Jack's flat was in Redcliffe Square—once-elegant houses of six storeys, fronted by marble porticos, built as homes for the larger upper-middle-class Victorian family and its attendant servants. As with most of London there seemed to be a coating of dust on every building, on every step and every windowsill, waiting like the rest of England for a real or metaphorical wind that would blow away the ashes of World War II. Redcliffe Square had escaped lightly, with broken windows, not ruined houses. In East London, Troy's old beat when he was a uniformed copper, whole streets, whole squares still lay as uncleared rubble, sprouting forests of buddleia and willow herb.

No doubt some of these dusty façades still concealed families, whether large or small, although few if any had servants. Most were in the process of being turned into flats. Jack had recently acquired what was known as a lateral conversion, that is, the entire first floor of one house and the entire first floor of the adjoining house. It was on the northwest side of the building, where a corner, for no other reason than architect's whim, became a delicious curve, and behind the curve Jack had a sitting room scarcely smaller than a tennis court.

Troy rang on the bell. A minute or less later a hand appeared over one of the balconies and a key-bearing sock floated down to the pavement.

It was perhaps an unexpected consequence of the curve in the conversion that the windows at each extremity faced each other. Troy stood in the sitting room and, looking idly around, found himself staring at Jack in what was clearly his bedroom window. Jack was almost ready, almost dressed but for a dangling tie and the absence of a jacket. She wasn't. She was stark naked, accepting kisses to her throat. As Jack's head bent, lips to nipple, she looked out of the window. Troy turned away, not quite quickly enough, as the woman fled. Jack simply tied his tie with not a glance in Troy's direction. He must not have seen Troy, and if he had, what did it matter? Jack was shameless, he'd never apologise nor expect an apology for any aspect of his love life—he had shagged his way through the world war with a particular fondness for the WRNS. Troy had bumbled into situations like this half a dozen times. But this was the first time he'd recognised one of Jack's lovers.

§3

Jack had never trusted Troy's car, nor Troy behind the wheel of his car, so Jack drove his own Scotland Yard Wolseley 4/44.

"How long have you had that car?"

"I forget," Troy lied.

It was a Bullnose Morris, a car almost designed to end up as a jalopy, which Troy had bought new over fifteen years ago.

"I mean," Jack went on, "it's not as if . . ."

Money, money, money.

When Troy lapsed into silence, unwilling to complete an obvious sentence for Jack, Jack bided his time. They'd reached the Elephant & Castle before Jack chose another obvious subject.

"This is a test, isn't it?"

"Is it?"

"Freddie, I'm up for inspector. And, if I may say so, an overdue promotion . . ."

"No, you may not. You've been a detective sergeant for five years, give or take. So was I. In fact, more, as Onions withheld my promotion for a year."

"All the same, this is minor stuff. It doesn't take two of us."

"If you think murder is ever minor—"

"We don't know yet that it is murder. Until then, does it really need a chief inspector and a sergeant?"

"How often have we gone out as a team?"

"Er . . ."

"'More often than not' would be the answer you're looking for."

"OK. OK. But if it's not a test, you're still monitoring, and Onions is bound to ask you, isn't he?"

Indeed he was. Indeed he had, and Troy had endorsed Jack repeatedly. It had crossed Troy's mind that Jack might be punished for Troy's sins. The less-than-flattering sobriquet "tearaway toff" had been coined in the locker rooms of Scotland Yard to describe Troy ten years ago, then it had been applied to both of them and now, on the eve of his promotion, seemed to be sticking to Jack like chewing gum on the sole of his shoe.

Their sins were of a very different nature—Troy's the more serious, a track record of disobedience and, if Onions only knew, some actual law-breaking, but a quiet life at home with the Metaphysical poets, a glass of claret, and the BBC's Third Programme. Jack . . . Jack was what another century might have termed a roister-doisterer. Troy was not even sure he could spell "roister-doisterer" and would hate to have to say it after a third glass of claret, but if it summed up a man who often came into the Yard hungover, whose free nights were spent in the clubs of Soho and Mayfair and whose track record with women, be it a Lyons Nippy or a debutante, might be the envy of Errol Flynn, then that was Jack Wildeve.

What was bothering Troy was Jack's current woman. How long had he been sleeping with Bryce Betancourt?

§4

Troy fell asleep before they reached Sidcup. He was blessed in that whatever he was dreaming about vanished the moment Jack nudged him to say, "We're just passing Battle. We'll be there in a few minutes."

He glanced at his watch.

"Good grief, it's almost one. How long was I out?"

"Best part of three hours. I don't know what you were up to last night, but not a word about what I was up to, because you haven't a leg to stand on. Besides, you snore."

Inspector Musker was waiting. He didn't strike Troy as a patient man.

Looked at his watch and said, "I should be at me lunch! The county pathologist left an hour ago."

Jack glanced at Troy. It was rare for rank to be so blatantly ignored.

"Don't let us keep you," Troy said.

With the added stare it was just enough.

"Hmph. You'll need me to bring you up to speed."

"Then you'd better lead the way."

In a cold, brightly lit back room, a body lay on a slab. A tall, over-weight, naked man. Aged fifty to fifty-five. Grey hair in his sideburns, white hair on his chest, a double chin and the sagging waistline of middle-aged spread.

As yet, there had been no exploratory surgery. The cuts were the injuries of assault.

Musker said his piece. The facts and speculations he had clearly been itching to utter all morning. The regional copper's resentment of Scotland Yard informed every syllable of his local report.

"Harry was our resident villain. Full name Harold Edward Edmondson. Traded as 'Gerald Gee—Bookmaker.' G. Gee, if you get it."

"Of course," said Troy, looking at Harry's throat rather than at Musker.

"He had a finger in a lot of pies. A chain of bookies all along the south coast as his legit enterprises and then the dodgy deals that weren't. Nothing we could ever nick him for. In fact, he could pass for respectable, but . . . but he was connected."

"Connected?" Jack said.

"London. London gangs. The big boys. He mixed with some of the new tearaways in the East End, and there were rumours he worked with the West London mob—Otto Ohnherz and the like."

Did Jack flinch at the name? Troy wasn't looking at Jack, he was looking at Harry's hands, at nicotined fingers, pumice-scrubbed and neatly clipped clean nails.

"If you want my opinion—"

A phrase Troy rather thought Musker probably had recourse to several times a day, uttered in the face of every indication to the contrary.

"—This was a hit."

Now Troy looked up.

"A hit?"

Had the idiot been watching too much Hollywood Noir?

"Gang killing. Plain as the nose on your face. He crossed one of the London mobs. They sent a hitman down from the Smoke."

The Smoke? Really?

"Took old Harry out to the beach after dark, then took him out."

"Where on the beach?"

"About two hundred yards west of here. Not far off the prom."

"Can you show us?"

In front of the police station Musker pointed to the spot.

"Mind—tide's been in and out twice. There's nothing left to see."

"But we'll look all the same," Troy said.

"Suit yourself. Waste o' time, to my way of thinking."

Why was it that "to my way of thinking" was so often spoken by men who did not seem much bothered by thought?

"Why don't you have your lunch, Mr Musker. We've already inconvenienced you. We can meet back here in an hour."

When Musker was out of earshot Jack said, "I know he's a first-class arse, Freddie, but he's right. We'll see nothing on the beach."

"We're not going to the beach. We're going back inside. I want another look at old Harry. You keep watch and see Musker doesn't interrupt me."

§5

Half an hour later Jack and Troy sat in the saloon bar of the Nag's Head.

Two rounds of egg and cress and two halves of mild.

"Well?" said Jack.

"I think Inspector Muskrat—"

"Musker."

"Whatever . . . He would dearly love to solve this one without us and wishes we'd just bugger off. But the chief constable told him to call the Yard so . . ."

"And his theory?"

"Poppycock."

"Isn't it just."

"So tell me why."

"Another test, Freddie? OK. The victim, Harry Edmondson, this G. Gee, was nothing but a small-town bookie. Musker talks of a chain of bookmakers all along the south coast. It's really just three, one here, one in Bexhill and one in Eastbourne. If you want to know how I know, just turn around: there's a flyer for 'G. Gee Turf Accountants'—ridiculous bloody phrase—tacked up on the wall. While you took another look at the body, I had a chat with the desk sergeant. Wouldn't quite say it but he thinks Musker keeps his brains in his boots. Gee was a boaster, inflated his reputation with hints of London connections—nods and winks and all that nonsense—and only Musker is dumb enough to believe it. I'd say the nearest Gee had ever been to a mob was probably joining the Rotary Club or the East Sussex Freemasons Lodge. It somehow enhances Musker's status if the criminals he deals with have underworld reputations. High time he grew up. There's no London end to this. It's a local killing. Now, your turn. Read me the corpse."

"Multiple knife wounds. Most of them shallow. Someone slashing rather than stabbing. None of them would have been remotely fatal but for a lucky hit on the carotid artery. Gee probably bled out on the beach while his killer looked on in amazement. I'd say someone he knew. No mob hit. They would have killed him with the first stroke of the blade—to the body, not the face and throat—or more likely they would have just shot him. They'd never have left the body on the beach. We'd probably never have found a body. I'd say Gee was lured—and I use that word with some precision—onto the beach, and if his killer intended to kill him at all—and I cannot state that that was the case—they probably hoped the tide would carry the body out to sea. As amateur as King Cnut."

"Hmm. Why do you say 'lured' is a precise term?"

"Because the killer was—"

"A woman."

"So glad we see eye to eye on this."

Troy glanced at his watch. Stood up.

"Now if you'll excuse me, I can be on the next train to Victoria and be back at the Yard before six. Musker's all yours and you're welcome to him."

"Seriously?"

"Jack, you've been telling me to get off your back all day. Consider it a free and unencumbered back. It's your case now, and yours alone. Find G. Gee's spurned mistress and wrap it up. If you can leave Inspector Musker with stale egg and limp cress on his face, call it a bonus."

§6

Not long after he returned to Scotland Yard, Troy called Inspector Kenneth Burdock in Criminal Records. He'd been at Hendon with Ken, refrained from using the nickname Dandelion, and respected Ken for recognising early on that he was a paper-and-numbers copper, not a pointy-hat-and-truncheon copper. Ken's memory was prodigious, his love of taxonomy awe-inspiring among the few who knew what taxonomy meant.

"Do you have anything on Bryce Betancourt?"

"You'd learn more by reading the *News of the World*."

Just after the war Bryce Betancourt had been living openly with one of West London's "Mr Bigs" (there were so many). In 1949 she had sued the *News of the World* over allegations of prostitution, won, dropped a similar case against the *Daily Mail* and magnanimously given her settlement to Dr Barnardo's children's homes. The press had poked around trying to find more about her and hit a brick wall—she was Swiss, she was French . . . she was a Jewish refugee from Austria . . . no doubt all fictions of her own devising—and within a few weeks she was yesterday's news wrapping tonight's fish and chips. Since then she had successfully dodged the spotlight. Troy himself had not had a single thought about Bryce or her notoriety until she had flitted across the window of Jack's apartment that morning. It was puzzling that he had recognised her immediately. More puzzling that he had recognised her stark naked.

"But," Troy said, "you'll have a file on Otto Ohnherz, and she might be mentioned in that?"

"Give me a few hours, Freddie. It's a busy day. Half my blokes want to leave early to vote. Why they can't vote first thing in the morning . . ."

Troy looked at his watch. It was almost seven. He hadn't voted. He'd gone straight to the cemetery. The polls would close at ten. He was registered at his mother's house in Hertfordshire, where his brother Rod was the sitting Labour MP. Rod would kill him if he didn't vote.

§7

It had been a sodden evening. Troy had got soaked dashing from his car to the polling station in the snug bar of the Blue Boar in Mimram, and soaked again getting from the car to the front door of his mother's house.

It was ten exactly according to the long-case clock that stood in the hall, five to ten according to the long-case clock that stood in Troy's study and "What fucking time do you call this?" according to Rod, who sat by a flickering, dying fire, listening or not to the news on the Home Service, gulping at a half-full brandy balloon.

"Tell me you got to the pub in time!"

"I did, and if you retain your seat by just one vote, that one vote will be mine."

Men there were who might say thank you and apologise now. Rod was just such a man, but no apology came forth. Troy sloughed off his overcoat and poked at the fire.

Rod turned off the radio.

"I hate pundits. Harding, Muggeridge—fuckemall. Do I really need anyone to tell me we're going to get our arses kicked? Where is Nancy Spain when you want her?"

"Right now, if I don't get some dry wood on the fire we're going to get our arses frozen."

Rod set his brandy aside.

"I've got to get back to Stevenage. The ballot boxes will start arriving in half an hour. I spent most of the day in Stepney. Only came home so Cid could change."

"Stepney?"

"As ever Freddie, out of touch with anything but guts and gore. Stepney, the soon-to-be constituency of your old sparring partner Billy Jacks."

"I wouldn't call him that."

Given a choice Troy would not call Billy Jacks anything. Given a choice Troy would avoid Billy like a dose of the clap. Billy's errant wife, Judy, had deflowered him on the kitchen table when he was nineteen. Best stick to politics—a subject of no controversy whatsoever.

"When did Billy forsake the beliefs of a lifetime?"

"As with so many, the war changed Billy. Went into internment a raving Tory—"

"To put it mildly."

"As I was saying, went in a raving Tory. Came out a convinced socialist."

"Congratulations."

"Earned and accepted."

Rod eased himself from the depths of his armchair, stood, looking slightly wobbly, and shook himself like a wet dog.

"Are you sure you're fit to drive?"

"Cid's driving. Wifely duty on such occasions, after all. And if you think I'm pissed, you're wrong. That won't be true for several hours yet."

"How long?"

"Quick, I'm told. We're not in any race to declare, but they reckon about two o' clock."

"Fine, I'll wait up."

"You don't have to do that, Freddie."

"I said. I'll wait up."

What was a couple of hours? In 1945 they'd waited weeks. Rod had still been in uniform. Instant demob if he won, back to the RAF if he didn't.

Troy stoked the fire, watched the cherry logs spit sparks, thought of Judy Jacks, dismissed the thought, thought of Diana Brack, could not dismiss the thought, and reached for the inch and a half of brandy Rod had left in his glass.

§8

"And here in Eigg, Muck, Rum and Ardnamurchan (North)," said the radio, "a Liberal gain as Murdo McDonald loses to Sir Grahame Ramsay-Muir, with the Conservatives trailing third, the two independents losing their . . ."

Troy was only half asleep, still half listening. He didn't hear Rod come into the room and was startled by a sudden hiss and roar from the fireplace. Rod was leaning, one hand on the mantelpiece, watching his red rosette burn.

"Don't tell me you lost?"

Rod said nothing for the best part of a minute, let the radio burble on.

"No. In fact . . . I increased my majority. Twelve thousand. Enough to make it officially a safe seat."

Inactivity had left Troy feeling cold. He prised himself out of the chair and stood at the opposite end of the fireplace, feeling the faint warmth of a burning symbol, more light than heat.

"Good news, then."

"Oh yes."

"And you heard about Stepney?"

"No. Tell me."

"Billy Jacks won by a landslide. Majority of thirty thousand. Tory lost his deposit."

Rod smiled, just when Troy was thinking he'd forgotten how to.

"Well, Billy deserves it."

"Honestly?"

"I see you finished my brandy. Pour us each another. If you're going to argue, I need arsy-li'l-bro fuel."

Seated either side of the fire, Troy still shivering, Rod stripped down to shirtsleeves, his Old Harrovian tie at half-mast, shoes off, odd socks on display.

Rod said, "I don't care what history there is between you and Billy. All to do with your time as a beat bobby, I suppose."

"To say nothing of a stint rounding up enemy aliens in 1940."

"Quite. Billy as an alien. He's more the Englishman than either of us, and as such he's got his finger on the pulse of the nation. Something I fear the Labour party as a whole managed to lose in a very short time. I can defend 'austerity' if you like, but now is not the time—"

"It's joyless."

"Yes. It is joyless. But that isn't my point. England will accept joyless if the rewards are evident—and they haven't been. For every bloke on the Clapham omnibus who sings the praises of the National Health Service, there's a housewife in Hackney who'll list you all things she can't buy to keep her family warm and fed. I spoke for Billy half a dozen times during the campaign and I saw more of the East End than I've done since you walked the beat before the war. It's . . . it's as though the war ended yesterday. The bomb sites are still there, just grassed over, there are houses without roofs or windows, standpipes in the street, loos that are little more than sheds . . ."

"Tell me something I don't know."

"And that's the pattern everywhere from Stepney to Glasgow. As a government we failed at the most fundamental level—in people's homes. If the Tories are voted in—and I might add that I think we'll scrape to victory—the first thing Churchill should do is announce a building programme . . . I dunno . . . a hundred thousand . . . a quarter of a million new homes a year."

"Instead Labour will say what?"

"I think an old idea is about to be revived. We will probably announce that we're throwing the country a party, an end to joylessness—a festival of some kind next year. Shades of Prince Albert, 1851, the Great Exhibition and the Crystal Palace."

"Papering over the cracks."

"You may very well think that, and for once we would be of the same mind, but I'd be in a minority in the cabinet. I'd like the cabinet to listen to Billy, but it'll be an age before they open their ears to him. I flatter myself mine have been open, and I've had both ears bent by him of late. What really hurt was something he said about ten days ago, not from the platform—he's learnt some tact—but to me, in private. He said Otto Ohnherz's rackets in Notting Hill and Bayswater have housed more people than Stepney Council have put into their houses. I doubt that's true, but it stings all the same. A Labour government achieving less than a wartime spiv and racketeer ought to be unthinkable."

Troy pondered his next remark, tossed another log on the fire.

"That name does keep coming up," he said.

"Ohnherz? Why so?"

"I asked for his file today."

"Really? What do you think you have on him?"

"Until I see the file, I don't know. Let's just say he is . . . of interest."

Rod straightened up, a look of something akin to shock on his face.

"You do realise he's a major donor to the party?"

"No. And it would never have occurred to me. But now you mention it, what does occur to me is to ask why the Labour Party takes money from an obvious crook. As you put it not thirty seconds ago, a spiv and racketeer."

"Obvious but unconvicted, and if memory serves, he's never even been charged with anything."

"He hasn't, but only because no one will testify against him. He's still running rackets. And in all probability the rackets themselves are not illegal, just the methods he uses. You know that, I know that and so does Fleet Street."

Rod sighed and sank again.

"I was against accepting so much as a farthing, but the party took the view that to turn him down would be tantamount to an accusation. Trial in the court of gossip. And . . . I've a sneaking suspicion he gave money to the Tories and the Liberals as well. The ultimate in arse-covering. Pay off everybody. Back every horse in the race."

"Have you met him? Is hobnobbing one of the perks of his donation?"

"Anyone expecting that would be disappointed with me as a nob to be hobbed. A junior at the Air Ministry? Not worth five bob to hob that nob. And no, I've never met him. He sends one of his blokes to meetings . . . I was at one in '48 or '49 . . . ducked out early and let Harold Wilson do the glad-handing. He seems to have taken to the bloke—Jim or Joe somebody. A Jewish name. Don't ask me to think clearly quite so early in the morning."

Troy shrugged. Blue fuse lit, time to stand back.

"I'm not expecting to find anything."

"So why are you asking? Suddenly he's moved up from housing rackets to murder?"

"It's . . . hmm . . . personal."

§9

Troy rose early and was back at Scotland Yard by eight thirty.

An angry Jack was waiting for him in the outer office. He snatched a piece of paper off his desk.

"You have one message. The Dandelion phoned: 'Tell Troy I have nothing on Bryce Betancourt and I'll get back to him about Ohnherz.' Freddie, what the hell are you playing at?"

Jack was a six-footer. Towered over Troy. Troy was hard to intimidate and simply met his gaze.

"Jack, do you want this promotion or not? Because if you do, I need to know everything Onions or the commissioner can find out if they decide to dig around."

"Dig around in my private life?"

"Yes."

"As you know, I'm not one to bandy around words like 'hypocrite,' Freddie, but right now that is the only word that comes to mind."

"Meaning?"

"Diana Brack. You had an affair with a suspect. And you have the fucking cheek to check up on my girlfriend."

"Your girlfriend is the mistress of a man considered to be a criminal."

"And Diana Brack *was* a criminal."

"Which I did not know. And when Onions found out he delayed my promotion for a year while he considered sacking me. And I don't know what bothered him the most—the utter cock-up that got her killed or my stupidity in being involved with her at all. Jack, I do not want to see anything like that happen to you. You've earned the promotion. Don't fuck it up."

Jack was not to be placated. On the other hand he wasn't going to retaliate. He stuffed his briefcase with a wad of papers from his desk and headed for the door.

"I have to get back to St Leonard's. May I take it you're not coming?"

Troy said nothing.

Went into his own office and called Burdock.

"There's a file on Otto Ohnherz—well, there would be, wouldn't there?" Burdock said.

"I hear a 'but,' Ken."

"But I don't have it. The Branch keep it."

"Why?"

"No idea. You could ask them, but you know as well as I do that no one in Special Branch would give you the time of day."

Burdock was stating a self-evident truth. It had been that way since the war. Troy had made enemies.

"You've got friends in MI5," he continued. "Whatever the Branch have, they have. You could get the file. Old pals act and all that."

Troy could have done without Burdock's last sentence, a scarcely disguised reference to class, but he was right.

Troy called Leconfield House and asked to speak to Jordan Younghusband. Troy had not known Jordan long, about two years, but long enough for the "old pals act" to kick in.

"I don't even need to look," Jordan said. "I know for a fact we have a file on Ohnherz."

"You'll understand," Troy said, "if I am curious to know why MI5 has a file on a man who is probably no more than a common criminal."

"As you say, probably. And perhaps Otto Ohnherz is an uncommon criminal. But—this isn't anything I'll talk about on the phone."

"Your place or mine?"

"Yours, I think. Do you have a bottle or two of your dad's 1929 claret under the sink?"

"Of course."

"And are you still getting off-the-ration veg from your mother's garden?"

"It's February, Jordan."

"Ah."

"I have eggs. And some salted bacon the Fat Bloke barrelled last autumn."

"Soooo—if you can work your usual magic of turning a packet of spaghetti into something resembling wallpaper paste, we might have makings of a meal?"

"See you at eight."

§10

An hour later Chief Superintendent Onions, head of the Murder Squad, appeared in Troy's office. Sat by the gas fire, trousers hitched up to half-mast above the tops of his boots. Pulled out fags and matches. Lit up a Woodbine. Coughed. Once, the last Christmas of the war, Troy had given Onions a silver smoker's kit from Asprey's, a tiny box to hold matches, with a compartment to tap ash into in the absence of any other vessel. He'd seen Onions use it twice before reverting to his usual box of Swan Vestas and dropping fag ash on the lino. He might as well have bought him a striped tie or a straw boater.

"Anything I should know about?" Onions asked.

"Probably not."

"Do you know owt I don't know?"

"Lots."

Onions drew deeply on his cigarette, exhaled a noxious cloud through his nostrils.

"Otto Ohnherz, for example."

Good bloody grief. Did everyone know?

"Just an enquiry," Troy said.

"About a murder?"

"No."

"Then why are you enquiring?"

"Personal."

"Personal? What does that mean?"

"Just a private matter, Stan."

"Then you'll be enquiring on your own time."

"If you say so."

"I do say so."

Fine. That was Troy's evening settled and sorted.

"And," Onions went on, "the lad's promotion will be through at the end of the week. Let's have a bit of a do for 'im. I reckon the lad's earned it. If he can only keep it in his pants, he might even make chief inspector one day."

The lad. Jack was twenty-nine. For years Troy had been "the lad." He was 99 per cent sure he was still "the lad" if his name came up in conversation between Stan and other senior coppers.

§11

Troy's house in Goodwin's Court might once have been a shop. He didn't know, nor did anyone else in the courtyard, but its bow-fronted window of spun glass, bulging with age and seemingly defying gravity, looked as though it might once have been a showcase for the latest fashions of the eighteenth century, all puff and powder. His mother had bought the house for him when he graduated from Hendon in 1935, almost fifteen years ago. It had been empty for "a while," and judging by the amount of pigeon shit he had swept out ahead of the fitters and decorators, that "'while" stretched back to the general strike of 1926 and perhaps beyond that to the antediluvian world of the teens and tens—a world of which he had no memory. The youngest of four—afterthought or accident, he would never ask—and the only one English-born, his mother always referred to him as her "little Englander," seeming anxious that he should adapt from the polyglot household she and his father ran at Mimram to England and the English, a journey she would never make herself. It might have helped if she'd spoken to him in English, but like many a Russian aristo-in-exile she preferred French. When he was a child she had made bedtime efforts to read to him in English, but her accent had been so atrocious he had wanted to put his fingers in his ears—"five" was always a county in Scotland and "sausage" utterly defeated her, "zozwatch" being about as close as she could get. The Englishman she might have wanted Troy to become Rod had half become—he was, after all, an eccentric, the abiding characteristic of a well-bred English gent, and had he not found his métier in being a member of parliament, he might have run an antiquarian bookshop or explored Antarctica. Becoming a Scotland Yard detective probably ruined her ambitions for Troy by being beyond her ken (there were only two types of copper, the Tsarist Okhrana agent and the Hertfordshire fat British bobby-on-a-bike) but she would never say so. Instead her admiration was saved for a type of Englishman epitomised by Jordan Younghusband—abundant without being ubiquitous. They had met the previous year, and he had charmed her to melting point, switching effortlessly between English and French, making her laugh . . . sending an eighty-year-old woman almost girlishly giggly. Troy had never thought she'd had a sense of humour.

"And what is your occypattzion, Mister Yunkzbun?"

Jordan could not answer that question honestly.

"Oh, you know, Lady Troy, this and that."

"Zees unt zat. What kindt of zees unt zat?"

"Oh, I've flown all around the world in a plane, I've started revolutions in Spain, even charted the North Pole . . . once upon a time . . ."

His mother wouldn't recognise a song lyric from *Don Giovanni*, let alone Ira Gershwin, but she knew a tease when she heard one—she laughed out loud and handed her empty teacup to Troy without taking her eyes off Jordan.

Thing was, Troy thought to himself, *Jordan probably had done all of those things . . . once upon a time.*

Waiting for him now, Troy wondered at the redundancy of his question about Bryce. Onions might just have nullified it with his "keeps it in his pants." If Jordan brought information that led to her name, Troy would listen, and whether he asked a question depended entirely on what Jordan said and how much of Troy's dad's claret he had necked.

§12

"You've improved."

"You mean, it didn't taste like glue?"

"Be fair, Freddie. I said consistency of glue . . . nothing to do with the taste."

"So happens it is just a cookery trick. You cool the pan before you drop the pasta back in and add the egg yolk, that way you don't—"

"Get scrambled egg? Quite. Of course, if we're going to be sticklers, the bacon should be pancetta—"

"Instead you get a fat man's best fatback."

"How is the old boy?"

"Getting older. Not slowing down. Wants me to keep my own pigs."

"You gonna do it?"

"Hmm . . . later perhaps. After I get one more promotion under my belt. And it might require my mother to shuffle off her mortal coil."

"Heaven forfend."

"She's a snob, Jordan. You just haven't figured her out yet. If I kept pigs at Mimram, I'd be reducing her family to the peasantry."

"My dad farms sheep."

"Never tell her. And when you say he farms sheep, what you really mean is he has a bloke on his estate on the Scottish border who farms sheep for him while he swans about in tweed and wellies saying, 'Jolly good, chaps. Keep up the good work.'"

"And you think your mother's a snob?"

"I have the antidote to all this guff breathing gently on the draining board."

"Eh?"

"You did say two bottles."

"I was being greedy."

"*Nessun problema.*"

§13

When Troy came back from the kitchen clutching a Château Ducru-Beaucaillou '29, Jordan had a brown cardboard file set next to his plate.

Questions, questions, questions.

First Troy topped him up. Decided to let him speak first. If this turned out to be a can of worms, he'd rather be the man uncorking the claret than the one reaching for the can opener.

A tissue-thin label was glued to the file cover—wartime economy paper—reading "Otto Oh$_n$herz," the *n* slightly dropped by a clapped-out typewriter.

Jordan flipped it open. Just one page. Badly typed. Every *n* dropped.

"Don't have much. As far as I can tell the file was opened in October '39, for no other reason than that Otto was technically an enemy alien. German, after all."

"Never applied for citizenship?"

"So many didn't. Your brother, to name but one."

"For which mistake Rod was interned for several months on the Isle of Man . . . And Otto wasn't?"

"I think age might have helped. He was already well over sixty . . . not much of a threat . . . and he was still, just about, respectable. He had one of the best escape clauses a man could have—a Ministry of Supply contract to manufacture RAF uniforms. I'd say Rod might have worn one, but I happen to know his tailor. If Otto was running rackets back in '39, most of us didn't know, and he also had friends, friends who would pull for him all the strings your father declined to pull for Rod. He spent the early years of the war at the BBC in a sort of psychological warfare unit, broadcasting propaganda. George Orwell was there, George Weidenfeld too, and William Empson."

"I don't remember any broadcasts by Otto Ohnherz."

"You wouldn't have heard them. Not for home consumption. He wrote scripts, in German, and apparently wasn't much good at it, so they let the arrangement lapse. He was gone by '41, and I am inclined to think that's when he got into the black market."

"A grudge?"

"If you like. A man spurned is a man . . ."

"Quite."

"Pretty soon he was the mirror image of Goering."

"Eh?"

"Butter before guns. He had a nickname, the Butterman. Half the housewives in London probably bought his off-the-record off-the-ration butter. However, our interest in him had lapsed by then. MI5 isn't bothered by spivs, and the ministry needed all the uniforms his factory could turn out. Ohnherz wasn't a threat to national security. Hence just the one page."

Troy had taken in the page in a single glance. Not a mention of Bryce Betancourt, and as far as he could see no longer any reason to mention her. He could just let it drop—after all, Jordan hadn't asked why Troy wanted to see the file, and might never ask.

Jordan set another brown folder on the table.

JAY FABIAN

It was a name Troy knew without being able to attach any specific memory to it.

"This chap, however, is of interest."

"Name is vaguely familiar. Who is he?"

"In the parlance of the New York mafia he would be the consigliere. He's Otto's right-hand man—"

Ah—the Jim or Joe that Rod had misremembered.

"And he is a person of interest not because of what he does for Otto, but for what he does that we don't know."

"Eh?"

"He is, or rather claims to be, a survivor of Auschwitz. To be precise, a survivor who was still there when the Russians arrived. Believe it if you will."

"Not something someone would make up."

"Perhaps, perhaps not, but it's enough to ring alarm bells. We're ninety-nine per cent certain that's when the Russians recruited Méret Voytek."

An involuntary twitch of the head, and Troy found himself focussed on one of the leafy-green Constables hanging on the sitting room wall. For a while, two years ago, a pastiche of the Botticelli *Venus* had hung there. He'd scraped dried brain from one corner. The last mortal remains of a Czech assassin who'd come for Méret Voytek, if only he had known who she was. Troy had helped Voytek escape to Paris. If Jordan had only known, and right now Troy thanked God he hadn't.

Jordan's eyes had followed his. He wondered: Did Jordan feel a frisson every time he set foot in this room—and he'd eaten with Troy on half a dozen occasions in the last two years—did he see walls splattered with blood and brains? If so . . . it didn't show. Troy thought he could still smell the smell every so often—not blood, not brains, but the Jeyes Fluid Jordan's team of "cleaners" had used to scrub away death.

"So," he said. "Anyone who fits that bill is suspect?"

"Pretty much."

"And you think Fabian is a Soviet agent?"

"Dunno."

"And what in his work for Otto Ohnherz is there that might be worth a spy's time?"

"That's wide of the mark. No, it's everything else he's up to."

"Such as?"

"He's a mingler. Ohnherz is semi-reclusive these days. Stroke in '49. Knocked him out of the loop. Fabian does almost everything for the business and goes well beyond anything Ohnherz would have done. He's a very different character. A charmer, whereas Ohnherz was always a bit of a curmudgeon. Fabian has a London social presence. Your brother's met him."

"'Met him' being different from 'knows him'? Rod's mentioned him just once. Couldn't even get his name right."

"'Know' is such a versatile word. However, there are rumours about Fabian and your sister. And in her case we'd need to define 'know' in its fullest and possibly most biblical sense."

"I don't need to ask which sister. The only surprising thing is that Sasha hasn't boasted about him."

"Quite. And there are also rumours about Fabian and the infamous Miss Betancourt, Otto being indisposed—'indisposed' as in 'probably can't get it up.'"

At last. After spag carb and the best part of two bottles of red . . . at last. The name.

Troy did not pursue.

"What you seem to be saying is that Fabian is, if this is the right word, infiltrating."

"Yes."

"Last night my brother told me Ohnherz is a donor to the Labour Party. In fact it's this Fabian chap, isn't it? If that's infiltration, I imagine he's in for the long haul. He's working his way into Labour while Labour are wondering how long they'll have in office. You seem to keep track of Fabian, so I can assume you know he knows Harold Wilson—Wilson's in the cabinet today . . . President of the Board of Trade . . . sounds far more important than it really is—"

"It has the word 'president' in it, after all. Must be so confusing for a foreigner."

"But in a year's time he could be on the back benches and in opposition."

"Well, agents like that aren't called sleepers for nothing. And that's the idea that has us worried. How sleepy a game might the Russians be prepared to play? You say Wilson might be yesterday's man in a year or so. He's only thirty-three. It's where he might be in ten or twenty years that matters. Fabian could prick his finger on a spinning wheel and still wake up in time."

"Rod thinks he's given money to the Liberals and the Tories too, backing every horse in the race, as he put it."

"That's true as well. Can't see the point in giving so much as a farthing to the Liberals, though. Labour will scrape home this time. Tiny majority. There'll be another election in a couple of years and the Liberals will get wiped out. They might hold on to Orkney and Shetland, who knows? The last bastions of the Asquith family. Meanwhile Fabian will have friends in government, right or left, whatever the shade."

"Let's go back to the beginning. If Russia has a Soviet agent in place, how did they get him here?"

"I don't know. Let me begin with the name. Jay Fabian is just one of the variations. There is also Jay Heller, Sam Heller and Sam Fabian. Our man is supposed to have used all four aliases in his time here but has apparently settled on Jay Fabian. I'm inclined to think none of them are real. We have no records of any of those names that we can be certain of. However, let's just call him Fabian for simplicity's sake. Fabian shows up in London in 1946. At that time Ohnherz's main racket was working the refugees. Finding jobs, skimming off their wages and so on. We think this is how he met Fabian. Problem is, there's no record of Fabian entering the country under the refugee quota. He was never issued an identity card and seems to have had no paper existence until Ohnherz used the refugee organisations and the Jewish lobby to get him papered—concentration camp survivor, trauma, amnesia and what have you—to take the pressure off him. And people—the little men with the rubber stamps, the state—do back off. No one wants to be called a Nazi. Fabian becomes legitimate with the start of the National Health Service . . . gets an NHS number and a National Insurance number . . . date of birth, dubious . . . place of birth, Berlin, also dubious. And 'Auschwitz survivor' becomes almost a war cry, a deterrent to any further probing.

"It's at this point that Ohnherz ups his game by starting his housing racket. The profits from the black market get ploughed into property in West London. He buys a house, then several houses, then a whole street in Notting Hill. Out go the white working-class tenants, in come all the Jamaicans and Trinidadians . . . paying through the nose because no legit landlord will take them in. I say 'legit,' but there's nothing illegit about anything Ohnherz is doing—and I should stop saying 'Ohnherz' because it's clearly Fabian who's the brains behind this.

"We tried tracing Fabian by all the names he's used—or more accurately, since he sticks to 'Jay Fabian,' all the names we've had reason to think might have been his. The name Sam has been thrown up from somewhere. And Heller. Sam Heller, Sam Fabian . . . nothing, not a damn thing. If he was in Auschwitz under any of those names, there's no way we'd ever find out. That nation of meticulous record-keepers was also a nation of mass record destroyers once they knew it was all over. They wiped Treblinka off the map, after all.

"We found what might be a Jay Heller in that there was a James Heller who seems to vanish off the face of the earth in the 1920s—and a Jacob Heller who joins the Ordnance Corps in 1940 and in 1945 transfers to UNRRA. At least that's the front. He was most certainly MI6. He gets his demob in 1946. Back to England from Germany on military transport, but between Dover and the demob centre in Camberley he too vanishes. Technically he's a deserter. Never even collects his gratuity or his badly cut suit. And if Jay Fabian really is Jacob Heller, he's applied for none of the benefits to which Jacob Heller is entitled. At best it's a tenuous connection. I cannot see Jay Fabian as an agent of Six, and if Six thought Fabian was really Heller, well . . . they've had four years to pick him up and reclaim him. As it is, I reckon they've taken a look and dismissed the idea that he is their missing man."

"They're not saying one way or the other?"

"Do they ever? Jay Fabian doesn't have a passport. In fact, he still doesn't have a national identity card—although to be honest I couldn't find mine if a beat bobby asked me to produce it. His only legit ID is his National Insurance card and equivalent NHS card, but he pays his taxes on time, and he banks with Coutts. Simultaneously he does and does not exist."

"While waving a Coutts cheque the size of a tablecloth? Very discreet. Perhaps Herr Fabian is Schrödinger's cat. But—he's what, an illegal immigrant? You could just deport him back to Germany."

"Why on earth would we want to do that? The whole point is to watch him. To find out how much he knows and to whom he tells it.

Besides, any move by us and he'll have lawyers onto us crying 'Nazi', and the next thing you know he'll have British citizenship."

"Somebody must be running him. If he's a spy he'll have some sort of embassy contact."

"None that we've found. Either he really is a sleeper, who'll report nothing until there's something worth reporting . . . or he isn't a spy at all."

Troy had been glancing through the file, ten times longer than the one on Ohnherz. He closed it. Dropped it back on the table.

"Jordan, this isn't anything I should bother with. Call me when Fabian kills someone."

"Au contraire, Freddie. Why don't you call me when someone kills him?"

§14

The next day Onions gave Jack the good news.

Troy hoped it would wipe the slate, but Jack seemed to be accepting with surly grace the promotion which he had long held to be his due.

Two days later in Sidcup Jack arrested Rebecca Brand, aged twenty-seven, half Harry Edmondson's age.

Time after time Harry told me, "I'll tell 'er this weekend." He din't love 'er no more. He said he loved me. "You're the only one, Becky, the only one." And then I found out I wasn't. I know 'cos his missis came round to my flat and laughed in my face. "You're not the first, dearie. And you won't be the last. And you sure as hell ain't the only one." Called me a daft trollop.

And then Harry suggested another of his moonlight walks along the beach. We did that a lot. The old trout never went near the sea, said it smelled. And then I asked him. "What other woman?" he says. And I say,

"Don't lie to me, Harry." And he slaps my face. Hard like.
So I slashes him. Only meant to stripe him the once. Just
a kitchen knife. Same one I use for spuds an' carrots.
But summink went wrong.

"At this point I found myself wishing she'd never mentioned the knife
in her handbag. A crime of passion suddenly turned into premeditation.
But . . . never thought she'd killed him with a nail file or anything else
you'd ever expect to find in a lady's handbag. I thought the tears would
never stop. Two cups of tea and a river of mascara later she told me
where she'd ditched the knife. In a waste bin outside the pub where you
and I had lunch. She went in for a large G & T to 'steady me nerves.' I
got helpful Mr Musker to send a uniform round. It was still in the bin
under the fag packets and used condoms. I have Rebecca Brand bang
to rights, and I wish I hadn't. Fukkit, Freddie—she could hang for this."

Troy said nothing.

It was far from unusual for a successful arrest to feel like a Pyrrhic
victory once the gallows loomed up, and it had taken the shine off Jack's
promotion. There'd be no "bit of a do," no celebration, no bunched
coppers at the bar of the Red Lion.

Jack's mood lightened a little over the next few days, and neither of
them felt it necessary to mention Bryce Betancourt or Rebecca Brand.

§15

September 1950

In September 1950, Otto Ohnherz died. He was seventy-three and had
been in poor health for some time. There were no close relatives. In
fact, no relatives at all.

Predictably the *News of the World* went to town, Ohnherz's death
knocking good-time girls and randy vicars off the front page for a day:

KING OF THE UNDERWORLD DEAD!

THE NAPOLEON OF NOTTING HILL!

AUSCHWITZ SURVIVOR!

THE MAN THEY COULDN'T CATCH!

It is a given of journalism that the dead do not sue. Wisely, having lost to her once already, the *News of the World* did not mention Bryce Betancourt.

"Auschwitz survivor" was untrue—lazy reporting, a confusion of identities that Troy considered had probably been encouraged by both Otto Ohnherz and Jay Fabian—but the *News of the World* didn't bother with obituaries, only headlines. Rackets made a headline. Auschwitz made a headline.

The *Post* did run obituaries, one might even say it specialised in obituaries, and they got it more or less right.

Otto, only son of Isaac and Hannah Ohnherz, born Charlottenburg, Berlin, 1877, had lived in London since the 1880s, when his parents had fled Germany in anticipation of the next pogrom . . . and blahdey blahdey blah.

Jordan had told him it was Fabian who'd been in Auschwitz. And if memory served, Jordan had ended his sentence with "believe it if you will."

Believe it if you will . . . Auschwitz?

Sam

§16

Oświęcim, Poland

January 1945

As the Red Army drew ever closer, the Germans marched all who could walk westward out of Auschwitz, across Poland. Samuel Fabian could not walk. This probably saved his life.

Fabian lay in a bunk in the infirmary. A strange institution in a camp designed for death. Fabian had never grasped the point of the SS treating illness when a bullet would suffice . . . but he was ill with he knew not what and stuck there in the pretence of recovery. Then the pretence stopped. Shots, single shots, rang out from the far end of the room and drew nearer with each squeezing of the trigger. As Fabian tried in vain to raise his head, a pair of dirty jackboots came into view, the ragged hem of a field-grey SS greatcoat and a hand in a tight black leather glove held out a Luger towards him.

Fabian felt nothing, heard nothing. The hammer had fallen on nothing.

The SS guard did not pull the trigger twice, let his hand fall to his side and spoke.

"It seems you get to live. Good luck with that."

Fabian slipped back into his sporadic coma.

He never saw the face of the man who had either spared his life or merely been too lazy to reload.

§17

When he awoke it was light, and he found he could move the muscles in his neck. He lifted his head to look out upon a shining sea of frozen shit and piss. He had no idea how long he had slept since the SS departed. Boots approached, stepping carefully round the slicks of shit. No greatcoat, no gun—the white quilted trousers of a winter combat suit.

"*Polski? Russki? Deutsch?*" a woman's voice asked.

Fabian was not at all certain he could speak, but did.

"*Deutsch,*" he said, then "*Jude.*"

Lest there be any misunderstanding.

"My German not good," she said.

He switched languages. "My Russian's fine. Talk to me in Russian. Just talk to me. No one has in weeks."

She perched her padded backside on the edge of his bunk.

Short, pretty, dark-haired and faintly oriental. A few acne scars on her left cheek, almond eyes and long lashes.

"I am Junior Lieutenant Riva Rifkin, NKVD. I too am Jewish."

"Amazing coincidence," said Fabian.

It was several seconds before she realised he was joking.

§18

"Can you walk?"

"I've no idea. Try me."

She held out a hand for him to grip. Short as she was, she pulled him up effortlessly. He sat on the edge of the bunk. Took half a dozen deep breaths.

"Еще раз."

One more time.

And she hauled him to his feet. Suddenly she looked even shorter. He was looking down at the top of her fur hat. A tad shy of six feet to her five foot nothing.

But then he sat down again with a bump, the wooden edge of the bunk digging sharply into his thighs.

"A moment. I can do this. I'll find the energy."

"When did you last eat?"

He shook his head. "No idea."

"Someone must have fed you. Or at least brought you water. The Germans left days ago. You'd be dead from dehydration . . . unless . . ."

How long had it been since the German had failed to kill him? Time was meaningless.

"I was delirious when the Germans dumped me here. I think I was delirious until you spoke to me just now. Or, then again, you might be part of my delirium."

"Oh, I'm very real."

"That is just what the angel of my delirium would say. Lately I have seen both demons and angels. The last thing I remember is . . ."

The Luger's hammer falling on nothing. He could neither believe nor explain the SS man's last remark.

He thought better of telling her.

"Еще раз."

And he stood. Her shoulder under his like a clothes prop.

Now he could see the length of the room. Bodies caked in frozen blood, stretched out on bunks where they had died . . . whenever . . . two days, a week, ten days ago . . . whenever.

Yes. Someone had fed him, or he'd be just another corpse.

§19

She mentioned fresh air as she draped a blanket around him and helped him out of the *Krankenbau*. The air was far from fresh. It was sticky with the stink of death, yellow with the clouds of ash constantly swirling above them. All but impossible to breathe.

Had he forgotten? It had never been as bad as this—but now there were bonfires everywhere, as though the Russians were trying to thaw out the camp, pouring dust and smoke into the air.

Where there had been huts, quite possibly including the one in which he had spent the last twelve months, there were now only broken bricks, splintered planks and dust, as raggedy women threw parts of Auschwitz into the flames.

"Let me see," he said.

A few yards away from the nearest bonfire he eased himself off Rifkin's shoulder and stood in the warmth of the blaze. A woman threw a straw palliasse into the fire and tried her best not to meet his gaze.

He turned to Rifkin.

"Poles," she said. "We needed workers. We rounded up Poles. The guilt was almost instant. So was the disgust."

"And the Germans?"

"There were a few, and what few there were we shot."

He bent to pick up a piece of paper that had floated off the bonfire, a relic of older flames, settling almost intact and freezing to the ground like an autumn leaf caught in a sudden frost.

A page from a ledger—columns, numbers and names.

He straightened up, feeling every muscle in his back ache to be free of his spine, and read.

"*Mein Gott.* The bastards burnt the records. They burn us and now they burn what traces we left. We are nobody, now. I am nobody. We never existed."

He folded the scorched piece of paper in four and slipped it into the pocket of his stripes.

Rifkin appeared at his side, silent but for the crunch of her boots on the frosted earth.

"I am nobody," he said. "One should never be a nobody."

Rifkin handed him a tin mug of something hot and pungent.

"Come. Sit. Drink. Drink slowly, Herr Nobody."

She led him to a makeshift plank bench by the fire. There were three people. Two he did not recognise, and Janusz Budziarek, a Pole from Łodz. He'd arrived on the same transport, in the same cattle truck.

When the train had stopped at Breslau the doors had been pulled back, and Fabian, like everyone else, assumed he had arrived. He hadn't. Two more Häftlings were prodded into the truck with bayonets: a hefty six-footer, as tall as Fabian—this was Budziarek, grinning like an idiot as he boarded hell's own handcart—and a smaller man Budziarek referred to as "Dog." Dog did not survive the journey and rolled onto the ramp four days later, dead.

Fabian had worked alongside Budziarek, had stood behind him in the endless pre-dawn roll calls. If constant enforced proximity, "the spontaneous nuclei of cohabitation," could be mistaken for "sticking together," then they had stuck together.

Budziarek looked up. Did not smile, did not speak, as though both actions would consume too much energy. But then he tapped the side of his nose gently, and Fabian knew who had fed him in his delirium.

"Drink slowly," Rifkin said again.

A sudden flash of memory and in his mind he heard those words in Budziarek's heavy Polish accent.

"Drink slowly, or you'll just puke it up," she said.

He sipped, felt steam in his nostrils, as pleasant as food itself, and tasted soup, thick soup with mutton and carrots and a delicious scum of fat floating up to the brim. A faintly rancid scent that he might now compare favourably to roses.

"Herr Nobody. Surely you remember?"

"Remember what?"

"Your name?"

"Oh yes. I used to be Samuel Fabian, professor of mathematical physics at the Humboldt University."

"Used to be?"

"Who knows? In Auschwitz you lose everything. Why should my identity be exempt?"

"Professor Samuel . . ."

"Sam. Call me Sam. Samuel no more. Sam will do until I find out who I am."

He did not tell her that one of the names on the piece of paper was his. She came from an ideology that professed irrefutable logic and spoke of the historical inevitable, where a physicist would speak of randomness and chance, of cosmos and chaos. The magic of coincidence might well be lost on her. Besides, Samuel Fabian, while not a common name, was hardly unique, and the number had burnt to black ash and crumbled away before he could read it. Some other Fabian? Long dead? Or living somewhere even now, as lost as he was?

"How many?" he asked.

"Survivors?"

"People . . . people like me. Häftlings."

"There were a couple of thousand yesterday. Fewer today. They die like . . ."

"Like flies."

"Yes. They do."

"War is over. Welcome to the war."

"No, no. You are free now."

"Of course, I was forgetting—*Arbeit macht frei*. How silly of me. Clearly I have worked hard enough to be free. A real Stakhanovite."

"No, no. Stop. You are free. Peace is freedom. Freedom is peace."

"Hmmm. Such a cute slogan . . ."

A long sip at his mug of exquisite grease.

"Now, why does it sound like a threat?"

§20

He must have fallen asleep for a moment. Hot soup over his thighs. For another moment he thought he had pissed himself. He'd done that often enough.

Budziarek set down his empty mug, hoisted Fabian up by his left arm, Rifkin on the right.

"No matter," she said. "Getting you cleaned up was always next on the list."

"What's she saying?" Budziarek asked.

Fabian translated.

"So, hosed down in the freezing cold—"

The SS had done that often. Just for fun.

"Or a bed bath with warm, soapy water from our new comrade?"

"Budziarek, the Germans should have put your libido up against a wall and shot it."

They lay on slatted wooden beds stripped of mattresses in the SS barracks, an iron stove roaring at each end of the hut.

Two Russian nurses followed Rifkin's orders. Stripped them naked and washed them down with yellow carbolic soap. At the smell of carbolic, the bawdiness seemed to leave Budziarek. All Fabian heard were groans.

When they were dry, sinking into powdery, bug-dusted mattresses, and warm beneath clean sheets and down quilts, a warmth Fabian felt certain had vanished from the earth under some Nazi rewriting of the laws of physics, Budziarek spoke.

"I don't have much Russian, but did I hear our comrade say '*mir*' and something else?"

"Мир—это свобода. Свобода—это мир."

"Meaning?"

"Peace is freedom. Freedom is peace."

"What's that? Marx or Lenin?"

"No, I think she just made it up. She's only doing what we all must do from now on—make life up as we go along. Glib aphorisms and all. Germany tore up the rule book."

"Svoboda . . . Freedom?"

"Да, свобода."

"Y'know, Fabian, even the thought of freedom scares the shit out of me."

§21

They—the whoever of they—let him sleep.

When he awoke, the room was full, another twenty or so Häftlings fortunate enough to have survived.

A Polish woman was shaving Budziarek's head. He grinned at Fabian.

"I'd pay a few złotys for this back in Łodz."

Another Pole was gathering up the striped pyjamas from the floor.

"What are you doing?"

"We have to burn them. Lice."

She held up his jacket. The superimposed red triangle and yellow star—political prisoner and Jew, not that Fabian had any idea why he had been classified as political—and his number: 155515.

"Please leave it."

"Orders."

Ah, orders, the way the German world worked.

The good fairy appeared out of nowhere. Lieutenant Rifkin.

"Can I help?"

"Ask our friend not to burn my uniform."

"We're burning them all."

"I want to keep mine."

Budziarek was laughing now. Throaty and bitter.

"Fabian, Fabian . . . do we really need souvenirs?"

"OK," Rifkin said. "I'll have it washed and returned to you."

The woman with the razor and the bowl of soapy water had finished with Budziarek and moved across to lather Fabian's stubble. He closed his eyes and said nothing.

Budziarek said, with almost a giggle in his voice, "Fabian, only you would manage to get room service in a *Konzentrationslager*."

§22

Came the thaw. Snow turned to mud. The bonfire the SS had lit to burn the evidence had been appropriated by the Russians to burn lice-ridden palliasses and had now been repurposed to roast a pig. Whatever—it was a source of heat.

Fabian and Budziarek sat on the plank bench once more, wrapped in blankets, while bad-tempered Poles milled around them and manic Russians ran around barking orders hardly anyone understood.

A mug each of scummy, deliciously muddy soup. An aesthetic delight to gaze into soup and not see the bottom of the mug. A tactile pleasure to feel a ceramic rim touch his lips after months of drinking from utensils improvised out of rusting tin. The only finer sensation had been the touch of cotton sheets when he had first lain back in bed, deloused and shaved. If there were such things as angels, the angels wore cotton and sat on clouds sipping mud soup.

"I got carrot, onions, potatoes and something that might once have been cabbage, or possibly a bat's wing," Budziarek said. "And I think the yellow scum is chicken fat. The Ivans are spoiling us. Next thing you know we'll have bananas."

"Budziarek, how long were you feeding me?"

"Since the Germans left. The passage of time isn't easy to keep in the mind. Everything kind of blurs. Maybe a week, could be longer."

"Was I conscious?"

"Not really. You were . . . how to put it . . . awake without knowing it. You sort of sucked at things more than drinking them."

"Yes. That might be one definition of delirium. I seem to have a memory, or an imagining, of a man with a pistol. A pistol pointed at me."

"Oh, that was real. Two days before the Russians arrived, an SD squad came back to finish us off. They shot everyone who couldn't run or hide, and started this bonfire. Half a dozen Häftlings were rounded up to pile on the ledgers. Then the SD shot them."

"And you?"

"The place was littered with corpses. I just lay down among them and played dead. I heard the gunfire from the *Krankenbau*. I saw one of the bastards come out of there buttoning the flap on his holster . . ."

It seems you get to live. Good luck with that.

"I lay a good hour after the SD left, just in case, then I went inside. Everyone but you was dead. And I knew you weren't dead because you were snoring."

"So you fed me gruel and water?"

"Yep. And then two days later the Russians arrived and we all lived happily ever after."

The short NKVD angel arrived.

"Все в порядке?"

Everything OK?

"Of course," Fabian replied. "We want for nothing."

Junior Lieutenant Rifkin still had not attuned to his sense of humour. Perhaps sarcasm was a vice unknown in the Soviet system.

"The major would like to see you."

"My door is always open. My bench and my bonfire too."

At last, a hint of exasperation appeared on her face.

"Could you report to hut 23 in fifteen minutes?"

Fabian held up a naked wrist. The one with the tattoo.

"Time is meaningless."

"О, черт возьми!"

For crying out loud!

She took off her Pobeda wristwatch and handed it to him.

"Keep it. I'm Russian, I'll steal another."

She left them to it, an angry beat in her steps.

"What was that about?" Budziarek asked.

"It seems her boss wants to meet me."

"Uh. That so? Try to come back with toothpaste. My mouth tastes like a midden."

§23

The Russians seemed determined to retrieve what information they could, anything that had survived the flames. Hut 23 was piled high with paper and cardboard boxes.

A scrawny girl with a dirty face and striking blue eyes sat bundled up in an SS greatcoat, sipping at the same greasy broth he had just downed. She looked simultaneously frightened and relieved. Fabian felt that good manners, if such things had survived mass annihilation, obliged him to speak.

"Sam Fabian. Berlin. Professor of mathematical physics."

"Magda Ewald," the girl said. "Vienna. Trombone player."

Suddenly it all seemed absurd to Fabian, like the moves in some silly party game, a playing card tossed down . . . sous-chef, saggar-maker, scrimshanker. He smiled. Fräulein Ewald did not return the smile and bent to her soup once more.

Another voice. "You must be Professor Fabian."

A different short NKVD woman had appeared in the doorway to an inner room. Ye gods, did the Soviet Union have no one over five feet tall? Fabian had no idea how to read the preposterous shoulder boards of the Russians. They seemed bigger than the woman herself, as though she were a cat fluffed up in anger or defiance. And perhaps that was the intention.

He'd take Rifkin at her word.

"Major?"

"Tosca. Larissa Tosca. Step inside."

She spoke German with the oddest of accents. One he could not place.

She beckoned to him. Closed the door. Pointed at a chair.

"You OK?"

"People keep asking me that question. Forgive me, Madame Major, but it's a stupid question. I'm in fucking Auschwitz. What can be OK about that?"

Against all expectation, she smiled.

"Okey dokey," she said in English, and then he could place the accent—American.

"Shall we begin again? And in what language?"

"I'm happy with Russian," Fabian replied.

"Which gets us straight to the point. Riva tells me you speak several languages. You care to tell me which?"

"My first language is German. I'm a Berliner. English I learnt in my teens—utterly essential if I was to keep up with academic papers in my field. Russian was a hobby. I adore Chekhov and wanted to be able to read him in the original. French I began before I could read in German. My mother told me it was the language of cultured people. I read Rimbaud before I ever read Goethe. Polish I picked up simply because I worked alongside Poles at the Humboldt, or at least I did until Hitler sent them all here. Yiddish, probably the least of my skills. My upbringing wasn't all that Jewish—just Jewish enough to land me here."

"Polish?"

"I get by."

"So you could interpret between Russian, German, Polish and English?"

"If asked, yes. Why English?"

"Because by the time we get to Berlin we'll be sharing it with the British and the Americans."

"We're going to Berlin?"

"Yep."

"I'd be inclined to say you just made my day, except that I am wondering if there's anything left of Berlin."

"Only one way to find out. Shake?"

She stuck out her hand. Fabian shook it. The merest frisson. A woman's touch.

"Oh—and we pay. You'll be on wages from today."

"I was salaried back in Berlin."

She switched to English once more, grinned hugely. "We ain't that grand."

"So . . . I am now a Soviet worker? One of the great Soviet proletariat at last?"

"Until we're through, yes."

"Through with what?"

"I don't know. Only time will tell. But you're a worker, not a slave. When we don't need you anymore you'll get your discharge, letters of identity and safe passage—our *Ausweis*—and you can be on your way to . . . wherever."

"My wherever has always been Berlin."

"Then you won't have far to walk."

Fabian paused in the doorway.

"I don't suppose you happen to have a tube of toothpaste about you?"

§24

Budziarek spat like a coal miner. Fabian's new watch told him it was eight in the morning, an unthinkably late hour, and already Budziarek had cleaned his teeth three times, noisily, gargling and spitting into his tin bowl. Such rare and simple pleasures.

The door was yanked open. A Russian soldier yelled, "*Raus! Raus!*"

A most unfortunate choice of phrase but quite possibly the only German he had.

"Немцы наступают. Немцы наступают."

"Oh fuck. Not again."

Budziarek spat one last time.

"What?"

"He's telling us to get out. The Germans are coming."

"What? Some sort of counter-attack?"

"You're asking me?"

§25

Outside, the sun was creeping over the horizon, slowly revealing a dirty grey everything everywhere.

The Russian who'd done all the shouting ran up to them still yelling "*Raus*," threw a couple of greatcoats at their feet, told them they had two minutes.

Fabian picked up a Red Army coat, shook it for bugs. No hammers, no sickles, no bullet holes.

Budziarek hefted his, a Wehrmacht field-grey with a number on each epaulette. He dropped it.

"I'll be fucked if I'll wear this."

Fabian had one arm through the sleeve of his, withdrew it and handed the coat to Budziarek.

As Fabian picked up the Wehrmacht coat, Budziarek said, "It doesn't bother you?"

"Cold bothers me. I've had over two weeks of relative warmth, enough to eat, and I am clean. If I have to wear something just to avoid slipping back into cold, starvation and dirt, I'd wear Hitler's underpants."

Budziarek told him he was crazy and buttoned up his Russian coat. "I heard something like '*dve minuti*'. Two minutes for what?"

A large dray horse lumbered into view, pulling a battered wooden wagon. The loud Russian just behind it, "*Raus, raus!*"

The wagon stopped. A dozen miserable-looking men on board.

The Russian urged them on, telling the men with gestures to move up and make room. Fabian and Budziarek sat with their legs over the tailgate. The horse moved off. The Russian stopped shouting, waved a friendly hand, smiled. Fabian would never understand Russians. There was no sign of his guardian angel or of her boss, Major Tosca, and he concluded the deal was off.

"I do hope this cart isn't our sole transport to Berlin. I'll rattle to pieces."

"We're going to Berlin?"

"Well . . . *I* was."

"Fuck Berlin. I'm going to Łodz and not an inch further."

§26

The sun shone without warmth.

Budziarek disappeared inside his greatcoat, only the top of his head and his eyes visible, but the eyes roamed wildly.

Every so often he'd leap off the wagon, snatch something from the roadside and have Fabian haul him back up.

The first time he held up an unopened tin of sauerkraut.

"Looks like this is the German version of a paper trail. The tin trail. Everything the buggers dropped or threw away."

Next, two cans of stewed beef. Then a jar of cherry jam, a can of peaches and finally a bottle of vodka.

"Would you believe it? Half a litre of Luksusowa. Spud vodka. Chilled, too. I prefer Żubrówka, but . . ."

He knocked back a mouthful, choked and coughed.

"First drink in nine months."

He coughed fit to bust. An explosive hacking that shook his ribs and turned his face to borscht.

"Heaven, absolute bloody heaven."

He handed the bottle to Fabian, who declined.

One more gulp and the bottle vanished into one of the huge pockets in his greatcoat before anyone else could notice what he'd got.

"Alcohol opens up your veins," Fabian said softly. "You need to conserve your body heat."

"Nah," Budziarek replied. "If that were true, all those dogs they have in Switzerland wouldn't go around with little brandy barrels on their collars rescuing people in the snow."

Wherever they were going, it was at less than walking pace, not that anyone felt like walking. They sat for five hours. Two men with four cans of food and no can opener.

Prolonged exposure to Budziarek's alternating silence and prattle— bon mots, aphorisms, homely wisdom—convinced Fabian of something he had long suspected: that there was such a thing as an affable idiot.

§27

Early that afternoon, the sun already dipping to a February dusk, the wagon stopped for the last time, at a railway junction.

Fabian was almost certain he'd passed this way en route to the camp. He'd been in a locked boxcar and had seen nothing of the journey except cracks of light flickering through the boards. The line led straight to the ramp at Auschwitz, which the Germans had built last year to speed up the killing of Jews. He had jumped down, a fit thirty-year-old male Jew, and had not been picked for immediate execution, just a brutal haircut and a check for gold teeth, of which he fortunately had none.

So . . . why the wagon? Had an Allied air force managed to lob one lonely bomb in the direction of Auschwitz? Had the Germans ripped up the tracks to slow down the Russians? Whatever—they climbed down, fell down, from the wagon. Two glistening steam locomotives, stark and black against the white of driven snow, purring and pissing on the track, one facing east, one roughly west, each with the too-familiar boxcars strung out behind it.

"I been here before," Budziarek said.

"Haven't we all."

A Russian came up waving his rifle as though it was an oar, paddling the air, herding them in the direction of the boxcars.

"Куда едем?" Fabian asked.

Where are we going?

"Краков."

Kraków.

Budziarek boarded first and was reaching down a hand to Fabian when a Soviet half-track roared up and skidded to a halt, slewed sideways on the railway embankment.

"No, no, no. Wrong train!"

Fabian turned to see a frantic Junior Lieutenant Rifkin waving at the Russian soldier.

"There's a right train?" Fabian asked.

Breathless, she paused to suck in air. "Yes. Of course. This train goes to Kraków. That one to Katowice. You should be on the other train."

"And after Katowice?"

"Not sure. We're aiming for Breslau. I have to rejoin my group. Failing that, Łodz. A roundabout route. We took Łodz more than a month ago. But the Germans are massing close to Breslau so . . . whatever . . . where I go, you go. Tosca's orders."

At the mention of his hometown, Budziarek leapt from the boxcar.

Everyone, Budziarek included, understood "*Niet.*" Particularly when accompanied by a raised hand like a traffic cop's at a road junction.

"What do you mean 'no'?" Fabian said, then for no reason he could be sure of added, "Where I go, he goes."

"О, черт."

All the same, she did it. Stopped arguing and walked with them to the other train.

"There'll be stops en route. I have no idea where or when. At the latest I will see you in Tychy."

"Where's that?"

"Ask your new friend."

She threw this over her shoulder as she walked back to her half-track.

§28

Budziarek said little till the train moved off. He grinned, held up his right thumb and said, "*Dom.*" Home.

Unlike the train to the camp, the boxcar had an iron stove. To light it they broke off bits of the carriage and fed them into the stove. The mathematician in Fabian wanted to calculate how long such wooden cannibalism could sustain them before they had a hot stove and no boxcar.

At the next stop, an invisible hand threw in two sacks of logs, and Fabian's inner calculator stopped. At the stop after that a babushka swathed in layer upon layer of ragged skirts and a Red Army tunic clambered on board with a sack of vegetables and a ham hock and settled down to cook.

The train sat an hour or more.

"Варю вам суп, польские бастарды!"

Soup, you Polish bastards!

Fabian did not translate.

With soup inside him, Budziarek became chatty.

"Tychy's about twenty K from here. Won't be long. We could be there in less than half an hour. It used to be famous for beer. I hope no one's bombed the brewery."

It was dark now. The train moved off for five minutes and then juddered to a halt, sending a Newtonian ripple through the chain of boxcars, and it did not move again until dawn. And when it moved, it crawled, stopped, crawled again and reached the outskirts of Tychy at noon.

§ 29

The train backed into a siding. Rifkin's half-track and half a dozen others were lined up in front of a vast building made of the dirty red brick in which Poland seemed to abound, a factory or perhaps a warehouse. Russian privates stood around a burning brazier, smoking.

"Any idea where we are?" Fabian asked.

"At the brewery. I said Tychy was famous for beer. This is the place."

"Beer? I'd kill for a slice of bread. Or half of your can of sauerkraut and a sausage."

"They'll have a field kitchen, an army marches on its wotsit . . . I forget who said that. In fact, I can smell it from here."

Before they could follow the coarsely aromatic trail of the field kitchen, a door opened and Rifkin beckoned to them.

Inside, in among the stilled paraphernalia of beer brewing, two of Rifkin's huge soldiers stood with half a dozen men—men with guns, men without uniforms—whom Fabian took to be partisans.

A shirtless man with a bloody face sat on an upturned crate, dripping into the sawdust and dirt at his feet.

"Now, Professor, you earn your wages. Find out what's going on. My men just stopped this lot from beating a man to death. I want to know why."

Fabian asked. Everyone talked at once. He calmed the gabble of voices with open hands and got one of them to tell the story—a boy of fifteen or so, in an oversize jacket and a bandolier of bullets.

"The man on the crate," Fabian told Rifkin. "He appears to be some sort of Gauleiter, a collaborator appointed by the Germans to this district. About a month ago the Germans marched Häftlings out of Auschwitz. That I know to be true. I saw them leave. A few days after they left the camp, they passed through here. A dozen or so women were not keeping up. The Germans abandoned them here. According to the Poles, this man lined up all the women and shot them in the back of the head. Then he had their bodies dumped in a mass grave. They say they can show us the grave."

Rifkin looked at the man.

"Tell him to lift his head up."

"*Podnieś głowę.*"

The man looked up. One eye closed, nose mashed.

"Ask him. What's his version?"

"*Mów mi.*"

The man breathed deeply—battered, weary, unrepentant. A cool disdain for his tormenters.

"They're wrong. I had nothing to do with it. I just found the bodies. The Germans shot the stragglers. All I did was bury the bodies. And then these bastards came along. They didn't believe me an hour ago. They won't believe me now. When you leave they'll ask me the same question over and over again and eventually they'll kick the last breath of life out of me."

"I saw him shoot them," the boy said. "He's lying!"

"Oh for fuck's sake, just shoot the fucker!"

Fabian had almost forgotten that Budziarek was there. Rifkin's head turned to him, then to Fabian.

"My friend Budziarek thinks you should shoot your prisoner," Fabian said. "What do you say? He's a POW now."

Rifkin said nothing. Looked at the man, looked at the partisans. Said nothing.

The boy spoke again, shouting in a language she did not need to understand—the meaning was obvious.

"He's right. Just shoot the fucker! Shoot the fucker!"

"Listen to the kid," the man said. "You'd be doing me a favour."

Then Budziarek pulled out a Luger and shot the collaborator in the chest. He fell backwards off the beer crate to land with his legs in the air.

§30

Fabian sat outside drinking beer.

Budziarek came to sit next to him, uninvited, clutching his tin of sauerkraut and a beer. He chinked bottles to no response from Fabian.

He finished his beer, shrugged off Fabian's silence and got up to leave, still clutching his tin.

Fabian called him back.

"Budziarek . . . before . . . well, just before . . . before everything . . . Budziarek, what did you do?"

"You mean my job? I was a thief."

"Professionally?"

"Like there's amateurs, sure."

"And you got sent to Auschwitz for stealing?"

"'Course not . . . they wouldn't have bothered . . . nah . . . I got banged up with you 'cos some stupid sod painted a pro-Soviet slogan complete with a hammer and fucking sickle on the outside of my house. So I got taken for a politico. I don't have any politics. I'm me. I look after number one."

"That in itself is a political position."

"Sez you. Why you asking so many questions?"

"The gun."

"Ah."

Budziarek hesitated. No shuffling of the feet, no sheepish glances, just a long look at the low horizon as he weighed up the wisdom of what he might say next.

"Picked it up in the snow, when I got the bottle of vodka, didn't I? Didn't seem wise to flash it about. Save it for when it's needed."

"And it was needed just now?"

"Damn right it was. I may be a thief, but shooting women in the back of the head? No, the bastard had it coming. Your girl was dithering, so I . . . took the initiative."

"Have you taken the initiative before?"

"You mean, have I killed anyone before?"

"Yes."

"In the middle of a fucking war you're bothered about my morals? Sam, if you get through this war without killing anyone, I reckon you'll be in the minority. No, enough questions. Sam, I am what I am."

"Sounds like a quotation. I forget who."

"It don't matter. I did what I had to do."

Rifkin emerged, flanked by her two dwarfing Red Army soldiers.

She held out her hand.

"Пистолет."

Pistolet needed no translation.

Budziarek uttered a simple "*Niet.*"

Rifkin looked a little incredulous but reached for her belt pouch and drew out a small Swiss Army knife. Fabian wasn't at all sure that Switzerland had an army but knew the knife had blades to prise things out of horses' hooves, overthrow dictatorships and . . . open cans.

"Давайте обменяемся," she said.

"She's offering to trade with you. Your gun for a can opener," Fabian said.

Budziarek slowly took the Luger from his pocket and handed it over. Rifkin held the knife by its chain and dangled it in front of him.

"Не вздумай еше раз возиться со мной."

Fabian said, "She—"

"No need. I get it. Her face says it all. "Beef with sauerkraut coming up."

Budziarek snatched the knife and went in search of the field kitchen. Rifkin waved her men away and sat down with Fabian.

"Скажи ему, чтобы больше не протрахал меня," she said softly.

Tell him not to fuck with me again.

Fabian ignored this. "You're not really bothered by what just happened, are you?"

"Should I be? Rough justice is still justice."

"Either that or it's murder."

"Professor, for a man who has lived through hell you seem strangely squeamish."

Fabian paused. He knew he'd underestimated Budziarek—affable idiot, thief and killer—and quite possibly he'd underestimated Rifkin too—with her beautiful nut-brown eyes, a smiling angel and a ruthless apparatchik. Had his guardian angel become his guardian imp?

"I thought . . . I thought I had seen the worst," he said at last.

"Who knows? Perhaps the worst is yet to come."

"Or perhaps you are invoking the worst. Will there be more rough justice before we reach Berlin?"

"We do what we have to do."

"Tell me, Junior Lieutenant Rifkin, who do you think was telling the truth in there?"

"Does it matter?"

"The truth matters."

"I don't know. Perhaps he did it, perhaps there were old scores of which we know nothing just waiting to be settled. I think we will encounter many more. The post-war world will be a world of settling old scores. Most of them small, petty and meaningless. Surely you can see that?"

Fabian sat in silence.

Rifkin held out her hand.

Fabian gave her the bottle.

"Or perhaps," he said, "just one very big score."

§31

Red Army rations consisting, as they did, mostly of bread, buckwheat kasha and lard, Budziarek's tinned food boosted their "lunch"—a concept that meant next to nothing—to the point of plenitude and taste.

He reappeared with wooden bowls of kasha and billycans of hot beef stew and cold sauerkraut, all balanced on a broken piece of wooden plank, like the world's worst waiter in the world's worst restaurant.

"You can dine on the smell alone," he said.

"Thank you," Fabian said softly.

"Oh. We speaking again, are we?"

"Of course."

Budziarek ate with his left arm curved around his bowl—a camp habit. Protection and preservation. Fabian had been about to do the same, but noticing Budziarek's gesture he refrained. There were habits that were worth losing before they became instincts.

"Just did what I had to, y'know?" Budziarek said across the top of his bowl, head down, elbow plying.

"Yes. I do know."

"I don't need your judgement."

"You haven't got it."

Rifkin passed by, also clutching a wooden bowl of kasha and lard and a hunk of black bread.

She stopped, sniffed the air.

Budziarek looked up, beckoned to her.

"Tell her she can have some."

As Fabian spoke, she was hesitant, until he shuffled along the bench and made space for her.

"Surely you have so little to spare?"

"If Joe Stalin can spare a slice of lard for us, we can spare a couple of ounces of beef for you. The Germans did not manage to strip us of all morality."

"They tried."

"Of course they tried. Perhaps my Polish friend and I are made of sterner stuff. On the other hand, perhaps he just wants something in return."

Fabian looked at Budziarek.

"*Breslau albo Łodz?*" Budziarek asked.

"Łodz," Rifkin replied.

Budziarek stared into his bowl, calculating, then spooned a third of his meal into hers. Fabian did the same.

She ate two spoonfuls, then she spoke. Picking her way through the Russian language as though it were a minefield.

"We . . . that is, the Red Army . . . we, the Byelorussian Second Front . . . have not yet taken Breslau. The Nazis are . . . resisting. We will succeed . . . our victory is inevitable . . . but it means we shall go north instead of west. To Łodz, and then to Berlin. The longer route."

Fabian translated.

"Do you reckon they're not allowed to say 'fail'?"

"Probably. All the same, you've got what you want. Łodz."

"Or what's left of it."

§32

They were three more days in Tychy. No explanation offered, and although he was visibly and audibly impatient, Budziarek did not ask again.

"Your girl's OK," he said.

"I'm sure she is," Fabian replied. "But she's not mine."

They wandered off into the town, separately. Insomuch as anywhere in Poland had escaped unscathed, Tychy had.

Anyone who had anything to sell was selling. In improvised stalls thrown up on the street—planks on barrels, the kitchen table or spread on squares of worn carpet on the cobblestones. The junk of centuries.

An old lady had a dozen or so books, a moth-eaten fox fur stole and a set of tarnished, monogrammed cutlery resting on what had once been the stand of a treadle sewing machine.

"I sold the machine," she said apropos of nothing.

Fabian picked up a book.

Step: Historia pewnej podróży. Anton Czechow.

A find. He'd not read a book since . . . since. And this was one he'd never read. Albeit in Polish, not Russian. It was the story of a journey. Apt. And the printed page had ever been his vice.

"I've no money," he said.

"Don't want money. Food."

"I've no food either."

The old lady stared at him, as though trying to read character in his face. He stared back, trying to achieve character.

"Take it," she said. "It was my husband's. The bastard used to sit around reading when he should have been working. I've no use for it or any of them. Books are for idlers. Are you an idler?"

"Anything but, madam."

She pointed at his chest.

"Open your coat."

Fabian obliged.

"I thought so. Lager stripes. *Żydem?*"

He opened his coat a little wider so she could see his star.

"*Tak. Żydem.*"

"I could ask you for your greatcoat, but I wouldn't be seen dead in it, and you'd freeze to death in your pyjamas. Take my advice, young man, burn that coat and get yourself another before somebody shoots you by mistake."

§33

The Russians had kept fires going all day. It was warmer outside than in the cattle trucks—a waning winter had not yet lost its bite.

He sat by a brazier until the light faded too far for reading. He closed *The Steppe* and looked up. Budziarek appeared, wrapping his greatcoat firmly around him. He sat on a beer crate opposite Fabian, and when Fabian thought he might reach out and warm his hands, he simply pulled the coat more tightly around his chest.

"Just in time for dinner. I'll ring for the butler," Fabian said.

"More kasha and more fucking lard."

"There was a mention of pork bellies."

Budziarek opened one flap of his coat.

"Could go nicely with this."

He was clutching a leg of preserved, salted ham between his right arm and his ribs.

"A bit manky, but we can scrape off the mould."

"Hmm."

"Hmm what?"

"Well. I've no money. You've no money . . ."

"You judging me again?"

"No."

"I didn't steal it. I would have stolen it, but there was an easier way. I just pointed to the uniform. These Tychy *głupeks* can't tell a real Russki from a hole in the ground—but they're scared shitless of them. My coat said it all. If I'd had my pistol and your girl's fur hat . . . who knows what I might have come back with. As it is . . . ham, and you're not going to say no, are you? Ham is ham."

§34

Rifkin pronounced the ham "вкусно"—tasty. A fraction short of delicious. She too asked no questions.

"Major Tosca mentioned something about wages when she recruited me."

"Correct," Rifkin said.

"We have no money. I have none. Budziarek has none. If he has no money he will steal."

"He stole the ham?"

"No. Let me say that he bargained for it."

"He should not steal. We have orders to shoot looters."

"Then you might as well shoot everyone in Poland. Starting with the Red Army. Meanwhile, if you pay me a small advance, I can share it with Budziarek. Then we will pay for what we want without bargain or barter."

"OK. But tell me, why do you like Budziarek?"

"'Like' would not be the word. He saved my life. He was the one kept me alive until I met you. But I might flip the question. Why does he interest you?"

"He doesn't."

"Junior Lieutenant Rifkin, are you lying to yourself or to me?"

§35

The answer came the following evening, just as dusk descended.

A woodshed—a low hut made of tarred railway sleepers—had appeared opposite Fabian's habitual spot outside the brewery. He hadn't noticed it before, but the Russians had just moved a row of wagons.

Budziarek had noticed it. He emerged from the hut, ducking his head, tugging up his trousers, picking his way carelessly across a dozen railway lines to Fabian.

As he plonked himself down, he was on the last button.

"She's OK, that girl of yours."

This needed no reply, so Fabian gave it none.

A few moments passed. Budziarek threw a log on the fire. The door of the woodshed opened again and Rifkin emerged. Fabian wondered how long it took to get in and out of a white romper suit—so many zips and buttons, such urgency—and he wondered how they'd managed without a common language.

Pieprzyć or *ебать* or fuck?

But perhaps this was the act that required no language, perhaps it was the universal language?

Rifkin looked to either side like a nervous child remembering her kerb drill, then she walked across the tracks and changed the subject that hung, like evening mist, so silently about them all.

"Tonight we have mutton."

Mutton needed no translation.

"And kasha and lard," Budziarek said.

"Of course," Fabian said. "An army marches on its stomach, even better if the stomach is full of lard. Perhaps comrade Budziarek will open the tin of fruit he's been hoarding. In celebration."

"I have no idea to what you are referring," Rifkin replied. "But fruit would be acceptable."

§36

In the morning, not long after first light, Fabian was awoken by the bumping of the cattle trucks, backwards then forwards then back again as the locomotive was fired up and stoked. Budziarek did not stir.

The train crawled out of Tychy at five miles an hour. Every few hundred metres it would stop for half an hour, an hour, and then begin to crawl again. Around two in the afternoon it stopped on the edge of a small town, somewhere on the vast Silesian plain, brooding and sibilant under a threatening sky. Fabian wondered if this was "it," if the train might never move again. He had little idea of the minutiae of Polish geography. The next obvious place they should arrive at was surely Katowice. Logically—and what was logical in wartime?—the train should have taken no more than an hour to reach Katowice. It had taken five hours and they weren't at Katowice.

He looked out of the open door, at giant winding wheels on pylons, arrows pointing to heaven, a kilometre or so away—they were in mining country.

Rifkin was walking down the track, stopping to say something at each open door. She reached Fabian.

"I'm not sure they understand me. Would you tell them all. We'll be here overnight. We have to take on coal."

"Where are we?"

She opened both hands towards him.

"Your guess is as good as mine. Just not Katowice."

"And not Łodz either."

Budziarek had awoken and appeared behind him.

"Be Polish, tell me where we are."

Budziarek rubbed his eyes, stared out at what passed for landscape.

"Boże Dary. It used to be famous for coal. Good, hard stuff, not that lignite rubbish. I should know, my dad was a miner."

"Are you joking?"

"O' course not, the old man spent twenty years down the pit and the next twenty coughing his lungs out in our apartment."

"I meant the name. Boże Dary? A gift from God?"

"I didn't name Poland. Not one square fuckin' metre of it. If I had, there'd be a suburb of Łodz called Satan's Arsehole. Have you had breakfast?"

"No. A month ago I'd have eaten it with a spoon, but now . . . I can't face unadorned lard for breakfast."

"Me neither. But if your girl is right, and we're stopping over . . . I'll nip into town . . ."

"She still hasn't given me any money."

"So?"

"Looters will be shot—Rifkin told us so."

Budziarek jumped down to the ground, shouldered his knapsack.

"Loot, shmoot, toot. You don't believe that, and if she believes it, she's the only Russian in Poland who does. Did we pay for the beer in Tychy? Her blokes drank enough to float a battleship. Did she turn down the ham I nicked? Gimme a break, Sam. It's steal or starve."

§37

Rifkin and Fabian followed Budziarek to the edge of the town. He soon lost them.

It was like a thousand other Polish towns, the urban settlement brushed out into rough countryside in broad strokes, where the industrial and the rural rubbed shoulders, where a man who spent his days down the pit would spend his days off tending a plot or raising a pig. In less than half a mile the height of the buildings in Boże Dary tailed off from the three- and four-storey structures around the pithead to the low shacks and pigsties in front of them.

"I grew up with this," Rifkin said.

"Mines?"

"Pigs."

"Where?"

"Bezumnizvinye. More than two thousand kilometres east of Moscow. On the other side of the Urals. Population about a thousand."

"Many Jews?"

"Oh yes. We are a far-flung outpost of Zion. A shtetl about as remote as you can imagine. Not a lot different from this. Flat. Wet. No coal, but plenty of pigs. That . . ."

She pointed at the pig ambling across its paddock of mud towards them.

". . . is a Siberian black pied. My job when I was a girl was to mind the sow."

"Not kosher, then?"

"Kosher is for the cities. We were peasants. The grass is too sparse for cattle. Sheep just die, it's what they do best. The pig is the perfect creature for a village on the Steppes. Eats what we eat, eats almost everything and shits everywhere. If God wanted us kosher he'd have plonked us down in Jerusalem, not halfway to Siberia."

"An interesting theory. I'd not have guessed you were a peasant."

"Why not? Nikita Khrushchev is a peasant, and he runs the Ukraine. But, since you ask, I am a college girl. Moscow State University, Lenin Hills. Until 1941 I was training as an engineer. In a socialist republic, birth is not fate."

Fate became all too apparent.

Fabian had observed a man in the partisan ad hoc uniform, one of half a dozen—no different from the men he'd seen in Tychy: leather cap, belted jacket, a bandolier of bullets—a man seemingly whittling at a fencepost with his bayonet. He thought nothing of it. People did the most pointless things, and whittling a fencepost to a point might be . . . pointless.

It wasn't.

A door opened in a shed on the far side of the pigpen. A huge partisan, the best part of two metres tall, ducked under the lintel and emerged dragging a smaller man by the collar.

The collar was attached to a Waffen-SS uniform, the uniform was worn by a man, the man was no more than a boy, seventeen or eighteen, it seemed to Fabian, scrawny and dirty, weighing about fifty-five kilos.

He looked terrified. If he had looked around, if he had had more knowledge or more imagination, he would have screamed.

He made no noise as the giant ripped his trousers from his body. He said nothing as two other partisans took an arm apiece and dragged him to the fence.

By now the man with the bayonet had whittled the fencepost dagger sharp.

Still the boy said nothing. Utterly uncomprehending.

Only when the giant slipped a hand under each armpit did the meaning of it all come clear to him, and he began to gabble in a language Fabian had never heard before . . . Magyar? Rumanian? The Waffen-SS had been recruited from most of Hitler's empire.

Then he began to scream.

"Does this have to happen?" Fabian said.

"Yes. It does. We are two against six. But we don't have to look," Rifkin replied.

"I do."

She turned and walked away, and as the Poles impaled the boy and his screams became ear-splitting, she broke into a run.

Fabian stood stock still.

The Poles noticed Fabian at last. Noticed his Wehrmacht greatcoat. One of them unslung his rifle and walked over to him, the barrel trained upon his chest.

This was the dangerous moment. Was he damned for the coat he wore?

Fabian had the coat unbuttoned. The Pole lowered the rifle a few inches and used it to lift one flap of the greatcoat.

"*Paski?*"

Stripes?

"*Auschwitz? Żydem?*"

Another dangerous moment. Poles had been, and could be, might be, more anti-Semitic than the average German.

"*Tak.*"

The Pole raised his rifle, aiming straight for the heart.

"*Boom,*" he said, then . . . "*W drodze, Żyd.*"

On your way, Jew.

And grinned as he said it.

A gentle tap in the sternum with the rifle.

Fabian walked slowly back the way he had come.

By the locomotive, he found Rifkin, dabbing at her eyes with a handkerchief.

"Tears, Riva?" he said.

"I am not . . . I am not heartless. Whatever you might think."

"What I think is that you should consider giving Budziarek back his pistol. Mercy killing might be his talent."

"Not funny, Professor."

"Not meant to be, Lieutenant."

And still they could hear the boy screaming. He would scream until his lungs gave out.

A gift from God?

§38

In the evening Rifkin had her men set up braziers along the length of the train and sat on a purloined beer crate by the fire nearest Fabian's cattle truck.

Fabian sat with her. Neither had anything to say to the other. His belly did the talking, grumbling with hunger, regretting he had not allowed it a breakfast of lard and kasha.

Out of the dimness Budziarek appeared with a full knapsack.

He upended it onto the ground. Tin upon tin.

Corned beef.

Frankfurters.

Sauerkraut.

Peaches.

Beans.

"And . . . for my next trick . . ."

He pulled out a lump of something wrapped in a dirty square of coarse linen.

"Ta-da! Zgorzelecki!"

Two uncomprehending gazes.

He peeled back the linen to reveal a speckled yellow wedge of mouldy cheese.

"Cheese, you dumb buggers! Silesian cheese! The local stuff. Must be a couple of kilos."

Rifkin got up.

"We need bowls and billycans."

She set off towards the locomotive and the improvised kitchen.

"Was it something I said?"

"No," said Fabian, and told him what had happened.

"Hmm."

"Hmm what?"

"So you stay to watch and she weeps tears of rage."

"That had not occurred to me, but yes, you may well be right."

"Sam, I don't care about the fate of one fucking Kraut, one Kraut less in the world . . ."

"He wasn't German. He was a conscript. Just like a million other kids."

"I don't care . . . if I'd been there I might have shot him myself . . . I'm an angry man . . . I hate Krauts, I hate fake Krauts . . . my rage against them is limitless . . . Łodz, Warsaw, Auschwitz . . . but you care . . . she cares . . . she weeps tears of rage. Sam, where is your rage?"

§39

Rifkin gave them a lecture as soon as the train stopped, at long last at Katowice.

"There is a large encampment here for displaced persons."

"What are they?" Fabian asked.

"They are . . . you. Except that they are not you in that they are mostly Italians. Some Hungarians, some Czechs, but mostly Italians. About a thousand of them. Many were forced labourers, some were Häftlings. Many were just criminals. The dregs of Milan's prisons."

Fabian translated for Budziarek.

"Good. I'm fed up to the back teeth with lardy kasha. A plate of buttered spaghetti . . . a dash of crispy sage . . . sliver of cheese . . . go down a treat, that would."

"Does he take nothing seriously?"

"Not much," Fabian said.

"However . . . you should have nothing to do with them."

"Why's that?"

"Breslau has not yet fallen, Berlin is . . . weeks away. We cannot send people west with so much territory still in German hands, so many will go east. I don't want you getting inadvertently caught up in a transport heading east."

"I'm sorry, Riva, I must have misheard. I thought the Nazis were on the other side."

"Not funny. There are hundreds of thousands of displaced persons. They need . . . managing."

"I don't feel the need of being managed at all."

"Professor, please stop. I know the games you play with words. Let me paraphrase—the policy of the USSR is to 'repatriate' where possible. To return people to their homelands."

"Except for those you'll be sending to a gulag."

"Oh for fuck's sake! Just stay away from the Italians!"

When she'd stomped off, sparking with melodrama, Budziarek said, "What was that about?"

"Not much. You want spaghetti, go out and get it. I'll be amazed if you find any, but I'll eat it all the same. So will Rifkin."

"We got złotys yet?"

"No . . . her cheque's in the post."

$40

Over buttered spaghetti with Silesian cheese, no sage, and the last of Budziarek's ham, Rifkin gave them the bad news.

"The track ahead of us is torn up. Sabotage. Clever sabotage. Only the odd rail here and there, but fifty or more over five miles. Makes it twice as difficult to repair. We'll be here a while."

"How long?"

"My people tell me . . . three weeks, perhaps a month."

Budziarek did not need or wait for a translation of месяц. It was the merest fraction different from the Polish miesiąc and all too painfully obvious.

"A month? I'm not waiting a month. I want to be back home, I want to be in my old apartment. If I've a home left, if I've still got a stick of furniture . . ."

In the morning Fabian awoke to find Budziarek stuffing his knapsack.

"Sam, you got pencil and paper?"

"Of course, here. But it's scarce, don't waste it."

"This is . . . fukkit, was . . . my address in Łodz. If you get to Łodz come and find me. I'm not waiting a month. I could walk there in less than a week."

He handed paper and pencil back to Fabian.

"11B Solna?"

"Yep. In Bałuty, the Jewish quarter, just south of the ghetto fence . . . that runs along the other side of the tram lines on Północna . . . if it's still standing."

"You lived in the shtetl?"

"Nope. Far too villagey a word. There was no shtetl, just streets where the Jews lived. But . . . Solna was cleared in 1940. All the Jews were fifty metres away behind the wire. My house in Śródmieście got blown to bollocks when the Krauts arrived. So I became a squatter. Was I going to live on the streets while apartments sat empty?"

"I suppose not."

"Sam, you're doing what you've never done before."

"What's that?"

"Judging me. But like I said . . . Come find me."

From somewhere Budziarek had obtained a leather jacket. It had bullet holes, and it occurred to Fabian that he might have stripped it off a corpse.

He slipped the jacket on and draped his Red Army greatcoat over Fabian's shoulders.

"Don't need it anymore. Put it on. Don't get mistaken for a German."

"I am a German."

"You know what I mean. If you go on wearing the Kraut one, you're just making yourself into a target."

"I know. I had that pointed out to me a few days ago in the most delightful way."

§41

Katowice pulsated. Katowice throbbed. Katowice buzzed. It heaved with *Sehnsucht*. If Rifkin had known the word, she would have agreed with Fabian. Katowice rippled with lust.

There seemed to be no shortage of food. Budziarek's contribution was not missed, although the man himself was. Rifkin seemed to Fabian to be struggling for Russian stoicism in the face of heartbreak. What he had perceived as a quick fuck in a railway hut was apparently a wartime romance. Of necessity they were usually brief encounters.

She sat silent over her pierogi for two nights.

On the third day, strolling—a concept all but alien to wartime—Fabian discovered that Katowice still had a functioning cinema. In itself this was a small miracle. The larger miracle was the sign outside:

Приветствуем товарищей СССР.
Будет неделя фильмов с русскими субтитрами.
Бесплатный вход великой Красной Армии!

WELCOME COMRADES OF THE USSR.
THERE WILL BE A WEEK OF FILMS WITH RUSSIAN SUBTITLES.
FREE ENTRY FOR THE GLORIOUS RED ARMY!

"I don't believe this," Rifkin said.

"What's to doubt? The gods of Communism have blessed you. We should see for ourselves. There's nothing else to do."

"Do I detect sarcasm, Professor?"

Fabian expected something like "classics of Polish cinema"—not that he was sure there was such a thing. Instead they watched a mixed bag of pre-war Hollywood—some in the original English, some dubbed into Polish, all with mangled, occasionally ludicrous Russian subtitles—while behind them was a constant susurrus of Italian, Polish and Wordless as the newly liberated fucked in the back rows.

It seemed to him that a hole—he had no better word—had opened up in space-time, concepts he had dealt with all his working life to no apparent conclusion . . . a hole down which they had somehow escaped from war, from Poland, into the joys of Tinseltown. In darkness war was not happening, in darkness Poland did not exist.

Tuesday: *Gone with the Wind*, which Rifkin did not care for.

Wednesday: *The Wizard of Oz*, which she liked even less. "Capitalist fantasy and a waste of celluloid . . . although I quite like the man dressed as a lion."

Thursday: *It Happened One Night*, which she utterly loathed. "Why is Hollywood fascinated by heiresses? They are just parasites."

Fabian was beginning to feel that this venture might not be the distraction he had hoped for. But . . .

Friday: *Gold Diggers of 1933*, which she declared to be a hidden masterpiece. Hidden from whom? Fabian wondered, but for days afterwards she hummed "Remember My Forgotten Man." She seemed to ignore "We're in the Money"; perhaps the translation—у нас слишком много валюты, "We Have Too Much Currency"—had been too clumsy to make either sense or a catchy song title, or perhaps it had deliberately defied any prescribed ideological stance.

And lastly . . .

Saturday: *The Roaring Twenties*. "A brave indictment of the failure of the USA. A nation betrayed by a corrupt and deeply flawed system. And the little guy, he is so cute. Such swagger. Has he been in anything else?"

As they emerged into early spring, late afternoon light and the creeping skyline, Poland came back, and with it, war: fifty, seventy—God alone knew—a hundred Russian planes roaring overhead.

§42

Their evenings had two rituals.

They would delouse.

And they would play chess.

Rifkin had seen chess matches but had never played.

"How do we play? I thought we needed a box of little wooden men?"

Fabian moistened some of their daily ration of rye bread—sour on the tongue, grey, almost stale—and twisted it into shapes vaguely recalling pawns and rooks, and a very poor semblance of knights and bishops. He drew the sixty-four squares of chess with his fingertips in the dust on the floorboards of the cattle wagon—then he taught her the rules.

"Do you need me to go over them again?"

"Nope. I heard you the first time."

Fabian had played all his life. A few times in his adolescence he had lost to his father, but no one had beat him since. Chess was second nature to him, like electrons and positrons. At the Humboldt it had been almost an initiation test for a new appointee to take on Fabian across the chequerboard.

Rifkin checkmated him in twenty minutes.

Back to back, delousing with the merest mask of privacy, she said, "A man and a woman pick lice together. It is a curious intimacy, is it not?"

"Did Budziarek delouse with you?"

"Only because I made him."

"Before or after?"

"Show me the man who will delay his passion for a louse and I shall show you a saint."

She turned halfway around, slipping her arms into her battle-dress. Fabian was still hunting for the red-spotted beasts in the seams of his jacket.

"Isn't it time you ditched your stripes?"

"Maybe later. Right now they are a *memento vitae*."

"You have to remember to live?"

§43

The next day Fabian stripped the bark off a birch tree and weighed it down with stones. When it was flatter and drier, he'd peel back the outer layer to expose the paler layer beneath and create brown and white squares for a much better chessboard. Not that he thought a proper board would make her easier to beat.

After nineteen days and a dozen chess victories, Rifkin announced that the track had been repaired. The locomotive that had stood cold and mute was fired up, and they began the slow crawl north to Łodz.

A hundred kilometres north of Katowice, the longest run without a break, somewhere west of Radomsko, the locomotive stopped again.

"We'll be here a while," Rifkin said.

"Why's that?"

"Come and look."

They had ground to a halt on a stretch of the flat Polish plain.

They walked to the front of the train. Soviet T-34 tanks were crossing the tracks ahead of them, bouncing, rocking, ten abreast like a wagon train. Fabian counted—280, roaring westward.

Rifkin grinned with pride, and in a gesture untypical of her, slipped her arm through his and drew him closer.

"It won't be long now. Soon you will have your country back."

Touched as he was by the sentiment and the affection in her gesture, Fabian was not at all sure he wanted his country back.

The engine driver came down from the cab, smelling sweetly, hauntingly, of coal and oil and steam. Then he spat black sputum on the ground.

Fabian had seen him many times. But never spoken to him. He was railway aristocracy, after all. He had been known to fling hot coals at Häftlings trying to steal water from his tender.

"Stop, start. Crawl, stop, start. What a way to run a railway."

Then he spoke to Rifkin, in Russian. "Is this your plan? To have us arrive at Łodz via Minsk and Moscow?"

Rifkin tightened her grip on Fabian's arm and told the driver to go fuck himself.

§44

They got to Łodz and found Solna. In the district of Bałuty, just a few metres outside the ghetto. The fence at the north end of the street lay in a tangle, as though a tank or several tanks had driven straight through it.

The door to 11B was ajar, a moraine of dust and rubble on the thrawl.

In the hallway of 11B, Solna, Budziarek sat propped up against the newell post, dead. Looking at the body, Fabian concluded he'd been shot in the stomach more than once. His hands were clasped to the wound as though he were holding himself together, fingers interlocked. Rats had taken his fingertips. He was caked in dried blood and sat in a crisp brown puddle a metre across.

Around his neck was a string suspending a cardboard sign at chest level:

Żydzi Won

"What does it say?" Rifkin asked.

"It's a very old slogan," Fabian replied. "In German it would be '*Juden Raus*.'"

A cry from the street behind them.

"Leave him be!"

Fabian came out into the light to see a tiny woman, no more than four foot ten, wrapped in rags, clutching an oilskin bag, wielding a walking stick of corkscrew hazel. She looked to be ninety. Her voice was like a frog's.

"Don't you dare move him. He is a warning to others! These stinking Jews, they come back and still think they own everything. Gone for years and now they come back to tell us what's ours is not ours. That it is theirs."

"What happened? Did you see this happen?"

"Of course I saw. This is the apartment of my grandson. He has lived here a year or more. Two weeks ago this Jew arrives and says no, this is his apartment. My grandson, my Piotr, tells him what is what and he should go back to Jew land. This is not a Jew house no more. And he goes away. Two days ago the Jew comes back, and Piotr finds him in the apartment, and he will not leave, he says everything is his—so Piotr shoots him. What did the Jew expect? That we would not fight for what is right? That we do not fight for what is ours? And Piotr has to run and hide in case the Russians come. But Russians do not come—until now."

She raised the stick and pointed past Fabian to the doorway. Rifkin had appeared, her face streaked with tears, brimful of rage.

Sam doubted that Rifkin had understood the words, but the stick said it all. She knocked the stick away and but for Sam's restraining hand would have knocked the old woman to the ground.

"Ведьма. Ведьма!"

Witch. Witch!

Rifkin suddenly collapsed onto Fabian, her head in his chest, buckets of tears and a wailing smothered only by his coat.

The old witch took her chance and hobbled off. At what she took to be a safe distance she turned and shouted at Fabian.

"I saw him die, you know. I watched the Jew die. I heard the Jew die. He cursed Hitler, he cursed the Germans, and with his last breath he cursed God and died."

And for a moment she switched to German: "*Gott verfluchen und sterben. Juden Raus!*"

Then she spat upon the ground.

Rifkin broke free and in what seemed to Fabian to be a single swift motion drew her gun and shot the old woman dead.

§45

Two streets away, in the doorway of a ruined shop, Fabian held her until she stopped shaking.

When at last she raised her head she said, "No questions, Sam. Not one. It is I who have a question for you. Sam, where is your rage?"

The same question Budziarek had asked.

"Shot for being a Jew. He didn't even look like a Jew," she said.

"What does a Jew look like?"

"OK. OK. I just . . . I just find it a dreadful irony."

"There's nothing ironic about it."

"I'm a Jew . . . you're a Jew . . . Budziarek was not . . ."

§46

They billeted in Harcerska and never went back to Solna. If the Russians, as the new rulers of Łodz, ever investigated the killing of an old woman there, Rifkin never mentioned it. Indeed she never mentioned it again, and he could not think that one more death would matter to them. The world had long ago become death.

At the end of Harcerska was a wall hundreds of metres long, the dusty, decadent beauty of flaking red brick. There was a bricked-up archway, lacking any insignia—no notice, no inscription, no memorial—but he guessed that it had once been the gateway to a Jewish cemetery and that the wall had been repurposed by the Nazis to keep the living in rather than to sequester the dead.

The apartment block had survived mostly intact even to the glass in the windows. Harcerska had been yet another Jewish-occupied street on the fringe of the ghetto. The Russians had commandeered the entire building, once home to dozens of Jewish families, now dispersed, now dead, and he knew that if he said this to Rifkin she would reply, "Are we not Jews?"

They stayed until late April.

Fabian gained weight.

Rifkin washed her hair every day and sang to herself as she did so. For several days it was a miserable song of death and loss and Mother Russia's sacrifices, so typically Russian since long before the revolution—then she switched to "Remember My Forgotten Man," although the only line she had mastered in English was the title. Either song seemed apt.

The roaring of the planes diminished, they flew over now in ones and twos, and looked to be transports rather than fighters or bombers.

"We will take Berlin soon," she said.

"Today, tomorrow?"

"Not quite. But the Red Army has crossed the Oder."

"Fierce fighting?"

"Many dead. The battle around Seelow Heights is proving costly. However . . . now you and I move on."

"What about our trainload of Poles and Germans? The Germans will be chafing at the bit."

"Then they can chafe. They re-enter Germany only when we say so. Meanwhile they stay. The Poles we already kicked off the train. They can have Poland back."

"When you say so."

"What's that supposed to mean?"

§47

"Why was Budziarek not your mission instead of me?"

She looked startled. He had refrained from mentioning Budziarek. If they talked about him, it was at her prompting. He missed Budziarek, the rogue who had saved his life, but his heart was intact, whereas Rifkin was holding herself together like a jigsaw puzzle—coherent, but with all the pieces visible.

"You're not my mission. You were never my mission. You're my ticket."

"Ticket?"

"To Berlin. I am . . . not lacking in ambition. When I told the major that you spoke so many languages—and that you were nobody's fool—she wanted you in Berlin, and hence I get to Berlin too. Berlin is where we need you, where you will earn your wage. Anything we do on the road to Berlin is really nothing. It won't matter. Like Tychy. Tychy was nothing."

"What happened in Tychy was not nothing. What happened in Łodz was not nothing."

§48

Commandeering was a Rifkin skill. She commandeered a jeep much as she had commandeered their apartment. "Jeep" had been merely a word to Fabian. He'd never seen one.

A Red Army private was hunkered down by the rear wheels, trying to apply dribbling, thin red paint to a recalcitrant, seemingly permanent white star.

"It looks brand new."

"It is. A gift from Uncle Sam, along with many tanks and hundreds of thousands of cans of tinned pork. If we run out of shells we will just throw pork at the Nazis."

"Where are we going, Riva?"

"Schwetig."

"Schwetig isn't Berlin. It's on this side of the river."

"We will get there, Sam. Believe me. When the last bomb has been dropped, the last bullet fired . . ."

"And the last tin of pork hurled."

"Sam, do you take nothing seriously?"

"I take seriously what needs to be taken seriously. The rest? A free-for-all. As whimsy takes me."

"Ух, какой ты капризный."

So capricious.

§49

Breslau did not fall easy.

Even as Sam had lain in his bunk in the *Krankenbau*, the Russians had taken Łodz. Two days later the Germans had forced much of the population of Breslau to flee—many died in flight and frost. The city itself—already a *Festung* on Hitler's orders, a fortress not to be lost, cost irrelevant—was now manned by a ragbag of Wehrmacht, Home Guard and Hitler Youth . . . encircled and under siege.

On April 30 Sam and Rifkin set off westward from Łodz, well clear of Breslau, heading to Schwetig via Kalisz and Glogau, to approach the village from the south.

"Why Schwetig?"

"I don't know."

"I went there once as a boy. It can be of no strategic importance . . . except perhaps for the bridge."

"The Germans blew up the bridge last week."

"But we're still going there?"

"I have orders to wait there."

"Wait for what?"

"Our escort into Berlin."

"Escort? Hmm. Should I feel honoured? I shall feel like the Kaiser or Franz Ferdinand, even Marcus Aurelius."

"Sam . . . please."

Glogau had fallen to the Red Army only days before and had become a giant crossroads with Soviet divisions arriving from the north and west to reinforce the final push on Breslau, roaring through the rubble.

A couple of hours before dusk, Rifkin stopped the jeep as tank after tank rumbled by.

Sam could not read every rank in the NKVD, too many pips and stripes and stars, but the man who approached them was clearly Rifkin's superior.

"Get off the road. And stay off."

"For how long?"

"Till they pass. Find a billet. You'll be here overnight at the very least."

"Billet?" Sam said. "Is there a house with a roof in this town?"

They slept in what remained of a church, among the bullet-riddled Madonnas, the splintered crucifixes and the million shards of stained glass scattered like petals. When they awoke, it was a bright May morning.

Rifkin had lit a fire in the font. It occurred to Sam that she might well not know what a font was, particularly one lying on the ground, chipped and split—a receptacle that had welcomed thousands of Christian babies into the faith now made coffee for two Jews.

"Another gift from Uncle Sam," she said, handing him a cup of real coffee in a real cup. "You know what today is?"

"Tuesday."

"May Day. Day of the Worker. Workers of the World!"

"And I have nothing to lose but my chains. Why do I not hear cheering?"

"Oh for fuck's sake."

$50

Schwetig was intact, mostly. Intact and empty. Empty of Germans, that is.

A squadron—Sam was not sure that that was the precise term—
of five T-34 tanks stood idle in the middle of the village, and—he
counted—sixteen Red Army soldiers, eleven men and five women,
were dancing and singing like drunks for the simple reason that they
were drunk. Drunk at three in the afternoon. All to the sound of a
concertina.

This brought out Rifkin's grumpy side, never far from the surface,
and rank clicked in.

"Who is in command?"

A man wearing a red dress and a tiny black hat, complete with hat-
pins, stepped forward.

"I am, comrade lieutenant. Stepan Poliakoff."

"Rank?"

He yanked down a shoulder strap to show his three yellow sergeant's
stripes on a black shoulder board. Then he held out the vodka bottle
to Rifkin.

"Drink, comrade? It's May Day."

She ignored this.

"Where are your officers?"

Poliakoff gazed around as though expecting to find them behind him
among the men and women as bizarrely dressed as himself, all looking
as though they'd just raided the washing line outside a brothel. Men
in laced corsets, women in combat trousers and high heels, the Folies
Bergère restaged on the baked earth of a German village square.

Then he turned back to Rifkin, arms spread wide, a grin of near-
apologetic helplessness on his face.

"Ah . . . we have every rank from private to sergeant . . . but no officers. There have been . . . casualties."

Sam wondered if Rifkin might be thinking what he was thinking.

She said nothing. Looked around.

"We will need billets."

The arms spread wide again, a May Day embrace of all humanity,
and the deceitful grin of helplessness returned.

"Take your pick. If there's one bed, there are a hundred. There's not
a Kraut in sight, they fled weeks before we got here."

"Assign someone to show me."

Poliakoff pointed at a woman as small as Rifkin and beckoned.

"This is Comrade Corporal Stanadyezhda. Vera, show the lieutenant to her quarters."

"What quarters?"

"Fuck knows, just find a place. Anything with a roof and running water."

§51

If Rifkin had ever heard of the *Marie Celeste*, she'd have mentioned it that day. She'd seen towns and villages in ruins, dust and ash—the hydrogen and helium of the feral world—but she'd never seen anything like Schwetig. A village whose villagers seemed to have been spirited away. No wake of chaos, no trail of confusion. They were here and then they weren't. In the house, Vera showed them a pan of beans growing mould on the hob—a tap dripped into booming silence, a half-eaten plate of blackened, maggoty porridge sat on the deal table, congealed around the spoon. Yet the inescapable reference was not history but fiction and fable.

"Goldilocks," she said.

"And you are the Russian bear. How very apt," Sam replied.

"Were they really so frightened of us?"

"Not to be frightened of the Red Army would be stupid."

"To just . . . just run . . . to just run and leave everything . . . all this . . . food . . ."

"All those dresses for your men to loot."

"Can I go now?" Vera asked. "Beds upstairs. Crapper out the back."

"Of course, Corporal. Dismissed."

If Rifkin was expecting a salute, she was to be disappointed.

"Do they have no discipline?"

"You're asking me?"

Upstairs they found a bed each, a room each. In a huge oak armoire—surely the prized possession of a German family?—they found clean sheets.

Rifkin sat on her bed. Bounced twice. Fixed Sam with her gaze.

"Do you suppose . . . ?"

"Of course," he replied. "They killed their officers. No question of it. But the next question is—"

"Will they kill us?"

§52

They didn't.

The fancy dress was put away and in the morning, routine—not quite the same as discipline—resumed. Tanks were cleaned and serviced, salutes given and returned. Rifkin sifted through a dozen messages handed to her by one of the radio operators.

"Each one the same. Оставаться на месте. Stay put. I'm beginning to think I'll never see Berlin. Reichstag taken—stay put. Chancellery taken—stay put. Stay put, stay put, stay put."

No sooner had she spoken than Vera Stanadyezhda appeared with another transcribed message.

"Came in very late last night. None of us were . . . sober."

Then she grinned, and as Rifkin read, her grin turned to smile, and when Rifkin leapt up and hugged her . . . to laughter.

"Hitler is dead!"

§53

Perhaps now the order to move on would come.

It didn't. Оставаться на месте.

Rifkin asked Vera Stanadyezhda about the bridge across the Oder.

"A construction crew arrived only a few days before you. They've floated out pontoons, but no one seems to know when it will be passable again."

Rifkin drove Sam to the river. The bridge, such as it was, was a latticework of wooden beams and struck her as being a house of cards built on floating shoes cast off by a giant in a Grimm's fairy tale.

"Oh shit. Is this all?"

"You're the engineer. What does your engineer's eye tell you?"

"That it will probably take the weight of a jeep, but our tanks will collapse it like—"

"A house of cards?"

"Exactly."

§54

A week passed in engine oil, axle grease and basic meals prepared by Poliakoff—a chef before conscription—to an inordinate, war- and ration-defying standard. Mercifully as close to lard-free as a Russian meal could get.

On May 8, in the first crepuscule of evening, one of the radio operators stuck her head out of the turret of her tank and yelled, "Война закончена! Бастарды сдались!"

War is over! The bastards have surrendered!

It seemed to Sam that it took only seconds for a bonfire to be lit, for Poliakoff to don the red dress and for a bottle of vodka to be stuck in his hand. Slightly longer for Vera to coax Rifkin into a flowery yellow dress.

He handed her the bottle.

She took one hefty swig and passed it back as the tears streaked down her cheeks. She leant on him as she had done the day they had found Budziarek's body, her forehead tapping lightly on his shoulder.

"Ладно. Ладно."

Enough. Enough.

He said, "There should be fireworks."

Without lifting her head she said, "Yes. There should be fireworks. Are you going to conjure them out of nowhere?"

In their billet he found baking soda.

From Private Smerdyakov he begged the bucket of rust he had been scraping off his tank all week.

From Poliakoff he scrounged a few emergency flares, which he opened into a bucket.

When they'd all got tired of firing bullets into the night sky and seemed sufficiently drunk he stood before the fire, wearing the outsize blue dress that Vera had threaded him into. He hoped he looked a little like a conjurer.

A handful of soda thrown into the fire produced yellow flames a metre and half high.

He took a mock bow to cheering.

A balletic pirouette, a big handful of rust and the flames deepened to burnt orange with a tinge of red. First one, then another and another till the bucket was empty.

"And for my last trick . . ."

A bucketful of the contents of the flares.

Flames five metres high and three across in every colour of the rainbow, scorching and contemptuous of night.

His audience erupted, more bullets in the air, empty bottles lobbed into the dark.

He rejoined Rifkin, her cheeks still wet, a smile on her face.

"What the fuck was that?"

"Potassium nitrate, mostly. A dash of magnesium, aluminium . . . boron . . . It's the boron that's burning green right now."

"You really are the conjurer, aren't you?"

"Just a professor of physics. Much as you are an engineer."

"Такой оптимизм."

Such optimism.

§55

A strange conversation took place with Vera Stanadyezhda.

"You are Jewish?"

"That's what the yellow star on my jacket means," Sam replied. "In fact, we are both Jews."

"The lieutenant too?"

"Yes."

"Then there is something you should see."

"OK, I'll get her."

"No, just you. She cries too easily."

Sam drove out of the village, less than two kilometres upriver.

Vera said, "Stop at the sign."

Before he could ask what sign, they were almost on top of it, strewn across the ground, a mass of broken birch, but legible.

REICHSAUTOBAHNLAGER
ODERBLICK

Vera said, "I do not speak German. What does the first word mean?"

"It was a concentration camp for road crews—the slaves the Nazis had building the autobahns. Jews, Poles . . . anyone they held to be inferior, but mostly Jews. You know . . . I've seen enough barbed wire for one lifetime . . ."

"Follow me."

Vera walked through what had once been the camp gates into a swirling dust bowl, the wind from the Oder whipping up and dropping back, past the burnt-out shells of huts to the far side of the compound.

A gallows stood intact. Two nooses swaying.

"This is what you want me to see?"

"There is more," she said.

She stepped into the remains of one of the huts, pointing at something hard and white sticking out of the ash.

Sam bent down to it, brushed away ash with his fingertips.

"It's a femur. A human thigh bone."

He brushed away more ash.

"And this is an ischium, part of the hip bone. Do you want me to go on?"

"Yes. Someone must see. Someone must witness, and I would not do this alone."

She dropped to her knees and scraped at the ash.

In a matter of seconds she had uncovered a skull.

Sam uncovered a piece of cloth.

"Do you really want to go on?"

"I want you to tell me what happened here. I know if we dig we will find more and more and more. And I want to know. You have been in a camp. You surely know what is here."

Sam sat down in the ash.

"When the Nazis fled Auschwitz they marched out all those who could walk. After that I don't know what happened to them, but the odds were against survival. Not long after, knowing they had left too many witnesses alive, they sent a death squad back to kill off the sick who'd remained in the *Krankenbau*. I alone am escaped to tell you. I don't know why. Why me?"

"Is that what happened here?"

"I think so."

They both stood up. She brushed ash from her uniform with her palms, hesitant at first as though aware that this dust, this anonymous dust, might be human remains, then vigorous as though cleansing.

"They burnt these people alive?"

"It looks that way."

"What is that you are holding?"

Sam opened his hand. A scrap of scorched cloth with a Star of David stitched onto it. Its survival little short of a miracle. Vera picked it up gently, but it turned to dust at once and slipped through her fingers.

Tears formed in the corners of her eyes.

A snort, a sniff and they were gone.

"Herr Professor, where are your tears?"

"No Corporal, the question is, where is my rage?"

§56

May 21
A Bright, Breezy Monday

Early in the morning a large plane flew low. The fact of surrender made little difference to the need to know, to be certain whose plane it was.

No one needed binoculars; as it swooped over the village square, rose again and looped back, the white star on the blue background was clearly visible. Americans.

Then the mini parachutes, no bigger than pocket handkerchiefs, fell like autumn leaves. The Russians darted about the square, gathering them up.

One fell at Sam's feet.

One fell at Rifkin's feet and was met with suspicion.

Round . . . like a small football.

"It's not a bomb," Sam said. "Open it."

She tore off the wrapper.

Sam translated the one word that mattered.

"Хаггис."

"Haggis?" she said. "What is haggis?"

"I've no idea."

"Yours?"

"A one-pound tin of Fortnum and Mason's Darjeeling tea."

"Masons? They were some sort of Christian sect in the days of the Tsars. What is a Fortnum?"

"I've no idea."

"Russian rules apply."

"Meaning?"

"If you can't eat it or fuck it . . ."

A blast of the horn on the lead tank demolished their conversation.

Sam had no idea tanks had horns. What would be the point?

Poliakoff stood in the turret waving at them.

"Let's roll! Before my boots take root in this German shithole!"

At the bridgehead, Rifkin's jeep leading the four remaining working tanks, Poliakoff took one look and pronounced the bridge to be a death trap. A god looking down from the heavens might have reached the same conclusion about planet Earth.

"We go north. The bridge at Küstrin."

When the dust cloud had cleared and the last tank was but a distant dot, Sam said, "I think I shall miss them."

Rifkin snorted, slammed the jeep into gear.

"So much for our escort."

"I don't think they were ever that."

"Then what do you think they were?"

"Deserters."

"The Red Army does not—"

"Riva, they turned south. Küstrin is north."

"South where?"

"Vera Stanadyezhda mentioned something about always wanting to see Florence."

"Florence? In a tank?"

"Stranger things have happened. Just wish them luck. I doubt the Ponte Vecchio is any stronger than this bridge."

Crossing the pontoon bridge put him in mind of trying to sleep on an inflatable mattress.

On the far side of the Oder, Rifkin pulled over to let him puke.

"Sam, you will never make a soldier."

He scarcely heard her, but one thought raced loudly through his mind, *Berlin, Berlin, Berlin*, until it became a deafening, silent roar.

§57

It was a slow crawl. So much traffic coming in the other direction to points east and who-knows-where. Rifkin lapsed into silence. Her first sight of Berlin, of which, Sam assumed, she had dreamed as much as he had, if for entirely different reasons.

They approached Berlin from the southeast, through the suburbs on the banks of the Spree, to Treptow. On every street, they passed through bedsheets hung from windows, as though, three weeks on, Berliners could not surrender enough or feel safe enough behind their white flags.

They had stopped so many times that it was several seconds after Rifkin turned off the engine before Sam realised that they had arrived at their destination—Hasselwerderstraße 38—an intact colourless building that might once have been the soft, flat yellow so favoured by Berlin architects, now coated in dust like a recently iced cake, but then, so was everything else. As he stepped from the jeep and stretched his legs, the breeze stirred up eddies of dust at his feet. The Third Reich—dust beneath his shoes.

"Sam. A kopeck for them?"

"Berlin did not deserve this. We were not Nazis . . . They came out of Munich like . . ."

"Like what?"

"I don't know, I have no ending for that sentence. Let us get on. Time for contemplation . . . later. The ruins will not vanish overnight nor the suffering with them. What is this place?"

"NKVD HQ, Berlin—and of my section."

"You've never mentioned a section before."

"Smersh."

"An acronym?"

"A contraction. Смерть шпионам."

Smert shpionam. Death to spies.

"Ah . . . am I to become a killer of spies?"

"No . . . that would be a waste of your talents. And I have known you four months, I have seen you almost every day—I doubt you could kill a fly."

"Don't be so sure," he lied.

§58

They were billeted on the top floor of a house in a side street that backed onto the railway lines that ran, if they ran at all, into the city centre.

They ran.

That night he heard the train that had taken him to Auschwitz, which then ceded place in his memory to the train that had taken him away from Auschwitz. One day, perhaps, a passing train would remind him of nothing.

In the morning Sam and Rifkin met over cups of American coffee in one of the many reception rooms at number 38—a room now crowded with boxes of paper, the filing cabinets of the Reich, a nation obsessed with records and names and numbers, right down to the one tattooed on his left wrist.

"We have a day in hand, maybe two," she said. "We are awaiting more . . . guests . . ."

"Such euphemisms."

"Точно."

Exactly.

"Your time is your own."

"How do you know I won't just vanish?"

"Are there locks or bolts on the door of your room? You could have vanished in the night. I would have been none the wiser."

His home in Eichkamp, the scene of both childhood and married life, was many kilometres to the west. He had no idea what might have survived of it, and, for reasons he could not analyse, he put off all thought of a return. He was unaccustomed to emotions he could not explain to himself. To the scientific mind there was a reason for everything. Even the big bang, physics' most intriguing mystery, would one day succumb to reason.

To his surprise, a feeling he soon learnt to suppress, trams still ran. He boarded one on the Reichsstraße. As he rattled past streets in ruins, armies of women, a sea of headscarves bobbing, were clearing and sorting rubble, and several times where a house stood mostly intact he could see carpenters and glaziers at work—where in the feral world did anyone find glass not broken into a thousand shards?

He rode as far as Friedrichstraße, where Rifkin had told him the American and Soviet sectors would meet in the near future, not that this seemed to matter—it wasn't as if either victorious army would build a wall.

He got off at the nearest stop to number 97, just before the railway bridge, more in hope than expectation.

A tank, just like Poliakoff's, was parked at the kerb. A dozen Red Army soldiers stood around smoking. A hundred women picked up bricks. And beyond them all stood Aschinger's Beer Hall. Its survival no less surprising than his own.

Throughout his imprisonment Sam had craved many things. Imprisonment itself was a condition of unrelenting craving—warmth, food, affection, food, books, food . . . any food . . . any food at all—but above all he craved Aschinger's pea soup, *Erbsensuppe*, served with pumpernickel.

He sat at one of the round, cracked marble-topped tables, much as he might have done before the war, breathing in the scent of soup, the rising, taunting steam—peas, carrots, a hint of cloves (?), a few slivers of wurst (?)—and touching, all but stroking the texture of fresh, moist brown pumpernickel.

He was aware that he was being watched. He was used to this. In the camp everyone watched everyone else if there was food. But they were not looking at his hands as he slowly spooned soup to his lips, with a delicacy that might in itself be worth the spectacle; they were looking at his ankles, where his prison stripes protruded from the Russian greatcoat. It was too warm a garment for the time of year, but until he got hold of something lighter it would have to do. And then his stripes would be even more on display.

He realised, as the heads turned away to sink behind bowls and glasses, that they knew nothing. Five years of war, however many millions dead . . . and they knew nothing, just the facts of their own suffering and survival. Rifkin had often urged him to ditch the stripes. Not yet. Not while they had a purpose.

§59

In the morning the other short Russian, the major, had reappeared to brief him. She had a name like an opera. Dido? Gilda? Violetta?

"Tosca. It's been a while," said Tosca.

"Quite."

"Sit down. This could take another while. I have to bring you both up to speed."

Sam and Rifkin sat side by side at the table, facing Tosca. Sam could feel Rifkin's caution in the presence of rank. She'd called him her "ticket"—ticket to what?

"You happy in those stripes, Professor? I thought we burnt the lot."

"He wasn't having it," Rifkin said.

"Jeez . . . so . . . suit yourself. Now—"

Tosca slapped a couple of inches of files onto the table, slid several large photographs out of the pile, fanned out half a dozen enlargements of things close to undecipherable.

Sam turned the nearest this way and that.

"Stop guessing, 'cos you never will. It's Hitler's left foot."

"What happened to his right?"

Tosca pushed another photo towards him.

"You have a Hitler jigsaw puzzle? Perfect for the children at Christmas."

He aligned the photos.

"But . . ."

"Yeah, but . . . I'm listening."

"Do you really think the Führer wore darned socks?"

"Straight to the point, Professor. Impressive. No, I don't think Hitler wore darned socks and I don't think Eva Braun darned his socks. We have his manservant . . . Heinz Linge . . . he says Hitler always wore black silk."

"Tasteful. Is this leading anywhere?"

"To bodies . . . We have at least a dozen bodies from around the Führerbunker . . . Which one is really Hitler? Any one of them could be Hitler."

"Perhaps none of them?"

"Which is why you're here."

"I'm a physicist, not a forensic biologist."

"We are trying to find everyone who was in the bunker at the end of last month. Most of them are utter nonentities. But we have Misch, we have Günsche . . ."

"Names that mean nothing to me."

"Sure . . . but you have the languages we need. And I think you have the intelligence we need too."

"So do you, apparently."

"I'm due in Vienna in two days. Lieutenant Rifkin will run this, Operation Doppelgänger. With your help we may well get what we need."

"Which is?"

"Certainty."

Sam nodded, paused.

"Which serves Russian interests the best, that Hitler is dead or that Hitler escaped? That one of these bodies is Hitler or that the whole thing is just a giant hoax?"

"We want the truth. No more, no less."

"You will understand if I remain sceptical."

Tosca stood up, pushed the pile across the desk.

"Everybody's a fuckin' cynic. Read, Professor. Study. By next week we'll have a roomful of Nazis to exercise your cynicism."

Then she was gone.

Silence settled like Berlin dust.

At last Rifkin spoke.

"Sam, please don't do that again. So far, all you've seen of her is the velvet glove."

"All Russia . . . wrapped in an iron fist."

"What?"

"Aleksandr Blok . . . but I may be misquoting him."

"I never had time for poetry and we haven't time for it now."

Sam nodded, paused.

"Doppelgänger?"

"For fuck's sake, Sam. I don't think these things up."

"Who are the men the major named?"

"Günsche was Hitler's adjutant. Misch . . . a relative unknown, but he manned the switchboard so I would imagine he has a hoard of secrets. Things overheard and never forgotten. But . . . they are both in Moscow. We get the lesser fish."

"We came all this way together for a jam jar full of tiddlers?"

Rifkin said nothing.

§60

The roomful of Nazis duly materialised.

Sam wondered how many of these unfortunate Germans were really Nazis. Whether in the Russian mind the two were not simply synonymous.

It seemed to Sam that the Russians had rounded up unsystematically. In the cellars at Hasselwerderstraße, and at half a dozen houses scattered around the city—those makeshift prisons—were men snatched at street corners, Home Guard has-beens, Wehrmacht nonentities, mostly men who'd been arrested in the vicinity of the Führerbunker as April had slid into May, loitering without intent. The lesser fish.

The routine rapidly became just that, routine. Rifkin had a clipboard, a pencil and a list of questions to which she added as the pointless question-and-lack-of-answer sessions went on.

"You could let most of them go," he said after ten days of asking, denying and new-found innocence. "They know nothing."

"No," she replied. "They are liars."

Another ten days later he said exactly the same thing to the same reply.

"Is that the official position of the USSR?" he asked. "That all Germans are liars? If you can believe nothing, you might as well believe everything."

"Philosophical twaddle. Let us proceed."

"To what? To more men who saw nothing, who know nothing, who say nothing?"

"To see nothing was the lie they told to themselves. To know nothing is a bigger lie, but the biggest lie of all is to say nothing, to say nothing now, to say nothing to us. Far better than I, you know that the three wise monkeys were all loyal subjects of the Reich. However . . ."

She flipped through her notes.

Hesitantly she said, "Downstairs. A new 'recruit.' But any day now he too will be sent to Moscow."

"Recruit?"

"Prisoner. Herman Humps. SS Oberschütze. A guard in the bunker gardens. He was found yesterday hiding in a house in Pankow. He has burnt his uniform but stupidly kept his boots. He might as well have had SS tattooed on his forehead."

§61

Humps had been knocked about. His cheeks were bruised, his lip was split and he looked as though he hadn't slept in days.

Sam stared silently at Rifkin.

"Don't ask," Rifkin said. "Stick to the script."

"If he won't talk to torturers, what makes you think he'll talk to us?"

"Stick to the script."

There was a carafe of water on the table. Sam filled a tumbler and pushed it across to Humps. Humps drained it in one.

"Thank you."

Their eyes met.

Humps was about Sam's age—mid-thirties, possibly older—and while Sam was reluctant ever to gauge intelligence from a man's features, a bad habit prevailed and the phrase "not all that bright" lodged in Sam's mind.

"Party member, Herr Humps?"

Humps turned the empty glass in his hand, looked into it.

"Never," he said.

"Conscript?"

"Why else would I be wearing . . ."

Before he remembered that he wasn't.

"What did you do before the war?"

Rifkin lifted her head from the scribbled pages in front of her. For a moment Sam expected another "Stick to the script," but even a phrase as simple as *"vor dem Krieg"* seemed to be beyond her.

"I was a baker. Bread, pastries . . . king of the apple strudel, that was me . . . and then . . . you know . . ."

"So you swapped white for black."

Humps smiled at this, then winced as the split lip stabbed him.

"Yep. Uniforms. Maybe the only things in this life that are black and white."

Perhaps not such a dimwit after all?

"Got drafted in '43, didn't I?"

"And your duties took you to the Führerbunker?"

"Yep. I got lucky, until now. Never left Berlin. Been at the bunker since January."

"And you were there on April 30?"

"Yep. Shift work. Just like in a factory."

"You know that is the day Hitler is supposed to have died?"

"Why 'supposed'?"

"We'll get to that. Tell me where you were."

"Mostly in the watchtower. If you've been there, it's that pointy thing like a castle turret. But I patrolled, and I took breaks every four hours."

"What time did your shift start?"

"At one."

"And at four, approximately?"

"I know what you're asking."

"I'm listening."

"More water?"

"Help yourself."

"At four o'clock the *Leibstandarte*, the bodyguards, came out and told everyone to bugger off. Not that there were more than half a dozen people. I just retreated. A few minutes later three more came out of the bunker. Two with a body, the third with a smaller body. There was a crater just a couple of metres from the door. They dumped the bodies there."

"Did you see faces?"

"No. Then Colonel Kempka and Unterscharführer von Niegutt started pouring petrol over the bodies."

Sam paused to give Rifkin the gist of this. She riffled though the pages on her clipboard, muttering, "Kempka, Kempka."

"And then?"

"And then the nobs appeared. I got behind a tree. It was all looking too important for an Oberschütze like me."

"You had a clear view?"

"Oh yes."

"Then perhaps you can give us a list of the 'nobs'?"

Humps counted off on the fingers of his left hand, the smallest finger locked at ninety degrees as though broken.

"Major Misch, General Krebs, General Burgdorf, a bloke I think was the Führer's butler or something, Colonel Städle—he was in a bad way—General Rattenhuber, Reichsführer Axmann, Reich-something-or-other Bormann, I forget what . . . same goes for Goebbels, Reich this Reich that . . . and some others I didn't know and some I probably forgot. And Kempka and von Niegutt, of course. They poured the petrol, but Bormann lit it."

Rifkin placed a hand on Sam's arm.

"We've been looking for Kempka, Bormann and Axmann for weeks . . . but there's no mention of a von Niegutt."

"Tell me about von Niegutt."

"What's to tell? Cypher clerk. Nice enough bloke. Bit too clever for me. Sort of bloke you'd say had swallowed a dictionary."

"Von?"

"Yeah. Von. He was some sort of count. But just an Unterscharführer, just another nerk, a couple of notches above me. He was the last to leave. Or was it Kempka? Easy to forget."

"And you never saw either of them again?"

"So happens I did. Von Niegutt came up about ten that night. Took a good look at what was left. Now, I don't know what was left. You couldn't have paid me to go over to that crater. But whatever it was, he looked. At half eleven I took me break. Tower was empty, but then, the bugger we were supposed to be guarding was dead so . . . anyways . . . I came back on at midnight and von Niegutt was there again. Only this time, there's nothing. Bodies have gone. Just dust and ash . . . and him. Then he turns and goes back down. That was the last time I saw him."

"In the dark?"

"Berlin burning was my torch. I could have read a newspaper by it."

"Do you think he moved the bodies?"

"Search me."

§62

Rifkin's policy was a day upstairs, a day downstairs.

Sam said, "Could you at least see that he's fed properly. Could you at least tell your goons to keep their fists to themselves?"

Summoned twice more, looking better, fed, cleaned up, his finger in a splint, Humps answered every question exactly as he did before.

"Do liars change their story?" Sam asked Rifkin.

"That is the received wisdom."

"Or do they follow a script?"

§63

A week passed.

Humps vanished.

No one answered Sam's queries about Humps, and he was not allowed in the cellar.

Alone in the interrogation room with no one to interrogate, Rifkin summed up several weeks of words with "We need to find Kempka."

"And Bormann?"

"Everybody is looking for Bormann. We've had sightings as far away as Paris and London."

"And the other one?"

"Oh, we'll look . . . but he hardly matters now."

Sam saw no reason to conceal his exasperation.

"It's been a waste of time, hasn't it?"

"You are a capitalist defeatist."

"A sentence utterly lacking in poetry."

"That's as may be but . . ."

Another file laid on the desk, another spread of photographs. She kept a hand in the centre of each shot, palm flat, fingers splayed, like a card sharp saying "find the lady."

"More socks?"

"Teeth."

She lifted her hands. Sam found himself looking at jawbones, both upper and lower mandibles. Visible bridgework, hints of gold.

"So, are we now collecting teeth like saintly relics? I suppose you are going to tell me they are Hitler's."

"Nothing of the sort. I have a question. Can this be faked?"

"Anything on paper can be faked. The jawbone is a hard fact. The dental records are not. And I am assuming you have Hitler's records? If you have, then it's a matter of what you choose to believe. After that, a matter of what you tell the world."

"You will understand . . . that won't be my decision. The Führer is dead, the Führer is not dead."

"Ah . . . the official Soviet position. That of Schrödinger's cat."

"You'll have to explain that."

"The baker's apron is white, the SS uniform is black. As Humps said, they might be the only certainties in life. Schrödinger's cat is the epitome of uncertainty."

"And I am still none the wiser."

"Riva, how long have Smersh had these teeth? A week? A month? Have they been picking over the bones of the dozen or more bodies Tosca mentioned . . . of Hitler's doppelgangers . . . while we wasted our breath on witnesses who witnessed nothing?"

"I cannot tell you that. And we did not waste our breath. Humps did witness the burning. So far, he is one of only three people who will admit to that."

"And do their stories match?"

"I cannot tell you that."

"What was all this about, these last few weeks? Was there any point in all those sessions with Humps?"

"Call it . . . mm . . . confirmation."

"Tell me . . . in Moscow . . . now . . . is Humps the Baker confirming again every time your people hit him? Is every bruise, every split lip, every pulled fingernail just extra confirmation?"

Rifkin said nothing.

§64

That night he heard the soft click of the latch and the softer padding of bare feet across the floorboards. The shoeless assassin? Or rather, the naked agent. A small, muscular body next to his, a hand pressed flat against his belly.

"This is not about satisfaction," she said. "It is about comfort."

"Well, that can make sense if you think about the etymology involved."

"Could you try to be less clever?"

"*Con fortis*. Latin. With strength."

"Ah, I see."

"An approximate derivation, of course."

"You can shut up now."

§65

In the morning he woke up alone, as he had expected.

He found her in the interrogation room. Yet another bundle of papers covering the desk. A glass of black Russian tea cooling in her hand.

He saw no necessity to mention the night before. She was in work mode, shoulder boards flared for take-off, a pencil tapping on the desk, impatient of its owner.

But—she looked up as he came in, smiled.

"Tea?"

"Russian tea is dreadful. Always overcooked. The samovar was invented just to kill tea. If you have a pot of Darjeeling on the go, with milk, English-style . . ."

"Ha bloody ha."

Another photo pushed at him.

"Socks, teeth . . ."

It was a close-up of a haggard, worried individual, baggy-eyed, five o'clock overshadowed.

"Who is he?"

"Erich Kempka."

"Congratulations."

"Ah . . . we do not have him. The Americans found him."

"Where?"

"Berchtesgaden."

"What? How did he get there?"

"He was Hitler's chauffeur. I might imagine he knew the route the way my dad's donkey knew the route from the market back to our village."

"Will the *Amis* share him?"

"Possibly . . . we have Humps's testimony to trade."

"So . . . it's the clincher? Hitler is dead."

"Schrödinger's cat," she replied.

§66

July 12, 1945

Somewhat to his surprise, Smersh handed over his back pay.

Just as he was wondering if the Reichsmark might now be worthless, Rifkin handed him fifty pounds sterling, in white hanky-sized notes. A small fortune—if they were real.

"I can't swear that they are," she said. "But who would ever know? You can swap them for pretty well any other currency in Europe."

He slipped the Pobeda watch off his wrist—the one she had given him months ago in Poland.

"No, it's yours. Keep it. I said I'd get another."

She pushed up her left sleeve to reveal a shiny man's watch.

"Rolex?"

"Omega," she replied, with just a touch of smugness.

"As real as my money?"

She ignored this.

"Where will you go?"

"To Eichkamp . . . I have resisted these few weeks . . . but I have to go. Either my house is still standing or it isn't."

"So you'll stay in Berlin? You'll go back to the Humboldt."

"No, I won't stay in Berlin, not while there are still lice to be hunted."

"What do you mean?"

"I'm not sure myself, but do you honestly think you or I could ever resume the lives we had before? The war is over. Welcome to the war."

On the doorstep of Hasselwerderstraße 38 they parted.

The hard affection of the night before already a memory at the end of a tunnel.

For months now, ever since the death of Budziarek, he'd found himself unable to imagine life without Rifkin. Now he could not imagine it with her.

§67

Since his return Sam had wandered around Berlin as far as the Reichstag and the Tiergarten and soon tired of it. How many reactions should a man have to such destruction? In a long afternoon—and in July one might even think afternoons were endless—he could walk to Eichkamp, but he'd seen enough. Instead he caught the S-Bahn from Treptower to Grunewald. Fellow passengers stared at his Red Army coat, at his Auschwitz stripes. He closed his eyes. The train had reached the zoo before he opened them again.

From Grunewald he walked to Großereichenweg.

Eichkamp had always seemed unreal to him, even as a boy when it had been almost all he knew. He could hardly remember the house they'd had before. He'd been nine when they moved to Eichkamp from Mommsenstraße in Charlottenburg. Berlin had been impressive, incomprehensible and overwhelming, Eichkamp the unreal suburb too remote, too quiet, too green, a Hansel and Gretel of a place where he was allowed out to play in the street. If the beauty of Berlin lay in its uniform apartment blocks, the beauty of Eichkamp lay in the small differences from one house to another.

He looked at the roof of his house. It had taken some damage—one great bite out of the gingerbread—as had many other houses in the street that had not been reduced to rubble. The roof with its bird's-eye windows tilted now, the windows askew and seeming to squint. He took the squint as an invitation.

§68

The bed had collapsed. It had been his parents' bed, and then his and Maria's. After her death he had never slept in it again. And then "they" had come for him and suddenly beds didn't matter.

The sitting room and dining room showed signs of having been cleaned—a mystery solved when he went into his study, a book-lined room not much bigger than a cupboard, the confines of which served to focus his mind—or so he told himself.

There was not a speck of dust on his desk, and one of his books lay open with a dozen bookmarks sticking out like flags—Dirac: *The Principles of Quantum Mechanics*.

And in one corner of the room a rolled-up quilt and a pillow.

He had a squatter—how could he possibly be surprised?

He was sifting through the contents of his desk drawers, the scraps of the life ripped from him, a puzzle to be pieced together, when a sound made him turn around.

A man of roughly his own age, roughly his own height, stood in the study doorway. He seemed to be wearing Sam's shoes.

"And who might you be?" Sam asked.

"Does it matter? I have potatoes."

Jay

§69

London

John Grant spoke excellent, if slightly accented, English. He was a French Catholic, born Jean-Jacques Granotier, had assumed his nom de guerre round about 1890, and round about 1912 was struggling to learn Yiddish.

In a converted—for "converted" read "abandoned"—Methodist chapel in Jubilee Street, London E1, a hundred yards from Stepney Green, Grant ran the London Anarchist Collective. Many if not most of his members were Jewish refugees from Eastern Europe—Latvia, Poland, Russia—some of the "most dangerous men in Europe," old men with neatly trimmed beards, who wore dark suits with waistcoats and watch chains, who doffed their hats to the housewives of Stepney, who smiled at children and ruffled their hair, who dreamed of Wiener schnitzel, pierogi or even a good cup of coffee, who were always clutching books or tightly folded newspapers . . . and who spoke softly to one another in Yiddish.

The common language, overriding German, Polish or Russian, was inevitably Yiddish. Grant wasn't much good at it. For him at fifty, it was a language too far, struggling for room in his head against French, English, Greek and Latin.

An educated man—he had long, long ago taught at the Sorbonne, and, however briefly, at the LSE—he now worked as a baker of bagels on the grounds that the work took up no room in his head. The collective was funded by Gabriel Heller, a Hatton Garden jeweller, descendant of immigrants who had arrived in London way back when, resident of St John's Wood, and wealthy man.

Heller was Jewish. He too struggled to learn Yiddish.

Attendance at meetings was variable. The hall would comfortably seat over a hundred, but frequently hosted only a dozen. Much depended on the speaker. Lenin had addressed them in 1903 and made it perfectly clear what he thought of Anarcho-Syndicalists—his final word to them had been "Вырастите!"—Grow up!

In 1907 both Grant and Heller had been convinced that the bearded surly bugger sitting in the third row at a talk by Sydney Webb had been Josef Stalin. He said he was called Ivanovich, but when approached in his own language by a fellow countryman had said only, "Пошел на хуй"—Fuck off.

Prince Kropotkin had been much the more affable. Heller had all but talked him out of semi-retirement in Brighton that year, 1912. Kropotkin had brought with him a surprise speaker in the shape of a young Russian, the newly exiled Nikolai Rodyonovich Troitsky, younger son of the well-known pamphleteer and prominent disciple of Count Tolstoy, R. R. Troitsky. The elder Troitsky was also the father of a rapidly rising force in English journalism, Alex Troy, who had settled in London a couple of years earlier with his wife, Maria; his twin daughters, Maria and Alexandra; and his son, Rod. His father and brother had followed at Troy's insistence, in the interests of their own safety, there being nothing to save them from the Okhrana once Tolstoy had died.

Out of nothing more than curiosity, Alex Troy accompanied his brother to the meeting. Once introduced, Heller and Troy became firm friends, meeting a couple of times a month either at Heller's house in St John's Wood or at the house Troy had bought from H. G. Wells in Church Walk. Troy would arrive with vintage wine, Heller with fresh bagels. Troy declined all invitations to attend more anarchist meetings but never seemed bored by any aspect of politics.

It was Troy who warned Heller, and Heller who warned Grant, in September 1914.

"You'll be shut down. It's already been raised in cabinet. The Home Secretary will instruct the Metropolitan Police to shut you down."

When Heller passed this on to Grant, Grant said, "But we've attracted no attention. The English authorities don't seem to give a damn. I could stand in the street wearing a black hat and a black cloak, clutching a black ball with the word "bomb" painted on it and—"

"John, that was in peacetime. Close the club before the police close it for you—or it could get nasty."

On September 24 Grant locked the doors on the old Methodist chapel for the last time. When the police finally arrived, in the shape of PC Walter Stilton, a portly constable who, as it happened, lived in Jubilee Street, he found a hand-written notice tacked to the door: "Closed for the duration. All enquiries to Berkoff's Bakery."

Stilton said no more about it, and thought little about it.

The next morning, only hours before the Jewish sabbath, Stilton bought his bagels from Grant, the shabbos goy—the *only* goy—in the bakery, as he did every Friday. The London Anarchist Collective was not mentioned and would not be for several years.

§70

In 1916 Heller's son—his only son—Adam was called up. The life expectancy of a subaltern on the Western Front at this point in the war was six weeks. His wife pleaded with Heller to "do something, do anything."

Against his better judgement Heller met with an old friend, a staff officer at the War Office, Colonel George Hedley.

"The life expectancy of a subaltern on the front line is six weeks," he said. "Adam is all we have."

Hedley said nothing.

Heller took a diamond from his waistcoat pocket and pushed it across the desk to him.

Hedley looked at it for a second or two, pushed it back to Heller, then stood up and opened the door, standing by it, ramrod stiff and silent.

Adam Heller lived more than six weeks—almost made it to seven.

That November his parents buried the bits of him that the army had been able to recover. For appearance's sake they buried him in a full-sized coffin—he would have fitted into a small suitcase.

In December, if a person can die of grief, Hepzibah Heller died of grief.

§71

With peace, horizons Heller had thought were shut forever reopened.

Late in 1920, at a socialist gathering in the home of Bernard Shaw in Ayot St Lawrence, Hertfordshire—ILP, Fabians, suffragettes, the odd Labour MP, the even odder anarchist—Heller, the oddity, met Christina Cave-Brown, twenty-two years his junior, the rebellious daughter of a country parson. They married in June the next year. Whilst disapproving, loudly then silently, the Reverend and Mrs Cave-Brown did not disown Christina. After all, Gabriel had not asked her to adopt the faith he had long ago deserted. They were married by her father's curate in her father's Anglican church. The heavens were not rent asunder. The spire was not struck by lightning.

In April 1922 their son Jacob was born. Neither parent wanted him christened but kept the peace by agreeing to do so.

By the summer of 1922, life seemed to blossom for Heller. A beautiful wife and a strong, healthy baby—bonny, as cliché demanded. By autumn he felt confident enough to reopen the London Anarchist Collective. There were fewer anarchists than before the war, old men had died, young men had other concerns, and in particular Grant had returned to France, and thence to Germany, where he eventually vanished into *Nacht und Nebel*. But a dozen Eastern European regulars came every Thursday and on intermittent Tuesdays. Heller's Yiddish had not been improved by eight years of neglect, but once he had mastered English, young Jacob seemed to soak up Yiddish from all those old men, who delighted in teaching. One old Russian, Moses Mirzoeff, who came only on Thursdays—Jacob thought of him as "the man who was Thursday" and called him Uncle Mott—took him in hand and would rather sit at the back of the hall teaching than listen to another anarchist lecture. By the time he was six Jacob was interpreting for his father.

It surprised Heller that no action had been taken against them during the nine days of the General Strike of 1926. Perhaps the police were far too busy . . . escorting non-striking workers to their workplaces, riding shotgun on trams and buses as Oxbridge undergraduates created dodgem mayhem in the streets of London and occupying the pavements with cries of "Move along now, move along now."

All Heller, or any other anarchist, noticed was the occasional slowing down of the beat bobby's already slow pace as he passed the doors of the chapel, paused and moved on.

In 1928, the collective decided that they would support the garment workers—the *Schneider* of the East End—in their strike for a living wage. The system of exploiting the workers was known as "sweating," whereby responsibility was passed down the chain from employers to workers, and wages were hammered into the ground. The anarchists had done this, or things like this—pamphleteering, joining picket lines—many times, both before and after the war to no noticeable reaction from the "authorities." But it was the dying days of the Tory government—perhaps a gesture was called for?

No notice was given. A Black Maria pulled up on the first Thursday in December, and a dozen truncheon-wielding coppers poured out and into the chapel, smashing chairs and cracking heads.

It was in Heller's nature to reason, to argue gently, in any confrontation. Thus he went down in the first rain of blows, blood pouring from his skull.

Jacob was hiding behind Uncle Mott. Mott picked him up and ran for the door. A policeman on the pavement whacked Mott in the knees and he went sprawling onto the cobblestones in the middle of the street. It seemed to Jacob, who'd been flung from Mott's arms, that he rolled like a ball, that he was curled up like a hedgehog, rolling, rolling, rolling. And he came to rest by the slippers, ankles, varicose veins and furled stockings of a large, angry housewife, followed by the stick-wielding policeman.

"Billy Roberts!"

The young copper stopped in his tracks.

"Does your mother know you're out, Billy?"

"Ed . . . Ed . . . Ed . . . Edna?"

"Mrs Stilton to you, you cheeky blighter."

Mrs Stilton picked Jacob up. The safety pins in the top of her pinafore stuck into his cheek.

"Billy, bugger off or you'll get the back of my hand."

§72

It was two hours before Detective Sergeant Stilton returned home from Scotland Yard.

Mrs Stilton told her eldest, Kitty, aged fourteen, to take her eyes off the penny dreadful she was reading and take Jacob upstairs.

"But . . . Mum . . ."

"No buts, girl. Upstairs now."

Stilton took off his hat but sat at the kitchen table in his macintosh as though he'd have to go out again any minute.

"Well, Stilton?" said Edna Stilton.

"Is that the Heller boy?"

"Yes."

"His father's dead. Three in hospital, one dead. The Commissioner's nearing his wits' end."

"If he ever gets there, let me know. Meanwhile, Jacob Heller?"

"All I know is the Hellers live in St John's Wood."

"Not that common a name. You'd better put your hat back on and start looking."

"A cuppa first?"

"Get out there, Stilton! Do your job and make coppers halfway respectable again."

It was two in the morning before he returned, accompanied by Christina Heller and her brother-in-law.

Jacob was asleep on the parlour sofa, wrapped in an eiderdown, clutching the yellow teddy bear Kitty had given him.

He didn't wake as Stilton carried him out to the taxi, still clutching the teddy.

Christina remained stoic—no tears. Her brother-in-law, the Reverend Eric Maugham, husband of her sister Jenny, looked grim, as though to speak would cost him.

"Mrs Stilton," Christina said. "I don't . . . I don't . . . I can't . . ."

Edna Stilton wrapped her in a fierce embrace and shushed her into silence. All bosom and safety pins. When Edna let her go, the tears were rising in Christina's eyes and she ducked into the cab without another word. The Stiltons watched the cab all the way down Jubilee Street until it turned into the Mile End Road.

§73

Weeks passed.

Jacob had told everything he remembered to a Scotland Yard inspector, in the presence of his mother, Uncle Eric and the family solicitor.

"This is leading nowhere," the solicitor said when the police had left. "The only witnesses are a bunch of foreigners and a six-year-old boy. There'll be no prosecution."

"You mean," Christina said, "that no one will be called to account for the murder of my husband?"

"I mean, Mrs Heller, that no one except you is calling it murder."

Afterwards, Uncle Eric said, "It's all for the best, you know."

"And what, Eric, do you consider to be the worst?"

Later that week, Eric and Genevieve Maugham moved the Hellers to the rectory at Chipping Ugley in Hertfordshire. Through the garden ran a small but rapid river, in which Christina Heller drowned herself.

§74

There was no formal adoption. Jacob fitted into the vacancy, perhaps the void, of a childless marriage.

The house in St John's Wood was closed up and put on the market. Jacob's clothes fitted into a single trunk, and he was allowed one box of toys and books, into which he put Kitty Stilton's teddy bear and the Yiddish Intermediate textbook Uncle Mott had given him—the book was beyond his age, but time would tell.

When the Great Depression hit in 1929, house sales stagnated. The Heller house, being at the top end of the market for the district, did not sell. It did not sell in 1930 nor in 1931. The Reverend Maugham had as one of many maxims "What's fair is fair" and would not lower the price, so the house stayed shut up and slowly fell into neglect and from neglect into decay.

The first few weeks the scullery maid, Brigid, doubled up as nanny, helping Jacob dress and bathing him. Jacob did not feel he needed either service but would not have missed her soft-voiced Irish songs for the world—"Carrickfergus" made him weep, "I'll Tell Me Ma" made him laugh.

But—one dull winter's day—Aunt Jenny said, "I should bathe the boy. My own flesh and blood, after all."

Jacob did not know what she meant by "flesh and blood." It sounded like something on a butcher's marble slab, like liver or kidneys—but flesh soon proved to be the problem.

After Jacob had been bathed and put to bed, Jenny remarked to the Reverend Maugham, "There's something not quite right about the boy, Eric."

"Eh?"

"I mean something wrong with his . . . thing."

"Thing?"

"Penis."

"I don't quite follow you, Genevieve."

She led him upstairs, peeled back the sheets and nightgown on the sleeping Jacob and said, "See?"

"My dear, the boy is circumcised."

"But . . . you baptised him yourself. He's a Christian."

"He's a Jew. Apparently."

"How could my sister do this? And not tell me?"

This deception hardened Aunt Jenny's resolve.

Jacob was not going to grow up a Jew.

And she began with his first name.

"From now on, young man . . . you will be known as James."

Jacob hid his Yiddish textbook behind the R. M. Ballantynes and R. L. Stevensons his father used to read aloud to him at bedtime.

§75

At school his teachers did not use first names for boys—he doubted any of them even knew his—a boy was "Smith" or "Jones," and in the frequent event of brothers in the same school, a major or a minor would be added. So with other boys he shortened his name to Jay. "James" or "Jacob" did not matter. "Jay" was short for both.

His identity was not in question in school or village. Aunt Jenny pursued her course by registering him at the local C. of E. infant school as Maugham, not Heller. He was James Maugham, the vicar's nephew (said aloud), son of that poor, unfortunate woman (whispered—"hysterical, you know") who had drowned herself in the river. And so a wall of silence was quickly erected around both subjects, his father's origins and his mother's death.

Aunt Jenny had a way of dismissing questions by changing the subject. She had a catalogue of inanities from which to choose, usually centred on personal hygiene or the vagaries of the bowel. She seemed obsessed with "regularity." She bought patent medicines—Carter's Liver Pills, Fennings' Fever Mixture, Blenkinsop's Bile Beans, various kinds of cod liver oil and ribbed brown bottles of kaolin and morphine. Jay found this baffling.

Any question posed to Uncle Eric would usually be met with "You're far too young. Boyhood years are the best years of your life. Best not to ruin them with too many questions." What he really meant was, best not to ruin them with answers. "Join in the cricket, ride your bicycle, study hard (not too hard, no one likes a clever dick) and, above all, do NOT play with yourself." The questions never went away, they lived with Jay in his waking hours and often as he slept—*Why did they have to die?* In a careless moment the Reverend Maugham had let slip an answer or part of one—Jesus had "wanted Mummy for his own"—which left Jay wondering what Jesus could possibly have wanted with his father.

§76

Life with Aunt Jenny and Uncle Eric, the Reverend and Mrs Maugham, made Jay into an easy liar. It was the line of least resistance to tell people what they wanted to hear.

"Everything tickety-boo, old chap?"

"Fine, thanks."

To have mentioned anything on his mind that might be deemed a worry was to invite accusations of mardiness, or worse, hysteria.

Becoming a day-boy at a nearby prep school when he was eight offered relief from the double life, the deceptions and sleights-of-mind of daily existence at the vicarage. No one demanded much of him, except that he pass tests and exams, of which there seemed to be hundreds, but he always passed, so the consequences were few. Of course they shouted at him, but that was what grown-ups did. It was their modus operandi—a phrase, like many others, that he knew because he was usually top in Latin and Greek.

His first term at Repton—Eton or anything much like Eton was beyond the family's means, "Church mice, y'know"—was a nightmare of violence and recrimination. It took Jay several weeks to realise that his saving graces (Greek, Latin and being top) would save him from nothing, because no one, not teachers nor pupils, gave a damn about knowledge. What mattered were prowess and deference.

Prowess—Jay couldn't kick a football to save his life.

("Two left feet, Maugham, you clumsy oik!")

But . . . he could slog with the best at cricket, out to the boundary for sixes. And he was a pretty good spin bowler, sending bales flying behind slow or complacent batsmen.

("You're a Bradman in the making, Maugham!")

Deference—he needed a defender. A senior, a bigger boy to bully bullies. He found one in the Hon. Piers Augustus Plunkett-Beirne, an eighteen-stone idiot, known as Jumbo, in need of a fag to warm the lavatory seat for him each morning. Jay considered this a fair price to pay for the pleasure of seeing both lavatory seat and enemies sat on, literally. Plunkett-Beirne regularly broke lavatory seats and ribs—no one seemed to care.

Thanks to Jumbo's protection Jay scraped through to seventeen, mostly intact both mentally and physically. The worst moment, in his first term, had been when a boy snatched a book away from him in the dormitory.

"What do you call this?"

Sensing an imminent exposure that might prove fatal, Jay replied, "Swahili. Daddy wants me to join the colonial service one day. You know, out to Africa to manage the fuzzy-wuzzies."

Thereafter he bound Uncle Mott's Yiddish Intermediate in brown paper, inscribed "Advanced Algebra Part Two." No one ever snatched it off him again.

At seventeen he saw his chance. He was due to sit Higher Matriculation in the summer of 1940. The head of Classics had assured him that a Cambridge scholarship at his old college, Pembroke, was virtually assured ("Already put in a word, old chap."). So, in December 1939, home for Christmas, in "civvies," the Repton blue uniform stuck back in the wardrobe, Jay donned a plain grey suit and joined the army.

He was underage and had plenty of lies well-rehearsed for questions that largely never came.

Birth Certificate—"Sorry, forgot."

Address—the old house in St John's Wood.

Next of Kin—his father. Would they ever check?

Educational Attainments—was it vanity that prevented him from lying? Was it hubris that he mentioned Cambridge as a prospect deferred?

Experience—"I was in the OTC at Repton? Does that count?"

The only reason Jay had ever been in his school's Officer Training Corps was that it was compulsory. He had been bored silly by rifle drill, marching and assault courses. His unuttered opinion was that he was being taught to fight an infantry war—the Boer War revisited—in the age of tanks and *Blitzkrieg*.

An officer—a crown on each shoulder: a major?—who had sat to one side of the desk saying nothing suddenly came to life.

To the two corporals hastily and illegibly filling in forms for Jay, he said, "Excuse us a moment, gentlemen."

He led Jay into a corner of the gloomy north London church hall and introduced himself.

"Burne-Jones. I'm in Intelligence."

Jay was not sure what this meant.

"If you say yes to what I am offering, then join a regiment of your own choosing—doesn't matter what, but the RAOC would be playing it safe . . . very little chance of combat . . . and at this stage of the war you'd be in training and when trained and commissioned you'd be training others—no matter, we will find you. If you say no, this conversation never happened."

"Offering?" said Jay.

"What?"

"You didn't say what it is you are offering."

"Military Intelligence, Mr Heller. SIS—or are you not as bright as you seem?"

Jay had assumed he was enlisting as a private.

"Commissioned? Don't I have to go before some sort of board to become an officer?"

"Yes. That would be me. Congratulations, Second Lieutenant Heller."

Five days later, on the second of January 1940, after a brief stay in the Herzog Jewish Relief Hostel in Fulham, Jay was in a charabanc bound for a training base in Surrey.

He never went back to Chipping Ugley, and while the Reverend and Mrs Maugham reported him missing, they never found him. It did not cross the collective marital mind that he had enlisted as Jacob Heller.

§77

Paris

September 1944

Jay—he had retained the abbreviation—did not rise rapidly. Burne-Jones told him this did not matter, that they were "Army" was a convenient fiction, SIS was what it was. Meanwhile Burne-Jones went from major to lieutenant-colonel and Jay to captain.

Jay saw no combat—though he read a lot about it, piles of bumf on his desk each morning. Jay ran no agents—though he read a lot about and from them too, piles of bumf on his desk each morning.

Since 1940 there had been Jewish battalions in the army, attached to the East Kents. More than ten thousand men, all volunteers from Palestine, had fought in Greece, some seventeen hundred captured by Germans—fate unknown.

It had crossed Jay's mind to volunteer, but he said nothing. Burne-Jones heard him anyway.

"You're not in a position to volunteer."

"I know."

"And . . . if I were you, I wouldn't get involved in anything to do with Palestine and the Mandate. It's the poisoned chalice. It's a quagmire."

That was undeniable—but it might be his personal quagmire.

In August 1944 Burne-Jones's unit transferred to Paris, to offices high above the Place Saint-Michel. It now seemed implicit that they would city-hop until they landed down somewhere in Germany.

It was in the Paris office, in September, that Jay first heard of the formation of a Jewish brigade of volunteers from Palestine under General Benjamin—unlike the earlier battalions, the new brigade would fight with the Star of David on their uniforms. They would, however, be led by English officers.

Jay raised the idea of a transfer with Burne-Jones.

Slightly to his surprise Burne-Jones did not stand in his way.

"I can forward your request, though I'm not optimistic, and nor should you be."

It took four weeks for the request to be turned down.

"The Jewish Brigade is infantry. They don't think you're qualified to lead infantry."

"I'm not . . . but how many Jewish officers can they recruit from England who are?"

"Haven't a clue, but there's more to it than that, and you won't like it."

"Eh?"

"You're only Jewish on your father's side, am I right?"

"Yes."

"Alas, that is not Jewish enough."

"Dare I say it's Jewish enough for Hitler? That were I anywhere in the Reich I'd be on my way to a concentration camp."

"Can't argue with that, but it remains you're not Jewish enough for Zion."

"As my chemistry teacher used to put on my reports, 'Must try harder.'"

"Do let me know how that works out, Captain Heller."

§78

Bielefeld

May 9, 1945

In November of 1943 President Roosevelt had established the United Nations Relief and Rehabilitation Administration—UNRRA. It was the kind of thing Roosevelt did—WPA, SSA, FSA: the New Deal seemed to revel in acronyms. Jay did not much notice. It was an organisation of hopeful anticipation in that, firstly, it was set up to manage the post-war refugee problem in Europe after a war that was still being fought, and, secondly, the United Nations existed only in FDR's imagination.

It was Burne-Jones who brought it to Jay's attention, both of them slightly hung over, the morning after VE night. They were by now stationed in Bielefeld in Westphalia.

"This changes everything," Burne-Jones said, seemingly apropos of nothing.

"I know," Jay replied. "From now on all the killing and dying will be done under the heading 'Peace.' *Plus ça change.*"

"Jesus Christ," said Burne-Jones, and reached for more coffee. "I've half a mind not to tell you."

"Sorry."

"UNRRA, which stands for . . . I forget . . . but you know what I mean . . . Now is when it comes into its own. According to the memos I'm receiving from SHAEF, they're expecting a tidal wave of refugees, possibly in the hundreds of thousands, some of them camp survivors; by far the majority will be people who got behind Russian lines when Poland was carved up."

"I see."

"Do you?"

"Of course. Jews."

"Quite. Polish Jews, German Jews, Czech Jews, Ukrainian Jews . . ."

"And their common language will be Yiddish."

"So glad you're on board. Jay, it's your chance. Not the one you've asked for, but a chance nonetheless, to do something for your own people. I can authorise a temporary transfer to UNRRA. All you'd have to do is get to SHAEF HQ in Frankfurt, sign on, collect your new shoulder flashes and see where they send you."

"What . . . what if they don't want me?"

"Oh, they will . . . eventually . . . they'll need all the Yiddish speakers they can get or they'll have to rebuild the Tower of Babel."

"How long is 'eventually'?"

"Dunno."

It took four weeks for the request to be accepted.

"Well?" Burne-Jones asked.

"Of course I'll do it."

Burne-Jones set the keys to his jeep on the desk in front of them.

"Steal a jeep. Get yourself to Frankfurt. Your papers are being typed up as we speak."

Jay did not need to be asked twice and scooped the keys up.

"I suppose you'll want it back."

"Not particularly. Jeeps are ten a penny. It's you I want back. Jay, this is strictly temporary. We'll review it in the New Year."

§79

June 1945

At SHAEF HQ a corporal-clerk handed him the red shoulder flashes of UNRRA. Jay did not know whether to add them to his RAOC flashes or unpick first.

"Dunno," said the corporal. "Some of 'em are Army—like you—some of 'em are civvies. So . . . suit yerself."

So saying, he handed Jay his marching orders, almost literally. A brown-paper envelope with his name on it marked "Re-use six times before discarding" and an inky, smudged War Office stamp over it. He was to report to Fuchsundachs.

"Where is Fuchsundachs?" Jay asked.

"It's a DP camp. "'Ere, I'll show yer."

He stuck his finger on the wall map behind his desk.

"Frankfurt . . . follow me finger . . . Fuchsundachs."

It was further north than Bielefeld—he'd driven a hundred and fifty miles for a pair of red flashes?—and about a hundred more to the east in Lower Saxony.

§80

Fuchsundachs Displaced Persons Camp
UNRRA

Lady Harriet Marsden, known to her friends, of whom there were few, as Hattie, appeared to have made up a uniform of her own—a battle-dress that had been dyed to a Bournville brown, with a touch of femininity in the white blouse and its forget-me-not pattern in dots of blue, Land Army girl regulation jodhpurs, with a deterrent array of buttons, and a pair of scuffed riding boots.

"Let me make one thing clear to you, Captain Heller, I am not a member of His Majesty's Armed Forces, but I'm in charge of Fuchsundachs and everyone in it. Rank and regiment mean nothing. You answer to me."

Burne-Jones had told him at the outset that rank meant nothing. Regiment: once he'd completed his basic training with the Royal Army Ordnance Corps he'd never seen them again, and wasn't entirely sure what they did. He was equally uncertain whether Lady Harriet was aware of the fiction written on each shoulder, RAOC rather than MI6.

He held up his new red UNRRA flashes, silently, feeling pathetic in the face of her verbal storm.

She pulled open a desk drawer and tossed a cardboard packet the size of a book of matches onto the desk—he flipped it open to see half a dozen needles and tiny skeins of thread in black, brown and blue.

"Can you sew?"

"No."

"Then I suggest you learn. Now."

"Now" went on for some time.

Fuchsundachs held fourteen hundred refugees. A former Wehrmacht training centre, it resembled every other camp Jay had ever seen, in its serried rows of wooden huts, except that it seemed somehow . . . worse, and he did not attribute that to the absence of a flagpole or of those dotted lines of whitewashed stones the British Army seemed so fond of.

"Fourteen hundred and we're full. It began in dribs and drabs as our boys advanced and people came in from the East. Then, almost as soon as the Russians took Berlin, it became a torrent. And more arrive every day. Huts designed for twenty now hold thirty. The sappers can't dig the bogs quickly enough.

"About seventy per cent of them are Poles, and about fifteen per cent are Jews. And the rest are a pot-pourri of what-have-you and scarcely comprehensible jibber-jabber.

"They're rogues, most of them. Scoundrels for whom the world is not enough."

Against every ounce of his better judgement Jay interrupted.

"I'm sorry?"

"They're the victims. Right now they're the victims. Many people have been victims before them and many more will surely be victims after, but right now they are dining out on it. An all but institutional self-righteousness."

"Dining out" struck Jay as a singularly inept metaphor for people who had but recently been promoted from "starving" to "rationed."

"There was a bugger here from Celle last week, a rabbi offering to convert Catholic Poles to Judaism in return for an orange. An orange! He'd had twenty idiots circumcised before I threw him out. Zionism is a maggot eating away at Fuchsundachs. And I will not tolerate it."

A fleeting image, one he could never have wished for, passed through his mind—a basket filled with orange peel and foreskins.

§81

He had heard of camps that were like mirrors of the world so recently lost, patient recreations, where committees were formed for this or for that, where string quartets got together, where brass bands were formed, university seminars held, schools and chapels opened . . . and where a pretence of normality might settle.

That was not Fuchsundachs. Fuchsundachs was defined by its rackets, by the dozens of dodgy deals taking place each day in conditions so factional peace was but a distant memory. Among these were a thriving black market—parcels from Uncle Sam that simply vanished from stores, coffee and tinned goods sold across the wire to German locals whose daily ration amounted to somewhat less than the two thousand calories afforded to the DPs—and a clandestine trade in fake papers, so that a Ukrainian born into the nascent USSR might, by a sleight of geography and a dash of the pen, now pass for a Pole . . . to say nothing of such commonplace acts as theft, violence and prostitution.

Dickens, he concluded, would have adored Fuchsundachs, and none of it would have struck him as preposterous in his haste to capture it in prose.

He had learned German at Burne-Jones's bidding in the middle of the war—now he added Polish to his fluent, if mostly untried, Yiddish, at least enough to intervene between one faction and another. He hated to agree with Hattie Marsden about anything, but they were scoundrels. Perhaps that was one of Hitler's lasting achievements, to have so abolished common morality, to have turned ordinary, decent people into rogues.

On the plus side . . . were he not acting on a daily basis as some kind of polyglot copper, he'd be stuck behind a desk with a rubber stamp, authorising this, denying that. Now he was metaphorically banging heads together, except when he was literally banging heads together.

With every train that stopped at the railhead three miles away, more Flüchtlings would arrive, almost crawling up the dusty track to the camp. Every hundred required four new huts, every new hut a ton or more of timber.

And so it went on. By August the influx of Flüchtlings from the East, those who had been behind Russian lines, pushed the percentage of Jews in the camp to over eighty—and given that many if not most refused to speak any language but Yiddish, Jay's talents were put to great use.

By October Fuchsundachs had tripled in size, and, keeping pace, its facilities had less than doubled while the rackets increased disproportionately.

It was not dull, but it wasn't rewarding either. The brief to disperse and repatriate failed at every turn and provoked Lady Harriet to rage. The Poles would not return to Poland, the Russians claimed they were Polish and the Jews just wanted to go to . . . Palestine.

§82

August 22, 1945
A Warm Wednesday
Quite Early One Morning

On a dusty, deserted road somewhere between Kunrau and Tülau, close to the new border between East and West, Sam, having passed no one and nothing since first light, saw something coming towards him. A young woman on a bicycle, one seemingly identical to his own.

She braked too hard and sent a cloud of white dust into the air, stuck out her right foot to steady the bike and said, "Snap!"

"You're going the wrong way," he said.

"That all depends on what you think is the right way. I am a Berliner. I'm going home."

"I am a Berliner too. I'm leaving home."

Boldly—she did not look to be more than sixteen or seventeen—she stuck out her hand for him to shake.

"Christina Hélène von Raeder Burkhardt. Known as Nell."

"Sam," Sam said, suddenly self-conscious about the name, as though uttering it for the first time.

"And where will you be going so far from Berlin?"

"England, I think."

The girl stretched out her arm and pointed back the way she had come.

"I'm not sure how far I've travelled today, but if you do not stray from this trail, perhaps in an hour or two you will reach two huge stone gateposts and a set of iron gates. That's Schloss Verrücktschwein. It's guarded by the British, who may be able to help you—and it's owned by an old count; he is the soul of generosity. You'll be there in time for lunch."

"I don't have a ration book."

"He won't ask. And if you have had enough of pedalling for one day, I'm sure he'll find you a bed for the night."

With that she was gone, and he never saw her again.

§83

The girl calling herself Nell must have pedalled faster than Sam cared to. It was three hours later, according to his Pobeda watch, when the gates of Schloss Verrücktschwein came into view.

As he drew level with the gates a jeep roared out and knocked him off his bike with a crack that could only mean a broken bone, and as the sound burst in his ears and his left tibia snapped, his head hit the ground and the world turned blue and green and red. He blinked, surprised to find that he was not unconscious, yet the world remained blue and green and criss-crossed with red and white.

The colours seemed to retreat, and his eyes focussed once again. All the colours were still there. A less than intricate pattern of geometric simplicity that he had heard was known as tartan. The colours retreated a little further and revealed themselves to be a pair of baggy trousers, the sort an American might wear to play golf. Yes, he definitely wasn't unconscious.

But then a voice began speaking in tongues:

"'Ere Fred, get yer skates on. I just knocked some poor bleeder orf of his clever mike."

But then again, perhaps he was unconscious after all and his mind was conjuring up gibberish.

§84

January 7, 1946
Fuchsundachs
The First New Year of Peace
A Bit Chilly

An odd character stood before him.

Five foot two, about twelve stones, double- if not triple-chinned and about thirty years old.

Jay could scarce remember when he'd last met a rabbi. Surely it had been back when his father was still alive? He thought of himself as an oddity—a self-taught Jew, a homemade Jew, who'd never had a bar mitzvah, could read very little Hebrew and who, thanks to the education afforded him by the Reverend Maugham, had a better knowledge of the New Testament than of the Old. And this man was yet another oddity.

He'd appeared in Jay's office unannounced, dumped his bag on the floor and said, "You're the adjutant?"

"We're not a military facility, Captain . . . er . . ."

"Gershwin. Ira Gershwin of Union City, New Jersey. US Army chaplain."

Jay stuck out his hand to shake, salutes seeming irrelevant.

"Jay Heller of Hampstead. Captain RAOC. Here on assignment to UNRRA."

"On assignment? Aren't we all? UNRRA is the whale that swallows everything. Jonah was just the first."

"But it ain't necessarily so."

Gershwin smiled at this.

"Touché, Captain Heller. Great song all the same."

"How may I help you? I assume you're here for the bris?"

"I am?"

"We've had two births this week, both boys."

"Surely you have your own guy for things like that? How many Jews do you have here?"

"Over three thousand. And while it's against all odds . . . no, no rabbis, no mohels. And improvisation hardly seems safe or proper."

"Sheesh. In my camp you throw a rock, you hit a rabbi. Well . . . of course I could do it, but it's not why I came. I came to talk to the Jews, to give a lecture, no more than that, about . . . the possibility of . . ."

"Palestine? You mean you're recruiting?"

"I'd rather not use that word."

"Quite. My boss would have a fit if you did."

"That's Mrs Marsden?"

"*Lady* Harriet Marsden. A fact she prefers we remember."

"Right. I wrote her. Didn't get a reply."

"Which means she didn't want you to come. I take it you're based in Bavaria?"

"Yep. Babelschnuck, north of Munich."

"Well, you may go back to Babelschnuck empty-handed. Lady Harriet sees it as her job to endorse the Mandate and right now the Palestine Mandate has a very simple policy—"

"I know . . . no more fuckin' Jews. But there are ways around that."

"Tell me more."

§85

"Lady Harriet, I'd like to have a word with you about the Jewish Brigade."

"Not again? You and your Chocolate Cream soldiers. I seem to recall they turned you down as you're not a combat soldier."

"The Jewish Brigade isn't fighting anymore."

"We're none of us fighting, Captain Heller. The war is over, perhaps you haven't heard?"

"I meant to say that they have other, new duties."

"Such as?"

"They are running a DP camp much like ours. There are several camps in the north of Italy . . . Florence . . . Cremona. The one in the South Tyrol is run by the Jewish Brigade."

"And how exactly do you know this?"

She'd had Gershwin thrown out, after the bris, before he could give his planned talk, yelling that he was "on a wild Jews chase" and that he should "bugger off back to Bavaria!" Jay thought better of mentioning him as his source.

"I'm in Intelligence, Lady Harriet."

"No, Captain Heller, you're in UNRRA. And I can tell you now there are no DP camps run by Jews."

"An inexactitude on my part. The Jewish Brigade is *involved* in the Bolzano camp."

"To what end?"

"I don't understand."

"Dammit man, if they're working with DPs, they can have but one purpose. They're recruiting for Palestine."

"There is that possibility."

"Are you just naïve or the most blatant liar I've ever come across?"

"Ma'am."

"Ma'am what?"

"I came to you with a request."

"Then get to the fucking point, Heller!"

"If I were to be released from my duties here and allowed to escort fifty DPs to Italy . . . it could be done legally and in an orderly fashion. There are many more than fifty willing to make the journey, but fifty is a manageable number. If we get to Bolzano I could hand over to Merkaz la-Gola—"

"What? Is that Yiddish?"

"No—it's Hebrew. The Jewish Brigade have established their own organisation to look after survivors . . . the new diaspora. They call it Merkaz la-Gola."

"For all I care, they can call it Coca la-Cola."

"May I be allowed to finish?"

"If you must."

"I know fifty is like a drop in the ocean compared to the numbers we have here, but if it works, it could be repeated time and again—with the added advantage that it might get the American rabbis off your back."

"Let me get this straight. You want me to allow the free movement of Jews halfway to Palestine—"

"That's hardly—"

"Shut up! Italy may not be halfway to Palestine geographically, but I'm talking intentions, not geography. It's not going to happen."

Marsden sat down. Interview concluded. Request denied.

Jay did not move.

Marsden pulled a sheaf of papers towards her and tapped on the desk with a pencil.

Not looking up, she said, "Heller. Just fuck off."

Jay did not move.

"What do you want, Lady Harriet? To turn this camp into a prison?"

Now she looked up, teetering on outright rage.

"What do I want, Captain Heller? What do I want? Most of all I'd like my own lavatory, preferably with a seat. After that . . . I just want you to bugger off back to Blighty."

"That's not going to happen."

"Unless, of course, I arrange it."

"I still work for Colonel Burne-Jones. He assigned me to you . . ."

"And you can be unassigned. Do not underestimate me, Captain Heller. When my brother says jump, even colonels do it."

He'd been slow. Not put two and two together. Desmond, Viscount Marsden. Recently appointed to the war office under the new prime minister, Clement Atlee. Back home the first general election since 1935 had changed everything. A few weeks ago Hattie Marsden had been an annoying loudmouth, now she was an annoying loudmouth with a brother in the cabinet.

"Don't make yourself any more of a nuisance, Captain Heller. You could do some good here, you know, but all you've done so far is to stir up the Jews. The Poles work. A few hundred of them are out there chopping wood right now, up to their ankles in snow. Do the Jews work? Half of them refuse even to register as displaced persons. It's as though a Jew can only be one thing at a time—a Jew! I wouldn't mind if you stirred them up into doing something right here, right now, but all you do is encourage fantasies about Palestine. For God's sake, Heller, grow up!"

§86

January 15, 1946
Fuchsundachs

She was smiling at him.

This could not be good.

"I have a mission for you, Captain Heller. You like the idea of missions, don't you?"

"Perhaps I read too much John Buchan as a boy."

"Very funny."

"But true all the same."

"I need someone to check out a castle near Wolfsburg. Schloss Verrücktschwein. Stupid bloody name. It's run by some lunatic one-legged nobleman named von Tripps who seems to be offering shelter to all and sundry. I have no problem with private enterprise, but I need to know how many Flüchtlings he's got and what happens when the place is full. We're up to four thousand here. If he dumps even a hundred more on us . . . Do I need to say any more?"

"Wolfsburg? I could be there and back in a day."

"Feel free to take your time."

"Fuck off" had been by far the neater and more accurate expression.

§87

Schloss Verrücktschwein

January 16, 1946

The schloss seemed to Jay to be an architectural hotchpotch. British artillery had done little to improve it. The slender, delicately tapering turret—reminiscent of a Grimm's fairy tale of rapid rivers and Rhine maidens—sported a huge shell hole, and a great many tiles had been blasted off the rest of the roof and windows blown in . . . or was it out?

The iron gates were propped open and looked as though they'd been that way since well before the war.

Leaning against a gatepost, having a crafty smoke on duty, was an outlandishly dressed individual—outlandish, that is, only to someone who'd never seen a corporal of the Seaforth Highlanders before, splendid in his khaki battle-dress and tartan trews.

One last deep drag on his cigarette and the butt was ground into the earth with the toe of a boot.

Jay stood at the side of the jeep.

A tense moment arrived only to vanish almost at once.

"If you're waiting for me to salute, you'll die upright. War's over, cock. I don't do salutin' no more."

"How very sensible," Jay replied, and stuck out a hand to shake. "Jay Heller, UNRRA."

"Beckwith Sharpe," the corporal replied over the briefest of handshakes. "Citizen of the People's Republic of Pimlico. Don't let the uniform fool yer."

Jay took a slip of paper from the breast pocket of his battle-dress.

"I have an appointment with . . . hang on . . . Captain Dobbin."

"That wanker. Through the front door, first right."

§88

Dobbin scrutinised the order and the signature.

"Marsden? She's not related to that twat at the War Office, is she?"

"She's his elder sister."

"Must make life awkward for you," Dobbin said, handing back the papers. "As of last week Lord Marsden has responsibility for the British Zone."

"All of it?"

"Alas, yes. Why do aristocrats toy with socialism? They should stick to huntin', shootin' an' fishin' and keep out of the way, if you ask me. However, I gather his sister wants a survey of the DPs at this castle. Have to say, I'm baffled as to why."

"Oh, I can answer that. She doesn't give a toss how many DPs you have. She just wants me out of her hair for a few days."

"Fine. Have a holiday. I'm sure I can find you a billet. The count keeps one or two beds free for his guests. He's a Great War veteran, interesting old chap. Indeed, some of the DPs are too. And who knows, perhaps you can be a fourth at bridge."

"Never played, sorry. Card games are a bit of a mystery. My stepfather was an Anglican priest. Cards were synonymous with gambling."

"Then keep away from my man Sharpe. He is very aptly named."

§89

Count Florizel von Tripps had only one leg. The chap sitting next to him at dinner had two, but the left was encased in a plaster cast.

He introduced himself as Sam Fabian, professor of physics at the Humboldt—"Or at least I was before the world went feral."

"Have you been here long?" Jay asked.

"Over four months. Ever since this idiot broke my leg."

"'Ere, less of the 'idiot,' yer tosspot!"

This from the tartan-trewed corporal seated opposite.

"Beckie . . . remember your manners, for God's sake," said Dobbin.

"He called me an idiot!"

"Well, you are an idiot."

"Oh yeah! I can outsmart the lot of you."

So saying, he produced a deck of cards and chose three.

"Oh, not again," Dobbin said. "It's just your party trick, not an intelligence test."

Sharpe ignored this and fanned out the cards.

"Eight o' diamonds. Four o' clubs. Queen o' hearts. The name of the game is Hunt the—"

"Sharpe!"

"OK. OK. Find the *Lady*."

He stuck his tongue out at Dobbin. "Posh git."

The three cards passed between his hands at speed. A couple of times he showed them face up to prove there'd been no substitutions, then he set all three face down on the table and said, in a parodic refined English, "Now Prof, faind the laidy."

Sam tapped a finger down.

The look on Sharpe's face said it all.

He flipped up the queen.

"You just got lucky."

"Perhaps, perhaps not."

"Yeah. But you can't do it twice."

Sam found the lady three times more, which set everyone but Sharpe laughing.

Von Tripps got to his feet, one flesh-and-bone foot, one tin.

"Enough. Gentlemen, as neither of our guests play, let us go in search of a fourth for bridge."

"Yeah. OK. How does he do it?"

And then Jay Heller and Sam Fabian were alone.

Jay broke a minute's silence with "Actually, how do you do it?"

"It's not infallible. I merely lower the odds. Sharpe relies on the hand deceiving the eye, and indeed it does. So . . . whichever card he has steered you towards is most certainly not the one. Which leaves two, so you have a fifty-fifty chance. He hasn't worked this out and thinks I can see through what he's done. I can't, of course."

"But you were right four times in a row."

"I got lucky. And I would imagine Sharpe is used to his marks being wrong every time. He's probably in shock."

"Intriguing."

"No, it's very simple."

"I was referring to you, not the game."

§90

Jay rose early and walked around the estate.

There were people everywhere, in every room von Tripps had not reserved for himself, in every outhouse and every shed, and even in the depths of winter there were still people in makeshift huts in the garden. It was Fuchsundachs writ small, perhaps no more than two hundred people, yet it lacked the tensions of Fuchsundachs and, he felt, not simply because of the scale.

He had no idea what von Tripps's policy was.

Anarchy might have been the answer.

In von Tripps's private kitchen he found Professor Fabian, hunched over a large café au lait, a chessboard set in front of him, every wooden piece impatient.

"You brought the coffee, surely, Mr Heller. It's too good for the German ration—or should I say 'too real'? Almost everything these days is ersatz. Life itself is ersatz."

"Meaning?"

"Only that I have been here too long, well-fed and sheltered, but also unreal. No matter, let us play."

Jay liked chess, without being particularly good at it. He'd learnt at school, where it was a social thing. Boys chatted over a chess game. Fabian said nothing but "check" and eventually "checkmate."

"However," Sam continued as though twenty minutes of chess had been only a momentary distraction, "my cast comes off tomorrow. I shall be free to set off for England once more. That's where I was headed until my encounter with Corporal Sharpe's jeep."

"England?"

"Of course."

Jay hesitated. Nothing he could say now could be considered good news.

"You've left it rather late. In the time you've been stuck here, things have changed. Immediately after the war ended Britain seemed to be open to, as they would put it, 'doing their bit' for refugees, but the gates have slowly closed. Even the term 'displaced person' seems like a notional shifting of responsibility from the aggressor to the victim—'you've only yourself to blame'; the logic of the English public school, along with 'consume your own smoke' . . . and I speak as one who was sent to such a place."

"Consume your own smoke? I've no idea what that means."

"I was never wholly sure myself, but England lives by such aphorisms. They pass for wisdom. Roughly it means handle it yourself—pain, poverty, whatever. Expect nothing from us and don't embarrass anyone by asking."

"And I thought Germany was heartless. So tell me, Captain Heller, how does this affect my pain and poverty?"

"The government of England now prefers to manage its refugee problem, and for 'manage' read 'constrain.' There are quotas in place, whether anyone admits it or not. The same is true of the USA. Yearning to breathe free won't get you in. First of all you have to get . . . out. Any day now you'll require something called a Certificate of Emigration to leave Germany, and it's not wholly certain whether it would get you into England, although its primary purpose—again, no one really owns up to this—is to keep you out of Palestine."

"I've no wish to go to Palestine. Never had a taste for milk and honey."

Heller smiled at this.

"Whereas I have. It seems to me that most of my life has been spent in what I would call Jewishness denied. I've had a bellyful of denying who I am."

"I have found—and my war has been very different from yours—that it pays to be a chameleon."

"I shall bear that in mind."

§91

The next day, Jay still practising the fiction of an "inspection," an RAMC doctor, summoned by the exercise of von Tripps's title, arrived to remove Sam's cast.

"It'll be another month before you'll really be able to walk properly. Exercise will build up the muscles, but you'll need a stick. I do hope you weren't planning any long journeys?"

This last remark was uttered with a pursuant smile.

"No," Sam replied. "Just to England."

"Glad you've kept your sense of humour, old man."

When the doctor had gone, Jay said, "He thought you were joking, but you won't be deterred, will you?"

"Can you think of any good reason why I should be? Everything you've told me so far—and believe me, I am grateful—amounts to just red tape, and all red tape requires is a sharp-enough knife."

A couple of hours later Sam had hobbled around the room, wincing at the pain, appalled at his own feebleness.

He sat back hard on the edge of his bed.

"A couple more days and I'll be fit to travel," he said.

"Really?" Jay replied. "Have you tackled a staircase yet?"

True to his own self-worth, Sam descended and ascended a staircase the following day.

"How would you feel about coming to the DP camp with me?" Jay asked.

"To what end?"

"I can't promise anything, but we might find that sharp knife."

"Explain."

"The camp commander—my boss, as it were—wields a lot of influence. She can cut though the red tape . . . if she chooses."

"What is she?"

"An English aristocrat."

"Ah."

"And a bit of a bitch."

"You give with one hand, you take with the other."

§92

A Few Days Later

Jay set his report in front of Lady Harriet.

She feigned interest.

"How many does he have there?"

"A hundred and forty-two. Actually, a hundred and forty-one now."

"What?"

"I brought one DP back with me."

"Heller, for crying out—"

"A special case, Lady Harriet."

"What?"

"He's a professor of physics. He's the sort of chap England needs."

"What?"

"People like Sam Fabian built the bomb that ended the war."

"British Tommies foot-slogging across Europe ended the war, Heller. The atom bomb was just the icing on the cake."

"I can't argue that with you. Nonetheless, Professor Fabian is a special case and I would like to ask you to use your influence to expedite his entry into Britain."

She'd been holding his report in her left hand. Now it slapped down as proof of her mounting exasperation.

"A small iota of me is flattered that you should think that, but influence is a currency which one has to spend carefully. If one's influence is to remain influential, one becomes a miser.

"Your concern is almost touching. But let me ask you: Can this man dig coal in Wales? Can this man plough a field in Kent? Can this man operate a loom in Lancashire?"

"He's a physicist, Lady Harriet."

"I say again: Can this man dig coal in Wales—"

"And I say again: He's a physicist. A professor of mathematical physics."

"Then what fucking use is he?"

Jay left it a week. The volcano cooled.

"May I take it that you would not object to Professor Fabian applying for an emigration certificate?"

Jay did not have her full attention—a fussy pretence of 'busy' that amounted to no more than shuffling papers.

"I've no authority to stop him. It's of no matter—"

—Now she looked at him.

—"—Because he won't get one."

§93

Jay's quarters had two beds. As an officer he was not obliged or expected to share. He'd given the spare to Sam.

When he got back from his fruitless meeting with Harriet Marsden, Sam was on the floor in his underwear, stretching his leg muscles.

Jay found himself staring at the tattoo on Sam's left arm and politely looked away.

"I got nowhere with her," he said. "But there is a plan B."

He waved the emigration certificate application forms vaguely in Sam's direction.

"We have paperwork to do. Do you have a *Persilschein*, the piece of paper that washes all stains away?"

"Jay—I have nothing. No ration book, no ID, no *Persilschein*."

"Oh."

"Von Tripps never asked for a ration book and he never bothered to register any of his Flüchtlings as displaced persons. I say 'nothing'—I have documents in Russian. Would they count?"

"We'll have to make them count. Who issued them?"

"Field Marshal Zhukov."

"Good bloody grief! Are you kidding?"

§94

It took almost a month for Sam's application to be received and rejected.

Several times Jay dissuaded Sam from setting off on his own.

"I should never have left my bike at the schloss."

"And you should never try to go anywhere in Europe without proper papers."

"Of course, I was forgetting—one should never be a nobody."

"Eh?"

§95

Jay showed Sam's rejection letter to Lady Harriet.

"Told you so."

"Your endorsement would have helped."

"Close the door on your way out."

"He just wants to get to England."

"So you keep saying."

"There is a plus side to this."

"And that is?"

"On the plus side—it's one less Jew wanting to go to Palestine."

Jay had experienced her rage before, but never on this scale.

Where a lady with a small *l* might have slapped his face, the lady with a large *L* hauled off and punched him in the jaw.

"You snivelling little shit! That is the last, the absolute last fucking straw!"

She reached for her telephone.

"Heller, get out of my office!"

§96

"You'll travel under escort back to Camberley. Once there, you have a choice. You accept your demob or you report back to Burne-Jones. After that I don't care what you do, but as long as you remain on my staff you will cease stirring up my Flüchtlings. If I catch you so much as talking to a Jew I'll have you clapped in irons. Do you understand me, Captain Heller?"

Jay kept his head down but did not take her caveat literally. Not to talk to Jews in Fuchsundachs was a physical impossibility, and there were no irons to clap him into. He was certain she'd love to use the word "brig," but they didn't have one of those either.

Three days later she sent for him.

"Pack, Captain Heller. MPs from Hanover will be here at first light. You will understand if I say that this is our last far-from-fond farewell. I won't be getting up at the crack of dawn to see you off. If you're not there, you'll be reported as a deserter. As simple as that. And I surely do not need to explain the consequences of desertion to you, do I?"

"Goodbye, Lady Harriet."

"Fuck off, Captain Heller."

§97

"Sam—I've led you on a wild goose chase."

"How so?"

"It appears I will be the one going to England, not you."

"Please explain."

"Lady Harriet has . . . fired me. An imprecise term, but that's what it feels like. She's called in the military police to see I get back to England."

"She has that authority?"

"Yes."

"But your real boss is this man you mentioned, Burr-something . . . ?"

"Burne-Jones. Yes, he is my boss. And my position here was due to be reviewed a few weeks ago."

"So?"

"He didn't remember, and I didn't chase him. His reaction would most likely have been to take me back to his unit, which is currently based in Berlin. It was not, is not, a convenient time to leave. But I don't think I have another choice. I'll have to call him."

"Or?"

"Or what?"

§98

A full-length mirror would have been useful. All the same, Sam got a good idea of what he looked like as Jay moved the shaving mirror up and down.

The uniform fitted well.

They were the same height, and Sam reckoned there was less than a couple of kilos difference in their weight. That they were both fair-haired and blue-eyed was a bonus.

"Am I the officer type?" Sam asked.

"We are both Hitler Youth archetypes," Jay said. "Everything the Führer thought Aryans should be."

"Race, shmace. Are you certain Marsden won't see you off?"

"In her own mind it's an insult and she is determined to inflict it on me."

"And the military police?"

"Never had any dealings with them. They won't know me from Adam, or in this case from Sam."

Jay stood in his vest and underpants.

His army dog tags dangled on a cord.

Sam held out his hand.

"What?"

"Details, Jay. They could be our undoing."

"Oh. Of course."

Jay slipped the cord over his head and dropped the tags into Sam's open hand.

"A baptism," Sam said.

"A farewell," Jay said.

"To what?"

"No, to whom. To Alec Burne-Jones . . . But for whom . . . ? Is there anyone in your history you'd like to say farewell to?"

"Yes . . . almost too many to mention . . . but I think Sam Fabian might now be saying goodbye to Krankfuß."

"And?"

"A nobody, an old man, a rogue. He kept me alive in Eichkamp, the first weeks after the war. They were starvation weeks, but he had an abundance of potatoes, eggs, pork . . . the list goes on. Perhaps I owe him my life. No matter . . . we haven't finished yet. We agree I can pass for you . . . now we have to be certain you can pass for me."

He slipped off the battle-dress and rolled up the shirtsleeve on his left arm.

"Oh shit," Jay said.

§99

Δ-155515

"You will not be able to pass as a survivor of Auschwitz without this."

"Tell me what you need."

"Ink. Preferably black. And a fine-nib pen."

Jay rummaged in the desk drawer and produced a jar of Pelikan ink and his father's old Waterman fountain pen.

"Too broad. Do you have anything finer? Needles, perhaps?"

"It just so happens . . ."

And he set the army-issue sewing kit Harriet Marsden had given him on the desk. Sam chose the largest, the one with which Jay had sewn his UNRRA flashes, discarded the loose red thread and said, "Get comfortable. This is going to hurt."

There was very little blood. And surprisingly little pain. Jay was amazed at the neatness.

He clamped blotting paper to his arm.

Sam said, "It may sting for a while, it may itch for an age, but it should heal in about ten days—after which, when the scabs fall off . . . well, who would ever be able to tell?"

§100

Jay described the route to England as much as was possible.

"This is educated guesswork. It is probable but not certain. The journey can be done in one day. You'll cross the channel from Belgium, and most likely land at Dover. From somewhere like Ostend one of the MPs will drive the jeep back to Hanover, the other will cross to England with you. You will need to pick your moment. If they overnight on the Continent, then it is not, absolutely not, your moment. Wait until you're safely in England. There'll be chances. It'll take a couple of changes of train to get to Camberley. That's when you lose the escort. In a London railway station."

"I understand. And you?"

"I won't hang around. I'll go out through the wire as soon as you're gone."

"If it helps, I left my bike in a tool shed at the schloss."

He reached into his open suitcase. The repository of all he possessed.

"And you'll need these."

"What?"

"My papers of passage, I suppose you might call them. As I said, official Soviet stamps and Zhukov's signature. They might just scare the hell out of any underling asking questions, at least as far as Italy. And I assume you are heading for Italy?"

"Yes, Bolzano . . . and after that? Who knows?"

§101

There remained the problem of accent. Sam's English was grammatically perfect but tinted with Berlin inflections.

Jay sacrificed his one apple.

A sliver placed between mandible and cheek made Sam's jaw look swollen.

"There," Jay said. "You have a toothache, an abscess or some such. And you mumble. And you say as little as possible. The MPs won't want to talk anyway. They'll be NCOs, and the English class system will erect an instant barrier. Just remember to return their first salute. Prisoner or not, you're still their superior officer."

"I have so much to learn about the English."

§102

The English hardly spoke to each other, let alone to Sam. He sat in the back of the jeep, nursing his "toothache." In the front seat the corporal might grunt or mutter to the lance-corporal and in return the lance-corporal might mutter or grunt something back.

Only when the lance-corporal had left them at Calais and Sam and the corporal stood on deck as the ferry approached Dover's cliffs was anything remotely chatty said to him.

"Blighty. Good to be back, innit?"

"Yesh," Sam mumbled through soggy, masticated apple, staring at the gateway to a country he'd never set foot in.

"I got another nine months in bleedin' Germany. All right for some."

Dover was not the opportunity.

Nor was Victoria Station.

Clearly the MP had no expectation that Sam would make a break and run. Without handcuffs his only restraint was his sheer size—looking as though he could snap Sam like a twig.

He flagged a taxi, told the driver, "Waterloo, cock."

Sam was momentarily puzzled.

What was a Waterloo cock?

Then he recalled that the English named railway stations after Napoleon's defeats, much as the French named them after his victories.

Waterloo was the opportunity.

It was the biggest railway station he'd ever seen, dwarfing anything in Berlin.

"I need to pish," he said, hoping the reply would not be "Me too."

"I'll be right outside, sir. So . . . no funny business. Know what I mean?"

Past a long row of backs as twenty men pissed, he found a vacant cubicle. He spat out his last slice of apple, opened his suitcase—a prewar relic with stickers, all those triangles and circles from hotels in Vienna, Paris, Milan and Bologna—inside which was his black suit, a trilby hat, horn-rimmed spectacles and a shabby briefcase devoid of labels, inside which were fifty pounds in white five-pound notes and the address of a Jewish hostel which Heller had given him.

He stuffed the uniform into the cistern.

Picked up the small, plain suitcase.

Caught a glimpse of himself in a mirror and wondered, as he would every time he looked in a mirror for the rest of his life.

He'd taken far too long to change, but the corporal had not come looking for him. He was outside, watching the crowd. As Sam passed him, he looked back at the "Gents" with not a flicker of recognition.

Fabian

§103

West London

March 1946

Sam found the Jewish Relief Hostel. It hadn't moved. It hadn't been destroyed by the Luftwaffe. It still stood in Disraeli Road, a hundred yards from Parsons Green, exactly where Captain Heller had said it would be. Neither ruin nor vacancy would have surprised him—after all, Goebbels had assured Germany that London was rubble by 1941—but the hostel was merely careworn and frayed. A patched and darned building in a patched and darned city.

There was much less damage generally than he had expected. London had not been levelled—there was rubble, but nothing on the scale of Berlin. There were gaps between houses, like pulled teeth, and what London and Berlin had in common was the light dusting of everything not in motion, as though a culinary god had taken a runcible spoonful of ash and coated the world like a doughnut.

The sign, chipped black on peeling green, read:

THE HERZOG: JEWISH HOSTEL

לעטסאָה רעשידיא :גאָצרעה רעד

est. 1882

1882—just in time for the first wave of pogromed Jews from the Ukraine.

A young man, no more than a boy, not more than twenty, stood behind a counter in the lobby, pen in hand, ticking off items on a list. Sam could see from the look on his face, before the man even spoke, that the absence of any luggage, bar one battered briefcase, was a cause for suspicion.

After a melodramatic pause, the man-boy asked, "How may I help you?"

"I am just arrived in England. I need a bed."

"Papers?"

How very German, how very Russian.

Sam shook his head.

"Well," said the man-boy, but he got no further.

Behind him had appeared a tall, stout woman in her forties, grey hair pulled back into a bun, deep blue eyes flashing.

"Michael—questions, questions, questions. How many times have I told you? We are not here to ask questions. We provide answers."

And to Sam, "Deborah Geffen. I'm sure we can help."

"Sam Fabian. I'm sure you can. I just need a bed until . . . until . . . I don't know until what, alas."

"We have space. Limited space, but the rules we go by are one week without question, and if, after a week, you are still without work or a room, we talk again. No one is ever kicked out on my watch."

Leading him up the stairs, Deborah Geffen threw over her shoulder, "Berlin, am I right?"

"Oh yes. And you?"

"I'm thoroughly English."

They reached a door, one hand poised above the doorknob before she offered the inevitable qualifier.

"Or as English as any Jew can be. We were Germans once. *Es war einmal.* Herzog was my mother's father. Fled Breslau. Must have seen it coming."

"And England took him in."

Once uttered, it seemed to Sam to be neither question nor statement.

"Yes. With bad graces. Only the onset of the war convinced the boarding houses to take down the signs that read, 'No Blacks, No Irish, No Jews, No Dogs.' A small mercy, we were above dogs. The signs are going back up now without us—progress, we've been delisted. I feel sorry for the dogs."

She thrust the door open onto a dark, clean room, carved out of a much larger space with plasterboard and studwork. It differed from his stall in the camp only in that someone had seen fit to paint it—a flat coating of streaky magnolia emulsion—but the change was immeasurable:

someone had thought it worth the effort. There was a cot no more than two feet wide, a chair, a washstand with jug and basin, and just enough room to walk between them all. Ah . . . a second difference he would come to appreciate, curtains.

She read his mind.

"In my grandfather's day it was a dormitory. We broke it up last year. People who've been through . . . whatever . . . People arriving now need privacy."

For a moment Sam thought she might ask what he'd been "through." But . . . questions, questions, questions . . . She would not ask. Just as well, he could not answer.

"Beautiful," he said, and meant it.

"Basic," she said, and meant it.

"You're late," she said. "The Jewish flood was last summer. But then the quotas came in."

"Yes, I am . . . post-diluvian. Nothing to do with quotas."

"Really? Well, good luck with that."

A phrase all too familiar.

§104

He did not sleep well. His room backed onto a railway line, the same line he had travelled on from Victoria Station, the Wimbledon branch of London Underground's District line—underground except that it sat on the surface.

He looked out of his window at first light. An old, dirty red train with a clerestory roof screamed past on tortured rails.

It was as though recognising the enemy was relief enough, and he slipped into a fitful sleep for an hour, and by the time he had queued for the bathroom it was close to 10:00 a.m. when he set foot on Disraeli Road in search of breakfast, or if not breakfast, coffee, or if not coffee . . . no, that was the bottom line, no substitute accepted.

He wandered north, away from the river, deeper into furthest Fulham.

On Dawes Road a sign above a corner café caught his eye.

HARRY THE GREEK'S CONTINENTAL CAFF
PROP. ARISTOTLE PANTELIDES
EST. 1920

Promising.

The apron on the man behind the counter was spotless, as was the café itself. No film of English grease. No chipped and cracked melamine. A clean, well-lighted place, as Hemingway would have it.

On the counter was a Gaggia coffee machine, a complex mystery of stainless steel and tubing. No doubt it made espresso Italian style, which was close to what his heart and digestion craved.

"Please. Might it be possible for me to have a . . . a Brauner. A Brauner is—"

"I know what a Brauner is. This is a continental caff. Vienna, Berlin, Rome. I do the lot. I know 'cos I painted the sign myself."

A cockney voice tinged with Harry's Mediterranean origins.

"Besides," he went on. "Him. He orders one every morning, and if he dawdles over his chess set or his newspaper he buys a second. And a bun. Always has a bun."

So saying he pointed to the café's only other occupant, an old man sitting alone at a round table, playing himself on a pocket chess set. The man looked up. Looked at Sam. A big bald head looming over a double-chinned face and a fat torso. *How could anyone*, Sam thought, *stay fat after six years of wartime rations?*

He beckoned.

"Berliner—join me."

"Is it that obvious?" Sam replied.

"*Ja. So unverwechselbar wie eine Tätowierung.*"

As obvious as a tattoo.

Ouch.

Before Sam could say more, Greek Harry said, "You wanna bun with that?"

"Might there be a choice?"

"O' course. Currants or no currants, possibly in the singular. A game of hunt the currant. Hours of fun."

Sam sat down opposite the chess player, who stuck out a hand to shake: "Otto Ohnherz. Charlottenburg."

Sam paused. Who was he? It had never been his intention to go on being Sam Fabian, and to be the man he had been so recently, if only for one very long day—Jay Heller—seemed like asking to be caught.

A silent, spontaneous merger took place.

"Fabian," he said. "Jay Fabian. Eichkamp."

Die cast.

"You've been here a while?" he asked.

"Since 1889. I scarcely remember Berlin. Or to be more precise, I struggle every day to remember Berlin, as I have no wish to forget it. I was twelve. Old enough to see, too young to understand. And you?"

"I am . . . relatively new here."

"How relatively?"

"Yesterday."

"Ah. The Herzog. A job?"

"Not yet."

"Are you looking?"

"Perhaps I finish my coffee first."

On cue Harry set an espresso and a small jug of cream in front of Sam-now-Jay—the do-it-yourself components of a Viennese Brauner.

"Perhaps we play chess while you do."

§105

How little he had thought his plan through came home to Jay when, an hour or two later, after diplomatically losing to Otto Ohnherz, he found himself looking in the windows of shops at the JOBS advertisements, at SITS. VAC., tacked up on cork-boards or simply taped to the glass. Not one in ten was offering work, most simply stating the availability of a tradesman and looking as though they'd been there for many dusty months.

He walked the streets of Fulham. Londoners were, he concluded, less efficient than Berliners—where were the teams of *Trümmerfrauen*, women swathed in layer upon layer against the late winter chill, filling truck after truck with rubble? London rubble had sat so long it had sprouted green shoots of he knew not what. But—if Nazism had had a saving grace, and it had not, might it have been "efficiency"?

And where the rubble had been bulldozed, strange box-like structures had appeared—one-storey instant housing for cockleshell heroes, looking prefabricated as though they had arrived flat in cardboard boxes to be assembled with a spanner, to last long enough for the first big bad wolf to come along to huff and puff.

Back at the Herzog he told Deborah Geffen of his first day's failure.

"Believe it or not," she said, "England is short of workers. So short we are hanging on to POWs simply to put them to work. To me that's cruel once a war is over, but I've heard that some of your lot don't want to go home anyway. Through with Germany. You're probably here for much the same reason. But a POW is legit, and you're not, are you? Don't get me wrong, England is not Germany. No one will just stop you in the street and say '*Papiere?*' They do that to the average Englishman and he'll just say, 'Bugger off.' The English don't take kindly to authority or uniforms. But the minute you get involved—I mean registering for work or housing—that's when your problems would start. No identity card, no proof of anything."

"Do you think the English might deport me?"

"I don't know. Do you have a talent they'd want?"

"I speak several languages."

"Hmmm. Anything else?"

"Science. I was a professor before the war. Mathematics is my strength."

"Clever dick, eh?"

"Very much so."

"Well, Professor Cleverdick, you'd be better off right now if you'd learnt bricklaying or carpentry, or any practical skill. Algebra builds no houses, geometry doesn't get your walls whitewashed."

Pretty much the same as Heller had told him not that long ago.

§106

The next day a circuitous route took him back to the Continental Caff. Ohnherz sat cocooned in his own silence, staring at the chess set, while at other tables the working men of Deborah Geffen's prescription rowdily took their morning tea break, rehashing last night's wireless programme, which Jay had heard through the tissue-thin wall—"Can I do you now, sir? Don't mind if I do"—a rapid-fire sequence of double entendres that weren't quite double enough.

"Ah—I thought you weren't coming. Get your coffee and we can start afresh."

The assumption was surprising, but then so was Ohnherz. To find this old Berlin Jew in a Fulham café was in itself surprising.

Jay asked for a Brauner and sat down as Ohnherz reset the board.

"This time try to win. You threw me yesterday's game far too readily. I don't simply wish to play—I can do that alone—I want an opponent. As ruthless as I may find him."

"I sit chastised."

"Indeed, you do."

§107

Jay won.

"Perhaps tomorrow I win," said Ohnherz.

"We can hardly take it in turns or the idea of an opponent vanishes."

"You misunderstand me. I meant that I have your measure."

"Really?"

"Oh yes. The mathematical mind. I know you far better than you imagine."

"I'm listening."

"You are an illegal. Looking for work half-heartedly. I had you followed yesterday."

"Followed?"

"One of my men. If you did not spot him, I must give him a bonus. And this morning while you were wending your way here, another of my men—a woman, in fact—had a chat with the Widow Geffen. What little England knows of you, I now know."

"Oh, there's much more to know."

"I'm sure. Join me for dinner this evening and tell me."

Ohnherz put a small business card on the table and closed the lid on his chess set.

OTTO OHNHERZ LTD.

THE SURABAYA SPICE HOUSE

LOT'S ROAD

LONDON SW

"*Surabaya-Johnny. Warum bin ich nicht froh? Du hast kein Herz, Johnny*," Jay said lyrically.

"*Und vielleicht bin ich auch ein Schuft?* You never can tell," Ohnherz replied.

Yes, perhaps he was a scoundrel.

"And happy?" Ohnherz said, standing, and patting down his pockets—glasses, cigarettes, wallet. "Do not ask for so much, Herr Professor."

Over another Brauner, Jay wondered about Ohnherz. A well-fed man, to say the least, in a well-cut bespoke suit, who played average—no, mediocre—chess, spoke with a middle-class Berlin accent and recognised a line of Brecht when he heard it. Perhaps a scoundrel? Perhaps not?

§108

"You had a caller."

"I know. He told me."

"Two days in town and you meet Fulham's Mr Big. It's tempting to ask whether you've not had enough trouble in your life, but it's a begged question. I'm sorry if I've made a problem for you, but I've learnt from experience that you don't lie to the Inland Revenue, Fulham Borough Council or Otto Ohnherz. Or for that matter, his representative on earth."

"A woman, he told me."

"Yes. It was young Bryce. God alone knows how she got mixed up with Otto—nice enough kid. All the same, I'm sorry."

"Nothing we have discussed was confidential. And the upshot is I am invited to dine with him at what I take to be his home."

"The Surabaya? Yes, it's where he lives. Top floor of an old East India spice importers. A warehouse. I almost said 'converted,' but from what I've heard, he hasn't bothered."

"You've been there?"

"No, but it's a local legend. Fulham's own Medici Palace."

"I'm sorry? What?"

"It's supposed to be full of junk. He's some sort of collector."

"Ah . . . and now he collects me."

"Will you go?"

"How could I not?"

§109

Deborah Geffen lent him a street map, folded many times, cracked, torn and taped.

"Or you could just hop on a 22 bus along the King's Road. If you find yourself in Sloane Square you'll know you missed your stop."

"Hop?"

"Yes. Hop. Londoners hop."

"Thank you, but I shall walk. How else will I get to know London?"

As he was trying to unfold the map on the corner of Fulham Road, the wind caught it, and by the time he'd folded it back to the right quarter, he realised he could not tell north from south and had walked a hundred or more yards in the wrong direction.

But—London was once again lit by its streetlamps, feeble though they were, and the buses rumbled by packed to the limit at the end of the working day, yellow fog licking at the windows like tongues of dogs—and indeed, people hopped on and hopped off while the bus was still moving as the buses appeared to have no doors.

He felt more certain of his way when he found himself on a flat plain, a park of some sort . . . a playing field . . . a slight rise in the centre, a flattened dome vaguely like an upturned saucer, concealing what? Then he saw the skewed sign that no one had bothered to remove or even straighten, England's war as permanent detritus and not a *Trümmerfrau* in sight:

EEL BROOK COMMON AIR RAID SHELTER
CAP. 120

He put his head into the low doorway for a moment and reeled back at the stench of stale urine.

He found Eel Brook on the map—north-northeast of the common ran Chelsea Creek, which he assumed flowed into the Thames, and following the northern bank of Chelsea Creek was Lot's Road, and in Lot's Road stood the Surabaya warehouse. Five floors of blackened brick interspersed with the odd cast-iron column—windows too high to see through even if a century of London dirt were to be scraped away, a double door fit to withstand a battering ram.

He yanked on an iron bell pull, heard no ring, then from nowhere a voice said, "Look to your left, Herr Fabian."

He looked. A numerical pad and an electronic Bakelite box from which the woman's voice was squawking.

"Press 1877 and the door will open. Just inside to your right is a freight lift. Wait there. I'll come down to you."

Why did a line of Coleridge suddenly come to mind: "caverns measureless to man"? It was a cavernous place, a single room, although that word seemed inadequate, a space broken only by more of the iron columns he'd seen on the outside. And the penny dropped. He was not thinking of Kublai Khan but of Xanadu, and not the Xanadu of the poem . . . the one in the film that UNRRA had shown one Friday night in the camp, *Citizen Kane*, directed by one of Hollywood's young Turks—the name escaped him—depicting the self-indulgent Californian palace of an American newspaper magnate—again the name escaped him—into which the rich man had packed his riches, pile upon pile upon pile. Here were a hundred or more packing cases. Some opened, some split, some unopened. He wandered through statues by the dozen as though Ohnherz had looted Florence or Siena—half a dozen she-wolves suckling a dozen boys, a reclining Leda and a priapic swan . . . and Donatello's *David* . . . the queerest statue . . . the first nude in however many hundreds of years.

"It's a copy," said a voice behind him.

"I should hope so."

"A good one, of course. Bronze, not paste. Otto paid the earth to have it cast in Florence and shipped here just before the war. I've always loved the hat."

Jay turned to look at her.

A woman as tall as he was himself, robed in some Turkish-looking dress-cum-tent, thick black hair piled high, a couple of porcupine quills stuck in the topknot, red and blue scarves entwined, making her hair into something resembling half a turban—appropriate to the poem he had half remembered only moments ago. A damsel sans dulcimer.

"I'm Bryce," she said, accent vaguely European, far softer than his own, and the merest hint of a lisp. "You took so long I thought you'd got lost."

"No, not lost, just intrigued."

"Then perhaps we should take the stairs. There are three more floors like this."

On the third floor his eye was caught by a very English oil painting, not hung, lying on its side on the dusty warehouse floor among pigeon shit and feathers. He twisted his head. Something in the style of Gainsborough, one of those portraits of boys in red, blue . . . whatever he had on his palette at the time.

"No," Bryce said, although he hadn't spoken, "that one's real."

"Real, yet lying in the dust?"

"Otto's gone off his English. There's a Constable back there some-where. They were both on the wall upstairs until last summer. Now he's into Picasso and Kandinsky."

"Real Picassos?"

"Oh yes. Personally I liked the English paintings. But they're all 'too green,' according to Otto. They'll be off to Sotheby's . . . if he can be bothered."

The top floor was graced with light. The windows were clean. There were roof lights. There were floor lamps and table lamps dotted every-where. Not quite an ascent from Hades, but close enough to spark the idea in Jay's mind.

Ohnherz was seated at the dining table, that morning's *Times* spread out in front of him.

"You're late," he said, not looking up. "You got lost?"

"No, merely intrigued."

"Whatever. Bryce, tell Chan and Maurice we will eat in five."

He gestured for Jay to sit opposite him, centre table. Jay noticed that it was set only for two.

"The lady will not be joining us?"

"Bryce has an overnight train to Paris. She is a model. Now that khaki is last year's colour—so drab, although, God knows, it was profitable—fashion is being resurrected in Paris. It's where she needs to be. Madame Vionnet has retired . . . Chanel is disgraced . . . Lanvin at death's door . . . but there are others waiting to fill their shoes, their dresses and any other garment that might spring to mind. Does the name Dior mean anything to you?"

"None of those names meant anything to me."

"No matter. The man bursts with ideas. He has been sending Bryce sketches for weeks. Apparently she is the shape of things to come. But I digress. Were Bryce not off to Paris, I might be offering her your job."

"My job?"

Whatever Ohnherz might have gone on to say was forestalled by the appearance of a small Chinese man in a starched white jacket, pushing a service trolley.

"Maurice say sorry, Boss. Pork will take a little longer."

A green soup was set in front of Jay.

"You don't mind Chinese food?"

"Never tried it."

"Or pork?"

"Never been particularly kosher."

"Nor I, but speaking of which . . . your credentials?"

"My what?"

"The Widow Geffen told Bryce you'd been in the camps."

"A deduction, not a quotation. But . . . since you ask . . ."

Jay rolled up his left sleeve.

Δ-155515.

Ohnherz smiled a downturned smile, if such, and nodded.

He looked up sharply.

"I forget myself."

And pushed the claret jug to Jay.

"Serve yourself, Herr Fabian. It's a 1929 Château Cheval Blanc Saint-Émilion. I rarely drink these days. I find alcohol and cocaine do not mix well."

"May I ask what job?"

"No questions about the vintage?"

"Surely wine is wine?"

"Oh dear—so much to learn. Tell me, have you learnt any Italian?"

"Some. I'm not fluent, not as fluent as I am in English or Russian, but I'd get by."

"In my line of work I need . . . shall we say . . . enforcers."

"Thugs."

"No, not thugs. Thugs are not in short supply, and since the fall of the Reich, you might say fewer vacancies than applicants. I have Marco and Bruno, former Italian POWs—I'd never hire anyone who'd been in the Wehrmacht or the SS. No, these are men whom life has hardened to the point of usefulness, but the job isn't all brute force and ignorance. It requires intelligence. You would be the Jewish intelligence releasing and restraining their Puglian peasant brute force."

"Why me? Why not someone not so new to the country?"

"I had Mr Bibby. He worked for me after he was invalided out of the British Army in '43 . . . but he met with an accident in February . . . very tragic."

"What kind of an accident?"

"An unfortunate accident. What other kind is there? . . . So you see . . ."

"You need me."

"I need someone with the mind of a chess player. I need someone who has known pain and danger."

"And—I'm sure I should have asked this earlier—what is the nature of your business?"

"Ah. You mean the Widow Geffen didn't tell you?"

"Only that you are Fulham's Mr Big."

Ohnherz laughed out loud, and when his vocal cords exhausted themselves he beat the table with the flats of his hands, and tears of laughter streaked his cheeks.

§110

Over off-ration pork—that it was off ration was the only part of the recipe Jay could grasp as Otto rattled off a list of ingredients appropriate to the Surabaya Spice Warehouse—Jay learnt about his "empire."

§111

Otto Ohnherz was atypical of an immigrant Jew in the late nineteenth century. His father had quit Berlin, not a city known for anti-Semitism (it was not Warsaw, it was not Munich, nor was it Vienna), ahead of even the possibility of a pogrom and had arrived in London with his wealth intact (and soon enhanced) and his furniture shipped—no battered suitcases or brown-paper parcels.

London needed dentists, and the sale of the house/surgery on Mommsenstraße easily paid for a share in a Harley Street clinic and a semi-detached Regency villa on Rosslyn Hill, just around the corner from a Congregational church in which no Ohnherz would ever set foot.

Harley Street soon became a lucrative practice, although the elder Ohnherz was wont to remark to his son that there was more money in plumbing.

"Imagine, Otto. A Jewish plumber in north London. You'd make a fortune."

His father placed Otto in a very reputable local non-denominational school. "Non-denominational" meant that in theory it admitted Catholics, of whom there were none; a few non-conformist Protestants, that is, Baptists, Methodists, Congregationalists, Unitarians and so on ad infinitum; C. of E., the overwhelming majority; and the odd Jew, if, that is, "odd" meant one tall, fat Jew with a strong German accent. That was Otto. Good non-denominational intentions did not change the law. Each morning began with prayers from the Book of Common Prayer and hymns from the Anglican Hymnal. Otto mouthed the words silently—his first lesson in crime, the art of deception.

Good intentions did not change bad traditions—specifically the olde Englishe tradition that the different were fair game . . . to be bullied.

It took three of them to do it, but on his second day at school they upended him into a lavatory pan until he choked and spluttered. On his third day they debagged him and wrote "Yid" across his buttocks in red ink and attempted a Star of David, which proved too complex a design for such simple minds, and on the fourth, managed to tip hot custard into his lap at lunch, after he'd asked what the "yellow water" was that came with every dessert.

To be effective, vengeance should be subtle. There is little room for immediate gratification or the personal touch. It would have been too easy for Otto to corner one of his tormentors alone and sit on him, and just as easy to be caught and deemed the oppressor. Instead, his second lesson in crime was getting away with theft, the secret of which was never to be caught with something you'd stolen. Otto robbed them of expensive pens, pocket watches, newfangled wrist-watches, even caps, gloves and football boots—none of which he kept. All ended up in the dustbins and drains of Hampstead. Vengeance, if paramount, is incompatible with profit. The double-edged delight of throwing away a pen worth two or three guineas was as nothing compared to watching his tormentor being beaten for not being able to explain the loss of his striped school cap.

Thus began a life of crime—immaculate crime.

Otto shone at school, partly because he knew that nothing he could do would endear him to the bullies and hence felt no compulsion to shy away from learning or succumb to peer pressure (he had no peers) and pretend to be fashionably stupid.

Otto would not follow his father into the practice. His father did not urge this upon him: "Why choose to spend a life staring down people's throats?" Instead Otto read economics, one of the first students at the newly founded LSE, an institution that would become more familiar with Jews than any school of dentistry. Yet, when he graduated in 1899 Otto showed no inclination to do anything. He did not become a decadent, never hung around the stage doors of West End theatres in top hat and cape wooing actresses, never blew his allowance at Epsom or Sandown Park. He sat in cafés, reading half a dozen newspapers and playing chess . . . pretty much as Jay Fabian would find him half a century later.

In the hope that travel would both broaden and sharpen the mind, Dr Ohnherz sent his son on a latter-day version of the grand tour, the idea being planted in his mind by the funeral of Queen Victoria in 1901, not quite the last time the crowned heads of Europe would turn out en masse but far and away the biggest show of royalty and aristocracy the world had ever seen, including the German Kaiser, the king of the Belgians, the king of the Hellenes, the khedive of Egypt, the king of Portugal, Grand Duke Michael of Russia and the man whose death would end the parade, Archduke Franz-Ferdinand of Austria. In his mind's eye he could see a map of the Europe he had left behind. He explained this to his son—"So much to see, so much to learn"—and met no resistance from Otto.

What Dr Ohnherz had not anticipated was that he would never see his son again.

Europe delighted and consumed Otto. Paris, Orléans, Bordeaux, Genoa, Milan, Vienna, Prague, Cracow, Venice, Bologna, Florence, Arezzo, Siena, Rome, Amalfi, Naples. After two years he had landed in Palermo, when news of his father's death reached him. His mother had died while he had been studying at the LSE. He did not feel like an orphan. He felt nothing much at all.

The sale of the Hampstead house and of his father's share of the practice left Otto comfortably off—an English euphemism for "rich"—with enough money to buy the redundant Surabaya warehouse and to play the stock market. In ten years he had quintupled his worth, and in 1913 made the shrewdest move of his life by buying shares in Birmingham Small Arms. His habitual, constant reading of newspapers and journals left him in little doubt: the Europe he had toured was going to war, if not now, then next year or the year after; the map his father had seen and explained would be ripped up and rewritten.

The second shrewdest move was to sell his shares when the United States entered the Great War in 1917—he was rich beyond his wildest dreams, but then he'd never dreamt of being rich but simply expected and accepted it. He was, not that anyone would know, a war profiteer, an occupation in which he saw further merit.

In 1934, having waited a year or more to see if what remained of liberal democracy in Germany would unseat Hitler, Otto bought an East End clothing sweatshop. A mistake. A factory making cheap dresses, manned by a recalcitrant socialist workforce, would prove impossible to reconfigure for uniforms. Speed seemed to mean nothing to them.

He did not sell the sweatshop, he let it be, a memento to his own folly, left the Eastern European Jews, the Poles and the Russians, the Flüchtlings from the Tsarist pogroms of fifty years ago, to turn out the frocks and run at a marginal profit. Meanwhile he bought bigger factories in Middlesex and out along the Thames Valley from Ealing to Slough and Reading, and when he landed his first modest War Office contract in 1937 he was ready. The Twickenham factory turned to khaki, and after the Anschluss of 1938 every factory followed, in khaki, navy and RAF blue. Rich again.

It was temptation, vanity, and knowing someone who knew someone that led Otto to the BBC Propaganda Unit, where, despite fluent German, a good education and his grasp of the economics of warfare, he was a disaster. George Orwell noted in his diary that "Ohnherz is stubborn, highly opinionated and perhaps the most erudite Philistine I have ever met. Clever, angry and blunt as a poker."

Otto stole Orwell's tweed jacket off the back of his chair and abandoned it on a number 38 bus. Breaking his own rule, he kept the ten shilling note he found in the inside pocket.

As the war ended Otto found himself richer than ever. "Butterman" had been true, was still true and would be true as long as rationing continued. Otto ran the biggest black-market racket west of the park. It sat comfortably with running factories, which acted as almost invisible marketplaces—shame he'd lost the BBC job, but the market for butter and eggs wasn't particularly large at Broadcasting House, although his clothing coupons went down very well with the production secretaries.

But . . . but . . . the switch to peacetime production was fraught. The War Office contracts for uniforms stopped overnight, and in the weeks following VE night there had been a steady drift of woman workers back to home and to eventual husbands. It was not a local problem; it was recognised by government as a national labour shortage. Otto considered selling up. He was talked out of this by his factory manager, Aleksandr Bibbicuk—a Pole or Ukrainian depending on which dictator was pushing the frontiers around that day—who had been in England since 1938 and in Otto's employ since 1943. He was known to everyone who worked for Otto as Mr Bibby.

"I can make it pay."

"How? I'm not working a sewing machine myself."

"More Flüchtlings. They've been dribbling in ever since the fall of Paris. Right now it's a flood."

"A flood the British will dam, a fat finger in the dyke. I wouldn't be remotely surprised if they set up a quota system like the one they had for Jews before the war. It makes me wonder what they expect of a Jew. They'd be furious if we all went to Palestine. Perhaps we should all sit in displacement camps until we rot."

"I agree, but until they do introduce a quota . . . well, we can recruit a workforce. In fact, we can have the British do it for us. Just let the ministry know we need workers."

By November 1945 all of Otto's factories were fully manned again.

By February of 1946 Otto was aware of the racket Mr Bibby was running. He had set up a fake employment agency and took commission for placing workers in Otto's factories. He then set up a fake housing agency and took more commission for finding rooms in a seriously depleted market, in a country where one house in three was bomb damaged. None of this was shared with Otto.

Mr Bibby had his accident.

Otto considered selling up.

He sat most mornings in the Continental Caff.

But the racket Mr Bibby had set up appealed, as rackets always did, to the curious, devious, anarchic side of his nature.

So he sat most mornings in the Continental Caff.

Then Jay Fabian walked in.

"Mr Bibby ran a bad racket. I could not permit that."

Jay said, "So you shut it down and, dare I say, preserved respectability."

"Dare all you like but you're wrong. I couldn't give a fuck about respectability. It is an illusion to be fostered and distorted at whim. No, what bothered me was that it was a bad racket. Bad as in inefficient, not bad as in wicked. I run good rackets. Rackets that make money. And . . . he cheated me. Kept two sets of books. You could run a better racket. I almost said you can have a free hand, but my conscience would not let me. Run Bibby's rackets, make them pay, see I get my share."

Jay paused.

Filled his glass and chose his words as carefully as Otto seemed to choose his wine.

"I'm not a thug, Herr Ohnherz."

"Did I say you were? I thought I'd mentioned intelligence, pain and suffering. I also told you I had the Italians for thugs. To be honest, I'd prefer a couple of Russians. They are suitably heartless. But . . . never a Russian around when you want one. The Italians are just about bright enough. They can show restraint when they need to, and they deploy or restrain the half dozen Polacks who work under them and actually collect the money—the Polacks are neither bright nor ruthless, but they are obedient. Bibby recruited them. They know only as much as is necessary. They were loyal to him. Marco and Bruno I recruited around the time of Bibby's accident. They are loyal to me.

"Of course, if you do not care to take the position I am offering, then I can offer you something really respectable. You can live in squalid respectability in the East End . . . four to a room, twelve to a bog . . . knocking up cheap frocks in a Schneider sweatshop for Petticoat Lane. Many a wave of immigrants has passed through Whitechapel and

Stepney . . . Huguenots, Jews and now Poles. The old Jews who used to work for me are dead or decrepit. Stepney is chock-a-block with Polacks . . . refugees from the Polish 2nd Corps . . . the one that fought in Italy . . . some of them regarding themselves as heroes . . . some of them may well be heroes . . . who knows? Heroes now living in houses so dark and damp even Fagin would reject them . . . and working for pathetic wages. I should know, I'm the one paying pathetic wages."

"Really?"

"Yes, really. Dog eat dog, Herr Fabian . . . or if you prefer it, winner takes all. Whatever. I should care. They're Polacks—born Jew-haters."

Over pudding, a pie of some kind laden with marzipan, Jay said, "Thank you. I accept. What's the pie?"

"They call it Bakewell tart. Bakewell is in Yorkshire or possibly Scotland. I have hardly ever ventured north of Hendon. No matter. They make excellent tarts. Maurice has no idiotic French patriotism about food. He'd open the Eskimo cookbook if I asked him. You will eat well here, Herr Fabian."

"Ah, I am to be a regular guest?"

"Have you not been listening? You will move in tomorrow. There is a suite ready for you on this floor. Collect whatever bags you have at the Widow Geffen's. If you need transport, Chan can collect you."

"I have one small suitcase—and the suit I'm wearing."

Ohnherz peered at him across the table.

"Not a bad fit, but it does look as though it was made for someone else."

"It was," Jay replied, realising that the only safe response had been silence.

"You can do much better. Tomorrow, after you drop off the bags you say you do not possess, Chan will take you to my tailors in Cork Street. Lambert and Stamp. Get measured. Pick two swatches. Mid-grey perhaps, dark blue certainly. Two-piece. Three-piece is for Wichsers and should have disappeared with the pocket watch. Two-button jacket—leave the bottom one undone. Faintly, just faintly American would be good. What I believe is now called 'mid-Atlantic.' Nothing flash, no zoot suits. No Cab Calloway. The right side of smart and casual. I don't want you looking like a solicitor, or worse, a bailiff."

"Anything else?"

Ohnherz laughed.

"Bravo—most men would be muttering embarrassed thank-yous. Good. Take what's on offer. It's what I would do. Shoes."

"Shoes?"

"Yours look like they have shuffled here all the way from Berlin."

"They have. The left has a hole in the sole."

"A hole in the soul. Such a notion. OK. Lobb's in St James's. Two pairs. Size nine, am I right?"

"Close."

"Then to the Burlington Arcade: shirts . . . perhaps a dozen . . . cufflinks—silver, gold is just vulgar . . . and no diamonds, I'm not that generous . . . a couple of ties . . . nothing in paisley. OK?"

"Of course."

"The thank-you might be appropriate about now."

"Thank you. I'll earn it all."

"Indeed you will."

§112

On the way down, Ohnherz stopped the lift at the first floor.

"Did Bryce show you my prized possession?"

"Aren't they all your prized possessions?"

Ohnherz threw back a grubby tarp to reveal a shining scarlet monster of gleaming metal. A dazzling sculpted blend of curves and corners that seemed to go on forever, to delight the eye to vanishing point. No pigeon shit. No feathers.

"What is it?"

"It is a 1926 Bugatti Royale. Fourteen point seven litre engine. Capable of one hundred and thirty-five miles an hour—or so I'm told. I've never driven it."

Jay was pacing out the length.

"It's over twenty feet," Ohnherz said. "Don't ask me what that is in metres, I wouldn't know."

"You've never driven it?"

"Never. I do not know how to drive. Why would I? I have Chan."

"But this has no miles on the odometer."

"The Rolls—we keep one for everyday journeys. Just, as the English say, to run about in. I'd hate to take the Bugatti out onto London streets, so much dirt . . . so many unfortunate possibilities. After all, you can replace a Rolls, you can't replace this. Chan polishes it every couple of weeks . . . every so often he puts air in the tyres . . . and so . . ."

"And so here it sits?"

"Exactly. Would you take *Le Déjeuner sur l'herbe* or *Les Demoiselles d'Avignon* on a London bus?"

To Jay this was a total non sequitur.

At the door, a chill wind slicing into them, Ohnherz reached into his pocket and pulled out what appeared to be a small notebook in a fading shade of green.

"You'll need this."

"Will I?"

"It's a ration book. My ration book."

"Won't you need it?"

"Do you think I live off wartime rations? Do you think I queue for butter and lard? The black market isn't out there, it's in my pantry."

"Of course. Stupid of me."

"How have you lived the last few days?"

"Coffee and a bun requires no points, and keeps me going longer than you might think. Last night I ate solely by the generosity of the Widow Geffen, as you call her."

"Ah. Send Deborah my best wishes. And be careful of her. She's far too honest."

Jay held up the ration book.

"Will this work? Won't people get confused? Who is me and who is you?"

"Yes—and I should care? Let them be confused. There is profit in confusion. Go forth in disguise. *Larvatus prodeo.*"

§113

The door closed with all the force of a descending portcullis. Jay stood in the street and watched as one by one all the lights on the top floor went out.

Profit in confusion. Of course—and profit in the hiring of a man without identity, a man seemingly untraceable, a man with possibly as much to hide as Ohnherz himself.

In the morning he told Deborah Geffen he would be leaving at once.

"Mr Ohnherz has offered me work and a room in his house."

Did she snort?

"Fine. Fine. But are you sure you want to do this?"

"No."

"He'll use you. That's what Otto does. He uses people."

Ohnherz was right. She was far too honest.

"You look like an innocent to me."

"Far from it, Mrs Geffen. There is guilt you may not imagine."

"Guilt about what?"

§114

On the top floor of the Surabaya warehouse Chan showed Jay to his quarters. He was expecting something small and boxy.

He thought of the study back in Eichkamp, where he had slept for fear of the house collapsing. Just enough room to roll out a quilt. Old neighbours lived on their allotments, in wooden shacks and tin huts. He stuck with the house, watching dusk, waiting on dawn. How often had he dreamt he was back in that room? A hundred, a thousand? In the dream he was not as he had been then, in 1945, but as he had been ever since, ageing in a room that never changed—the fixed point to which his dreams returned. Time after time.

The contrast could scarcely be greater. His new rooms were palatial. His own bathroom with both bath and shower. A bedroom with a bed that must have been two metres across, fifteen or sixteen square metres of old, threadbare Persian carpet. A dressing room with a wardrobe that might hold twenty suits. An anteroom that served as an office, with desk and typewriter, an armchair with a seat so long it could pass for a divan and a divan lacking only an odalisque . . . a huge window with a view of the creek . . . and just as he was noticing that the walls were bare brick, Chan reappeared.

"Boss say you have these."

He set what appeared to be small framed photographs or paintings facing the wall.

Jay approached, somewhat puzzled, and turned them around.

The first was obviously a Picasso. Blue period—whenever that might have been. A man with a cello or something very like a cello, hunched over, skeletal, his arms and fingers seeming unnaturally long.

He wasn't wholly sure who had painted the other, neither being signed, but he'd guess at Kandinsky if only because Bryce had mentioned him. It was bright and blobby, with lots of criss-crossing lines and what he thought might be the staves of sheet music. If he could work out which way was up he'd hang it on the wall. The Picasso he thought depressing and it could stay facing the wall.

"Boss want see you."

"Where?"

"Today Boss work in bed."

§115

Good God, the man was wearing a fez. Perched atop the vastness of his hairless pate like an inverted flowerpot on a football.

The rest of him was wrapped in a blue velvet quilted smoking jacket, at least to the waist, from which point downwards he wore baggy *lange*

Unterhose—a garment the English called longjohns, not that Jay knew the word. If he were naked it would have seemed less bizarre.

This was not a room with a woman's touch, any woman's. It smelled of old cigars . . . there was no dressing table, no mirror, just a tallboy littered with collar studs, no earrings or necklaces. Jay concluded Bryce had her own room or, bearing in mind the quarters Ohnherz had assigned to him, her own suite. It would have made him rethink his idea of her relationship with Ohnherz, but on that score he had no idea.

From the cabin of his four-poster bed, heavy with embroidered drapes, Ohnherz gestured at the two figures to his left.

"Meet Marco and Bruno. These gentlemen collect for me."

Jay doubted very much that they were gentlemen. Good suits, not as good as the ones Otto had bought for him, under which they rippled with muscle, barrel torsos straining at the buttons. Short and stocky, small men and big men at the same time.

He searched his expanding vocabulary for the word Ohnherz had used to describe them, the equivalent of a *Schurke*—German had so many words for men like these, the 1930s had been a prolonged field day for *Schurken und Schläger*—and retrieved *thug*. Yes, they were thugs.

"They're a couple of Italian thugs with fuck-all English. They know 'Fancy a shag?' and 'Pay up or else.' They are, shall I say, an essential part of my workforce, but they are not management. That is now your prerogative."

"*Buongiorno, signori. Sono Jay Fabian, piacere.*"

"Was that your meaningless pleasantry? Fine. Tell them they can fuck off now. *Raus!*"

"*Il signor Ohnherz vorrebbe restare da solo ora. Sarebbe così gentile da lasciarci soli per il momento?*"

One grunted, the other said nothing, but they left obediently. Jay still did not know which was Marco and which Bruno.

Ohnherz pushed his breakfast tray to one side, scattering crumbs, and swung his legs to the floor.

"*Ich muss scheißen.*"

He disappeared into the bathroom behind the bed and proceeded to speak from his seat on the lavatory.

"Questions, Herr Fabian? Surely you have questions?"

"I can come back later."

"You never heard a man shit before?"

"Not lately."

"Ha! No matter. From now on the wops report to you. They collect from my investments—call them rackets, if you like, I'm not a snob—and they deliver my share of the hits."

"Hits?"

The lavatory flushed and Ohnherz emerged hitching up his *lange Unterhose.*

"Robberies. Back in Italy they were smash-and-grab men. I have not discouraged them. Every man should have a hobby. Just accept my share. No need to ask them where or what . . . it will be in the newspapers one way or another, and don't quibble about any idea of a percentage. I'm not in it for the money."

"I should ask why you are in it."

Ohnherz sat on the edge of the bed and pulled on his trousers.

"Of course. It's a matter of psychology. They feel better for it and it amuses me. I like to be amused. But you've already worked that out, haven't you?"

He stood up, jerking his belly into the trousers, flies gaping.

"*Ach. Genug.* Find Chan. Just tell him: buttons and cufflinks."

"Buttons? Cufflinks?"

"The small things I cannot do for myself. Fortunately I can still wipe my own arse. The day I cannot, Chan gets a pay rise."

$116

Chan came into Jay's room and slapped down two heavy ledgers, the be-all and end-all of double-entry bookkeeping.

He left at once.

"Chan!"

"Wait. Boss send more."

Jay opened the top ledger, a spider scrawl of numbers, a few ink blots, a scattering of Polish names.

Then Chan was back, a dozen or more loose paper folders dropped onto the desk with a gentle thump.

"Read, Boss say."

So he read.

The ledgers had only eight completed pages. The numbers did not match, and it was obvious that Ohnherz had obtained the real books as well as Mr Bibby's fakes. Jay could not see the point. If you think up a vital lie, stick to it. Two sets of books is asking to be caught.

The Bibby method lacked any sophistication. The Poles collected commission from around three hundred of Ohnherz's factory workers, in shillings. An apt English phrase came to mind—bits and bobs, Mr Bibby's bits and bobs. Bibby kept the books, and at "point of entry" skimmed off the top. Again Jay could not see the purpose. If Ohnherz knew nothing of the racket, who was Bibby skimming from? Only himself. As crooks went, Bibby seemed amateurish. If the workers missed a payment, he hardly ever followed up. And the last page of receipts looked as though moths had eaten the money and left blank upon blank, yawning gaps among the numbers. Then the columns emptied completely, and he realised this must have been when Mr Bibby had had his unfortunate accident and the Italians had been hired. Whatever duties they performed for Ohnherz, bookkeeping was not one of them.

He turned to the paper files.

A meticulous record of black-market goods in and out of the warehouse. He didn't need to read any more. It was a simple conclusion—the factory racket made very little money, the black market was a licence to print it.

Just before lunch, Ohnherz appeared.

"Well? Can you do it?"

"Do what?"

"Turn Bibby's racket around."

"Perhaps. But I wonder if it's worth it."

"And the market?"

"You want me to run that too?"

"Of course. It runs well, but it isn't clockwork. Mistakes get made."

"Such as?"

"Stuff comes in from the river at the jetty, on high tide. Convenient, almost invisible, but sometimes it sits in the warehouse too long and rots. That sort of thing."

He shrugged, as though "that sort of thing" covered a multitude of cock-ups.

"I can fix it, but I've been running things on my own for five years. I intend to live a little. The door to Europe is open again, after all."

Jay thought Ohnherz had already lived a lot.

"Aren't you worried about getting caught? I had two hours with your accounts and already I can see that the turnover of goods is huge."

"You mean the police? No, they leave me alone. Fulham and Chelsea police stations are among my best customers. A healthy discount on cheese and butter, the odd bottle of scotch gratis . . ."

§117

Ohnherz spent most of the summer in Paris with Bryce. Often the sum total of Jay's communication with Otto was reading about Bryce in the *Mail* or the *Express*—photographs of Bryce on the catwalk or Bryce accompanied by "well-known London entrepreneur" Mr Otto Ohnherz (well, English probably had a euphemism for everything). At best Bryce was an intermittent visitor at the Surabaya. It was August before Jay could pin Ohnherz down to a discussion.

In the meantime he ate meals cooked by Maurice and served by Chan that left him wondering what rationing had ever been—and he had visited all Otto's factories and addressed meetings of fifty or so at a time, with an offer: "Appoint a delegate to speak for you and collect what you owe. Whoever takes on that job, we wipe his slate. The rest of you, a fifteen per cent reduction. But there will be no more late payments. I say again, no more late payments."

On cue Marco and Bruno stepped forward. Neither spoke nor so much as twitched but the message was received.

He then cut the Polish team back to two and moved the other five to the black market, which he deemed to be undermanned, hence the problem in distribution.

Marco had appeared at the Surabaya with two large sacks of coins. "*Due settimani di soldi*," he said. "*E altri in arrivo*."

He put down an old crisp bag, inside it was a gold-plated Bulova watch lightly coated in salt. Otto's "percentage." Jay would have liked to ask, but Otto had made it clear he should not, and Marco vanished like a *Nebelstreif*.

He counted the bags of cash, mostly half crowns—tedious, boring, and it took over an hour.

If this was two weeks' money, Bibby's racket was yielding less than a thousand pounds a month.

But by July the factory racket was up to date and had swallowed up the incentive discount he had offered. All the same . . . come August . . .

"It's not worth the effort," he told Ohnherz on his next visit. "It was Bibby's folly. It should not be yours. Let it go."

"No. Let it run its course."

"What might its course be?"

Ohnherz mused on this.

"Not sure. There's still a labour shortage. I anticipate it not being solved for five or six years. The glut of returning soldiers was not the solution after all. Our workers could move on at any time, and the racket begins and ends with them—but they hardly speak English and I offer no encouragement to learn. I even built a recreation hall in Twickenham so they might mix freely with one another, and by 'freely' I mean 'exclusively.' The less contact they have with the natives, the better. Europe displaced these people. I place them, but then I also get to choose where to place them."

"So they're trapped?"

"A harsh word, but if the cap fits."

Jay wondered if it fit his own head. The "job" was a bore, simple bean counting and crude man-management on a level two rungs above outright thuggery. There'd been two or three times during Ohnherz's prolonged absences when he had wanted to quit and take his chances in the outside world—but he was a man without identity, housed and clothed and fed by Ohnherz on a borrowed ration book. He lived permanently in disguise. He was as trapped as the clothing factory workers, just much better dressed.

"The black market?" he asked simply.

"Oh, that will surely end. Normality will return. It's inevitable. Bread was the last item to be rationed and so will be first off the ration. Would you believe we now export flour to Germany while rationing bread at home? But everything will come off eventually. I just don't know when."

"Would you like me to find out?"

"Eh?"

"I have joined a political party."

"Really? Which one?"

"All of them—not the Communists, of course, but any with a chance of gaining power at the next election—Labour, Conservative, Liberal— although the latter is a bit of punt, as the English say."

Ohnherz laughed.

Jay resumed, "I've paid my subscriptions, but I'd like to use funds to make a donation. A substantial donation. Big enough to get me consideration and, better still, invitation. Meetings with the great and not-so-good. With men who think the opinions of the rich matter. That wealth is wisdom. Men who might care to air future policy matters with a sympathetic benefactor."

Ohnherz laughed and beat the table with the palms of his hands.

"Ah, Herr Fabian, how quickly you see through the English façade. 'Sympathetic benefactor'? You mean you'll bribe them!"

"*Genau.*"

Exactly.

"And if anyone asks if you're naturalised and actually have a vote?"

"Their manners are far too good for that. I am just a well-dressed Englishman who talks funny—and the Lambert and Stamp suit talks louder."

§118

November 1947

Jay persuaded Ohnherz to attend the London Auction Mart in Queen Victoria Street in "the City"—the heartland of London money, a square mile with its own mayor and its own police force. The same streets Dick Whittington thought would be paved in gold.

"It's November. It's freezing out there."

"Humour me, Otto."

"I been there before. Nothing will happen I haven't seen before . . . all those north London Orthodoxers, the Stamford Hill Cowboys . . . all looking like they stepped out of the eighteenth century in Poland . . . black beards, black hats and black coats . . . Ach! Idiots."

"Perhaps, but warm idiots."

"Ach!"

"And canny businessmen."

"You think so. The Americans have a word for it: 'penny ante.'"

"Meaning what?"

"Nickels and dimes . . . threepenny bits and tanners."

"Aren't we in the nickel-and-dime business? We collect in shillings, florins and half crowns."

"No . . . Think of the scale. That is what matters."

"Come and see."

"Alright. If I die of exposure . . ."

"But first . . . a short diversion to Notting Hill."

"Notting Hill? Why Notting Hill?"

"A plan. I have a plan."

"Do I pay you to have plans?"

"You pay me to use my brain."

"*Klugscheißer.*"

Flattering, in its back-handed way. Ohnherz had just called him a smart arse, or in the always more direct German, a clever shitter.

§119

Coburg Street W11

Jay had walked the street every day for a week, sidestepped every pothole where a century of neglect had stripped the tarmac back to cobblestones. He knew next to nothing of London history, but surely it was a logical conclusion that slums were not built as slums, that these six- or seven-storey bow-fronted houses with their temple-like porticos, their half-basements, their servant's entrances, and their attic bedrooms for maids and footmen had once housed "well-to-do" (an Englishism he had learnt was meant to suggest the not-quite-rich yet richer than the "comfortable"—there was, indeed, a "euphemism for everything") middle-class Victorian families on the floors between? Now, the exterior of every house resembled a badly done jigsaw puzzle, as the render fell off in chunks the size of dinner plates. Now, every window was bare, with rotting wood, half of them without glass and making do with tacked-up cardboard. Now, the drains stank, the cockroaches scuttled up the area steps and onto the pavement and the rats rattled the dustbins.

On the corner was a dairy, shuttered as though it might be open tomorrow or it might not. On the opposite corner a functioning public house—the Coburg Arms—its windows so mired in grime as to be impenetrable to light.

Jay and Ohnherz stopped in front of number 11. Jay wishing to gather his thoughts and be as clear as he could in the face of such visible obstacles to his purpose. How to . . . sell an idea?

A door slammed. He turned his head to see a bickering Black couple in their twenties.

"You just like ya father. A lazybones who sit under a mango tree all day a-pickin' da nose. Well, mistah, dere ain't no mango trees in West Eleven."

Another distraction. And then they were gone, around the corner, out of earshot.

At last he said, "Notice anything?"

"You mean all these fucking shvartzers? There's no money in shvartzers. They ain't got pots to piss in."

"It was two, Otto. Just two."

"So?"

"So look down the street. Twenty-two houses . . ."

"And twenty-two thousand sitting tenants on sublets going back to before Noah's ark set sail. I wouldn't buy a house in this street. Never! *Gar nicht!*"

"Twenty-two houses . . ."

"So you say. Which of these *Mietshäuser* you want I should waste my money on?"

"All of them."

"What?"

"Twenty-two now . . . seventeen next week."

Jay unfolded the auction catalogue. A boxed advertisement, lined in black like a death notice—Coburg Street W11.

Ohnherz took it in at a glance. Paused, looked again, then he raised his gaze as though raking the street in a searchlight.

"The whole street is for sale," Jay prompted.

"All of it?"

"Yes. And we'll get it cheap."

"Who would be so stupid as to sell a whole street rather than house by house?"

"The Church of England."

§120

The inclement weather kept the numbers low. The auction room was far from crowded. All the same, one of the Stamford Hill Cowboys spotted Ohnherz at once. A tiny man in, as Ohnherz had predicted, Hasidic black.

"Ah, Otto. What brings an old momser like you down among us riff-raff. The quest for a bargain?"

"You want the whole show to yourself, Eli Wilsek?"

"No, just my share of it. Stamford Hill, Stoke Newington, Clapton. Why don't you fuck off back west and leave the rest of London to those that know it?"

"Suddenly he's the cockney sparrow? No, Eli, you and your bunch of penguins can fuck off back to Łodz or Warsaw . . . if you can find a ghetto still standing."

Wilsek did not take this in his stride. He flinched visibly and turned away without riposte.

"You can take the man out of the ghetto," Ohnherz muttered. "You can't take . . ."

An auction catalogue had fallen from Wilsek's pocket. Jay picked it up and was about to call to Wilsek, when Otto's hand closed on his arm.

"Leave it. I cannot be bothered with these Polack penguins."

Jay handed him the folded catalogue.

"He's ringed one property."

Ohnherz studied it for a moment. Item five. A house on Newington Green.

"If this is what he wants, let's see he doesn't get it. What item is your street?"

"Fifty-one."

"If they crack on, that's still more than an hour from now."

Wilsek had evidently set himself a top limit. Ohnherz came in at thirty pounds. At thirty-five Wilsek turned to see who was bidding against him. At fifty he looked angry and at fifty-five pulled out.

"He does not know the price of spite."

"Do we?" Jay replied. "We now own a shambles of a house way off our patch. What do we do with it?"

"Nothing. Let it rot. It can fall down for all I care. If it crushes a few penguins as it falls . . . Now . . . Coburg Street. You still want to spend my money on it?"

"It's why we're here."

"OK. Time to prove your mettle. You've got about an hour and a half. Get back there and make a pre-emptive strike."

"I'm not following you."

"Go backstage. Ask the auctioneer to call the owners and make them an offer they can't refuse. Pre-emptive. Convince them they'll make more than letting it go under the hammer. Cash today, no waiting on a mortgage. They'll take it out of the auction."

"Is this regular practice?"

"No. But if you're going to spend my money, this is how I want it spent. Cheap, you said. So get it cheap. And this plan you have for the street—it had better be good."

§121

The Plan

"There's a high turnover of tenants. As you said, sublet upon sublet. As they leave we step in . . . put in your clothing factory workers . . . proper kitchens, working bathrooms . . . collect rent, not commission. May take a year or two, and it will cost us initially, but the profit will show. There's a hard core that will not move on, but thirty per cent of the rooms are empty as we speak. Next week that could be zero or it could be fifty. If we can stop the illegal sublets and get control of fifty per cent by the spring . . . well . . . at fifty per cent we'll be making far more than we ever would by skimming."

"These tenants. Londoners?"

"Well, mostly. A few Blacks, as you saw for yourself, Jamaicans, Trinidadians . . . most landlords will not let to Blacks, after all . . . but mostly Londoners."

"What sort of Londoners? What are we talking about here? Bus drivers, cabbies . . . butchers, bakers, candlestick makers?"

"If that's English for 'aus allen Gesellschaftsschichten,' then yes and then again no."

"Riddles, Herr Fabian. Riddles."

"There is a certain . . . criminal element. That's why the Church commissioners were keen to sell."

"Oy gevalt."

"But . . . the largest proportion by far is white working men."

"And white working girls?"

"You mean prostitutes?"

"Of course I mean fucking whores!"

"Yes. Them too. The damage to the Church's—"

"Do not tell me it's their reputation at stake. Fuck their reputation. Priests are nothing but hypocrites. Forget the clothing workers, just get the Londoners out."

"What?"

"Get them out. Every last one of them."

"Some of them will be protected by law. I believe the term is 'statutory protected tenancy.' We can't evict them."

"Then you'd better think of something. Thieves, burglars, murderers, I don't care. Bus drivers, shopworkers, streetsweepers, I don't care. Statutory? Stat *mein Arsch*. So de-stat them. I don't care how. But . . . leave the whores. Whores are good for business."

"Really?"

"Yes. Really."

"Everyone except the whores?"

"This is getting boring."

"OK. Everybody out and forget the clothing workers. We then have twenty-two empty houses. So what do we do with twenty-two empty houses? Almost empty—but for whores."

"Did I say empty? Did you hear me say empty? *Gott in Himmel!* You said there were shvartzers. What we want are shvartzers. Shvartzers and more shvartzers. Get the Londoners out. Leave the whores. Move in the shvartzers. Whores and shvartzers. Great combination."

"Shvartzers who hadn't got 'a pot to piss in' this morning."

In as much as Ohnherz ever smiled, he was smiling now, leaning forward slightly, elbows on knees in what Jay took to be a faux intimacy.

"Herr Fabian," scarcely more than a whisper. "You just bought them the pot."

He straightened up, the smile had become the grin of the Cheshire Cat.

"And next week you'll buy another seventeen pots. It was a good plan, Herr Fabian. But mine is better. The Jews and the Poles are down to a dribble, the dregs of Eastern Europe, the detritus of Hitler's war, the permanently displaced and the readily forgotten, the human rubbish—all stymied by quotas. The shvartzers? The fucking shvartzers! No quotas. They're British, every last one of them. British and Black and they'll arrive in boatloads. The old black market is dead or dying. Long live the new Black market."

He tossed down the late edition of the *London Evening Standard*. A photograph of a ship a docked at Southampton. A parade of black, baffled, tired faces . . . men and women in their best clothes, clothes too thin for an English winter, half a dozen of the men wearing the most impossible hats for England on a cold, wet November day—straw boaters. The caption, with defiant optimism, read "England is the place for me."

The mask of pleasure was complete. A ripple of satisfaction that spread to Ohnherz's jowls in a tide of fat man's mirth.

"That ship docked this morning. Fifty-seven shvartzers from the West Indies. By now some of these buggers will be freezing their balls off at Waterloo. They may be the first, but they won't be the last. Believe me, they will come and they will come in hundreds."

It occurred to Jay that Ohnherz had been one step ahead of him all along, almost from the moment he saw the Black couple emerge from number 11. Everything else had been bluster and manoeuvre. And when Jay had told him it was a whole street rather than a single house on the market, he'd gone two steps ahead, and it had taken Jay far too long to catch up. He'd already bought the pot for the shvartzers to piss in. Ever after, when he wasn't calling them shvartzers, Ohnherz referred to West Indians as *Strohhüte* (straw hats)—perhaps marginally less insulting.

§122

December 1947

Chan said, "Boss gone caff."

Clear enough.

"May I borrow your bike?"

Jay found Ohnherz at his usual table, a quiet moment after the rowdy elevenses of the working men.

"Sit."

Imperious.

"Sit, tell, play."

"I'm not sure I have the time to play."

Ohnherz's look told him otherwise.

"I bought the other side of the street. Another seventeen, but there's more."

The merest flicker of an eyebrow as Ohnherz pegged the pieces into the chessboard.

"In the new year two sides of Colwyn Square will go under the hammer."

"Interesting. How many houses?"

"Twenty-six."

"Cheap?"

"Not as cheap as Coburg Street, but . . . yes."

"The Church again?"

"No. Some sort of aristocratic estate. Lord Ecclesbourne. Whoever he might be."

"Toffs. England is full of impoverished toffs. Ownership without understanding. Capitalism, which served them well for four hundred years, is through with them. The power base has shifted. And they are baffled. They have their titles and their stately homes rotting around them, and they are baffled."

"They should blame the Jews."

"Ha! They should read a little Marx and then they might just get it—meanwhile we get what they can no longer keep."

"As you said, dog eat dog."

"Or in this case, Jew eat toff. Now—play."

Within sight of mate, Jay losing in the interests of diplomacy, he said, "I'm going to need an office."

Ohnherz, head down, contemplating his next moves.

"Surabaya is vast, pick a corner."

"I mean, I will need one in Notting Hill."

"So—kick out a goy. Your move."

Leaving after losing, Jay encountered Deborah Geffen.

She glanced through the window at Ohnherz beckoning for another Brauner.

"It's been a while," she said.

"I'm sorry about that. I had meant to keep in touch, but . . ."

"Don't apologise. I know Otto's world swallows people. It's all a game to him. All some kind of vicarious pleasure. Take care, Mr Fabian. It's when the game is over and he spits you out you're in trouble."

Jay tried to ignore this. One of the six impossible things before breakfast.

§123

February 1948

Jay was sweeping out the ground-floor front at 9 Coburg Street—the office Ohnherz had dismissively agreed to. A large room, facing the street, a few feet above pavement level. There was no goy to evict. At some point in its ninety-year history the room had been the nosy domain of a caretaker—a *Hausmeisterin*, a *concierge*, such an un-English notion—and since the departure of the last and the rapid decline of the street it had stood empty, gathering forty years of dust, the original Victorian wallpaper fading to flowery nothingness, the spiders spinning a silken empire, dead pigeons in the fireplace.

A tall, muscular Black man appeared in the doorway—pork pie hat, gabardine suit in American sky blue and snakeskin shoes. Pretty well defying the Ohnherz prescription that had led Jay to be in sober dark blue and Lobb brogues. It was the same man who had been in the street the day Jay had shown the building to Ohnherz.

"You the man?"

"No, just *a* man," Jay replied.

"But you the owner, right?"

"Wrong. I just work here. And you?"

"Valentine Langrishe. I live next door. First floor front."

"Really? I heard you sat under a mango tree and picked your nose."

Langrishe laughed.

"That gettin' to be her catchphrase. Not true. Not true at all. I'm a driver on the District line, morning shift, Edgware Road to Wimbledon. So most afternoons I'm under Winsome's feet and she give me shit. Speakin' o' which . . ."

"Yes?"

"The shitter's blocked again. We share with two other flats, and . . ."

"And?"

"And I dunno."

"I do. In the past the landlords did nothing for you. But new ownership, new broom . . . you're hoping."

"Actually, I was hoping for a new plunger."

§124

Jay bought a rubber drain plunger in Woolworth's for one and sixpence. The following afternoon he called at number 11.

Winsome Langrishe opened the door, less angry than the last time he had seen her. She seemed surprised to see him, but then, she had no idea who he was. He held up the plunger.

"Oh. Langrishe boxing down the gym."

"Then I'll leave this with—"

"No, no, no!"

She grabbed him by the arm and pulled.

Jay had not yet seen the inside of any of the flats he had acquired for Ohnherz. They had bought bricks and mortar, not wallpaper and lino. Might this be typical? A big central table, far too many chairs, as though twelve might sit at a table made for six, a double bed shoved into one corner, a Utility fold-up pantry. A gleaming gas stove, looking as though it were scrubbed daily. A Blaupunkt radiogram the size of a blanket chest. A dozen framed family portraits on the wall. A few more that he thought might be of the great and the good.

He looked a moment too long and Winsome noticed.

"You don't know who they are, do you?"

"No."

"No? Where you been all your life?"

She tapped each one in turn: "Marcus Garvey, Learie Constantine, Sugar Ray Robinson. Langrishe's heroes. Them and Charlie Parker."

"Ah."

"Ah what?"

"I have heard of Sugar Ray Robinson."

"I should think so. The crapper out on the landing."

When Langrishe returned twenty minutes later, Jay was yanking on the chain for the first flush through.

"Must admit I warn't expecting this."

"Good. That'll make it easier for you not to expect it next time."

"There gonna be a next time?"

Jay handed him the plunger.

"I won't know because you won't need to tell me. A man in London with his own plunger could go far."

Langrishe laughed.

"Hey man, you got some brass lip on you. You sure you ain't from Trini?"

"I'm German. I rather thought that was obvious. Jay Fabian, Berliner."

"You a refugee?"

"In a manner of speaking. Now if you'll excuse me—"

Winsome intervened.

"No—you must stay for a cuppa."

"I don't want you wasting your ration on me, Mrs Langrishe."

"'Tain't wasted. You done Langrishe's job, you can drink his tea."

$125

"So you're from Trinidad?"

"Nope. Nevis. Trinis is known to be lippy, that's all I meant."

"Nevis? Never heard of it."

"An island about the size of a tablecloth in the Lesser Antilles."

"What's an Antille?"

"Dunno, but the Caribbean got lots of 'em. I left mine in '38. Think of me as a Londoner. Winsome, she come over in '45. Straight after VE Day. We moved in here when I got demobbed."

"So, two years. On a sublet?"

"O' course on a sub. You think the Church of England lets to darkies?"

"And the neighbours?"

"What about the neighbours?"

"Some darkies?"

"Some."

"Resentful Londoners?"

"Lots. But there's a difference between resentment and hostility. Resentment is a quiet thing. A shifty look, a 'good morning' not returned. Hostility—you gotta bang a few heads together. Hasn't come to that yet."

"Prostitutes?"

"The girls are OK. Never had any trouble with them. The pimps— they're lowest of the low. They really would just sit under a tree while their women earned a living on their backs. Most pimps act tough, but they're not. One or two took me on. Big mistake. I did three years in the Pioneer Corps, '42 to '45, and while I was at it I was regimental welterweight boxing champion—same weight Sugar Ray fight at. I thump a feller, he goes down."

"Pioneer Corps is British Army?"

"Trench diggers . . . I dug holes for fellers to shit in halfway to Germany. Now I got a German to unblock my shitter. Life's little ironies."

There was a moment's silence in which Jay thought he might be able to get up and leave, but it occurred to him that he was not through with Langrishe nor Langrishe with him.

"And your war?" Langrishe said.

Jay supposed this was a question men of his generation would ask each other as long as they lived. At least the British generation would—Germans might never mention it again.

"You could say I had an interesting war. Look, I must go now, but if you are free this time tomorrow, call by the office."

§126

"Do you know who Otto Ohnherz is?"

"Everybody heard of Otto Ohnherz."

"Well, he's your new landlord."

"Jesus . . . we just jumped out the dutchie and straight into the fire. And I reckon you gonna tell me he wants all us darkies out?"

"No, I'm not."

Jay told Langrishe "the plan," wondering whether he would just walk out. Instead he was pragmatic.

"So Otto wants more like me?"

"He calls it the new Black market."

"That's really funny, but forgive me if I don't laugh."

"I thought you might question his motives."

"I probably will . . . eventually. But if there's one thing I've learnt as a Black feller in London it's that we look after one another . . . or go under."

"With that in mind . . ."

Jay paused, wondering how to continue, wondering how far ahead of him Langrishe might be. Langrishe said nothing. What seemed obvious to Jay apparently was not obvious to him.

"I'd like you to come and work for us."

"Us?"

"Otto and myself."

"As what?"

"Is there an English word 'fixer'?"

"Yep. And there's also an English word 'nark.'"

"I do not know that one."

"Someone who . . . sells out his own kind."

"Ah . . . I see. No. I would be asking you to be anything but that. You would be a liaison between us and the newcomers. Part-time, of course. You could still drive your Underground train."

"You reckon you need . . . what did you call it . . . a liaison?"

"Yes. But I also need help to get rid of the oldcomers first."

"No such word."

"Well . . . how about 'natives'?"

Langrishe laughed out loud.

"Natives? Natives? Oh sweet Jesus, tell me I get to call these old Cockney bastards natives and I'll sign up right now."

§127

"Otto calls them 'stats,' from statutory protected tenant. We need, his words again, to de-stat."

Langrishe sucked his teeth, like a recalcitrant plumber confronted by a paint-encrusted stopcock.

"You got something in mind?"

"I was rather hoping you might . . ."

"Yeah. Yeah. OK. Leave that one with me. I got cousins further down the street. Jellicoe and Nelson."

"They are . . . gangsters?"

Langrishe laughed louder than before.

"No. They're musicians, man. Neither of them would harm a fly. You know what a steel band is?"

"Like a brass band?"

"Nothing like. A steel drum is a homemade instrument back in the islands. Specially Trini. We make 'em from oil drums. Been around since the start of the war, maybe a bit less. Jellicoe and Nelson got more than half a dozen fellers in this street playing over the last couple of years. They rehearse in a church hall down Ladbroke way. They could be persuaded to rehearse here."

"A pleasing sound?"

"If you like—but loud, very loud."

§128

April 1948

With a parting bribe of fifty pounds per family, Jay had thought the "natives" might be only too willing to escape the nightly noise of a steel band. Langrishe carefully moved the Rum 'n' Boogie Brothers, as they called themselves, from house to house that none might sleep. Jay thought of it as Notting Hill's "Nessun Dorma"—a song the band did not know. But . . . but there was resistance unto stubbornness. Some took the money. As many did not.

"We got a problem," Langrishe said.

"Anyone I know?"

"Number 44, other side of the street. Fat bastard name of Albert Patterson. Professional dole claimer. I reckon he's not had a job since he got out of the army in 1919. All the same, he reckons every Black man is a welfare state scrounger, charged up on hemp and wanting to fuck his daughter. Not that I think he has a daughter, and if there was ever a wife she left before my time, but you know what I mean."

"Yes. We've met. I got a silent sneer."

"Well, he's one of the stats and he's threatening to go to this new-fangled tribunal."

"Fangled? I do not know fangled."

"English word. Adds nothing. He means this thing the government set up a couple of years ago to set rents and look after tenants' rights.

London's full of renters, not one in a thousand has a clue about the tribunal. Be years before it can show teeth. Even longer till it bites."

"I get it. I just didn't recognise the terms."

"He's the one behind the resistance to your offer. He tells the other tenants to stick it out. I think some of them are scared of him. It's a bit like being scared of a blancmange, but . . . you never can tell how people think."

§129

Jay called on Patterson.

He was accustomed to the low standard of living in Coburg Street. Many tenants coped with the decrepit buildings with the scrupulousness of Winsome Langrishe. Cleanliness in the face of dirt, order in the face of ever-encroaching chaos.

Albert Patterson was not one of those.

Jay looked at the cracked windowpanes; at the damp, peeling wallpaper; at the stains around the chimney breast where the roof clearly leaked, and knew where the responsibility lay. With Otto and, since he was Otto's representative, with himself.

The rubble of Berlin had seemed preferable to this. He remembered the openness, the vast expanse of sky that seemed to be revealed by the destruction; he remembered the exposed interiors of houses and apartments as though the city had been turned inside out—an illusion, a fraudulence of light and air.

This was darkness made visible.

A room aching to be rubble.

Come, friendly bombs.

He breathed in the smell of kerosene from the two-ring cooker, overlaid with the smell of burnt lard. He looked at the rugs, which had not seen a broom in months; at the layer of dust over everything; at the pile of dirty, encrusted dishes on the table; and at the unemptied chamber pot sticking out from under an armchair, and knew where the responsibility lay. With Patterson.

And the threadbare shred of sympathy he had felt for the man began to evaporate.

"I would like to discuss my offer with you, Mr Patterson."

"I already told your tame wog. I'm not leaving. How many times do I have to say it? You can install all the jigaboos you want to bang on a can all night long, I don't—"

"It's a more than generous offer, Mr Patterson."

A fat finger poked Jay in the sternum.

"You wouldn't be so cocky—"

Poke.

"—if I went to the tribunal about the rent."

Poke.

"—Or if I called the rozzers about all the tarts you got working these flats."

Poke.

Patterson was a big man, a six-footer, an inch or two taller than Jay, a man possessed of lots of spittle and big hands with which to poke a finger, but he wasn't fit—most of him was belly and chin—he had bulk without muscle and, Jay thought, words without force. If the man had any further knowledge of what a tribunal was, bar the word itself, Jay would be amazed.

"Do make your mind up. Which is it to be? The tribunal or the police?"

"What?"

"Mr Ohnherz would not be the one to take a threat lightly. If you feel you have a grievance, he would encourage you to air it. So which is it to be? The prostitutes, of which neither he nor I am aware, or the tribunal, which will undoubtedly endorse your right to live here but will also tell you that as an unfurnished tenant you are responsible for the condition and, dare I say, cleanliness, of your own flat."

The finger stabbed Jay in the sternum once more. He could break the finger and brush this blowfly away with a single punch.

He said, softly, "You're a big man, Mr Patterson, but you're in bad shape."

"What you saying? Speak plain, yer fukkin Kraut! You threatenin' me?"

"No. I am only saying that we have our lawyers standing by, so take your pick. I had hoped for an arrangement of mutual benefit, but . . ."

Jay reached for the doorknob, turned, pulled and paused.

"Not so bleedin' fast. 'Old yer 'orses. What arrangement?"

$130

Four Days Later

Albert Patterson stood just outside the office door, a look of contrived fury on his face. All but spitting at Langrishe.

"Is the bastard in there with you?"

"Which bastard you mean, man? I'm the Black bastard, so they tell me."

"The white bastard, you arsy sod!"

Langrishe swung the door open so that Jay and Patterson could see each other.

"Hidin' behind your minstrel show again, are you, you Kraut cunt? Well, I've had enough. You win. Gimme what you promised and I'll load me everything into the van and bugger off. That's what you wanted, isn't it?"

"Cash or cheque?"

"Stop pullin' my plonker."

Jay opened the top right-hand drawer of the desk and took out the cash box, and from the cash box took an envelope of white five-pound notes the size of pocket handkerchiefs.

Patterson opened the envelope, didn't count the notes, hefted it as though weighing it momentarily and stuck it in his pocket.

"I do 'ope that tin o' yourn is bottomless. There's two dozen blokes out there, all wanting their fifty knicker—and all waiting for the day they get to piss on your grave."

The room shook as he slammed the door.

"I hope you know what you're doin', boss. That's an awful lot o' piss."

"I'm doing what we're both doing. Following orders. It's the German disease."

"Not funny."

"Wasn't meant to be. Show them in one at a time."

Two dozen was an understatement. By seven in the evening seventy-two Ohnherz tenants had claimed their quit money. One or two simply held out a hand without a word and looked at Jay with hatred. One spat at Langrishe, who wiped his face on his sleeve and said nothing. Most, lacking imagination, settled for calling Jay a Kraut cunt or Langrishe a Black bastard. No one even attempted negotiation.

The last, Malachi Gold, a man simultaneously old and ageless to Jay, took his money in silence. Counted it in silence, slowly. Stared at Jay. Would not look at Langrishe.

Then he spoke.

"Have we learnt nothing, Herr Fabian? Surely the lesson of the twelve years of the Reich is that we . . . that we . . . look after one another . . . or perish."

Perish? Or go under? Much the same thing.

As Gold left, Langrishe shrugged in incomprehension, as though he had not recognised his own words on another's lips, then he slid the bolt on the back of the door behind their righteous abusers.

"You got good English. Know the phrase 'water off a duck's back'?"

"No, but I can guess. Something like *'Es ging ihm am Arsch vorbei.'*"

"Meaning?"

"Went right past his arse. Couldn't give a—"

"Shit? 'Cos that was everybody but that last bloke. It's like they were beyond anything we could do. Indifferent. Immune. I'd feel better if just one of them had taken a swing at me. Spit? Fukkit. I been spat on all my life—"

"*Genau.*"

Langrishe's mood shifted, visibly. Part of the performance lapsed. Any hint of pidgin abandoned. He sat down opposite Jay.

"It went easy, didn't it? Far too easy."

"It went as planned."

"Meaning?"

"When I was young, Germany was full of men like Patterson. Swagger without substance—"

"All mouth and no trousers, the English call 'em."

"Men almost pathetic on their own, brave in a mob. The basic quali-fication for wearing the brown shirt. I simply encouraged Patterson to rustle up a mob. I gave him . . . *einen Anreiz* . . . an . . . incentive."

"What?"

"He didn't count his money. Probably because he didn't want you to see. There was two hundred in the envelope, not fifty. A deposit."

"A deposit on what?"

"On every tenant he brought with him. Five pounds per person. How many were there?"

"I dunno. Fifty?"

"Over seventy. When no one's around he'll be back for another two hundred or so. More if he persuades others to take the fifty and leave. All depends on how scared they are of the blancmange, as you called him."

"You're a clever bugger, aren't you?"

Jay said nothing.

"How long do we have to keep this up?"

"Till Otto says we can stop."

"Till white is black?"

"If you insist on putting it that way."

"Are we doing the right thing?"

"No. We're doing the wrong thing, for the right reason."

"One day, if none of these buggers kill us first, you must explain that to me."

§131

Two days later, around ten in the morning, Albert Patterson appeared in Jay's office. He pulled out the envelope of money, peeled off fifty and threw the rest onto the desk.

"Fuck you."

It seemed to Jay that someone had worked Patterson over pretty badly—his nose was mashed, his right eye closed up, and the fingers of his left hand bandaged around tiny splints as though each finger had been broken individually and systematically in a vicious game of This Little Piggy.

"Why?" Jay said.

"Why? You fuckin' bastard. Why? I got told to, that's why. But you knew this would happen, didn't you? You come in and play the soft man, and all the time you've got two wop hard men waiting for me. Fuck you, Kraut, fuck you! You know what? We should have killed the lot of you in 1918. Fuck you!"

Jay called the Surabaya.

Chan answered, "Boss out."

"Boss out where?"

"Sotheby's. He buy Pissarro."

§132

He waited on the pavement in Bond Street, outside Sotheby's Auction House. It was almost lunchtime. The occasional well-heeled buyer-in-person and all the agents of absentee bidders emerged in a babble of chatter, mostly in English, but one or two in languages Jay had never heard before.

Eventually Ohnherz appeared, stooping slightly and speaking softly with rapid hand gestures to a much shorter man, who nodded as though listening to whatever bee was in the bonnet.

Ohnherz caught sight of Jay.

The look was not welcoming, but then, and purely for the sake of his companion, a practised bonhomie took over.

"Let me introduce you. Sir John Cary . . . Jay Fabian. Herr Fabian is my right arm. Sir John collects for the Duke of Derbyshire. I just cost the duke a Pissarro. A railway station in Dulwich—not that we either of us know where Dulwich is."

Cary's good manners were instantly eclipsed before he could say a word or extend a hand. Ohnherz steered him ten feet away, let his bee fly again and returned to Jay a few moments later looking smug.

"Doesn't know his arse from his Pissarro. Now, something on your mind, Herr Fabian? *Spuck's aus!*"

Spit it out.

"You can't send in Marco and Bruno to beat people up."

"Really? Since when?"

"Otto, it will attract the police."

"No, it won't. If the Met gave a damn about Notting Hill, they'd have cleaned it up long ago. Besides, if you wanted that fat fool Patterson left alone, you should not have told me about him."

"Otto—"

"No. No 'Otto this, Otto that.' Patterson got taught not to fuck with us. Now every man in Coburg Street knows not to fuck with us. Besides, the Italians need to keep in practice. They are sharks. It pays to throw them a sprat once in a while. Now, I have lunch with this English dummkopf at the Ivy. So, go back to Fulham, forget about Patterson . . . and take the painting with you."

Jay hung the Pissarro above his desk. Ohnherz came in and looked at it once. A long, appreciative gaze at a steam train puffing through a cutting in the leafy London suburbs fifty years ago, then a hand clapped to Jay's shoulder in approval.

"Looks good," he said, and then never enquired about it again. Not for the first time it occurred to Jay that for Ohnherz the chase mattered far more than the kill. The sweatshop in the Mile End Road he never visited, the house on Newington Green he would let fall down, the Kandinsky he never looked at, the Bugatti he never drove.

§133

It was the day after when Bryce appeared. He never knew when Bryce might appear. Otto never told him in advance. Sometimes there would simply be a third place set for dinner. Sometimes she would appear in mid-morning mufti—her antidote to the catwalks of Paris and Milan—clutching a huge café au lait. Sometimes she sounded almost English.

Sometimes he could not tell one Continental strand in her accent from another, and fought shy of thinking them all a pretence. Sometimes she would say no more than hello. Sometimes she would strike up a conversation that almost inevitably left him feeling ill at ease.

Today was one of those days.

She perched on one corner of his desk, long legs crossed, barely hidden by another of the voluminous oriental robes she favoured off duty, today something in wine-bottle green with a splash of gold. One hand gripped the desk, the other twirled a wayward lock of hair. For a full minute she said nothing while she gazed at the Pissarro, then:

"You're foolish to go up against him, you know."

"Really?"

"Yes, really. What do you think Otto wants of you and me? What is it we have in common? I was sixteen when he found me. I was malleable. You were—"

"Thirty-four and not malleable."

"Hear me out. Age is not the issue with you and Otto. You were, in his words, 'a man on the run.' That made you willing, and willing is much the same as malleable."

"On the run? I'm a *Flüchtling*, a refugee. Otto must have met hundreds of refugees, people like me."

"Refugees, of course. People like you? No. Jay, he chose you, just as he chose me."

"Is all this relevant to my, as you say, going up against him?"

"Yes. What Otto can shape, he can bend, and what he can bend, he can break."

"Yet . . . I appear to be his representative on earth."

Jay opened the desk drawer and took out "his" ration book. Bryce gave it a cursory look, smiled at the name and threw it back on the desk.

"Jay, if you were Otto's representative on earth he'd have given you a passport too. He has half a dozen of his own—"

"Fakes?"

"Of course they're fakes. Fake passports are a lucrative line for Otto and one that amuses him no end. You know what Chan's passport says? George Butterworth from Oldham. Chan has only limited English and has never been north of Finchley since the day he jumped off a Chinese freighter in the West India dock. But if Otto gave you a passport . . ."

"I'd no longer be a man on the run."

"Yep."

"A man on the run spends his life looking over his shoulder. I haven't had to do that. I have Otto."

"Or rather, he has you, as he has me. But . . . as I said, it amuses him."

"So we're a game?"

"Of sorts. Otto always needs a game or two or ten. I think he has the lowest boredom threshold of anyone I've ever met."

"You know Deborah Geffen?"

"Of course."

"She too thought of Otto as a player of games. She once told me that all Otto's pleasures are vicarious. I had to look the word up in a dictionary."

"I might have to do the same."

"He lives . . . by proxy. I am his proxy. You are his proxy."

"I am his . . . proxy doxy."

Where some might giggle at their own joke, Bryce just grinned.

"I'll have to look that up too," Jay said.

§134

When over a hundred and twenty tenants had taken their fifty quid, cursed Jay, and quit, there remained several immovable, protected families. At each daily briefing Ohnherz's frustration seemed to grow.

He was not to be appeased.

"*Verdammt nochmal.* What can be so hard? You want I should send in Marco and Bruno? They could solve this in minutes!"

"No. I don't want that. Not now, not again, not ever. But . . . you should know . . . we're evicting Jews too."

"So? Are all these diehards Jews?"

"No. About half of them—but all I have to go on are names. If Schneider has become Taylor . . ."

"Don't ask me to care. Don't ask me to have a conscience. I pay you for that. Next Yom Kippur you may atone for me. Take on the burden of my sins. Just send me the bill."

§135

Jay sought out Councillor Derek Harrison at a Saturday-morning surgery—Surgery? Why surgery?—which took place in his front parlour in Radnor Terrace, the street door propped open with a flat iron, a VOTE LABOUR poster, faded by three years of sun and dirt, still taped to the window.

"Rehousing," he said. "Coburg Street, Colwyn Square."

"Good God, are you the wicked landlord I've been hearing about?"

"No. I merely represent him. Call me Mephisto. I believe you have an obligation to rehouse private tenants in council flats."

"Get to the point. You bastards are evicting people."

"Of course. It's what bastards do."

Jay spread eight white postcards out on the parlour table. Each with a name and address.

"All these families will need rehousing."

Harrison looked at the names.

"I know some of these people. Vogel . . . that's Jack Vogel. And Goldberg . . . Syd Goldberg . . . both on protected tenancies. We don't rehouse people who voluntarily give up a protected flat. They can't just make themselves homeless and expect—"

"These families, all of them, are still in residence, but believe me, they will leave and they will become homeless."

"You can't just evict them."

"We won't. All the same they will leave."

"I'm not with you here, son."

Jay took a fat envelope from his jacket pocket and set it on the table.

"A contribution to party funds. Do the decent thing. Bend the rules."

"You're bribing me?"

"No, Councillor. I am bribing the Labour Party and for far more than it is worth. In the envelope is one thousand pounds. Put these people on the list and bump them up it. Offer them flats in the block you've just completed in Siddal Street. And be quick about it. They'll need a roof over their heads by the end of the month."

"Who the hell are you to talk to me like that?"

Jay said nothing.

"How do you know they'll even accept?"

Jay said nothing.

"And if we don't? And I just tell you to bugger off?"

Jay said nothing.

Moments faded into the nothing.

Harrison took the envelope.

Jay phoned Ohnherz from a box on the street corner.

"You can call off the Italians."

"You trying to spoil my fun?"

§136

"*Ein* Tausend? A grand? A whole fucking grand!"

"We'll have it back in six months."

"How so?"

"I did the maths. Eight flats at two pounds ten shillings a week would be twenty pounds a week, or eighty pounds a month. But they are not single rooms at thirty shillings a week, they are big flats and each flat is divisible. We split them all into two, and that comes to forty pounds a week or one hundred and sixty a month. In six months we will have recouped the thousand and everything else is pure profit."

"That's six months and one week, not six months."

"Roughly speaking. There is still a profit to be made at the end."

"Then let us not speak roughly. Profit shmoffit! What would it have cost just to block up the shitters with cement?"

Jay refused to be drawn.

"OK. OK. *Genug*. The thousand is spent. So . . . you got the shvartzers?"

"Langrishe has two cousins working Waterloo whenever a ship docks at Southampton."

"Hustlers?"

"Word has spread. They hardly need to hustle. People look for them."

"How do people know them? Do his cousins wear pink suits?"

"Nelson does."

"You pulling my shlong?"

"Jellicoe has a more sober taste. Pinstripes and a bowler hat."

"Now you're definitely pulling my shlong."

§137

February 1949

It was a blissfully warm February this year after the ice hell that had been February '48. A cold start that rapidly rose to the illusion of an early spring.

All the same, that second Sunday they breakfasted in the sunshine with the windows onto the Thames firmly closed.

Bryce had returned from the Continent in November, after more than two years, seemingly glad of the break. Her days were now her own, even if her nights were spent on Ohnherz's arm at one London gathering after another—the clubs, the receptions, the soirées. Jay accompanied only if Ohnherz insisted.

"He has quite enough decoration as it is. And I'd hardly be a trophy worth sporting."

Bryce had said nothing to this, not compounding his lack of tact with her own.

She had quite an appetite for one whose figure was her living, Jay thought. She had tucked into porridge and had just bashed the top off a second boiled egg when Chan appeared with the Sunday papers.

"Boss still sleep. You read."

The table all but groaned as four inches of solid newsprint landed down.

Bryce showed no interest and egged on.

Jay spread them out: *Sunday Post, Sunday Chronicle, Sunday Times, Sunday Pictorial*, the *Observer, Reynold's News* and two papers local to Fulham or Chelsea. Seeing them fanned out, his eyes were drawn to the front page of the *News of the World*—a pseudo-newspaper that seemed to have titillation as its raison d'être, naughty vicars and bus stop flashers, and a political content readily exceeded by the *Beano*.

The photograph that took up almost a quarter of the page was of Bryce in a swimsuit she had modelled one summer or another that left little to the imagination. A second, smaller photo showed her leaving the Tumbling Dice club in Mayfair on the arm of a man whose face had been blanked out. Yet a third showed her leaving the same club with a much smaller man, face also blanked. The headline read LONDON COURTESAN and for the benefit of 99 per cent of the *News of the World's* readers, who would otherwise be baffled, went on to explain "courtesan" in terms that implied "prostitute" whilst not actually using the word.

Jay never thought he had a face that was easy to read, but Bryce said, "What's up?"

"I think we need to wake Otto."

She pulled the paper towards her.

Why does Bryce Betancourt go home with a different man every night? Until recently she graced the cover of *Vogue*—twice!—of *Femmes Françaises*—three times!—and countless lesser magazines. Now she is to be found in the seedier parts of London, escorting men twice her age. Has the "Newest Look" lent itself to the oldest profession?

"You understand what they're saying?" Jay said.

"Of course I fucking understand it! They're calling me a tart."

"I'll wake Otto."

A restraining hand dropped lightly to his arm.

"Don't. Well, not yet anyway. He'll hit the roof. Honestly, he'll be volcanic."

§138

Chan had the hide of a rhinoceros. Once Ohnherz had stopped smashing the breakfast crockery, he silently swept up the wreckage and reappeared ten minutes later with a fresh pot of coffee and a jug of cream for the mid-morning Brauner.

Rage being both ecstasy and exhaustion, Ohnherz was lying in an armchair, head back, still swearing, now softly, merely to himself.

"Wotta bunch of . . . wotta bunch of . . ."

Jay was pleased that he had given up on the ending of that sentence. "Cunt" had been one of the last words he'd learnt in the English language, and he'd never yet found an appropriate occasion to use it. Perhaps it was the last word any foreigner learnt. To hear it used fifty times in five minutes seemed more than enough.

"I shall sue," said Ohnherz in hardly more than a whisper.

Jay wondered. The wisdom or lack of it in intervening now. But Bryce spoke first.

"You can't sue, Otto. You haven't been libelled. You're not named. Only I can sue."

"Then I shall pay."

"Offer accepted."

"I shall call Cyril Stetner today."

"It's Sunday."

"I don't care if it's the day of his mother's funeral. The cunt is a lawyer on retainer."

One too many.

§139

"Of course," Stetner was saying. "It's clear-cut. Completely clear-cut. Unquestionably libel. Open and shut."

"So we'll win?"

"Ah, Otto . . . not what I said. Open and shut. It all depends on what's in the doorway."

"For God's sake, man. Is English not your first language?"

"I do see an obstruction. Bryce—"

Bryce cut in: "Otto, Cyril is trying to tell you that I cannot go on living here and sue the papers for libel. They would have a licence to rip my private life and yours apart."

"Let them try!"

"No, Otto. Absolutely not. I should be Caesar's wife. There must be no reason for suspicion, no gift to the enemy. In fact . . . I should move out today."

Jay thought a second set of crockery might be reduced to shards any moment, but as Ohnherz stood, the rage seemed to drain from him.

"Herr Fabian. The key to the square. Bryce, pack what you need for the night. Tomorrow Chan will bring the rest—the anything and everything of what you need. Herr Stetner . . . to my study . . . there are battle lines to be drawn."

It was so abrupt that neither Bryce nor Jay spoke for a minute.

"I'm not even dressed," she said at last.

"But the fuse has been lit. Pack. Do as he says."

"I don't even know where we're going. The key to what, for fuck's sake?"

"Lowndes Square. A top-floor apartment."

"Whose apartment?"

"Otto's. He had me buy it last summer."

"Why?"

"I don't know. Perhaps for just such a contingency as this."

$140

Jay drove. Bryce sat beside him on the front seat of the Rolls.

"Do you not think dark glasses a shade melodramatic for February?"

She snapped them off. Snapped at him.

"For fuck's sake, Jay. This whole farce is melodramatic. You know how the *News of the World* got those photos? They had a chap stand outside the Dice like some vulture with a camera. They saw me go in with Otto. Not a photograph they'll print. And they saw me leave . . . One of those two chaps in the photos is Oscar Mackie, the other is the Hon. Bertie Norman. Scions of the English aristocracy, the penniless younger sons, but both old friends of Otto's. You've seen what nights at the club are like. I look bloody good on his arm for an hour and two martinis, then he wants to gamble in the back room . . . and I don't. Bores me silly. But Otto trusts almost nobody, so Oscar or Bertie and half a dozen others see me to the door of the Surabaya and then they go back to the Dice or some other gambling club, bankrolled by Otto and forever in his debt, and I go to bed with a good book and a mug of cocoa—metaphorically speaking. You should know. On at least two occasions that man was you."

Jay said nothing.

A lengthy pause—the length of the King's Road.

"I'm not a tart, you know. I'm not even a mistress."

"Really?"

"You've never asked. Surely you've wondered?"

"I wonder about many things. But the beauty of wondering is its intensely private nature."

"Jay, sometimes you are too damn clever for your own good."

Outside the block at the southern end of Lowndes Square Jay parked and handed Bryce her overnight bag.

"Have you ever been inside?" she asked.

"Oh yes. Once we got rid of the sitting tenant, Otto brought in furnishers and designers. You will not be disappointed. You will want for nothing. And if you do, Harrods is a short walk away."

"Got rid of? Really, Jay?"

"He needed some persuading."

"And you were the persuader? Notting Hill methods in Knights-bridge? Where will it end?"

Jay said nothing and handed her the key.

She looked up towards the top floor, then back at him.

"Forgive me, Jay, if I do not ask you in. This is so . . . strange."

"I wasn't going to come in. I was going to leave you with your thoughts."

"Tomorrow. Come with Chan tomorrow. By then I might just know where I am and what I've done."

§141

Influence, persistence and bullying got the case to the courts by April. Bryce won substantial damages, which she promptly gave away. Otto won his costs.

That night they dined well from Maurice's infinite menu. Ohnherz broke his habit of preferring drugs to alcohol and opened champagne. He was like the king in some mediaeval drama or a latter-day Roman emperor—defying both decline and fall, displaying a brutal bonhomie.

Bryce remained subdued.

At ten thirty, just as Ohnherz was suggesting, in English parlance, that they "go on somewhere," she said, "I am done. I need my bed. Jay, please take me home."

Jay looked at Ohnherz to see if the word "home" had registered with him. It hadn't.

When he let himself in around midnight, the house was quiet as the grave. The revels had moved elsewhere.

Bryce did not move back in.

She ate with them when invited, which was most of the time, and she performed her duties on Ohnherz's left arm unfailingly, with both charm and grace—for the few months that remained to them.

§142

August 3, 1949

About eleven in the morning the telephone rang in Jay's office in Coburg Street. Chan was never at ease with the instrument and tended to gabble.

"Chan, slow down. Say again."

"You must come to Surabaya. Boss dead. I think."

"You think?"

"He lie on floor and he not move."

Jay dialled 999 for an ambulance, phoned Ohnherz's doctor, drove the Rolls at breakneck speed to Chelsea and arrived as Ohnherz was being stretchered into the ambulance.

His eyes were open. Far from lifeless, they showed fear for the first time in the years Jay had known him. His left hand came up in some sort of gesture that meant something or nothing.

"You family, mate?" one of the crew asked.

"No, no. I work for Mr Ohnherz."

"Then I can't let you ride along. But if you want to follow, we're taking him to the Marsden."

"What is it? Do you know?"

"Not supposed to guess, but . . . I seen it before. Lotsa times. Stroke."

§143

Nikolas Fischer, Ohnherz's personal physician, emerged from consultations at three that afternoon. Jay and Bryce had swapped newspapers an hour ago, read to the point of boredom rather than distraction and sat in the corridor in silence.

Now Fischer sat, assuming gravitas.

"It's bad," he said. "Otto cannot speak. Cannot move his legs but has some limited movement in both arms."

"Does he know you?" Bryce asked.

"Oh yes. He can see and hear."

"Does he know what has happened to him?"

"Yes. His rage against the dying light is almost palpable."

Jay pondered the unfamiliar phrase.

"Will Otto die?" he asked.

"He is in no immediate danger, but the chances of recovery are slim. He has a private room here, and we both know he has the funds to stay here forever, but he'll only be here for tests and therapy for a week or so. After that he'll be able to come home. You'll need to hire someone, of course. If not a nurse then a helper of some sort. And physiotherapy several times a week is thought to retrain the brain and the muscles. I can recommend someone to you. Above all, he cannot be left alone. He is close to . . . helpless."

Palpable rage, helpless. Jay had no difficulty in imagining the rage.

"As I said," Fischer repeated, "he cannot be left alone."

He looked pointedly at Bryce.

Bryce met his gaze, stood up and said, "You will understand, Dr Fischer, when I say that Herr Fabian and I need to talk. We'll be in touch in the morning."

§144

"No," she said, sitting next to Jay in the motionless Rolls. "I can't do it."

"Who is asking?"

"Isn't it obvious what Fischer meant? He wasn't looking at you, he was looking at me. I won't move back to the Surabaya. It's not that I don't care . . . It's . . ."

And the sentence went nowhere.

Jay reached for the key in the ignition.

"Do I need to ask where?"

Bryce did not answer.

He drove to Lowndes Square.

§145

The following Thursday Ohnherz returned to the Surabaya. In eight days in hospital he had managed no coherent speech, but his right hand beckoned, plucked, seized and silently pleaded.

Jay had prepared.

The nurse was hired and lived in on the floor below, the therapist was booked for every morning bar Sundays, and he had made a quick visit to Hamleys toy shop in Regent Street, where he had bought a plywood drawing board and three sets of Scrabble.

Ohnherz was propped up with pillows, almost dwarfed by the vastness of his bed, a room within a room.

Jay set the drawing board next to him, tipped all three sets of wooden alphabet tiles onto the board and discarded the boxes.

"Jay?" Bryce's voice querying.

"Bear with me. Help me group the letters in order. You know, a pile of *a*'s, a pile of *e*'s. And so on."

This took several minutes.

When they had done Jay said, "Otto, what would you like?"

The right hand reached out and pointed. Slowly Jay assembled letters to read MARMITE TOAST.

The hand pointed again.

W-H-I-S-K

Ohnherz seemed to inch up from the pillows and the hand stretched to its furthest for the letter Y.

Jay sent for Chan.

The evening meal was perplexing. Maurice and Chan carried on as normal. No one had told them otherwise.

Beef bourguignon for two, served with a 1929 claret.

Neither had an appetite, each of them far too conscious of the empty chair.

Jay picked up his plate.

Bryce said, "You're going in? We can't just take our meals sitting around his bed like he's some sort of invalid."

"But he is an invalid."

The nurse was feeding Ohnherz bourguignon purée. Taste without substance. Every so often he would drool. The nurse simply wiped his chin and proffered more.

When she had finished, Ohnherz's right hand made circles in the air and pointed at nothing.

Jay set the board of letters in front of him again:

BABY FOOD, YOU BASTARDS.

And it seemed to him that the eyes might be smiling.

Then the hand moved again:

TAKE HER HOME.

Bryce said, "It's OK. I can stay."

TAKE HER HOME.

§146

Chan had taken the Rolls to the chemist's with a prescription. Jay called for a cab.

Again, they drove the King's Road in silence.

In Lowndes Square Jay paid off the cab.

"I'll take the bus. In a cab I'd be alone with my thoughts. I'd rather not be alone with my thoughts. I would prefer the inanity of overheard chatter."

"Me too. I dread being alone with my thoughts, which is why I'm going to say to you . . . come inside."

Jay said nothing.

"Come inside, Jay."

§147

At first light Bryce awoke, ran her fingertips along Jay's belly to touch his left arm, stroking lightly across the tattoo.

"Was it dreadful?"

"I can't say."

§148

A week passed. Ohnherz's condition did not improve, nor did it deteriorate. Between them Chan and the nurse would lift him on and off a commode and at mealtimes his right hand was just capable of lifting a spoon to his mouth, sloppiness notwithstanding, and a giant linen napkin served as a bib by any other name. Chan got his promised pay rise.

The Scrabble alphabet also served its purpose. On the next Monday morning Jay followed the moving finger and spelled out the word STETNER.

By eleven o'clock Cyril Stetner was closeted with Ohhnerz, the door to his bedroom closed.

Just before noon he emerged.

"I am invited to lunch with you and Bryce. Would you mind giving her a call? We can talk over lunch, but it is a conversation we need to have together."

Bryce showed no surprise.

"I was expecting this."

"Expecting what?"

"I don't know. Perhaps just the summons from Stetner."

Over bangers and mash—transformed by Maurice with parsley, wine and garlic into something quite un-English—Stetner said, "Otto has made changes. He is nothing if not a realist. The changes to his will need not concern you. Wills are the documents of death, and Otto, however weakened by recent events, is very much alive. It is the matter of the power of attorney that brings us to this table today. Now, do you know what the term 'power of attorney' means?"

"No," said Bryce.

"Yes," said Jay.

"Ah," said Stetner.

Jay turned to Bryce.

"Essentially, and for legal purposes only, we become Otto. We have the power to sign documents, pay bills, acquire and sell on his behalf. It's more than a formality, but given that Otto is still capable of a straightforward yes or no, still a formality."

"Could not have put it better myself," Stetner added. "Except that there is no 'we.' Otto has asked that the power of attorney be vested in Jay alone. You, Bryce, would of course be the counter-signatory to any large transfers of money, but no one is anticipating that necessity quite yet."

"That's a relief. I would never want the responsibility. I would never want the involvement."

When Stetner had left and Chan had cleared the table with optimum invisibility, Bryce said, "I thought I'd be curious about Otto's will. I find I am not. I was never 'in it for the money.' If Otto ever thought that, then he doesn't know me."

"Perhaps he will leave the empire to Battersea Dogs' Home."

"If that's anything more than an off-the-cuff joke, then you don't really know him. But . . ."

"But? I'm listening."

"Power. The power to buy and sell. Did you ever dream of such power, Jay? Of the changes you could make?"

§149

"Now things gonna change," Langrishe said.

"Obviously. Otto isn't going to get any better. But that's between you and me."

"Why? It's bound to get out sooner or later."

"Then let it be later."

"You staying on?"

"Not sure I have a choice. I can hardly leave him now."

"Not so, but I won't argue the toss. I do have choices."

"Obviously."

"I can stay."

"Get to the point, Mr Langrishe."

"Or I can go . . . or I can do neither."

"OK. You just lost me."

"Would you say you needed me here?"

"Yes."

"But I'm not irreplaceable."

"Who is?"

"So replace me."

"This might be the most elliptical conversation I've ever had in English."

"I'm starting a tenants' association. Something to look after the rights of Otto's tenants."

"If Otto were dead, he'd be, in that strange English phrase, turning in his grave. Instead I hear him raging within the coffin that his body has become."

"Yeah, well. I think I get that. 'Cept they're not his tenants anymore. They're yours."

"They're still his. And still he rages. And when that rage is stilled by death . . . then they might be mine or Bryce's. Who knows? Until then I do as he would have me do. Valentine, Otto would never pay you to do this, and neither will I."

"'S OK. I don't expect that."

"Then what?"

"I passed my accountancy exams. I'll be quitting London Transport at the end of the month."

"Got any clients?"

"Every self-employed trader in this street, and every other street you own."

"Impressive. Can't be many, but impressive all the same."

"You'd be surprised at the enterprise of West Indians. We're not just barrow boys—though some of us are barrow boys, even then we're self-employed. It'll be just income tax returns at first. I'd offer to do for you . . . but . . ."

"You think Otto pays income tax?"

"Yeah. That was a dumb remark."

"Quite."

"And there's one favour I'd like to ask. I'd like to be able to keep the office, or rather, an office. Doesn't have to be this one."

Jay had grown accustomed to Langrishe's modus operandi—bright and brash. Just now he was neither. He was asking for something, which he hardly ever did, and was not comfortable with the question. Cap-in-hand did not sit well.

"You can have the room across the corridor. On the house. No charge. Put up a sign if you like."

"Really? I was thinking of just 'Coburg Street Tenants Association.' If I can work out where the apostrophe goes. Don't really want to use Otto's name—unless you insist."

"I don't. However, I do have a question."

"Yeah. I knew you would."

"Why did you never ask Otto?"

"Had to get qualified first. Couldn't do it while driving an Underground train on shifts. And . . ."

"And he'd have said no."

"Not exactly. Otto would have had me shot."

"A metaphor?"

"No. Otto would have had me shot."

"Do you honestly think Otto had people shot?"

"What do you think Marco and Bruno do, Jay?"

"General enforcement and a bit of smash and grab, which benefits their income and Otto's ego. A vicarious pleasure for an old man who hates the idea of respectability."

"I can't say it was a regular thing, but Otto had people bumped off. Marco and Bruno are his hit men. Mr Bibby?"

"Otto did mention him. An accident of some sort."

"Nope. Bruno shot him on Otto's orders."

"How do you know?"

"'Cos people tell me things they wouldn't tell you."

A raised eyebrow by Jay said more than words.

"You've been Otto's man from the start. If folk are being polite, you're 'that Kraut cunt.'"

"Yes. Heard that enough times. And when they're not being polite?"

"Then you're 'Jew Boy Junior.' Sometimes just 'Jewnior,' but you have to imagine the spelling to get that one."

"So you're . . . let me get this straight . . . setting up in business in opposition to Jew Boy Junior on behalf of tenants, ninety-nine per cent of whom are Black?"

"That about sums it up. I'd query the word 'opposition,' but yeah."

"Hmm . . . Jews against shvartzers . . . ?"

"No. 'Jews against shvartzers' was the way Otto thought. We can make this work, Jay."

Jay knew he was right. In the brief year or so he had "owned" Notting Hill, Otto had derived a perverse pleasure from pitting Jews against Blacks, as though he relished the prospect of violence. Neither Jay nor Langrishe had ever offered more than token resistance, and but for the stroke he might have succeeded.

All this time Langrishe had sat clutching a cup of tea that must be stone cold by now.

He raised the cup in a toast. Jay, puzzled, raised his empty cup.

"The king is dead," Langrishe said. "Long live the king."

"How quickly we blast a living man into the past. *Prost.*"

$150

"Let's have dinner," she said.

"Of course. Tell me what you'd like and Maurice will have it ready for eight o'clock."

"No. Not there. I meant . . . take me out to dinner. A restaurant. We've never eaten in a restaurant together."

"There have been many things which until lately we never did together. However. You have somewhere in mind?"

"Do you know Prunier's?"

§151

Prunier's was a corner-house restaurant in St James's, almost opposite Lobb's, where Ohnherz had sent Jay to buy shoes, and Lock's, where he had not sent him to buy hats.

It was the kind of restaurant Ohnherz had favoured, where head waiters would greet him by name and have a reserved corner table for him. They did not know Jay from Adam.

Bryce was there ahead of him. Light summer dress—cosmic swirls rather than flowers—very little make-up, a pair of dark glasses resting on the menu. Incognito, but not quite enough. As he sat down Jay could see heads turning with an "Is she?/Isn't she?" query on their faces.

"This was one of Otto's favourites," she said. "We're in Ottoland."

"Ah? This is a wake for the living?"

She did not flinch at his phrasing.

"Of a kind."

"He did invite me once, but when I told him caviar was not, shall we say, 'my cup of tea' he never asked again."

"Well, I never thought you were stuck on wurst and schnitzel. Take a look. It's a broad menu in a fishy sort of way. You choose for both of us."

Over a 1946 Château du Nozet Pouilly-Fumé, with filet de turbot Bréval (a fish for which he could not conjure up the German name) for him and sole bonne femme for her, they talked of nothing, avoiding, it would seem, the something for as long as possible.

"Bonne femme, Jay? Hausfrau? Are you trying to tell me something?"

And, without trying, they arrived at the something.

"Quite unintentional. But I did wonder if you had reconsidered."

"I have. And to the same conclusion. I won't move back to the Surabaya. However, I didn't suggest dinner to give you another refusal. I want to make an offer."

"I'm listening."

"Move out of the Surabaya and in with me."

Why had he not seen this coming?

"I . . . I can't do that."

"Can't or won't?"

Jay said nothing.

"I want, no, I *need* to be free."

"And to be free you must betray Otto?"

"That word has no meaning here. Otto has Chan, who would probably die for him, plus a qualified nurse and Maurice, who knocks every
other chef in London into a cocked hat. There would be, there is, no
betrayal. But I cannot be me at the Surabaya."

"That I understand."

"And I cannot be free if you remain there."

Yet another sentence not anticipated.

"Bryce, now is not the time."

She set down her glass, eyes on the tablecloth. Were those tears?
She looked up. Yes, they were.

"What has he done to you? What has he done to us? What is he still
doing to us?"

"From his deathbed? Really?"

"Jay . . . leave him. Please."

"The frog hasn't boiled yet."

"What the hell is that supposed to mean?"

Jay topped up both glasses with the last of the Pouilly-Fumé.

"A wake, you said. Of a kind. Otto is getting very short shrift at his
own wake. Let us raise a glass to him."

He held his glass out to her, the candlelight a flickering reflection in
the golden wine. A spirit dancing.

Her hand did not move.

§152

Langrishe said, "You need to get rid of Marco and Bruno."

"I am well aware of that. Their loyalty is to Otto, never to me. However, easier said than done."

"You got a plan?"

"Yes. They can resist everything except temptation. They've already pulled a couple of jobs without telling me or Otto. We just have to wait for them to fuck up."

"Like what? What would you consider to be a fuck-up?"

"I don't know . . . perhaps sticking up Mappin & Webb in the middle of Regent Street in broad daylight?"

"Yeah, just don't hold your breath while you wait."

§153

Six weeks later Marco and Bruno were arrested at four thirty of a Thursday afternoon in Carnaby Street, Soho, two hundred yards from Mappin & Webb's shop, apparently in possession of a briefcase containing twelve thousand pounds' worth of Mappin & Webb jewellery, seventeen Rolexes and a pair of Beretta 9mm pistols.

"I don't bloody believe this," Langrishe said.

"They were open . . . shall we say . . . to suggestion."

"You tipped off the filth?"

"No. Certainly not. I did as I said . . . waited for them to fuck up. All I need to do now is arrange for their defence."

"Not sure I follow you."

"Patience, Mr Langrishe."

§154

Otto had had Cyril Stetner, his solicitor, and Jago Margolies KC on retainer since the thirties. Each had other clients, but if Otto said "now," they were on his doorstep within half an hour. It was said of Jago that by the time he'd finished a cross-examination, the witness would be swearing Tom, Tom, the piper's son had been nowhere near the pig and had in fact been eating curds and whey with Miss Muffet at the time. Not to hire him would arouse suspicion in all who knew Otto.

The trick—if trick it was—would be to let "nature" run its course, let Jago give Marco and Bruno the best defence possible, and to put in front of him one unshakeable witness.

"You'd be better off bribing Jago to throw the case," Langrishe said.

"I doubt he can be bribed."

"Tell me you didn't tip off the filth. I mean, not 'honour among thieves' and all that crap . . . but there are things we just don't do."

"I told you yesterday. No. It was hardly necessary. They were going to get nicked regardless. Regent Street in broad daylight? I just made certain that there was one person in Mappin & Webb that Jago will not shake."

"You planted someone in the shop?"

"Of course."

"He'd better be good. Jago could shake the pope."

"I doubt he'll shake my man."

"*My man?* What do you sound like?"

"He's mine only in that I have forewarned him of Jago's technique and have paid him handsomely. Although why money is handsome is a quirk of English I will never understand."

"Money's not handsome. It's plug ugly. Who is this test, anyway? No—forget I asked. I don't want to know. We're into what you said a while back."

"Remind me."

"Doing the wrong thing for the right reason."

§155

Marco and Bruno each received ten years. After a violent altercation while on remand, Bruno was transferred to Broadmoor—once, long ago, defined as an asylum for the criminally insane, now merely a psychiatric

hospital. Marco was left to finish his sentence in the Scrubs "alone"—
something one never was in prison.

Ohnherz used his Scrabble tiles to spell out one word:

DUMMKOEPFE.

Alas, Scrabble had no umlauts.

Life in Notting Hill went on without them—not quietly, but perhaps
calmly, wrong things and right reasons still prevailing.

§156

Jay wound up Mr Bibby's "bits and bobs."

He did not mention this to Ohnherz.

He burned the books along with the bridges.

It was not enough for Langrishe.

"There's more you could do."

"Really? What happened to 'we'? Or are we back to Jews against
shvartzers?"

"No. We're not, but I'm not Otto's representative on earth. You are."

"Changes?"

"Improvements—or did you go into this racket blind?"

Jay thought about this. *Blind.* Odd choice of word.

"The frog hasn't boiled yet."

"What the hell is that supposed to mean?"

$157

September 1950

Jay was in a small room, a room he dreamt of often, back in time, back in Berlin. He was not alone.

Chan shook him awake.

"Boss, Boss!"

Jay looked at Chan, looked at the clock and the early-morning light bouncing up from the Thames.

"Boss, come quick. Boss dead."

"Again?"

"Real this time. Lotsa blood."

He dashed into Ohnherz's room, Chan at his heels.

Ohnherz wasn't there.

"Bathroom," Chan said.

And on the floor of the bathroom was the naked figure of Otto Ohnherz, lying on his right side in a pool of blood three feet across. The gash in his head was deep. Marble is such an unyielding material.

"Chan, Fischer now. Call Fischer."

He felt for a pulse and found none.

He'd seen enough dead men not to doubt any further—hope was not an issue. Mystery was an issue. How had he got out of his pyjamas? How had he walked to the bathroom? He hadn't walked anywhere in a year and more.

$158

Fischer said, "I have to report this."

"Otto would not be happy about that."

"As if that matters. Sudden death. Odd if not suspicious circumstances . . . but I wouldn't worry. The inspector at Fulham nick is
a . . . What should we say?"

"A customer of ours."

"Quite so. A customer. However, the rabbi at Fulham Synagogue
isn't."

"I'm not following you."

"Otto asked for a Jewish burial. If you don't believe me, ask Stetner.
Stetner probably has it in writing."

"When was this?"

"At the height of the Blitz in 1940. We'd both had too much to drink.
Bombs were falling close enough for the two of us to pay a moment's
notice to death. He told me then. He opted for the local Jewish cemetery.
Told me he'd visited it as a boy. I chose cremation up in Golders Green."

"Had he been in a synagogue since he left Berlin?"

"Not to my knowledge, but his exact words were 'I was born a Jew, I
shall die a Jew; meanwhile if I want third-rate theatre I prefer Shaftes-
bury Avenue to a synagogue.' If I were you, I'd pay a call on the Fulham
Synagogue and discuss terms."

"Terms?"

"They're a business just like any other. Make them an offer."

"For what?"

"Well . . . for one thing you'll need a key to the Brompton Jewish
Cemetery in the Fulham Road. They haven't buried anyone there since
before the war, and I don't mean the war that just ended. Meanwhile,
I'll sign the death certificate and tell the police they need not be concerned. Accidental death, unless you say otherwise."

"I don't."

§159

When he called Bryce she said, "Give me five minutes and I will call
you back. Or did you think I might not shed a tear for him?"

$160

As the clock ticked into mid-morning Jay began to call those he thought should know. There weren't many—Stetner, Margolies . . . and, for no reason he could think of, Langrishe.

"Fukkin' hell, man."

Then he set off on foot to find the Fulham Synagogue in Lillie Road.

It was a case of "blink and you'll miss it." To Jay it resembled a pre-war prefabricated petrol station, a dirty brick façade of flaking cream paint tacked onto a shoebox exterior, utterly dominated by the buildings around it. If St Paul's was a statement, this was a footnote.

Berlin or Prague it was not.

He thought at best he might find a caretaker who might tell him where a rabbi was to be found, but it turned out the man on the doorstep wielding a broom was the rabbi—skinny, sixtyish and grumpy.

"You want what?"

"I want the key to the Brompton Cemetery in the Fulham Road."

"What? I've been here man and boy since 1898. We shut the cemetery a couple of years later. In all that time no one has ever asked for the key. Who is so dead and so important I have to open up after fifty years?"

"Otto Ohnherz."

"Oy gevalt. That momser?"

"Exactly. But a Jewish momser all the same."

"But . . . the cemetery is full."

"Two hundred pounds."

"Impossible to find a vacant plot."

"Two hundred and fifty."

"Simply can't be done."

"Five hundred."

"Cash?"

"Of course."

"I'll open up at ten tomorrow morning. You get one hour."

"We'll be ready."

"For an extra twenty-five you get chairs too."

"Chairs?"

"Extra chairs, at home. For sitting shiva. In my experience, which is plenty, you always run out of chairs at shiva. You can't have enough chairs. Crazy Uncle Leo who you haven't seen since 1922 comes up from Manchester. Then six of your father's sisters come in from Dagenham. It all mounts up."

"We won't be sitting shiva."

"Not sitting shiva? What kind of Jew are you?"

"A very rich one."

§161

Lillie Road was less than half a mile from Disraeli Road. On something more than impulse he walked to the Herzog and called on Deborah Geffen.

"Thank you for letting me know. I'll be there. The only thing Otto would ever be short of is mourners. Who will speak?"

"I . . . er . . ."

"Then I will."

§162

Brompton Jewish Cemetery

This was Prague, this was Berlin. A hidden corner of the nineteenth century shut away from a busy London thoroughfare by a high wall of grey London brick. Tilting gravestones in Hebrew and English, fifty years of benign neglect. A place of repose and reflection, but for the pouring rain.

Langrishe, by his own admission having no clothes dark or dull enough for a funeral in a wet September, wore an Aquascutum overcoat Jay had lifted from Ohnherz's wardrobe. Jay had not asked why Langrishe wanted to attend. It didn't matter. Nor would he ask for the overcoat back.

Langrishe stood with the other "mourners" in the sticky London mud as the rain pelted down onto umbrellas and four men from the undertakers lowered the coffin into the ground with a defining splash. This was death. Unpretty, unromantic death. Ashes to ashes, mud to mud.

Stetner and Margolies stared at Langrishe, questions silent upon their lips. Langrishe stared into the open grave. Bryce was veiled and clinging fiercely to Jay's right arm.

Deborah Geffen stood at his left and began to recite. "*El Maleh Rachamim, shochayn bam'romim, ham-tzay m'nucha n'chona al kanfay Hash'china, b'ma-alot k'doshim ut-horim k'zo-har haraki-a mazhirim, et nishmat . . .*"

Stetner and Margolies had switched their wooden gaze from Langrishe to her. She stopped, looked at them looking back at her, her eyes accusing them both.

"*Et nishmat Otto!* Well? What? None of you buggers were going to say a word, were you? For fuck's sake. *Genug!*"

She beckoned. The gravediggers stepped forward and began to bury Otto.

Deborah clutched her umbrella in her left hand and with her right shielded her eyes, her voice now dropped to little more than a whisper: "*Shema Yisrael, Adonai Eluhanu, Adonai echad.*"

Then she left.

Stetner and Margolies tipped their hats and followed; Margolies slipped and narrowly escaped falling on his arse in the mud. Bryce stepped quickly round him and stood by the gate, waiting.

Only Jay and Langrishe stayed at the graveside.

"I was brought up C. of E., the faith of the mother country," Langrishe said. "Back on Nevis when the vicar had done his bit, before the shovels came out, it was the custom for us all to chuck in a trowelful of earth, even the pickney, and some of us would chuck in flowers or something personal."

Jay heard something land in the grave with a gentle, wet slap.

"A memento?"

"Yeah. My rent book."

At the gate Bryce said, "There are reporters out there. Just when I thought they had forgotten me."

Jay held out his arm once more.

"And they will forget you again."

As they stepped into the street to the crackle of flash bulbs, Langrishe appeared, took Bryce's free arm and gave the press a shot Jay knew they would be loth to print.

§163

The reading of the will was a lesson in brevity.

Stetner told Bryce and Jay that they inherited almost everything, with no covenants of any kind. It was theirs to do with as they wished. He put no value on the estate.

Then he read out a very small list of minor bequests. It would not have surprised Jay if there had been none. Chan and Maurice would receive ten thousand pounds each if they now chose to leave, twenty-five thousand if they chose to stay working for two years or more. Aristotle Pantelides—Harry the Greek—received one thousand. No dogs' home, no cats' welfare, no Jewish Charities—bar one.

"Fifty thousand pounds to the Herzog Foundation. A person Otto refers to only as 'the Widow Geffen.' I take it she is the woman who sought to put us all in our place at the burial?"

"Yes."

"And she is known to you?"

"Yes."

"Then if you would supply me with a name and address, I will draw up a cheque as soon as probate is cleared. In the meantime feel free to give her the good news."

"Good news" might have been less than precise.

§164

"Typical. A lifetime of crime, abuse and all-round bad behaviour and he thinks his sins can be wiped away with a cheque."

"Are you declining the legacy?"

"Of course not. It's not mine to refuse. I will take Otto's blood money—that is my obligation—but . . . are you the heir to everything else?"

"Me and Bryce, yes."

"Then I would ask you this: What will it do to you? What has he done to you, Jay?"

It was a familiar question and one he would prefer to dodge.

"Not sure I understand you, Deborah."

"Otto is dead. I came to see for myself. Otto is dead. But his reach is longer, deeper than any grave, so I say again: What has he done to you?"

§165

At the Surabaya Jay sifted through box file after box file of papers.

"I thought I knew everything. At least everything that ever got written down."

"Something surprises you?"

"Many things."

"Such as?"

"An apartment in Paris, fourth arrondissement."

"It's where I lived in my Dior years."

"A castle in County Cork. Where the hell is County Cork? Surrey I know. Middlesex I know. But Cork?"

"It's in Ireland. I didn't know about it either."

"A pair of semi-detached houses in Chelmsford."

"You are kidding."

"Would I make up a word like Chelmsford? And there's more—a ruined farmhouse near Valence in France and a house on Mommsenstraße in Berlin."

Bryce snatched the pages from him.

"My God. He bought back his father's old house. Who would have thought Otto sentimental?"

"Look at the date and the price he paid. He bought five minutes after the last bomb fell on Berlin. Sentiment had nothing to do with it. It's an investment. He bought something he knew would be worth a lot of money when Germany recovers."

Two hours later Jay still had no clear idea of Otto's worth. There were assets and there were hidden assets. The castle in Ireland might be worth a fortune. The farmhouse in France might be worthless, as might the streets of Notting Hill. He knew exactly what Otto had paid for Notting Hill, but he had no idea of its value now, and what it might be worth in 1960 or 1970 was beyond guessing.

Then Bryce said, "Sell it all."

"What?"

"You must sell it all, or if you can't do that just give it away."

"I don't think I can or should do either."

"Jay, if you want to stay with me you need to be free of Otto. Otto is wrapped around us like Marley's chains. Cut us loose."

He did not understand the reference to someone named Marley, but her point was clear enough.

"Deborah called it blood money. Is that your thought too?"

"No. It can't be. I've lived off it all these years. If I were more moral I might think like Deborah . . . but I took the Otto shilling in 1938. The paint dried on my whited sepulchre years ago."

"If it's penance you seek, we could always live in the semi in Chelmsford."

"Stop! This is going nowhere."

"But I'm sure you'd prefer the castle in Cork."

She hit him, for the first and last time. A stinging slap to the cheek.

§166

When he awoke she was still wrapped around him.

§167

October 1950

Winsome Langrishe was waiting in his office, seated in the chair opposite his, as severe and upright as the governess in a nineteenth-century novel—a straight spine and a letterbox mouth, as though to smile would offend God.

"I hoping I not too soon for you, Mr Fabian?"

"No, no. I'm often in at this time."

He turned, looking out of his office door and into Langrishe's, where the man stood waving frantically.

"I meant, too soon after funeral. After all . . . you is in mourning."

He wasn't, but saw no point in saying so.

The folder she had been holding on her lap was set upon his desk and the contents spread out.

"Langrishe! Don't try to hide, feller. I hear you breathing. Get in here this minute."

Jay found himself looking at a collection of catalogues for bathroom fittings, most in black and white, one or two in lurid pink.

Langrishe stood silently at his shoulder.

"Now," she said. "The time have come."

"What time?"

Langrishe slipped into view.

Jay looked at him quizzically.

"That damn frog you been on about. Man, it just boiled."

And the penny dropped. Lavatories, washbasins, sinks.

He picked up the nearest brochure.

In pink.

He read out, "'Make your bathroom blossom with Armitage Shanks.' Armitage Shanks?"

"He'll go blind," Langrishe said.

In a split second Winsome was on her feet and clipped him around the ear as if he were a ten-year-old.

"Langrishe, you wash the filth outa ya mout' wi' soap an' watter!"

Jay turned the pages. An arcane and previously unconsidered vocabulary nestled there.

"Pan connector?"

"Is the thing what connects the pan," Langrishe said.

"What's a pan?"

"Mr Fabian, it the thing what you does your business in, and not to be mentioned in p'lite company," said Winsome.

"Flush plate?"

"Search me."

"Ball cock?"

"Don't look at me, man. I too scared to speak."

Winsome biffed Langrishe once more.

"That hurt!"

"It were meant to. Now, speakin' o' balls, if we must. Ball in your court, Mr Fabe. When you made up your mind, pot will be on hob next door. Pig tail, rice an' peas. You welcome to join us for luncheon."

They heard her feet clatter down the steps, along the pavement to number 11.

Only when the door banged to did Jay speak.

"Luncheon?"

"Posh word she just learnt. 'Omnibus' could be next."

"Pig's tail? Does your wife not know I'm Jewish?"

"Jay—do you know you're Jewish?"

Jay sat in the chair Winsome had vacated, looking into the hidden mystery of bathroom fittings. A world he had never bothered to imagine.

Langrishe gripped his shoulder as he headed for the door. In the doorway he turned.

"Like she say, ball in your court. You brought this on yourself. Y'know, right things, wrong reasons. All Winsome saying is, time to do the right thing for the right reason."

"She's telling me she wants a proper bathroom?"

"No. She telling you we all want proper bathrooms."

Jay did not move.

He sat a while, with a new world of shining porcelain and gleaming copper laid out before him. A world of close-coupled cisterns, bottle traps, pink basins, U-bends . . . and Ascot water heaters over the kitchen sink.

Still he did not move.

Silent upon a peak in Notting Hill.

Bryce's words came seeping back to him.

You must sell it all or if you can't do that just give it away.

But he didn't.

$168

December 1950

For weeks now the rift had been healing—a slow process he thought better of hurrying along. Bryce's tears had become rage, had become tears again and had then subsided into a melancholy manifesting itself as silence and affection. She clung to him. Clung to him but would not spend another night in the Surabaya.

On Christmas Eve he awoke late to find her kneeling on the floor of the sitting room at Lowndes Square with a hundred or more photographs spread out before her. Every one was of her.

He had never seen the unpublished ones before—the try-outs and rejects for magazine covers, some shot on a motor drive so a strip of stills looked like a frozen movie, alternating between the formality of a pose and moments in between when she was off duty for a few seconds at a time. The moments showed him how much she liked the work, and he realised he had never asked how she felt about giving it up or why she had given it up.

"I was wondering if I could go back to fashion."

She cupped her hands and scooped up a couple of dozen photographs, then let them drop to the floor like paper drizzle.

"Really?" Jay said, picking one up.

"Yes. Really," she said, snatching it back.

Then she suddenly grabbed a pile and began tearing them up, then another and another. Then she threw them in the air to land like confetti all over them.

"But it's all just a fucking fantasy. Isn't it? Just a fucking fantasy!"

"I don't—"

"Paris is what I have done, not what I will do or should do. Surabaya is what I have done, not what I will do or should do. I will not go back. I cannot go back, and if I stay, I will . . . fester."

Jay slipped from the chair onto the floor.

She leant her head against his chest, speaking scarcely more than whispering: "Jay, I have to leave. I will leave. I will leave *you*."

But she didn't.

Bryce

§169

Mimram, Herts

April 1951
A Pleasant Meal Ruined by Politics

The Labour government limped on—a majority of five seats. The lows had been low to bring them to this—a lunatic scheme for growing peanuts on a gigantic scale in Tanganyika in 1947, a projected three million acres that took no account of the prospect of drought in East Africa and ended up as a pathetic hundred fifty thousand acres, roughly the size of the Isle of Man, and a far from pathetic thirty-five-million-pound bill for the long-suffering British taxpayer.

Rod had been a vigorous advocate of the scheme, as had John Strachey. Rod was Air Minister, the bloke responsible for the RAF, in which he had served during the war—a chestful of gongs to show for it. As secretary of state for war, Strachey was his boss, and as a former Communist, a highly unlikely ally. Still, they had stuck together until the inevitable.

For reasons Troy could never quite grasp it came up at dinner in the spring of 1951, but Rod was always one to be licking old wounds.

"What a fucking fiasco."

This at dinner with their mother, by now somewhat deaf and, as ever, a bit deaf to anything said in English.

"*Que viens-tu de dire?*"

Troy gestured at his plate.

"Too much Tabasco," he said.

"*Tabasco? Qu'est-ce que le Tabasco?*" she said and did not even pretend to care about an answer.

"Dare I say . . ." Troy began.

"Never been able to stop you daring anything," Rod replied. "So . . ."

"There was a certain symbolic value to it, almost poetry."

"I'm rapt. Tell me."

"The Shervicks."

"The Shervicks?"

"All those American tanks, the Shermans you had converted into ploughs."

"It was bulldozers, and they never worked."

"Isaiah. I forget the chapter. Something about beating armour into ploughshares."

"I forget too. But it was swords, not armour, and I had sniggering back-bench Tories quoting it to me every five fucking minutes when the shit hit the fan. Poetry? Thirty-five million quids' worth of poetry! Ye gods, Freddie!"

The highs of England's first fully-fledged socialist government had been celestial—or perhaps it was only one high, the creation of a National Health Service in 1948. Monumental, indestructible, and not enough to save its creators. Rod knew that a five-seat majority was a parlous condition for any government, and Troy knew that at every meal between now and the next election . . . be it August (daft idea . . . too many voters on holiday . . . Margate . . . Skegness . . . Ilfracombe) or September (better by far) . . . bugger-all else would be on Rod's mind.

He saw little or no fraternal duty in being a distraction, as their current conversation was proving.

Troy had distractions of his own.

Or, in the interest of precision, Troy had *a* distraction, in the shape, the rather comely shape, of Valerie Clover, wife of Corporal Kenneth Clover RAF and mother of four-year-old Jackie. If this were not sin aplenty, Valerie was also the daughter of Chief Superintendent Stanley Onions. It was one definition of double jeopardy. Onions didn't know, or Troy thought he didn't know. Ken certainly didn't as he'd been posted to Korea six weeks ago—thereby creating the space in Valerie's life for Troy to fill.

§170

Valerie had never been good on her own. She and Troy had had a fling in the last summer before the war. Onions didn't know, or Troy thought he didn't know, and Ken had not yet appeared. It had fizzled out by the Christmas of '39, and as far as Troy could tell—Valerie being at best an irregular communicator—her war had been as liberated as that of his own sisters. Only an unwanted pregnancy had led her to marry Leading Aircraftman Clover in 1946. And then . . . a much-wanted Jackie, who nonetheless could not fill the space in Valerie's life. Valerie wanted to be a good mother, and tried to think of herself as a good mother, but once Ken was posted abroad Jackie saw more of the babysitter than of her mother.

"I can get away tonight."

A phrase that concealed as much as it revealed.

Away from what? Away from whom? Troy had no idea who babysat Jackie—nor would he ask. He wasn't Valerie's moral judge any more than he was her fairy godfather. Stan was a widower. There was no Granny Onions eager to help.

Ken's ship had sailed only forty-eight hours before Valerie had called with her telling phrase. Onions had insisted Troy attend the farewell "bit of a do." He hadn't seen Valerie since Jackie had been born.

"You were friendly once upon a time."

Onions didn't know, or Troy thought he didn't know. Now was not the moment to tell him. That moment simply did not exist.

Sherry from the wood, brown ale and fish paste sandwiches around the dining table in Onions's cramped Acton terrace. Ken's big, swaggering mates from his RAF ground crew unit towering over Troy. Valerie's childhood friends, all now young wives with young children, eyeing him up in such a way that he was left in no doubt. They knew. Ten years and more ago these girls, as they had been, probably had no secrets from each other. He felt like a specimen—and it was hardly far from the truth. Posh, rich, small enough to bring out the maternal. A specimen.

"I can get away tonight."

"Are you sure?"

"'Course I'm sure. I got the sitter all lined up."

"I meant . . . are you sure this is what you want to do?"

"Never bothered you before. You never cared if it was me made the first move. After all . . . if I'd waited for you to . . ."

"Different times. Ten years ago . . . we were both kids."

"I need you now. For Christ's sake, Troy, don't push me away now."

And he didn't.

For a while it was bedroom bliss.

It remained blissful through April, through May.

One Friday morning in June, Inspector Wildeve came in from the outer office and quietly closed the door. This was not Jack's typical modus operandi. He left everything open, doors, drawers, cupboards, button flies . . . and seemed not to understand the principle of the hinge. Occasionally he slammed a door, but close one gently?

Rats, thought Troy.

"Rats," said Troy.

"Rats?" said Jack.

"I smell one."

Jack pulled a chair up to Troy's desk and sat down.

"In a word . . . Bryce."

"Not a name I've heard in a while. Not since Ohnherz's funeral. Is Miss Betancourt well?"

"No idea. That affair lasted about a month. Haven't heard from her since."

"Sorry. Wasn't my intention to kill it off."

"Actually Freddie, it was. And whatever I might have said at the time . . . you were right and I am grateful, if undemonstrably so. But . . . but it is in that same spirit of friendship that I sit before you now."

"Jack, who's writing this script? It sounds like discarded pages from some long-forgotten Victorian melodrama. Oh, Sir Jasper, do not touch me."

"Our Valerie."

This got Troy's attention. He stopped twirling his pencil, impatiently leaned back in his chair and said, "Tell me."

"You left early yesterday—"

"I was over the road. In Rod's office. Family stuff to sign. Pile of bumf a mile high."

"Your phone rang shortly after six. I picked it up. Before I could say anything a woman's voice said—"

"I can get away tonight."

"Yes. And in exactly that sexually loaded tone. Seduction down the copper wires. Freddie, if I can recognise Valerie Onions's voice, so can the girls on the switchboard. I can keep a secret. They can't."

"They're paid to be discreet. This *is* Scotland Yard."

"I'd laugh, but it's no laughing matter."

"Stan doesn't know."

"You'd better be right."

Jack was right and Troy knew it. In 1939, he and Valerie had been young and single. Had Stan known, his parental sense of propriety might have been triggered, as the guardian of his daughter's virginity, his class-consciousness too—"Stick to your own kind, our Valerie"—but now, whilst Troy was nakedly single, Valerie was a married woman in her thirties with a daughter of her own, and Onions's wrath would rise out of his Lancastrian Methodist (or some such Protestant faction that Troy had not fully grasped) upbringing to bring forth thunderbolts of moral rectitude. He'd probably thump Troy and then put him on point duty in Catford.

"I'll stop her calling."

"Would it not be better to stop *her*? Full stop?"

"I've no wish to do that. Besides, she'll dump me just like she did last time."

"That, Freddie, is because you always manipulate the circumstances to get yourself dumped. It's a form of constructive laziness. Comes without effort or guilt."

Such insight in one so young.

"And," Jack went on, "I've met 'our Valerie.' What do you see in her? And don't say 'What does anyone see in anyone?'"

Troy spun his chair around and looked out at the Thames, bright and sluggish at the same time, avoiding Jack's gaze for a moment.

"What you see is what you get with Val. She is not much of a dissembler, and while you—that is, I—have her attention she makes me feel that I am the world to her. But it's a tap. One she can turn on or off at a moment's notice. She is a creature of conviction, although I could not tell you what that conviction is, only that she draws clear lines for people she meets and woe betide the man who crosses them. She draws no such lines for herself, of course."

"My God. She's a chip off the old block, isn't she? Stanley Onions's daughter. To a T. How many times has he laid down Stanley's Law to us then ripped it all up a week later?"

"And Bryce?"

"Eh?"

"To return to your opening word."

"Eh?—again."

"What did you see in Bryce, Jack? You knew the risks at the time, and you might have brought Ohnherz down on you as well as Stan."

"As they say on the Cambridge entrance paper, this is a two-part question. What did I see in Bryce? Not what you see in Valerie. She is very far from being "what you see is what you get." I knew her no better at the end of the affair than at the beginning. She is . . . what? She is a masquerade of a woman. She is Pirandello with a cupboard full of commedia dell'arte masks to choose from. In that sense she's much more like you."

Such insight in one so young.

"As for the rage of the dads . . . can't argue with you about Stan . . . I was playing with fire and with my own prospects. But Otto Ohnherz? The press had that wrong all along. She was never Ohnherz's mistress. That was another of the masks. She was, nay is, Jay Fabian's mistress."

"I'm beginning to regret that I never met her," Troy said.

"Don't. You have enough problems without Bryce. Freddie, you can't dump Valerie. So I hope she dumps you."

§171

Troy "saw" Valerie well into July. Then she stopped calling. Troy did not mention this to Jack. Onions seemed none the wiser.

The last he heard from Valerie was a scrawled letter in biro to his home in Goodwin's Court, at the beginning of October, rage in every twisted word.

You won't believe this. Ken is back. I ask you what was the bloody point. Six weeks it takes to get to fukkin Korea and he's back in six months! Not worth unpacking his kitbag.

But there's worse. He's taken a posting in Cheshire, RAF fuckin Cranage. Ken is a mechanic. Trained on all them fighters during the war. Cranage got no planes. Not a single fukkin one. All that training, all that knowledge and he takes a job running stores and spares. I do not fukkin believe this!

But there's worse. We're not living on the base. It's only a dozen miles from Salford . . . we'll be living two streets away from where my dad grew up, two streets away from where I was born. What is the bugger trying to do to me?

I gotta sign off now. I'd say I'll miss you Troy, if I thought for one second you'd miss me.

Valerie.

§172

Six weeks later, on August 29, after trial, retrial, conviction, appeal and press furore, Rebecca Brand was hanged at Maidstone Gaol.

Jack said, "We need to get drunk."

Troy, being adept at dodging drunk, gave the impression of matching Jack drink for drink whilst staying relatively sober.

"What have we done, what have we done?"

Jack knocked back a double Laphroaig and called on the barman for another.

"What was it you said about her, Freddie? An Ibsen heroine?'

"Just a coincidence of names. It had no meaning. You run two Ibsen plays together you get the name Rebecca Brand."

"Well fukkit! We turned her into Tess of the d'Urbervilles. I feel like quitting. Fuck this job. I feel like quitting."

He didn't. Troy saw him home. Stretched him out on the bed and dished up the Alka-Seltzer at the Yard the following morning.

§173

On September 19 the Prime Minister announced that he would "go to the country"—not a declaration of his holiday plans but of the next general election, which he called for October 25.

On the morning of October 25 Jay Fabian was found dead in front of one of his many houses in Coburg Street West 11. For a moment Troy thought of Bryce Betancourt and re-ran his conversation with Jack. To no conclusion.

He had the day off, at his brother's insistence.

"Be there or else. Last time I had to whip you in myself! Do your bit, Freddie."

So . . . it wasn't his case. It was Jack's. He'd drive out to Mimram, vote, do his "bit," whatever that was, and watch the Labour government sink like a Spanish galleon hit with a broadside.

Then Jack phoned from a police box on a street corner in Notting Hill and said, "I really can't do this. I really shouldn't be doing this. Can you take over?"

§174

Coburg Street was, in an English phrase that almost defied meaning, much of a muchness. A Victorian street that had arrived, risen, fallen and might be about to rise again.

Troy could not recall that he'd ever walked down it. He had "cut his teeth" as a copper at the opposite end of the city in Stepney and

Limehouse. Coburg Street had suffered a brief notoriety a few years ago, just before the death of Otto Ohnherz—brief because the London press was scarcely concerned about the exploitation of immigrants. It looked better than he might have imagined. No boarded-up windows, very little rubbish in the streets, the odd lick of new paint on old doors.

Jack was leaning against the bonnet of his Wolseley.

"It's at times like this that I wish I smoked."

"Where?" said Troy.

"Number 13. At the bottom of the area steps."

"You've looked?"

"Yes. It's Fabian. Just about recognisable. A seven-storey fall from the roof. Messy. Look, I need to get away from here. I've leave backed up. If it's OK with you, I'll take three days and be back on Monday."

Jack opened the car door.

"One thing," Troy said. "Bryce Betancourt's address? You surely weren't intending to tell her yourself?"

§175

The body lay under a tarp. A congealing puddle of blood on the cobblestones.

"Messy" was accurate. "His own mother wouldn't know him" sprang to mind only to be readily dismissed—after all, Jack had known him.

Two of Troy's squad, Detective Constables Thomson and Gutteridge, stood at the top of the steps, waiting.

"Mr Wildeve told us to do a house-to-house," Gutteridge said.

"Then why are you standing here?"

"Boss, these is all flats. There must be, well . . . hundreds of 'em. There's only two of us."

"Ring the Yard and have half a dozen uniforms taken off traffic duty or whatever . . . Just get it done. I want the last person to see Fabian alive."

"That would be him."

Thomson pointed to the doorway of number 9, where a tall Black man stood next to a sign that read COBURG ST. TENANTS ASSOCIATION.

"Name of Langrishe. Says he was on the roof with Fabian last night."

Troy introduced himself.

Langrishe said, "I got an office. You better come inside."

The doors either side of the hallway were open.

"I'm on the right," Langrishe said. "Jay was on the left."

Troy looked in.

Spartan. A desk. Three chairs. A spotless blotter on the desk. No ashtray. A kettle on a single gas ring in the corner.

"I suppose you'll want to search it?" Langrishe said.

"Would I find anything?"

"Probably not. Just plumbing catalogues and paint charts. Jay kept everything back at the Surabaya. He only used this office if people wanted to see him. Hence the three chairs. Folk usually come in couples."

"And yours?"

"Stuffed. I dealt with every complaint from serious issues to petty whinges."

He led Troy in.

Half-open filing cabinets, bursting with paperwork. A cluttered desk. An overflowing ashtray. A chaise-longue. Half a dozen chairs. An Armitage Shanks promotional calendar—bathroom fittings rather than scantily clad models. A boxing poster—England's own Randolph Turpin versus Sugar Ray Robinson, that summer. Langrishe had thought enough of the occasion to frame the poster.

"My job is to handle everything I can," he said. "Most things never got to Jay. If they did, I wasn't doing my job."

"But some did?"

"Yes."

"Was he responsive to complaints?"

"Mostly—but let me ask you a question. I've heard of you. You're Murder Squad. So is this a murder case?"

"That's what I'm here to find out."

"And you think it might be someone with a grudge . . . one of my people? 'Cos I can tell you now . . . that is very unlikely."

"Fabian kept his tenants happy?"

"Mostly. But it took two of us."

"And what took the two of you to the roof of number thirteen last night?"

§176

Troy had not thought he had any problem with heights, but this was vertiginous. A gently sloping lead roof, slippery with overnight rain.

"It started to rain about ten. Jay and I were in the pub on the corner. Brendan Riley came looking for us. Said the roof was leaking again and old Mother Riley was bashing his ear about it. We went back to number nine. Jay had this rubber mallet in his desk just for flattening lead, 'cos this sort of thing happens a lot."

"You're not telling me Fabian fixed things in person?"

"Yep. His first day here he came round with a rubber plunger and unblocked my crapper. Last night he walloped the lead—himself. Rain had stopped by then. He told me he was on top of things and I should go home to the missis. I did. I live at number eleven—between here and the office. I went down through the roof door—left the door on number nine open so Jay could go down the way we came up. First I knew something wasn't right was about seven this morning. I went to the office. Door wasn't locked. I went up to the roof. Door was still open. Then I heard old Magenta screaming."

"Magenta?"

"Magenta Christmas. One of the Trinis. Widow in her eighties. Basement flat. Pulled back the curtain and . . ."

"Quite," said Troy. "So . . . anyone could have come up the way we just did, any time after you left?"

"I suppose so, but then every house in the row has a roof door and you can just walk from one roof to another."

"That opens up too many possibilities."

"Yeah. I figured."

§177

It was late morning when Troy arrived at Lowndes Square.

Bryce answered the door, faintly bedraggled in some sort of voluminous oriental gown.

She looked at him quizzically for a moment.

"Do you know who I am?"

"Freddie, isn't it? Sasha's little brother? Sergeant—"

"Chief Inspector."

"This can't be good news."

"It isn't. Jay Fabian is dead."

The hand that had been holding the door let go and it swung open as she walked away. She fell onto the sofa, head in hands. Then she leaned back, eyes on the ceiling, and breathed deeply.

When she straightened up Troy was sitting opposite her.

"I've always dreaded this," Bryce said. "That one day . . . one day what? I don't know what I'm saying. Jay is dead . . . Jay is dead. Three little words and a world ends."

Troy said nothing.

"Tell me. When?"

"Around eleven o'clock last night."

"Where?"

"Coburg Street. Apparently he fell from the roof of number thirteen."

"'Apparently' is copper-speak, isn't it? Slipped or shoved or jumped? Why?"

"I don't know why. I have several questions to ask you, but I can't go into that right now."

"Neither can I. I must go weep for my man."

She stood up.

"Please see yourself out, Mr Troy."

And she vanished into the bedroom.

§178

Troy called the Hendon laboratory. A few years ago, at the inception of the National Health Service, Anna Pakenham, assistant to the Met's chief pathologist Ladislaw Kolankiewicz, had left Hendon to become an NHS physician, and thence to private practice, thus skewing the rather odd relationship ("Shall we, shan't we, shall we, shan't we?") she had had with Troy since the middle of the war. Zuzanna Zarnecka, a fellow Pole, the new *kundel*, as Kolankiewicz habitually called her, answered the phone. Compared to Anna, she was brusque, quite free from Anna's flirtatious banter.

"He's in Dundee, Troy. Some case the locals couldn't crack, although to be honest I think he agreed to go simply because he'd never been to Scotland."

"How long?"

"He reckoned it would be four days away. Which means he'll be back tomorrow. I can assume this is urgent? Is it the Notting Hill body?"

"Yes, and urgent as it is, it will have to wait a day. Could you get the body on a slab? I'll take a look myself this afternoon, but I want Kolankiewicz to do this one in person."

"If you think I'm not good enough . . . of course."

"Not the point, Dr Zarnecka. Think of it as teamwork."

"Trying very hard, Troy. And failing."

The clunk as the phone went down was deafening.

§179

Troy found himself looking at a corpse about five feet ten inches tall, and about twelve stones in weight. Good musculature—a man who took care of himself without becoming a fitness fanatic—a few scars, an inevitable mass of broken bones and a gash in the skull that was surely the fatal wound.

He lifted the left arm.

A tattoo: Δ-155515.

"What do you see?" Zarnecka asked. "Kolankiewicz reckons you can read a corpse as well as he can."

"It's baffling," Troy replied.

"At this stage isn't every body baffling?"

"Yes, but this is baffling baffling."

"OK. I can take a hint. I am the apprentice, Kolankiewicz's 'mongrel.' One more question and I'll shut up. Left leg. A bullet wound?"

"Yes and an old one. Lots of men who served in the last war will have something like it."

"So . . . not necessarily a clue, then?"

"Now you're taking the mickey."

"I most certainly am, and you've asked for it. Or perhaps I'm just flirting. Troy, let's have a drink sometime or lunch . . . without either of your dreadful sisters."

"Of course."

But neither of them named a day.

§180

Troy went back to Coburg Street.

Thomson and Gutteridge met him outside number nine.

Gutteridge said, "We've drawn a blank, boss. Nobody saw anything, nobody heard anything."

"Not even the scream as the bugger fell," Thomson added.

Troy ignored this.

"You've been at it less than eight hours."

"You said it. Our shift's over."

That sort of jobsworthism usually exasperated Troy. He strove for patience.

"How far did you get?"

"Both sides of the street, as far as the pub. The Yard sent two uniforms. If you want us to do the rest of the street, they'll have to send more."

Troy had worked with Thomson and Gutteridge since 1944. He had often come close to loathing both of them. They were too old to be constables—both older than Jack, and Thomson had even turned down promotion. Dealing with them meant a frequent battle with laziness and lack of imagination. But—they were right. This was going nowhere.

§181

Going from nowhere to somewhere meant knocking on Valentine Langrishe's door.

Troy said, "I am trying to understand why a man might kill himself."

"How many angels can you fit on the head of a pin?"

"Let's whittle that down to two for purpose of argument. You and Jay."

"I'm listening."

"You took drastic measures to get control of this building and dozens of others like it."

"In Otto's time—yes. I won't deny it."

"Any regrets?"

Troy had weighed up the question on his way to Notting Hill. He'd expected hesitation.

Langrishe didn't even blink.

"Do I feel regret at what we did? No. Never. We put roofs over the heads of Black families. I'd never regret that. You want regret, remorse, guilt . . . you talk to the buggers who wouldn't let to us. Talk to the Church, talk to the English toffs, the chinless wonders who own half London. The only thing I would regret is if what we did got Jay killed."

"Did it?"

"You tell me. All I know is there was a man found in bits in the yard of number thirteen. If you know how he died, tell me."

"I don't, but the options are simple. Slip, push or—"

"Jump? Get to the point, Mr Troy. Ask me if Jay was the type to kill himself."

"Was Jay the type to kill himself?"

"The fuck I should know. What I do know is he was a survivor, war, Nazis, death camps . . . a survivor."

"None of which would rule out suicide. Quite the opposite, in fact."

"How many death camp survivors have you met?"

"Some."

"Some? Yeah, right. Neither you nor I know what goes on in the mind of a man who survived Auschwitz."

"Of which he never spoke?"

"Not a dicky bird."

Langrishe seemed to gather his thoughts for a moment or two.

"I suppose you could say a man who'd been through what Jay had been through was shaped by it."

"It would be extremely odd if that were not the case."

"But . . . he never mentioned it. And there was a shaping, if that's what we're calling it, that was much more apparent."

"And?"

"Otto Ohnherz. A lot of what you might have heard about Otto was bullshit—he fostered his own myth. All the same, he was a crook. No two ways about it. If you've heard the same rumours about Jay, double bullshit. Jay ran a straight operation. A good operation—just not as good as he thought it was."

"Meaning?"

"Things in this street could have moved a lot quicker without Otto lurking in the background. He's been the ghost in the machine as long as I've known Jay. Jay was an honest man, Otto wasn't. And the Jay who was in Otto's grip was a man compromised."

"How long has Otto been dead?"

"Don't matter—his reach stretches beyond the grave."

§182

Troy left it until early evening before he called Bryce.

If she didn't pick up by the third ring, he'd give her till morning.

"Miss Betancourt? Frederick Troy."

"Of course. I've been expecting your call. I suppose you'll want to hear my alibi? Haven't got one. I was here alone. All night. Can I go now?"

The twist of bitterness cut through her audible exhaustion.

"Actually, that's not why I called. I need the name of Jay's doctor."

"Ah . . . I might have known . . . heart attack, strokes . . . whatever. But I can tell you now, there was nothing wrong with him."

"That he mentioned."

"Yes. That too. Isn't this where you tell me it's just routine?"

"It isn't."

"Jay was with a Harley Street doctor . . . Anna something or other. I'm sure he told me her last name, but I forget."

"Pakenham?"

"Yes. That was it."

Anna Pakenham was also Troy's doctor, and ten years ago, before the arrival of the "mongrel," she'd been Kolankiewicz's assistant. Not that London was a small world, but Harley Street was.

§183

Troy called the Fitzpatrick Clinic and asked for Anna.

"Out on a house call. May I take a message?"

"If you'd just tell her Troy called."

"Troy? Just that? One word?"

"Yes."

He'd been home about an hour when Anna appeared on his doorstep in Goodwin's Court.

"You rang?"

"I did. It's been a while."

"It has, you fucker."

"Are you coming in? Kettle's on."

"Of course I'm coming in, and the sun is over the yardarm so turn off the kettle and open a bottle."

Anna sat clutching a glass of lukewarm white wine.

"Buy a fridge, Troy."

"One day," he said.

"It wasn't a chatty call, was it?"

"No. Jay Fabian is dead."

"Oh hell. Do you mean he's a case?"

"Yes."

"And my erstwhile employer, the Polish Beast, is on it?"

"He will be. We have a day in hand. All the same I'd have called you anyway . . . as his GP. He took a fall. All of seven storeys, broke half the bones in his body. Probably died instantly."

Anna sighed.

"I liked him, you know. All the rumours. All the gossip. All the same . . . I liked him."

Another sigh, another swig of wine.

"OK. I'll tell you what you need to know. Jay was fit as a fiddle. Played tennis at Queen's every summer. Not a pound overweight. Blood pressure 105 over 70. A low risk for sudden stroke or heart attack. I first saw him in 1949. I last saw him six weeks ago. If anything, he was in better shape now than then. But you're not asking me about his body, are you?"

"Actually, I am. We can get round to his mind later."

"Ask away."

"The scars."

"He'd been in one of those camps, Troy."

"In particular the one on his left arm."

"That's a tattoo, surely you—"

"*Upper* left arm."

Anna set down her glass.

"Oh. Oh. I never noticed any scar there."

"More like a burn."

"Nor that. You see, there's no real reason to strip a patient naked. You examine them bit by bit as . . . well . . . as ailments demand. I never saw the whole of him, certainly never saw him naked."

"The circumcision?"

"He was Jewish. Of course he was circumcised."

"But you never saw the scar?"

"No . . . there was never a necessity for him to drop his pants. Now, top me up. I find all this beating about the bush rather tiresome. And open a red. I hate drinking alone."

Five minutes later, corkscrew still in hand, the same corkscrew with which he had killed Milos Danko three years earlier, Troy pondered. He could not use the implement without pondering—but he snapped to and said, "The mind."

"Jay's mind? So much more interesting than his body. Almost makes me wish I were a psychiatrist, not a physician. Jay Fabian was a Chinese box or one of those Russian doll thingies you used to have on the shelf."

"Matryoshka."

"If you say so. Layer upon layer . . . saucers full of secrets."

"Any clues?"

"Not a sausage. Of course there was his war. It's a given, a constant with men of his age—dinner with your brother, for example, or my husband after the fifth or sixth Scotch. Jaw, jaw, war, war. Rod will never shut up about his war, Jay would not talk about his—which is understandable. What German had a good war? Some of them might talk about it—I've met so few Germans, after all—but Jay didn't. And could not be lured. The most I got out of him was 'I survived.' Or 'Let us live for the day.' The no-go areas were clear. If conversation was steered or drifted where he didn't want it to go, he would abruptly change the subject. But I didn't have the relationship with him I have with you. Indeed, Paddy Fitz told me I should not have taken you on. Sociability has its limits. Jay was my patient—pure, if not quite simple. Sociability should have its limits. Angus and I went to dinner just the once at the Surabaya and Jay and I lunched together maybe twice a year. Not much to it. He never chatted me up. Who knows, if Angus were on walkabout I might have welcomed it."

"The Surabaya. Was Ohnherz there?"

"In another room, I was told. Bedridden. Never met him."

She knocked back her wine and held out the glass.

A steely pause and a steely gaze.

"Angus is on walkabout right now."

"I see."

"Do you, Troy? When my husband is on walkabout . . . spare tin leg and a bottle of twelve-year-old Strathnoddy in his cricket bag . . . is when we are most . . . ."

Fearing her pause might stretch into infinity, Troy said, "Most what?"

"At risk."

Troy topped up her glass and ignored his own.

§184

What was it Jordan said a couple of years ago about Jay Fabian?

Why don't you call me when someone kills him?

§185

"When was this? I've seen nothing in the papers?"

"This morning. What time is it now? Half past ten? So he was found about fifteen hours ago."

"And?"

"Smashed to pieces after a seven-storey fall from one of the houses he owned in Notting Hill. I need to ask: Have you added anything to his file since we last spoke about him?"

"No. He wasn't of much interest. After Ohnherz died everything went quiet. There's been no buzz about the rackets they ran—if indeed they were rackets."

"They were, but that's hardly a legal term. So . . . my lot weren't watching him and yours weren't either?"

"This is beginning to look like a bit of a cul-de-sac."

"Except . . . if he was a sleeper for the Russians . . . what is the fate of old sleepers?"

"Hmmm."

"Hmmm what?"

"If the Russians wanted shut of Jay Fabian, there are two ways they'd go about it. He'd vanish without trace or his murder would be made to look like an accident. Now, tell me that's helpful."

"It isn't."

"Good night, Freddie."

Anna leaned across the bed and took the receiver from his hand.

"Do you have no sense of priority, Troy?"

§186

After such a long train journey, Kolankiewicz broke the habit of a lifetime and arrived late.

"I do not know why that train is called a sleeper. Sleep is impossible."

It was eleven o'clock before he and Zarnecka were ready for Troy.

"My glamorous assistant will lead," Kolankiewicz said.

"I—"

Zarnecka cut Troy short.

"Troy, I lived in Poland throughout the whole of the war. I did not leave until 1946. How many death camp survivors have you met?"

Langrishe's question to the letter.

"Some."

"A few?"

"Yes."

"I've seen hundreds. I treated men, women and children straight out of the camps."

"And?"

"This man was never in a death camp."

Such a show-stopping line required a pause. Troy looked at Kolankie-wicz, who nodded, whether to Troy or Zarnecka he could not tell.

"I'm listening," Troy said.

"The marks of malnutrition are with them forever. The sheer lack of vitamins and proteins . . . muscle wastage, hair loss, deformed nails, loose teeth . . . you can sum it all up as the premature, the enforced advancement of ageing. How old is this man?"

"I don't know.

"How old would you say this man might be?"

"Thirty."

"A camp survivor of thirty might easily have had you guessing at fifty." Troy glanced at Kolankiewicz.

"She's seen it first hand, my boy. We have not."

"Oh, I'm not arguing. If anything, I'd like more detail."

Dr Zarnecka picked up her notepad—to Troy just a mass of Polish scrabble.

"No old contusions, no dental bridges, no plates, only two missing teeth, just three scars—the one we agreed was a bullet, minor scar tissue above the right eye and one that looks like a burn. Just one old break, on the left tibia—well treated, I'd say, properly, professionally set—but of course he broke bones the day he died, most of them by the bye. Put simply, bluntly, this man has never been beaten or whipped, has been well-fed and probably never missed a meal in his life. Auschwitz, Auschwitz is something a man wears forever . . . a shroud for the living."

"Is there anything *I* can tell *you*?" Troy asked.

"I do not know, but it's hardly a competition."

Troy turned to the body.

"I would not have been able to draw the conclusions you just did. But this much I can say: The tattoo is a fake. Very well done, but a fake. Handmade, homemade if you like. Not a machine tattoo or a brand. A sequence of discontinuous, uneven pinpricks.

"The circumcision I hold to be self-inflicted—if not, his parents brought in the world's worst mohel for the bris. It's far too ragged."

"Self-inflicted? What man would—"

"Lastly, the burn . . ."

Troy produced a Sherlock-sized magnifying glass from his coat pocket and held it over the burn on the inside of the corpse's upper left arm.

"Does that look like a cigarette burn to you?"

"Of course," Dr Zarnecka replied.

"Look at the edges, where the burnt flesh puckers and becomes normal again. What do you see?"

"I don't know. Black specks of some sort."

"Ink."

"Another tattoo?"

"Yes. But this one is real. Now—what kind of person has a tattoo in exactly this place?"

"I don't know."

Kolankiewicz spoke for what seemed the first time in an age.

"My dear, I am sure there is no reason you would know this, but it is the blood group tattoo of a member of the SS."

She looked shocked.

Troy said, "It all fits together. You gave us the half of the puzzle that completed the picture."

"So," she replied. "He's not a camp survivor, he's not even a Jew. He's a fucking Nazi."

"How aptly you put it," Kolankiewicz said.

§187

Surabaya

Chan let him in.

"You Mistah Troy?"

Troy held up his warrant card. Chan seemed none the wiser for it, but beckoned him in.

"Lift. Top floor. Boss office."

Troy glimpsed treasure through the lattice of the lift gates. Good God, was that a Bugatti? Was that a Cézanne?

In contrast, "Boss office" was spartan, as though less than fully inhabited.

The desk was a work of art. Troy guessed at Arts and Crafts, in walnut, from about fifty years ago—not what Troy would have chosen for himself, with lots of little drawers he found too fiddly—but the only other works of art, the only other reflections of what he thought to be inordinate wealth, were paintings. Kandinsky or some such. Lots of blobs and . . . stuff . . . and a painting of a steam engine by an artist he did not recognise.

Chan was standing behind him.

He pointed at a bank of filing cabinets.

"Biz papers," he said.

Troy wasn't interested in biz—he wanted the personal, something that might give him a handle on the late Jay Fabian. And he could do without Chan.

"What chance of a cup of tea, old chap?"

Play the Englishman as time and place demand.

He wanted the personal, but so much was impersonal. As though Fabian left as little trace as possible. Life packed into a suitcase, but no suitcase. No love letters, no memorabilia, no memoranda, not even a note jotted to the man himself. Just a calendar that was largely blank and a diary not of record, of things done or said, but of appointments, some of which raised an eyebrow.

In one of the small drawers where one might expect to find paper clips he found paper clips and a wrist-watch—rather dusty and rather scratched and missing its crown.

He wiped it with his hanky and took out his "Sherlock."

Beneath the scratches, doubtless a puzzle to most, but clear enough to Troy, the word Победа—Pobeda—the Russian for victory.

This was a standard-issue World War II Red Army officer's watch. Oh shit.

In the drawer beneath was an envelope with twenty pounds in white fivers.

Hardly surprising, but that the envelope was as dusty as the watch, as though it had lain there some years, and he was 99 per cent sure the notes were fakes. Why would anyone as rich as Jay Fabian have fake money?

They were not modern notes. There was no metal thread, which would have marked a real note as post-war, and the signature was almost an antique.

A telephone sat on a corner of the desk.

He waited while Chan set a tray in front of him with teapot, cup and milk, then dialled Jordan.

"Does Russia make fake English money?"

"Of course. What have you got?"

"Pre-war fivers."

"You're sure?"

"Sure they're fake? No. Sure they are pre-war or meant to look pre-war? Yes. The cashier's signature on them is 'Catterns'. When did he last sign a note? 1936? 1937?"

"Dunno. You're the copper. But speaking as a know-all spook, I can tell you that when we got to Berlin in '45 it was awash with fake fivers the Germans had made. Now tell me why you're asking me, not the Fraud Squad."

"I'm in Jay Fabian's study. He had four of them . . . and a Red Army wristwatch."

A silence, that Jordan eventually broke.

"I do hate it when you put a cat among my pigeons, Freddie."

§188

One personal element emerged, or rather fell into his lap as he opened the last drawer.

An LMS Railway postcard.

"Explore the Peak District from Sunny Miller's Dale."

He'd been to Sunny Miller's Dale. It had rained non-stop.

On the back was just a signature, "Bryce," and single X kiss.

Troy had only two "witnesses." It was not that Langrishe knew nothing, but that Bryce might know everything.

He called her.

No one picked up.

She could have another night to grieve.

§189

Troy had not seen much of Johnny Fermanagh since their last graveside
reunion—Diana's forty-first birthday—and when they had met, Johnny
had hardly been sober. He wasn't sober now. Troy had sat down in the
back room of the Salisbury in St Martin's Lane—the velvet box, as some
raconteur had dubbed it—simply to buy time, to sum up, to postpone
the inevitable. What was the inevitable? A confrontation with Bryce?
Telling her what in all probability she already knew in order to learn
exactly what she did know?

"Can I get you another?"

Johnny looming—nay, swaying—over him.

"Just a small one, Johnny, easy on the gin."

Johnny waved at the barman and held up two fingers without a word
exchanged.

"My condolences."

"On what?"

"The election."

Troy had not given a second thought to the election. Second that
is to the phone-bollocking he had received from his brother, and the
cross-patch exchange with his sister Masha—"Freddie, it's the least we
can do for family." Neither of them had ever seemed able to grasp that
murder was . . . well . . . murder.

"Oh, Labour will be back," he said. "Rod is exhausted. A spell in
opposition will do him good."

He paused before the prospect of his own lies throttling him.

"Yes, old man, but for how long? I mean . . . 1956 . . . 1961?"

"1970. Let the bugger have a lie-in."

This set Johnny giggling just as the barman brought them each a G & T.

"On the slate, please, Sid."

"Boss would be happier if you cleared yer slate, yer Lordship."

"Really? And less of the 'Lordship', if you don't mind. Freddie, I don't suppose . . ."

"How much is Lord Fermanagh's bill?" Troy asked.

"Twenty-two pound ten an' six."

More than a week's wages for the successful middle class. Beyond the cherished target of the "thousand-a-year man."

Troy took four fivers out of his wallet and handed them to Sid.

"On account," he said.

"Very decent of you, Freddie. I'll pay you back, of course."

"I doubt that, Johnny."

Johnny giggled and sprayed gin and tonic across the table.

"However, I'll wipe your slate here and in every pub between here and Seven Dials if you do something for me."

"Just name it, old man. Anything, anything at all."

"Put on the ermine and take up your seat in the Lords. You won't be disappointed, they have an excellent bar. But . . . no Tory nonsense . . . no cross-bench pretence . . . you sit for Labour and you do what my brother tells you."

Johnny didn't even pause for thought.

"Done. Marquess of Fermanagh, Labour peer. May my dad turn in his grave and spin like a bloody top. Now. Clean slate. Can I get you another?"

Troy had often wondered at Johnny's sporadic attendance at the House of Lords since he inherited the title. It was as if he didn't realise they paid. He didn't doubt that Johnny would fit neatly into the upper house. Peer and piss artist of the realm.

He left him to it. At some point he'd find it convenient to tell Rod he'd recruited a new Labour peer, some moment when he needed brownie points.

$190

An hour or more passed to no conclusion.

A gentle tapping at the door.

Let it not be Johnny Fermanagh. Tired and pissed.

It wasn't.

It was Jack, tired and pissed.

"Don't tell me. You were just passing."

Jack threw himself down into an armchair, got up at once and wrestled out of his overcoat, tangled up in sleeves. Troy peeled it off his back and he flopped down once more.

"I went into the Salisbury for a drop of Dutch courage before I came here. Johnny Fermanagh emerged from the back room . . . buying drinks all round. Some idiot had paid off his slate. Had more than I meant to and about half what the bugger would have poured down me."

"You need Dutch courage to talk to me?"

"Any kind of courage."

"I'm listening."

Jack rubbed at his face with both hands, willing his brain and tongue into coherence.

"Bryce," he said at last.

"Not your case," Troy replied.

"Brack."

"That was your case, but that was 1944 and this is 1951."

"Becky."

"Who?"

"Rebecca Brand. You may recall we hanged her? Two months ago."

"Jack, is this leading anywhere?"

Jack's arms flailed in mid-air, grasping at nothing."

"All these . . . dead women."

"I think you'll agree Bryce Betancourt is very much alive. Only the murderers are dead."

"Dead . . . because we killed them."

"No, Jack, the legal system killed Rebecca Brand. I killed Diana Brack because she was trying to kill me."

"And that doesn't bother you?"

"Not for a moment," Troy lied.

"OK . . . OK . . . Becky Brand's death bothers me, fukkit it . . . haunts me."

"You want me to tell you it shouldn't? That we were just doing our jobs?"

"No. True as that cliché is, it matters not a jot. A young woman who acted on impulse is dead. As is the gobshite of a man she killed."

"And there's not a thing we can do about either of those deaths."

"Bryce."

"As I said, I'm listening."

"If . . . if . . . Fukkit, could I have a glass of water?"

When Troy brought it, Jack downed it in one and belched.

For more than a minute he was silent, eyes closed. When he opened his eyes, he looked into Troy's.

"Freddie, I can't go through that again. Becky Brand nearly killed me."

"Jack, you're going to have to be a bit more forthcoming."

"You think she did it. You think she killed Jay Fabian."

"Forty-eight hours into the case I do not know who killed Jay Fabian."

"Dammit, Freddie, you suspect her."

"I suspect anyone that ever met Jay Fabian. He was a public figure, he aroused a whole spectrum of reactions in people, some of them most certainly violent. It seems to me that you're the one who suspects Bryce, and I think it's time you told me why."

But Jack had passed out.

Troy draped a blanket over him and went to bed.

§191

Even the telephone ringing didn't wake Jack.

"Freddie? Jordan."

"You're up early."

"That's because you cost me a good night's sleep. I find it very hard to sleep if I think Five has fucked up on my watch."

"How are your pigeons today?"

"Roosting, if that's what pigeons do. The answer is no. I got three buggers out of bed at sparrowfart this morning—all Soviet-watchers—and everyone agrees that if Jay Fabian was a sleeper, he was the Rip Van Winkle of sleepers. And I have insider confirmation of that."

"Insider?"

"For fuck's sake, Freddie. On an open line?"

"Ah."

"Ah indeed. Now what are your colleagues at the Yard saying? Was this a plain, ugly London underworld hit? Mugsy, Spanner or Joe the Greek wanted Fabian out of the way?"

"No, they're not. They're saying Fabian was clean, that he wasn't on their radar and that his rackets were legal—if not very nice."

"So pass the case on to the Not Very Nice Squad?"

"I will refrain from laughter."

"OK. OK. We both know what's next. Forget foreign countries or criminal gangs—you're looking for an individual now."

"Alas, yes. A conspiracy would have been so much simpler."

§192

He nudged Jack awake.

Wafted a cup of coffee under his nose.

Troy gave him five minutes and then switched to copper mode.

"You described Bryce to me as a set of Pirandello masks."

Jack shook his head like a wet dog.

"Eh? I did? When was that?"

"The last time you were worried about women, alive or dead. You compared her one way or another to 'our Valerie.'"

A gulp of coffee, a self-pitying sigh. Both hands wrapped around the cup.

"So I did."

"And Anna told me Jay Fabian was like a Chinese box or a Russian doll. It seems he and Bryce were very much alike. I have been unable to arrive at a consistent picture of Fabian for that very reason . . . he is a Chinese box, a Russian doll . . . a Pirandello mask."

"I didn't know him that well."

"I didn't know you knew him at all."

"We met. Once or twice. That was inevitable, I suppose."

"Once or twice?"

"OK. Half a dozen times . . . a dozen . . ."

"And what else are you not telling me?"

"Eh?"

"Last night, in your cups, you told me I suspected Bryce."

"I did? Oh fuck."

Head back, staring at the ceiling, avoiding Troy's eyes.

"And I replied that it was you, not me, who had suspicions. I think you'd better tell me what brings you to suspect a woman you say you haven't seen in the best part of two years."

"I was lying."

"I know."

"We've met, we've . . . well . . . from time to time."

Jack jerked himself upright. Another wet-dog shake.

"Freddie, I don't want to be responsible for another woman hanging. We should stop now."

"Just tell me."

"No."

"Jack, whatever it is I will find out one way or another."

§193

"There were tensions between Bryce and Fabian. She wanted him to give up everything he'd done with Ohnherz and start afresh. Needless to say, he wouldn't. A couple of times . . . she said that she'd do anything to be free of him."

"Exasperation? A figure of speech. Will no one rid me of this turbulent priest?"

"I don't know. And I never wanted to tell you."

"Then what did you want?'"

"I suppose I wanted to know what you know."

"I know what you have told me."

"Oh Jesus Christ."

§194

Troy called the "individual."

"I have to talk to you again. In person."

She trounced him with a single phrase.

"Will you be arresting me, Mr Troy?"

"Not today."

And she trounced him with a second.

"Then take me to dinner and ask all your questions. Otto and I always liked Prunier's. Jay was indifferent. He'd go there if I dragged him. And this may be the last time I ever go there. I'd prefer it if that were with you. I don't have to drag you, do I, Troy?"

Fukkit. The bloody woman was flirting with him.

§195

Troy almost flinched when he saw *Consommé Tosca* on the menu. Once, not that long ago, he'd had a Russian lover named Tosca. He had last seen her in Berlin at Christmas 1948. They'd never meet again. He knew it in his bones.

Surely he could eat tapioca in a chicken broth without thinking of her?
No, he couldn't.

He should not have ordered it.

He pushed it aside.

Waited for his *Coquilles Saint-Jacques* while Bryce finished her Colchester oysters and quaffed a 1950 Orvieto. He knew "quaffed" was a cliché, but she wasn't sipping.

He did not need, as yet, to ask questions.

She talked, unprompted.

"I was never Otto's mistress. You do know that, don't you?"

"Jack did mention it."

"If I say it was always Jay, it's because it feels that way. In fact, Jay and I did not become lovers until I moved out of the Surabaya two years ago. I would never have had an affair under Otto's roof. It would have been too strange. I moved out in 1949 when the press got too nosy—the day the *News of the World* finally called me a tart. It was fairly easy to convince Otto that something like that was inevitable. I'd been followed everywhere by freelancers looking for a shot—the shot—while I was in Paris, and in London it was scarcely different except perhaps the motive was different. They weren't looking for the off-guard, no-make-up, messy-hair shot of a celebrity; they were trying to brand me with the scarlet letter. Otto had already bought the flat in Lowndes Square. Forward planning or what? I don't know. I only found out that day. By the time it all got to court, I was there, and . . . Jay was back at Otto's and, yes, we were lovers. But it was something the press never picked up on—they were quite convinced Otto had me rented out as some sort of high-class call girl. And after the court case most of the papers steered well clear of me. 'Once bitten' isn't a bad maxim. They missed the truth, because the truth was not obvious. That I was in a loving relationship with Jay."

"A loose loving relationship?" Troy ventured.

"Don't be coy. You know about my affair with Jack. You saw me tit-naked that day, after all."

"Jack was not the only one."

"I can't hear a question there, Troy. At the same time, you don't seem to be judging me."

"If it worked for you—"

"And it worked for Jay. Ask your sisters. It was something we agreed on. Now, am I a suspect? Are any of my lovers suspects?"

"I only know the name of one, and I am inclined to rule him out."

"I could give you a list, if you like, not half as long as the one you're imagining right now."

"I don't need it."

"Yet?"

"Yet."

"Would it surprise you to know your old pal Charlie is on it?"

"Not in the least."

"I liked Charlie. As cads go, he was alright. Couldn't resist any passing skirt, but . . . we sort of lost touch. I was sad about that."

"He's in Washington. Been there since the spring."

"He talked about you a lot, you know. Not like Jack. You were a taboo subject with Jack. Your sister introduced me to Jack. Almost the first thing—although logically it was later —almost the first thing he said was 'We don't talk about her brother.' Fine by me. I'd never met you. He was . . . is . . . what's the word? In awe of you."

Troy did not think that was the word.

"Can we skip coffee?" she asked. "It's better at my place."

§196

"You never answered my question. Am I a suspect? Do you suspect me, Troy?"

"Would I be here with you if I did?"

"According to Jack and your sisters, that's exactly where you'd be."

"What has Jack told you?"

"Nothing. And I haven't asked. I've not seen Jack since August, and when I say 'seen,' it was a phone call asking to meet. He just needed to talk. To meet. I had something on. I said something like, in a day or two. He put the phone down."

"Do you remember when in August?"

"Towards the end. Thirtieth or thirty-first."

"The twenty-ninth, perhaps?"

"Possibly."

"That was the day Rebecca Brand was hanged."

"Oh. And he wanted to pour out his heart to me?"

"Yes. Instead he got drunk and I put him to bed."

"I'm sorry. I should have, shouldn't I?"

"And I put him to bed drunk last night too."

"Me?"

"Of course."

"I am surprised."

"Don't you think it's time we put our cards on the table?"

"Flip you for it."

She lost.

"You first," said Troy. "Who are you?"

"Am I not who I seem to be? Am I not the reputable Bryce Betancourt who saw off the *News of the World* and then retired young to live modestly with twelve volumes of Proust, two Picassos and a pair of Siamese cats?"

"Proust? Really?"

"Call me an optimist."

"The newspapers have trucked out every nationality this side of the Urals over the last five years. *Paris-Match* thinks you're Belgian. MI5 knows you're not Russian or else they'd have a file on you, and I can assure you they haven't. My brother thinks you're Italian . . ."

"Does he not talk to your sisters? They know exactly who I am."

"And . . . ?"

"I'm Betty Pryce from Swansea."

§197

"I grew up in Town Hill—a housing estate thrown up in the twenties as homes fit for heroes. Instant slums. Just add heroes. If we'd had a bob or two more we might have lived in the next suburb, Sketty, and then I'd be Betty from Sketty. But we never had that bob or two. Da worked—he wasn't lazy—the only time he took off was the nine days of the big strike when I was four. He drove a steam shunter in Swansea harbour—the Swansea Harbour Investment Trust. For three weeks they had their initials painted on the side of the engine. People said it summed up life in Swansea, but it was not bad money, although there was never such a thing as good money in Wales. Most of it went down his neck, and when he was drunk he'd relive his personal battle with the Kaiser and knock Mam about. She put up with it. For far too long. I left school at fourteen, got a job in the stock-room at Woolworth's, scraping the green mould off the biscuits. When I was fifteen they put me behind the counter, broken biscuits, crisps and crackers. Wouldn't trust anyone my age on make-up. When I was sixteen Da lost his job, leaving me the sole breadwinner. The week after he was laid off I came home on the Friday, put my pay packet in front of Mam like I always did. Usually she'd hand ten bob back to me. This time, she didn't even open the packet. Shoved it all across the table. 'Just go,' she said.

"Well, she was right. I knew she was right. Things could only get worse, Da could only get worse. But I wasn't going to blow everything in one go. I got onto the London train with a platform ticket. I dodged the inspector as far as Reading, but I was fairly certain there'd be checks between there and Paddington so I got off. No idea what to do next. All I knew was London in big letters, like the Hollywood sign. I wasn't even sure where Reading was. Just not London.

"I was sitting on the platform. Otto came out of the first-class waiting room. 'Stand up,' he said. I was sixteen, five foot ten and still growing, and I looked twenty. 'Are you looking for work, child?' he asked me. I gave him a childish response. 'Depends,' I said, and he said, 'Then depend on me. I have a factory not half a mile from here turning out dresses. I could use someone to model them for me.'

"Of course I said yes. It was the middle of winter and the alternative was freezing to death. Otto found me digs. I strutted the length of his workshop in one hideous frock after another. That lasted about two months, and then the Anschluss changed everything. No more frocks. Thousands upon thousands of uniforms in khaki and several shades of blue. I was redundant. Besides, I didn't look good in uniform. So Otto moved me to the Surabaya. I didn't think I'd be there long, but my time there ran to eleven years.

"I was not entirely ornamental—he taught me bookkeeping—but being ornamental was part of the job. Once London had settled down to enjoying its war, I was always on his left arm, leaving the right for all the glad-handing. By this time I was Bryce, a merging of my names, and Betancourt with its silent *t*, adding what Otto called the 'vital element of mystery.' And he spun and he spun and he spun. I was the daughter of a Swiss diplomat, I was a French countess who'd hitched a ride on one of the little boats of Dunkirk—the missing chapter from *Mrs Miniver*—or I was a desperately poor child from Naples whose parents had been killed by Blackshirts. And once or twice he tried the missing Romanoff princess line but there were already far too many people playing that one. I faked the accent—having a bit of a lisp helped, and losing South Wales was far easier than I'd ever imagined. I wonder sometimes, if there hadn't been a war on, whether Otto might have tried to have me come out, you know, 'the season,' all that debutante nonsense."

"My sisters did it. I can't repeat to you what they said about Queen Mary."

"I can imagine. Now, if you say you hadn't heard tittle-tattle about me during the war, I'd say you led a sheltered life . . ."

"I had and I did. I heard the version you gave my sisters."

"I also told them the truth."

"Which, out of character, they have kept to themselves."

"Even now?"

"Oh yes."

"The only time I ever felt the illusion come unstuck was in '42."

"Of course."

"Of course what?"

"The Town Hill case."

"I didn't realise you knew."

"March 1942. Mrs Enid Pryce stabs her husband eight times, and then drowns herself in the Bristol Channel. The missing daughter is never found, but the Swansea police stop short of assuming she's dead. I was already at Scotland Yard. We were asked to search for Betty Pryce—I say 'we,' it was not my case—and failed to find her."

"When did you put two and two together?"

"A couple of minutes ago. But . . . we digress."

"Not really, there's very little left to tell. Otto got me through that, through Mam's death, I mean. He stuck me in his library and told me to educate myself. So I did. Proust isn't a joke. It's an ambition. I read most of the greats. Even now I reread Chekhov. Otto taught me German so I could read Goethe in the original. What was odd was that until Jay came along there was almost no one I could talk to on that level except Otto himself. If your sisters had read more I might have had a very different relationship with them."

"Me too."

"And through it all, I remained an ornament. Otto had no interest in me sexually. My war was . . . sinless . . . although there must be a better word. Paris wasn't, of course, nor was Milan, but Otto didn't care. As long as I showed up when summoned . . . to meet a Rothschild or a Gulbenkian . . . but it was peacetime again and he did with me what he'd had in mind from the start."

"The catwalks?"

"And Monsieur Dior. I gave Christian two years of my life. I might even have gone back to him but for the *News of the World*. In '46 I left a vacancy at Surabaya. Otto found Jay much as he found me. He said it was in his favourite café in Fulham, but it could have been anywhere. Otto and truth were ever strange bedfellows.

"I thought I was free of Otto at the moment of his stroke. I wasn't because there was Jay, and if Jay wasn't free of Otto, I wasn't free of Otto, and it occurred to me that to be free of Otto I had to be free of Jay. It wasn't a pleasant thought. It ripped into me like a knife. I pushed that thought to one side, to the back, to the other side . . . and still it came back. So I tried to lose Jay. To . . . to bury myself in a new love."

"And you thought that was Jack?"

"Yes."

"It didn't work?"

"Question or statement? After all, you know the answer. No. I was a fool to think it would. You know Jack far better than I do. I would never be his all, his everything, as long as there was another woman on the planet. He's a kid in a sweetshop sucking on a Nuttall's Mintoe, then he notices the liquorice allsorts . . . then the walnut whips. He can create the illusion that you're all the world to him as he looks across your shoulder at the totty on the other side of the room."

She paused, drew breath as though approaching a difficult sentence.

"And he thinks of you and himself as two of a kind—the tearaway toffs. That is just about the sum total of all he's said about you. But he's wrong, isn't he?"

"Yes. But again we digress."

"Perhaps. Perhaps not. Jay—Jay was a good man but not as good as he might have been. He thought he was immune to Otto. He wasn't. So I had to break free. Last Christmas, a couple of months after Otto died, I made up my mind to leave him, and I told him so. I didn't. I couldn't. That changed nothing. I still had to break free. But, since I know you are wondering, that did not include acts of desperation such as pushing him off the roof. I needed to be free of Jay as I needed to be free of Otto—simply to be me.

"It was a matter of identity. Who was I? I certainly wasn't Betty Pryce from Swansea. Council houses, each one identical to the one next door—all pebbledash and privet. Not a thing worth imagining. Not a place to foster imagination. Otto gave me Bryce Betancourt, a woman of his imagining, an identity of his making."

"So, who are you now he's dead, now Jay's dead? Not Bryce Betancourt?"

"Oh, I very much am Bryce Betancourt. I am she and she is me."

§198

"The coin has flipped, Mr Troy. So—who are you?"

"Wrong question. Who was Jay? That should be the question."

"You've had three days to find out."

"And that's not enough. However . . ."

"However?"

How much to tell to get what he needed?

"I had expected—given what seems to be the joint reputation of Otto and Jay, a confusion I think both of them fostered—to find plenty of resentment. I talked to the man who runs the tenants' association. I found none. My constables called on everyone in Coburg Street. They did find resentment and anger, greatly outweighed by something only a fraction short of gratitude and affection. Mostly along a colour divide. Few white people were singing his praises. I have little or no reason to think that any of Jay's tenants killed him.

"Unlike Otto, Jay seems not to have mingled with London's borderline criminals, the Soho racketeers marginally on the right side of the law. Hence I would rule out anything as melodramatic as a gangland hit. Otto's reputation as West London's Mr Big was a myth. A potent one. People, even some coppers, believed Otto was responsible for half the crime south of Watford.

"Jay preferred a different kind of hobnobbing—politicians. He was a major donor to all three main parties. He was cultivating influence, and what he might have done with it had he lived is anyone's guess. He knew my brother, he knew Hugh Gaitskell, Harold Wilson and probably half the present shadow cabinet. According to his diary he had appointments with Rab Butler and Harold Macmillan last summer. And the name Enoch Powell was pencilled in for tomorrow. None of them likely suspects.

"However, MI5 have a substantial file on him."

"Really? Now there's a waste of the taxpayers' money."

"I quite agree. They don't know who Jay was. They clutch at straws. They confuse him with some Englishman named Jacob Heller. Their only real reason to suspect him is that he was a prisoner in Auschwitz and it is a fact that the Russians recruited survivors of Auschwitz. But . . ."

"But what?"

"Jay was never in Auschwitz."

§199

"How can you be sure? It was . . . central . . . integral . . . God, I can't find the word . . . it was an essential part of Jay. The experience made him what he was."

"Yet he never talked about it."

"He couldn't. So many of them couldn't. He mentioned dreams, the kind of dreams you'd associate with . . . well, with the camps, I suppose."

"Can you remember any?"

"Oh yes. It was only ever one, the same dream over and over. A small room, somewhere. He was in it, not as he was then but as he was now. Like seeing yourself back at a classroom desk, and all the time knowing you're thirty-five or forty, not ten or eleven."

"He woke up screaming?"

"Never. He just calmly told me if he had the dream. After he described it the first time, he'd just say he'd had 'the dream' again."

"And that was all he said?"

"Yes. There was no other reference to the war or the camps in the dream . . . just this one small room."

"So you filled in the blanks. Just as he intended."

"No . . . no . . . it wasn't like that."

"Did you ever have a conversation about the war that went beyond hints and assumptions?"

"No, no, no. Cards on the table, Troy. We agreed. You're holding aces you're not playing. Tell me. You must tell me."

"I thought the tattoo was fake. I thought that the first time I saw it."

"You've seen lots?"

"I have seen some . . . and this was . . . unconvincing."

"But you could not be certain."

"No, I couldn't. But there is a young pathologist at Hendon who came over from Poland just after war. She has seen many survivors. The tattoo was not an issue for her—but everything else was. Musculature, skin condition, teeth, nails . . . the absence of any signs of abuse. And then there was the burn."

"What burn? I knew Jay's body like a road map. He had no burns."
"Upper left arm on the inside."
"That's a birthmark."
"No, it's not. It's an attempt to obliterate another tattoo."
"What tattoo?"

$200

She wept buckets.
Laid her head in his lap and wept buckets.

$201

When he awoke he was alone in her bed.
All too familiar.
And the phone was ringing.
The clock read seven thirty.
He let it ring five times to see if she might answer from some other room and on the sixth picked it up.
"Troy."
"Bryce, I'm baffled. Where are you?"
"At the Surabaya. Just jump in a cab, Troy. Chan has coffee on."

§202

Surabaya

Chan let him in, rode to the top floor in silence, the lift rattling slowly past the treasure trove of West London's own late Kublai Khan.

"Let's eat," she said. "I'm starving."

Chan set a feast in front of them.

A pot of Blue Mountain, scrambled eggs, smoked salmon and a choice of bread—dark, moist German pumpernickel; crisp French baguette; black, molasses-laden Russian Borodinsky with its hint of coriander. It was the way Troy's father used to start the day.

He must have stared too long.

"Chan still caters to Otto. If you see what I mean. It's a gourmet breakfast. Neither Jay nor I are gourmets by any stretch of the imagination —in fact, Jay expressed a preference for Weetabix, and I'm a salted porridge girl—but . . ."

"The dead hand still grips."

"Too profound for me. Perhaps after a second cup of coffee?"

After that second cup, she said simply, "Jay."

"Jay is why we're here."

"Yep. Now . . . let us establish a fact. Jay was German. He never pretended otherwise. At least we can agree on that?"

"Of course, perhaps an Austrian . . . but . . ."

"No buts, Troy. No split Teutonic hairs. Just bear with me. Let us say that Jay was a German who latterly played the Englishman without ever quite becoming one. A disguise that never quite fit. Do we still agree?"

"I'm listening."

"Playing the Englishman. In that sense, isn't he rather like you?"

"You tell me. I'm not going to fill in the blanks."

"I quote your sister, more or less. Sasha said her brothers were so unalike she thought one of you might be a changeling. Rod has perfected his performance as an Englishman. It confuses no one. Took his impersonation right to cabinet and the front bench."

"But it isn't an impersonation."

"That was your sister's point and is mine now. When the mask fits, it—"

"It is no longer an impersonation? I couldn't agree more."

"You, she reckons, do *not* play the English game. You regard your Russian self as a dressing up box you can dip into whenever it suits you . . . to find aspects of character Rod either does not have or is very capable of ignoring . . . to pull out and put on the masks. There is what she called a Russian Darkness to you . . . capital *D* . . . a Raskolnikov or a Rogozhin. And no mask ever quite fits. That was Jay too, I think. Very different masks, of course. Sasha says you are often angry, deceitful, vengeful . . . those are a few of your masks."

"According to her. And I think you both have this the wrong way around. If my sister and you are right about masks, and I do not say that you are, then the mask is the man you see before you, and the 'dishonest, conniving little shit'—Sasha's words, not mine—is the real Frederick Troy . . . a Raskolnikov or a Rogozhin by a much neater name."

"And if memory serves, they were both murderers."

"Raskolnikov killed the moneylender for her money. Rogozhin killed the woman he loved, Nastasia Filipovna."

"We each one kill—"

"It's OK. That's a line I know by heart. Oscar Wilde wrote it just for me . . . but I'm still not sure where this is leading."

"To more masks . . . to . . . the evidence. If you've finished, follow me."

§203

Fabian's study.

Bryce stood by the desk.

"I searched this room," Troy said. "I searched this desk."

"I've no doubt you're good at your job, Troy. After all, your reputation precedes you . . . but you've never been a little girl with a jewellery box.

"I had a jewellery box long before I ever had any jewellery, but that's never the point of little girls having jewellery boxes. The point is secrecy. A place your mum doesn't know about. Some acute maker of boxes worked this out and made them with hidden compartments, specially for adolescent girls like me. Nothing even the worst amateur detective couldn't crack, but I had one, my friend Maggie had one, and we wrote notes and hid them. We'd nothing to say in those notes . . . but as I said, that was never the point. We hid nothings, private little nothings. This . . . these . . . surely are somethings."

She pressed the side of the desk, on what Troy took to be just the end of a dowel or joint, and a drawer the size of a pocket edition book shot out on a spring. Then she upended the drawer onto the desktop blotter.

A small brass canister and a tarnished oval metal disc with numbers stamped into it.

"Feeling foolish, are we? Now is your opportunity to reclaim your reputation, because I've no idea what they are, but apparently they were worth hiding."

Troy gently picked up the brass tube, something that had been fashioned from a cartridge case. One end unscrewed on a fine thread and inside was a tiny glass phial.

"It's cyanide," he said. "The sort of thing that was issued to the Nazi hierarchy towards the end of the war. I gather it was Himmler's idea. In some cases it was hidden in a tooth filling. All the would-be suicide had to do was prise out the filling and bite down on the glass. They'd be dead in seconds. Both he and Goering used them. Eva Braun too."

"I will save the obvious question. The disc?"

"Yes. It would match the cyanide. It's the dog tag of a Waffen-SS soldier."

"Rank?"

"It would never say. These numbers just identify the individual. The British ones are much the same, except they would also have a name. I don't know what was typical in the German forces. This just states a number and a regiment, although that's a poor comparison. Waffen-SS was huge."

"Hierarchy? You said hierarchy."

"A loose term. It could be just that the—the whosoever—was simply around when the cyanide was being handed out."

"So we don't know whether the owner of this dog tag was a general or a lance-corporal. A mass murderer or a hapless squaddie."

"Correct."

"But we agree that Jay was German. After all, that was never in doubt. But you say he wasn't Jewish. This was his desk . . . so it's within reason to say these things were his. If so, we're saying that Jay was in the SS? The tattoo, the dog tag, the cyanide all point to that."

"Correct."

"Would you stop saying that. You sound like the speaking clock."

"Then yes . . . a plain and far from simple yes."

"SS? Perhaps the ultimate disguise for a Jew?"

"Perhaps. But unlikely. I am inclined to reverse your question."

"What? Jew is the ultimate disguise for an SS member?"

"As I can't say 'correct' again, shall I say it's looking like a plausible theory?"

"Troy, that's preposterous."

"Bryce, we have spent three days discussing disguise, masks, impersonation. What about any of this strikes you as preposterous? The man was a chameleon."

"So who was he? And now the delayed but obvious question: If he had cyanide, which you say is instant, why jump off a roof? If we've spent three days on disguise, masks and whatever, we've also eddied around 'pushed, jumped or slipped' for just as long to no conclusion . . . but you have reached a conclusion, haven't you?"

"The same one you are holding at arm's length."

"It was just an accident, oh God, it was just an accident, wasn't it? Although I've no idea why I just said 'just.' But . . . then . . . there is this."

She dropped an envelope onto the desk.

"This was in there too. Open. Read."

The letter had been tightly folded four times, was from a rabbi, and was dated May 1948.

West Central Liberal Jewish Congregation
82 Charlotte St. London W1

Dear Jay, friend and benefactor, may I say it is far too soon for one as young as you to be planning your funeral. However, since you ask, no, we have no cemetery of our own, being as we are far too new an organisation, but your request will be recorded and either I or my successors will honour the terms of your request and your very generous bequest.

My very best wishes to you,
Rabbi Julius Bresslaw

Bryce looked over his shoulder as he read and as he set down the page, she said, "If he wasn't Jewish, why has he requested a Jewish funeral?"

Klaus

§204

Berlin

May 1945

When his great-grandfather failed to come back from the Franco-Prussian war in 1871, the estate that might one day have passed to Klaus Linz von Niegutt went to pot. The old man had left debts that were unimaginable if only because no one, including his wife, the Gräfin Clara Linz von Niegutt, had bothered to imagine. They had hectare upon hectare, Arab horses, a staff of twenty, a schloss and several donkeys. And when the debts revealed and overwhelmed, the horses were sold, the staff was let go, the schloss fell down and the donkeys ran away.

All that remained of the estate in Baden-Württemberg were a couple of dozen hectares and several pigsties utterly devoid of pigs. Sometime in the seventies Great-grandmama had moved her family—four girls and one boy—to Potsdam in Brandenburg, buying a modest lakeside villa—seventeen rooms, four hectares, two maids, one cook—with what remained of the family fortune. In the eighties this had passed to his grandfather, who had raised his family there—five girls and one boy—while working in the Imperial Civil Service in Berlin, a forty-five-minute commute each way—enough time for a newspaper word-square puzzle, the passion for which seemed to run in the male line, as his only son, Klaus's father, passed the gene to him a generation later. Klaus often accredited his fluency in English to the crossword puzzles of the *London Times*, the much-evolved version of the simple word square, even though some of the words he learnt were so arcane as to be useless.

His father too worked in the Imperial Civil Service—but, when he was finally released from a prisoner of war camp in 1919, two years after Klaus was born, there was no empire left to serve. It was at this point, odd-jobbing in low-paid clerical work, selling family heirlooms for ready cash, one or two of which dated back to the reign of his remote

ancestor Eberhard the Illustrious, that Graf Ludwig Linz von Niegutt
abandoned the use of his title. Germany was a tumult of factions and
paramilitary groups all at war with each other.

"It could get me shot," he told his son. "Freikorps, Communists and
these new chaps calling themselves National Socialists. They've all of
them no reason to like the aristocracy."

By the time Klaus finished school in 1935, the "new chaps" had
gained imaginable power—imaginable in that they had imagined it
right from the start. He might have stayed in education—he excelled at
mathematics and modern languages—and become, perhaps, a school-
teacher, but the inclination was not there. Klaus, by his own reckoning,
only "played" with languages and with numbers, a hobby rather than
a calling. Besides, teachers were required to join the National Socialist Teachers League, party membership by any other name, which his
father was keen that young Klaus should avoid, just as he had kept him
out of the Hitler Youth, although it seemed inevitable that membership
would soon become compulsory. When it did, Klaus was no longer
"youth," he was of conscription age, and in 1938 found himself drafted
into the *SS-Verfügungstruppe*.

"What the hell is that?" his father had asked.

"A black uniform and jack boots," Klaus replied.

"So, is black the new brown?"

The black was soon swapped for *Feldgrau*, as the SS and the Wehrmacht swept across Poland with Klaus very much in the rear. He was
not, he thought—as did everyone else—much of an SS type, being as
he was five feet eleven inches tall—taller than the German average,
shorter than the *SS-Verfügungstruppe* average; most of the men he had
trained with at Lichterfelde topped six foot four or more. Long, short
or tall, they all had one thing in common: they were happy to escape
the Reich Labour Service, which had become compulsory in 1935. For
his part, Klaus had never much liked wearing shorts anyway, whatever
the shade of brown. All the same, to be stuck at the back, in a service
unit, seemed to be missing something.

"You're tall enough to die in battle, if that's what you want," one of his
officers had told him. "But you're far more use to us as a translator than
a rifleman. Most of these pigs don't speak German, let alone Polish."

Klaus had long since added some Polish, good Russian and fluent French to his English—which talents kept him in the rear, which talents had no more ability to stop a bullet than a papier-mâché shield. All it took was one, to the left thigh, leaving him imperceptibly if occasionally painfully lame for the rest of his life. "Rear" had not proved rear enough, as his curiosity had led him to stray far too close to the front line and into the sights of a Polish sniper. He was shipped back to Berlin, given a medal—"What for? I did nothing, absolutely nothing!"—and assigned to the Reich Chancellery. He spent the rest of the war in Berlin. No jolly jaunts to the Wolf's Lair or the Eagle's Nest ("Is there a place called the Dog's Kennel?") and as the SS reorganised he found himself in the *Leibstandarte SS Adolf Hitler*, part of the Waffen-SS assigned to be Hitler's bodyguard and technically a panzer unit.

"Panzer" means "tank." The next tank Klaus saw would be Russian. He saw much more of the cypher-encoding machines, as an inordinate facility with codes, statistics and languages finally found a niche for him—neither hobby nor calling, but a job. What use did Hitler have for yet another bodyguard? He had Misch and Günsche, both of whom were close to six foot six. Sturmbannführer Günsche was referred to as Hitler's adjutant, but those around him called him Hitler's doorpost, as he always seemed to be propping up the door. Once they had all moved into the bunker, in January 1945, Oberscharführer Misch became the one who manned the telephone exchange, and the least of Klaus's jobs was to stand in for Misch while he took a break and not mix up the plugs and wires. He liked Misch. He didn't think he was very bright, but he liked him. They had three things in common, perhaps more, but three were certain: they had both been wounded in the first weeks of the Polish campaign and reassigned to the *SS-Führerbegleitkommando*, neither was a party member (no one had asked), and both were determined to avoid the peril of promotion. Klaus remained an Unterscharführer. And from Misch he found out why the two of them were not at the front, east or west: the last sons of their respective families—as with the previous generations Klaus had only sisters—they were "reserved." Their duty was to serve—the oath of loyalty was quite clear about that—but also to continue the "line." So like it or not, he was part of the Nazi scheme to further racial purity.

"Mustn't get my balls shot off, eh?"

He was standing next to Misch on Hitler's birthday, the twentieth of April, when the building shook, as it often did, and flakes of plaster showered them like devil's dandruff. He heard someone say, "Bombers . . . *Amerikaner*,"—but he and Misch knew artillery when they heard it.

"My God," Misch said. "Can the Russians really be that close? If they are . . ."

He wouldn't finish the sentence.

"Go on," said Klaus. "Just say it. We're fucked. Rochus, we've been fucked from the day we invaded Russia."

"If you pretend you didn't say that, I'll pretend I didn't hear it."

§205

Klaus would never claim to know Hitler. He met him many times in the course of his work, but Misch "knew" Hitler. He'd travelled with him, until the Reich shrank and the travelling stopped, often in the back seat of the Mercedes, as one of Hitler's quirks was to sit with his chauffeur, Kempka, and map-read.

It was Misch who told him Hitler was dead.

"What? I heard nothing."

"Nor I, but I've seen the body. Just one shot, I think. It looks as though Fräulein Braun took cyanide."

Many, if not all, of the cave dwellers had been given cyanide capsules, handed out by Hitler as "gifts from Himmler." A glass phial in a tiny brass tube, made from the case of a 7mm bullet. Klaus had his. He'd no intention of using it.

The next thing he knew, he was standing in a corridor as Günsche carried Eva Braun's body up to the surface.

"Don't just stand there. You're needed up top."

What was needed, it seemed, was to pour two hundred litres of petrol onto the corpses, still wrapped in blankets, dumped in one of yesterday's bomb craters—not even a hastily dug grave. He never saw either face.

He stood behind Bormann—the man was overweight, sweating as if he'd lugged Hitler's corpse up the stairs personally. Obersturmbannführer Schädle was leaning on him, one hand on his shoulder, taking the weight off a shrapnel-mangled leg.

Bormann threw a burning rag into the crater.

The petrol exploded.

They saluted.

They all stood back, flinched as the smell of burning meat rose up to compete with the smell of petrol.

It was a mild late-April afternoon. He'd given his last straight-arm Nazi salute. It was all over. Schädle removed his hand, thanked him and went back into the bunker. One by one they all followed. Only he and Kempka remained, left in charge of twenty-litre jerry cans and the stoking of the funeral pyre. It occurred to Klaus that he could just walk away now. He could walk away into the stutter of machine-gun fire, punctuated by the frequent whizz-bang of shells and the banshee scream of the rockets Berliners had nicknamed Stalin's organs. He could just walk away. Which of them would shoot him in the back? He could just walk away. He didn't. He went back inside and left Kempka to it.

Around ten, curiosity got the better of him. He returned to the surface to look into the funeral crater.

Hitler was a charred, blackened, but mostly intact body. Eva Braun had crumbled. No one would ever recognise either of them.

Later, nearer midnight, amid a lull in the bombardment and with Berlin lit by its burning buildings, the need for cleaner air drew him to the surface once more. Never a pleasant place, never free from the smell of damp and diesel, the bunker now seemed less like a circle of hell than a long, crowded corridor to nowhere, a U-Bahn train that never moved, a bizarre Masque of the Grey Death, as every inch of space seemed to fill up with the "entitled," discussing when or how they might kill themselves and bingeing on wine and brandy and food looted from the Chancellery. The party had begun that morning, even before Hitler had pulled the trigger—the blaring swing music from every loudspeaker was probably why he hadn't heard the shot—and continued to roar on drunkenly.

The bodies had gone. There was nothing but scorched earth—Hitler's final tactic writ small—and ash tossed around in the breeze, a drifting grey wisp of cloud. Was this the last of Hitler? A handful of dust you could inhale? He'd rather not. He could just walk away. He didn't. He went back underground.

§206

The next evening General Mohnke took charge. Klaus's immediate superior, Schädle, unable to walk, had killed himself. Mohnke wasn't the type. He was a general, indeed the last general, the man entrusted by Hitler with the defence of Berlin, a notional place now reduced to less than a square kilometre—the "citadel"—now to be left to its fate.

Mohnke's plan was that those who could walk would escape to street level, go into the U-Bahn and seek out active forces to rejoin the battle. That was the way generals thought—or at least the way those that had not already blown their brains out, like Burgdorf and Krebs, thought—loyal to the end, stupid to the end. Klaus had no intention of rejoining any battle. He liked Mohnke. Mohnke was scarcely older than Klaus and already a full-blown Brigadeführer. He had always been good to Klaus, but the order to join the first group to attempt to escape from the bunker was the last order Klaus meant to obey.

The groups were to leave in sequence, varying from half a dozen to twenty people, spaced at twenty-minute intervals. This made no sense to Klaus, but one did not argue with a general. They would leave under cover of darkness. An hour before midnight. This too made no sense—it was a moonlit night, and either the Russians were out there or they weren't . . . but one did not argue with a general. They picked their way through the ruins of the Chancellery, ankle deep in water, over wrecked staircases and through shattered walls to the garage, in a darkness barely punctuated by burning pitch torches. Klaus held his up, feeling like an extra in some amateur staging of *Götterdämmerung*.

There was a bricked-up window at pavement level underneath the Chancellery balcony. Mohnke told Klaus to break it down, and when he'd done so he crawled through the gap into Wilhemstraße, followed by Mohnke, Hitler's secretaries Frau Christian and Frau Junge, his personal cook Fräulein Manziarly and about twenty others.

The U-Bahn had not run in he knew not how long. The plan was to cross Wilhelmplatz to the Kaiserhof U-Bahn, use the tunnel under the river and regroup somewhere in the north of the city.

Klaus paused and looked around in the moonlight, which seemed outshone by the glow of Berlin burning. He hadn't been out of the bunker in more than six weeks. The outside world was novelty and mystery. Nothing looked as it should look. Everything was dust and fire. The world seemed broken. A toy smashed by a peevish giant. He could taste the night. It was chemical and sickly, sweet and dusty . . . cordite, gypsum, open sewers, rotting flesh . . . a hint of sulfur . . . Perhaps this was brimstone on his tongue?

The first thing he saw was a dead horse, lying in a sea of rubble—a carcase all but stripped to the bone by hungry Berliners. An apt symbol for the city itself.

Frau Junge stood motionless next to him. Shock and disgust. The immobility of fear.

Behind her, Dr Schenck urged them on—he seemed to have taken personal charge of the women.

Everyone, even the secretaries, wore some kind of military uniform. Junge in a tin hat, Manziarly in a Wehrmacht jacket many sizes too big that she'd picked up somewhere. Schenck had swapped the bloody white coat he'd worn for days now for an SS greatcoat. This was the Führer's final ragbag army . . . women, clerks, telephonists, cooks and doctors.

§207

The staircase down to the U-Bahn was gone. Bombed to dust.

"Tell me, Graf von Niegutt, have you ever tobogganed?"

Klaus was momentarily foxed, not that Mohnke addressed him by his long-forgotten title but that he knew it in the first place.

"No. I'm a Berliner. Very flat, Berlin."

"Quite so, but on our arses shall we go."

Klaus tried vainly to control his descent, but in seconds felt his fall escape him and heard the ripping of his trousers and felt the first drops of blood on his arse. Then he stopped, feet rammed with all his weight against a moraine of rubble.

"Now!" Mohnke said.

They flicked on their torches, and he saw that he had reached the infernal circle that Dante had ripped from his typewriter and binned. Eyes, there were eyes everywhere.

Mohnke yelled, "We're Germans! No Russians! Germans!"

The eyes retreated. Klaus swept his torch beam across the faces. Impossible to count. Fifty people? A hundred? Hundreds? Women, children, old men—no young men.

"Germans!" Mohnke yelled again.

He turned to Klaus.

"Get the others down here. There's no danger."

"Yet," Klaus said softly, but not so softly Mohnke did not hear.

"Just do it."

Klaus signalled with his torch. Schenck came down first, catching Fraulein Manziarly as she tumbled. As the last of the twenty or so reached platform level Klaus brought up the rear. As they left the station Mohnke ordered, "Torches out," and they were plunged into darkness.

Klaus put out a hand to the shoulder in front of him, someone so shrouded in Wehrmacht grey that the only thing he was certain of was that it was a woman—he'd no idea which one—and they set off in a caterpillar heading north towards Friedrichstraße. It reminded Klaus of photographs he'd seen as a boy—a line of British Tommies blinded by mustard gas trailing along, hand to shoulder, sightless, helpless.

A few hundred yards on, perhaps more—pace and distance blurring into dusty, stinking confusion—part of the ceiling had gone and moonlight streaked in. Then once more into darkness, through the ruins of the stations, past a makeshift hospital set up in a U-Bahn car. Darkness, then more moonlight. Klaus relaxed his grip. The woman in front turned momentarily and he caught a glimpse of Frau Junge—one of Hitler's secretaries, and a war widow. He realised his hand might have been her only reassurance, but Mohnke was calling for him. He blundered his way to the front of the line.

"You're the Berliner. Where the fuck are we?"

"Not sure. Pretty certain the make-do hospital was Stadtmitte. We might be somewhere between Friedrichstraße and whatever's next."

"What is next?"

"I don't know. Oranienburger?"

"Shit, shit, shit! There's something up ahead."

"What?"

"That is what I'm asking you."

"I don't know."

"OK. Leave the others. Follow me. And draw your pistol. You do know how to use a pistol, don't you?"

"More or less."

"More or less? There's a war on, or haven't you heard?"

Up ahead was a steel barrier closing off track and tunnel. Two middle-aged men in civvies stood guard by the huge iron wheel, the turning of which sealed off the tunnel. They wore armbands, something embroidered in red on grey cloth, but unreadable by the light of a torch.

Klaus realised they had come further along the tunnel than he'd thought and in all probability they were under Berlin's river, the Spree.

"I'm General Mohnke. Who are you?"

The elder of the two men took his unlit pipe out of his mouth.

"BVG," he said, and stuck his pipe back in.

Klaus thought Mohnke would explode.

"BVG. What the fuck is BVG?"

Klaus had mad visions of a special SS unit of which neither he nor Mohnke had heard, so secret they lived underground like moles.

The pipe came out again, not a flicker of concern on its owner's face.

"BVG—Berliner Verkehrsbetriebe. City Transport Authority."

"Civilians?" said Mohnke.

"Of course." Uttered with pride in the face of a uniformed SS general.

"Fukkit. I'm the commandant of the citadel. Open this fucking gate!"

"And I'm assistant-deputy department head of city flood control. And this is a flood gate. Closes every night after the last train."

"But there are no trains. There haven't been any for weeks."

"No matter. Orders are orders. If you're a general you should know what that means."

Mohnke was clutching his Luger in his right hand, occasionally it moved off his hip as he spoke, but Klaus found himself half respecting Mohnke for not once waving it in the man's face.

"I don't bloody believe this."

"Nor me," said Klaus. "Are you going to shoot him?"

All Mohnke said was a sad and soft "Follow me."

He set off back the way they had come. Klaus holstered his pistol.

A few yards on Mohnke said, "How far would you estimate until we can surface?"

"Friedrichstraße Bahnhof. Unless it's been destroyed, the U-Bahn should connect with the main railway line. But we'd still be south of the Spree."

Mohnke had been clear in his briefing. They were not "escaping"— they were to find their way to Prinzenallee on the north bank, where a ragbag Wehrmacht unit was said to be still fighting. They would join the resistance, the last resistance, to the Russian advance. Likely as not, none of them would survive.

Klaus was not resisting. He was escaping.

§208

Mohnke had the idea that they might cross the river on the railway line—the line that led north and west out of the Friedrichstraße Bahnhof to the Lehrter Bahnhof.

"Half of us will fall in the water," said Klaus. "And the other half will be sitting ducks for Russian snipers."

"Perhaps, Graf von Niegutt, you are a real soldier after all. Find a way across."

It took Klaus about twenty minutes to report back to Mohnke.

"There's a catwalk below the tracks. Looks as flimsy as a fairground jay-walk but appears to be intact. It's about as close to invisible as we'll get."

From his haversack Schenck produced a pair of surgical snips—no doubt designed to cut bone or tendon, they also cut through the barbed wire blocking the catwalk.

Klaus lingered. He'd bring up the rear until Mohnke told him otherwise.

He looked up. Russian searchlights raked the sky above him and he knew he'd been right in urging this route on Mohnke. He looked down, and the river reflected the light from the burning station above in shimmering red and gold.

At the far end of the catwalk was more barbed wire, but a spiral staircase led down to ground level at Schiffbauerdamm. Mohnke took it and left the barrier intact.

Klaus reckoned Schiffbauerdamm to be about an hour's walk from Prinzenallee, although that might be a peacetime hour, along streets not littered with corpses and rubble, and bear little relevance to time as it now manifested itself. This might be his best, his only chance. He stayed on the catwalk, and when the last of the group had gone down the staircase he put a boot on the barbed wire and leapt—yet another rip in his trousers and a bleeding gash on his right leg, but he landed safely, crouched and listened. No one called for him, no one came back.

§209

He walked on, still high above ground level. In ten or twenty minutes he'd be at the Lehrter Bahnhof. He'd no idea what he'd find, but at this moment that was true of anywhere in Germany.

His right foot slipped on a wet rail and he found himself rolling out of control down the embankment. Something big and soft broke his fall. The combination of moonlight and a city burning was enough for him to see the corpse. He turned the head towards him. Bormann. He'd not been dead long. There was the almond odour of cyanide and slivers of broken glass on his lower lip.

He climbed back up the embankment.

He never knew what hit him. He didn't think he'd heard an RAF bomber overhead or the screech of an approaching Russian shell.

When he awoke it was light.

He realised at once that he could see very little but a blur with his right eye. His fingertips found an open cut in the brow above it, and the eye was clouded with blood.

The left eye showed him bricks. A sweeping curve in dirty Berlin brick. He appeared to be inside a railway arch. How had he got there? Had he walked? Had he been dragged?

A quizzical face appeared in front of him. Looming up, it seemed to be mostly nose. He slowly drew back his focus from the bricks and the arch to the face that peered into his and the truth became obvious. Not walked, not dragged but rescued.

A woman—old or young he could not tell—swathed in layers, crisped in mud. A gypsy headscarf in reds and blues the only splash of colour.

She stroked his eyebrow, told him to look down, then up and down again.

"Bloodshot. Red as borscht. But no splinters. I doubt you'll lose the eye. Trust me. I was a doctor . . . in a faraway country . . . once upon a time."

She leaned back. Now he could see her clearly. Her face like a brown berry, expressionless, compassionless, an almost clinical concern for the well-being of a total stranger.

She thrust a bowl and spoon at him. Steaming, salty buckwheat porridge.

"Eat, Unterscharführer. You look like death itself."

"Where . . . where do you come from? You're not German, surely?"

"Croatia. I was one of your slave workers. Free now, so eat up. If you can walk, bring back the bowl when you've finished."

The woman sat with a man and three other women around a fire. Broken furniture and window frames. Bits of Berlin burning. They were dressed in clothes that amounted to little more than rags. Age was impossible to tell. They could be thirty, they could be fifty. Not one of them looked to weigh more than fifty kilos.

The second day of May had opened with a Berlin chiller and an over-cast yellowing sky, as though the sun struggled to break through the cloud of dust thrown up by battle. His legs went from under him and he sat heavily on a piece of masonry next to the woman who'd brought him porridge. The man stared at him over the rim of a tin mug. The woman handed him a mug.

"Drink. It's coffee. Ersatz coffee, of course."

One sip and Klaus almost choked.

"Acorns," she went on. "I saved acorns last autumn. You've never had ersatz coffee before, have you?"

The cave dwellers had breakfasted on real coffee until the end. The Chancellery pantry seemed to have almost unlimited supplies of both coffee and champagne.

The man set down his cup and held out his hand, palm down. One by one all the women followed suit. It seemed clear to Klaus that he should do the same. Then they all flipped palm-side up.

Every hand was a brown mass of callouses and scars and chipped fingernails. The man was missing most of the little finger of his right hand.

Klaus's hand was hardly manicured, but the flesh was soft and pink, discoloured only by ink on his left hand where his fountain pen had habitually leaked. The hand told the Croatians far more than words.

They laughed out loud, drew their hands back and returned to their breakfast.

"Where did you work?" Klaus asked.

"Borsigwalde. Making Mausers," said the man. "Factory got blown to smithereens by the British ten days ago. Lots of us got killed, lots of your people too. No work—better still, no one to make us work—so we moved on, a day or two ahead of the Russians. They have come to set us free, but they might just kill us in the process."

"We are free," the Croatian woman said again. "So are you."

"Eh?"

"We are all Flüchtlings now, Herr Unterscharführer."

Tin mug back in hand, the man was once more looking intently at Klaus. Klaus knew what he was seeing. The tatty remnants of his SS field-grey uniform, ripped in half a dozen places, spattered with blood; the calf-high, itchy, uncomfortable jack boots—laughingly called *Marschstiefel*, marching boots, about as comfortable to march in as wooden clogs—the SS lightning flashes on his right collar; the single pip of his corporal's rank on the left and the blue ribbon of long service, a mere four years, on his chest. Something in Klaus must have appealed to Frau Junge's maternal instinct. She'd sewn it on personally. There'd been a brass wound badge from his brief spell on the Eastern Front, but he'd lost that ages ago and thought so little of it he hadn't requested a replacement. He had the scar and the occasional ache to remind him.

"No combat medals, then?"

"No," Klaus replied. "I was never much good at combat."

And the man, said, "Ditch the uniform. If you want to see tomorrow, ditch the uniform."

§210

Up on the embankment Klaus walked on the ties, poorly spaced for easy movement, requiring him to jump at every third or fourth step as though he were playing hopscotch.

The Lehrter Bahnhof hummed like a beehive, a low level of constant noise. Hundreds, possibly thousands, sleeping, dying, waiting—waiting for trains that would never come, under what remained of the roof. The RAF had reduced it to an iron skeleton. He stayed on the track. Going up to platform level would mean picking his way through the bodies.

Halfway across he heard a shout behind him.

"SS bastards."

Well. He couldn't argue with that. Then something hit him in the small of the back—then another hit, and another to the shoulder, to the head, and the one that brought him down hit him mid-calf.

What now? Would the aggrieved of Berlin leap down and kick him to death? Would he die under the boots of Nazism's fellow travellers?

It stopped. And it hurt like hell.

He stood, the blood in his right eye still made focus difficult. Half a dozen men on the platform stood motionless—and it occurred to him they had noticed his gun, and his dagger. If they no longer feared the uniform, they at least had the good sense to fear the weapons. He'd ditch them the first chance he got. He'd never used the gun, and the only use he'd found for the dagger was as a pencil sharpener—he would have left them in the bunker but that Mohnke was insistent they all be armed.

§211

Down below—somewhere in the rubble of Moabit, he thought, as he had not yet recrossed the river—a man was hanging from a lamp-post.

Toes down, feet swaying gently, one eye popping, the other masked by an eye patch.

Around the man's neck hung a scrawled cardboard sign that read simply: VERRÄTER, traitor.

He could guess who'd done this. He'd served with fanatics, men devoted enough, stupid enough, to kill and die in the name of a man who'd blown his brains out the day before yesterday.

The man was old, sixty or more. He'd probably been drafted into the *Volkssturm*, that ludicrous last-ditch attempt to save Berlin by calling up the very old and the very young, and in all probability he had run away at the first glimpse of the enemy. He wasn't tied to the lamp-post. His killers had simply thrown a rope over the crossbar, anchored it to the bumper of a burnt-out *Kübelwagen*, hauled him into the air and left him to die of slow strangulation.

Klaus cut the rope with his SS dagger.

The old man dropped softly, more crumpling down than crashing.

Klaus felt his wrist. The body was still warm. He looked all around him impulsively. It was very early in the morning, an hour or so after first light; all the same it was odd that no one was around, scavenging, escaping, surviving—were they all underground?—but if a bunch of marauding, murderous madmen had just passed by . . . ?

He tugged the body through an open doorway and into the ruins of a house. The old man was the same height as Klaus, somewhat thinner, but the clothes fit him, loosely and shapelessly. The finishing touch was the eye patch over an empty right socket puckered with ancient scars. Strangely appropriate. Klaus fitted it over his damaged eye, ran his palms down the front of the jacket to smooth it out and felt a sharp pinprick at the left breast and a lump in the breast pocket. He twisted the fabric upwards to look more closely. A metal pin, the kind of metal pin that had once held his wound badge. Inside the breast pocket was the missing medal, broken off at the hasp: Iron Cross, First Class 1914. Of the millions who had served in the First World War, not much more than a few thousand had received an Iron Cross, First Class. This man had been a hero. This man had lost his eye in the First World War—and had lost everything in this one.

There was no possibility of burying him. Klaus laid his uniform over the old man, and closed the fingers of his right hand around the iron cross. To take it, steal it, never crossed his mind.

The problem was . . . the shoes. Klaus wore a 45, and his late benefactor only a 42, so he kept his marching boots, draping the baggy woollen trousers over the scuffed leather.

Out in the street, just past the thrawl stone, was an iron manhole cover.

Klaus prised it up with his dagger. No smell. Coal, not sewage. He dropped his Walther pistol into the hole. It was an easy choice: the possibility that he might need to shoot someone versus the risk of patrolling Russians catching him with an SS-issued weapon.

Then the dagger, a ludicrous weapon in black and silver, engraved: *Meine Ehre heißt Treue.* My honour is my loyalty.

There remained his Waffen-SS dog tag, slung around his neck on a piece of striped twine and forgotten until now. He had slept with it, showered with it and scarcely noticed it. It wasn't something he strapped on each day like the dagger or the pistol. It was something he lived with. He snapped the twine, looked at the egg-shaped piece of steel in his hand. He was identified only by a number—something he'd been expected to know by heart but never had—and damned by the lightning flashes, the stylised *SS* of Waffen-SS. He should throw it away, but something approaching sentimentality surfaced. It wasn't him. It wasn't part of him. All the same he hesitated. He should throw it away, it should follow his dagger and pistol into the ditch for exactly the same reason. To be caught with it could prove fatal.

He shoved it into a jacket pocket and climbed back up the embankment. Let chance take its turn, if the dog tag fell out through a hole in the pocket . . .

§212

He was searching for a way up to the tracks again—found a rubble staircase, a man-made mountain, stone upon brick upon stone.

Overhead he heard a screeching noise, looked up expecting American fighter planes and saw a flock of wild geese. He watched them weave into the eastern sky in a V formation, then he pressed on. Stone upon brick upon stone. The screech returned. Back so soon. He looked up—the familiar V formation. Then the bullets ripped into the ground around him and in seconds the planes had passed in search of another target. He scarcely saw them. Eyes to the ground—a near-perfect circle all around him where the bullets had hit. Blessed or cursed. He hadn't a clue. He gained track level and set off along the S-Bahn, south and west, above the Tiergarten and the zoo.

He had no plan. Other than his own survival he had no plan. Why was he heading west? His reading of countless decrypted messages from the Wehrmacht commanders in the field had given him a very good idea of where the British and Americans were—not close enough, the Russians would take all of Berlin before the Western Allies were within striking distance. His reading of decryptions from the Abwehr gave him a fair idea of how the nation and the capital would be carved up by the victors—it would pay to be in the West. But . . . would it pay to be at "home," back in Potsdam, an inch beyond the city boundary on the far side of the Glienicke Bridge, in what would inevitably become Russian territory? Stalin might give the Americans and British their share of Berlin, but not one square metre more.

He'd heard nothing from his family since the end of February. Phone lines in Berlin had remained miraculously intact when little else had—but his father had not cared for the gadget and had never installed a telephone. The old man had died in 1942, of natural causes. Two of his sisters had married foreigners and emigrated in the 1930s. Mona to Switzerland, Cosima to Sweden. Both safely neutral countries. His eldest sister, Kirsten, had been so outraged by the Nazi victory in 1933 she had left for the USA, never to be heard from again. That left his mother and his middle sister, Gisela, in the villa in Potsdam. Since

February Berlin had been pounded—the USAF by day, the RAF by night. He'd no idea if there was still such a place as Potsdam.

§213

It was slow going, not even a kilometre an hour. By late morning he had got as far as Savignyplatz, in Charlottenburg.

All morning he had looked down on what appeared to be a human anthill, scattered by a giant's boot—people had emerged from the ruins in hundreds or thousands, deploying every form of transport from pram to donkey-cart, anything that didn't require petrol, all piled high with household possessions, all heading westward away from the Russians. Too late. In the middle of Savignyplatz dozens of tanks had rolled in from both sides of Kantstraße, east and west.

It was instinctive to duck, to lie flat across a railway sleeper—it had been a Polish sniper who'd picked him off on the Eastern Front, after all—but it was a reasonable deduction, when reason kicked in, to assume that no one was looking at him. He was a bird on the wire, all but invisible to the troops below. And as he lay watching it became clear that he was witnessing the meeting up of two Russian divisions. First the manly hugs, then the bursts of machine gun fire in the air, then the vodka, then the dancing . . . it spelled out one long word, writ large—encirclement. Berlin was now wrapped in the iron fist of the Red Army.

§214

At Deutschlandhalle Station he left the S-Bahn. One branch of the line turned east, one south, the route he needed to follow if he was to reach the bridge to Potsdam, but two hundred metres of the southbound track were now not much more than steel spaghetti.

Down at street level a remarkably orderly crowd was slowly following the autobahn to the Havel and the Glienicke Bridge. They seemed curiously restrained, speaking in low tones not much above whispers, and constantly scanning the sky.

If the old adage "safety in numbers" meant anything—there had been more than seventy million Germans before the war, so how many made a safe number was anybody's guess—he knew he should simply mingle, match their pace and lose himself. The things that made him stand out, as far as he could see, were his age, his health (not having spent the last four months on a diet of cabbage and potatoes, no doubt looked better fed than he should), and his empty hands. A risk, but everything was.

The woman ahead of him had several dresses draped over her right arm—perhaps her entire wardrobe. A small girl of nine or ten pushed a doll's pram holding nothing but a twitching white rabbit in a cage. An old man driving a donkey-cart had a double bed and a mattress stacked high while his wife and grandchildren perched precariously on the tailgate and the donkey struggled.

Several times they passed Russian troops, in half dozens, usually gathered around a tank. The level of curiosity varied. One group pressed bread and cheese upon the *Flüchtlinge*, another stared in silent contempt until one of them found a voice.

"Thousand-year Reich! So keep moving. Only nine hundred and eighty-eight to go!"

Occasionally a woman would be pulled from the line with cries of "*Frau, komm, Frau*," but none of them seemed quite to have the bravado for rape in front of an audience of hundreds.

And then, a couple of kilometres from the bridge, a Russian pulled him from the crowd. It was not surprising, if hardly inevitable. A man of combat age surrounded by women, children and old men.

"Солдат?"

Soldier?

"Nein."

The Russian lifted the eye patch. Klaus knew his eye must look a mess. "Even the Third Reich," he said, "had no use for a one-eyed man."

A remark the Russians took at face value.

A second, huge Russian was pointing at his boots.

"Ботинки, ботинки!"

Boots, boots!

Oh shit.

"Размер? Номер?"

Size? Number?

"Fünfundvierzig."

Forty-five.

"You got feet like a girl."

Compared to them he probably had.

Then a third Russian seized his left hand.

"Uhri, uhri, uhri."

And stripped him of his watch. An art deco Tissot, a fifteenth birthday present from his father.

"Swap?" said the Russian.

"Swap for what?"

He stuck an oat biscuit in Klaus's hand and slapped him on the back.

A few minutes later Klaus ate the most expensive biscuit of his life.

§215

Glienicke

The bridge was down.

Why was the bridge down?

More precisely, given that bugger-all in Berlin was still standing, why had anyone expected the bridge to be *up*?

The bridge was down. It sagged in the middle, broken-backed, half under water.

Disbelief was only momentary. They stared, they shuffled, they asked impossible questions, but disappointment drove. The crowd hung together and after a few minutes set off almost as one back towards the city.

Klaus sat in the dust, one of half a dozen stragglers, looking homeward. He thought the next bridge to the north might well be the Stößenseebrücke, linking Charlottenburg with Wilhelmstadt at the narrowest point of the Havel. From where he stood now, that was fifteen or sixteen kilometres distant, four hours on foot, boots and blisters not allowed for. No one, he thought, had turned south. Just as well. What he'd seen at Savignyplatz probably meant that Greater Berlin was completely surrounded by Soviet tanks. The safest thing was to stay put—something he was very reluctant to do.

One by one the stragglers got to their feet.

A man of seventy or so spoke to him.

"You think the Americans did this?"

"I don't know."

"I'll tell you who did this. Those fuckers in the SS. It's all over and they can't see it. I'll bet they got down here at dawn and blew the bridge. It's all over and still they can't see it. Hitler's still giving orders and they're still following. Idiots. Utter fucking idiots."

"You haven't heard?"

"Heard what?"

"Hitler's dead. He shot himself two days ago."

Incredulity, acknowledgement and joy all flickered briefly across the man's face.

"Good riddance. Good fuckin' riddance! Tell me where he's buried and I'll piss on his grave."

"I had that opportunity."

A joke too far, a risk too far, but the old man made nothing of it, laughed grimly and moved on.

Of course, he was right. Klaus had seen enough of the damage of war to know that this was not the work of a bomber. Bombers did not drop single bombs, they dropped clusters, bombs falling only seconds apart. If the USAF had bombed the bridge, the area all around would be cratered, whereas the bridge had had its centre span neatly dropped into the Havel. Dynamite. He'd bet that the SS had planted dynamite weeks ago.

He didn't want to be part of a ragbag crowd heading north.

Was he more likely to be stopped by Russians alone or mob-handed? How typical of the Red Army were the good-natured if light-fingered jokers who stopped him last time?

He must have dozed off. Forearms on knees, forehead on forearms. It had, thus far, felt like the longest day of his life. Something nudged him awake. Something wet and warm.

He carefully turned to his right.

A horse had stuck its tongue into his jacket pocket.

A large cart horse—he couldn't tell a Rhenish from a Schleswig from an Ardennes, but it was dark brown in colour with a heavy black mane that covered most of its face and eyes and it was between the shafts of a painted wooden cart. He stood up, brushed the dirt from his jacket, and the horse stopped licking.

Her name was on her bridle, picked out in studs, like a dog collar: SERAPHINE.

On the side of the cart was a brewer's sign, peeling yellow lettering on a chocolate background:

ENGELHARDT BRAUEREI, CHARLOTTENBURG

He climbed on, took up the reins and shook. Seraphine drew the cart around and slowly pulled away. Just when Klaus was thinking they'd catch up with the loose crowd that had left an hour before, the horse veered off into the woods, along a rough limestone track. He was not consulted in any way. If this was her route back to Charlottenburg, so be it. If Seraphine knew her way home, she might save him a long walk. If they stuck together, he might save her from getting eaten.

He fought off sleep, but the swaying of the horse's buttocks had achieved a hypnotic rhythm. He nodded off. Snapped to. Nodded off. And when he awoke, the light had changed. They were in the Grunewald. He was almost certain of that. Somewhere south of Charlottenburg, probably somewhere near the Olympic Stadium and the Deutschlandhalle, the point at which he'd left the S-Bahn line to join the pointless pilgrimage to the bridge.

He missed his watch. How long till dusk? How long till he'd need to find shelter?

The woodland had given way to more open ground, grass and shrubs, a dirt track along which the horse plodded her way unconcernedly, to what Klaus took to be allotments, almost a shanty town of sheds, a patchwork of cultivated plots, the emerald tops of potatoes, the sharp spears of leeks and onions, the dark-veined leaves of beetroot.

The horse stopped where a middle-aged man, with a Hindenburg moustache and a large cigar, sat on a bursting armchair next to a corrugated steel-roofed shed. He'd seen them approach but not yet moved a muscle other than to puff on his cigar.

"Where d'you find her?" he said simply.

"Glienicke."

"Might have known. We did that route twice a week before the brewery got bombed to buggery. They owed me back pay I was never gonna see, so I kept the horse 'n' cart. Hop down. She'll be wanting a drink."

The man got up. He wasn't hopping anywhere. His left foot was twisted inward at what looked to be a painful angle.

He unhitched the horse and stuck a bucket of water in front of her.

Prompted by the deafening slurps, Klaus realised that he'd drunk nothing since his ersatz coffee with the Croatians.

"May I?"

"O' course."

The man gently pushed the horse aside, plunged a ladle into the bucket and handed it to Klaus.

"Nothing to worry about. I collect rainwater."

Klaus downed it in one gulp.

"Klaus," he said as he handed the ladle back.

"Adolphus," the man replied. "Adolphus Zobb. Not that I answer to it. Ever since this . . ."

He touched his left leg.

" . . . I've been Krankfuß."

"You don't mind that?"

"Nah. Who will ever want to be named Adolf again?"

"He's dead, you know."

"I do. Died leading the last of the faithful into battle. It was on the radio."

Klaus shook his head.

"Not true. Shot himself."

"Coward's way out. Can't say I'm surprised. Couldn't stand him. Nor the Kaiser, for that matter—whiny little bugger. It was his war cost me this."

Another tap to the twisted leg.

"Western Front?"

"Nah. Did it myself with a sledgehammer. Kept me out of the last war and this one. Better a live cripple than a dead hero. An' you?"

"Er . . ."

"Make it convincing, son. Spin me a yarn . . . and then I'll tell you you should have ditched the boots as well the uniform. So . . . lose the boots."

Klaus glanced down.

How right he was.

"I haven't found anything that fits. I take a forty-five."

"Me too, but yer not havin' mine. So . . . you dodging our own or the Russkis?"

"Both, I suppose."

"Wehrmacht?"

"SS."

A plumber's sharp intake of breath.

"Well, you're not staying here. Russkis come through, they'll bust us both. Your lot . . . they're heartless, stringing blokes up all over Berlin."

"That will stop soon if it hasn't stopped already. The Russians are in control. They took Berlin this morning."

"If you're still alive on Friday, tell it to me again."

"I need somewhere to spend the night. I won't betray . . ."

"Nothin' doin'. But—you see the backs of them there houses over there. That's Großereichenweg. Bombed to bollox. One of 'em used to be mine. It was a good street back in the day. Mixed bunch. A few Catholics. Mostly Lutherans and about enough Jews for a Sunday-morning five-a-side football team. But there's good Jews an' bad Jews. We had good ones. House on the end was theirs. That was the Jew-house. I reckon it's the only one I'd lay my head in and not expect the roof to collapse. Family name of Fabian, that was them."

"What happened to them?"

"Now you're just being ridiculous."

§216

Krankfuß gave Klaus a kerosene lantern and a book of matches.

"It'll be dark as the grave inside. Mind, don't waste it. Kerosene costs more than schnapps and believe you me I've tried running lanterns on schnapps. Bring it back in the morning. And watch out for rats. There's a plague o' them on account we already ate the cats. Breakfast is at seven."

"Breakfast is at seven? You sound like a receptionist at the Adlon."

"Nah . . . much better than the Adlon. My chucks are laying. We got eggs."

The "we" was pleasing. Puzzling. It was the dawn of a new era, the age of every-man-for-himself, and yet here was a man he'd never met before offering to share food.

The house Krankfuß had pointed to was about 250 metres away. Klaus picked his way along the narrow paths between vegetable plots and past sheds of wood, steel and any other material that had come to hand. One was roofed in what looked to have once been a rather expensive Persian carpet. The value of everything had changed. Kerosene was worth more than schnapps, roofing worth more than antique carpets, and almost anything worth more than human life.

Occasionally a head popped out, did not speak and ducked back in. At the last hut another lone gardener was taking in the last of the day with a Meerschaum pipe and a bierstein.

"Is it over?" he asked.

"Oh yes," Klaus replied. "We can all go home now."

The man's croaky tobacco laugh followed him all the way to the street.

What to make of Großereichenweg? It wasn't his part of Berlin. It was one of those nameless suburbs he'd whizzed past countless times on the S-Bahn—nameless, that is, until you stopped and looked. It was, he thought, Eichkamp, a nonentity of a place, solidly built in the 1920s and only "put on the map" when the stadium for the 1936 Olympics was built there, then instantly "put off the map" when the S-Bahn station had been renamed Deutschlandhalle.

Quiet streets lined with laburnum and poplar, the occasional Brandenburg blue spruce—all blasted and leafless. Something . . . shells fired from a Russian tank . . . bombs dropped by a British plane . . . had ripped through here recently, leaving the street looking flimsy if intact. It wasn't the hollow crater that central Berlin had become—it wasn't Mitte or Moabit. Houses had roofs in part or in whole and no bodies hung from lamp-posts. Down the street a Red Army T-34 tank purred. Its crew stood around a brazier warming up tinned rations, roasting what smelled like lamb. One glanced his way but ignored him.

The villa he was looking at, the one Krankfuß had called the Jew-house, had bird's-eye windows set in a roof of scalloped tiles, half of which were missing. The joists and frame of one had sunk. The house now appeared to be squinting at him.

Only when he'd entered the Jew-house did Klaus light the lantern.

He hadn't asked Krankfuß how long the house had been abandoned, but there was a thick layer of dust over everything—months, possibly years, not days. What was surprising was that the house did not seem to have been looted, or perhaps only things of practical use had been looted. On a heavy nineteenth-century oak sideboard stood a nine-pronged menorah, the symbolic candelabrum of the Jewish people. In a drawer below was a full set of silver cutlery, in a cupboard below that Meissen bowls and Spiegelau crystal wine glasses.

It was tempting—or just plain nosy—to search the whole house, but his priority had to be to find somewhere dry to sleep. Upstairs moonlight streaked in through the holes in the roof and the smell of roasting lamb curled in through the broken windows.

The Russians had begun to sing:

Письма твои получая
Слышу я голос родной
И между строчек синий платочек
Снова встаёт предо мной
И часто в бой
Провожает меня облик твой
Чувствую, рядом с любящим взглядом
Ты постоянно со мной.

Predictably sentimental stuff—no doubt fuelled by vodka, schnapps or even kerosene—about a girl with a blue handkerchief, the girl someone had left behind. Well-fed and drunk, they'd not bother him tonight.

On the collapsed marital bed, supported only by three of its four legs, was a pile of plaster, and beneath the plaster was what appeared to be a goose-down quilt. He shook it loose, took it downstairs, still in search of the dry spot to lay his head. This turned out to be a study of some sort—with a desk, an upright chair, one armchair and three walls lined floor to ceiling with books. It was cleaner than the rest of the house, and when he pushed the chairs aside he had just enough room to roll out the quilt.

He held the lantern high to see the spines of the books: Whitehead and Russell's *Principia Mathematica*, Max Planck's *Treatise on Thermodynamics*, Paul Dirac's *The Principles of Quantum Mechanics*. He'd heard of all of these writers and read not a word of any. He wondered what kind of person had lived in this house, worked in this study—study? His father's house in Potsdam had bigger closets. Was this Krankfuß's "good Jew"?

Too late.

He was exhausted.

Blow out the light.

§217

Klaus awoke as lost as he had ever felt. It took a few seconds to find himself.

I am . . . where?

In a cupboard? In a closet?

Then he noticed the books.

A study, someone's study.

He felt for his watch, then remembered that it now adorned the wrist of a Red Army soldier, along with half a dozen others.

Uhri, uhri, uhri.

The sun had hit the wall above the desk. He had lived so long underground . . . to be woken by a sunbeam . . . to be able to read the time . . . give or take . . . by the slanted sunbeams and dancing dust motes upon an accidental dial.

It was still early, he concluded. Not yet seven o'clock.

He threw off the quilt, was about to reach for his boots when Krankfuß's warning came back to him: "Lose the boots."

In the bedroom closet he found a pair of dusty but hardly worn brown Dinkelacker brogues, size 45, made in Sindelfingen, Baden-Württemberg . . . a pleasing coincidence . . . his hometown a couple of generations removed . . . where once was the family schloss. Of all the shoes, in all the world, he should walk in these. They were utterly at odds with his stolen rags, as he realised when Krankfuß laughed out loud.

"Knock me down with a feather, you look like the best-heeled scarecrow in Berlin. Take a seat, m'lud. Yer repast will be with you shortly."

Krankfuß had a small open fire burning, a drop of lard melting in the pan, half a dozen shit-speckled eggs nestling in the dried grass at his feet.

"We may not all be lords, but we might dine like kings."

"How long have you lived like this?" Klaus asked.

"What? In the open air? More than a year. You lot couldn't protect us after all. What was it Fatso Goering said . . . 'If a bomb drops on Berlin, you can call me Meyer'? Nah . . . once the British started on the night raids it was safer out on the allotments. It'd be November or December of '43 when things got really bad. I moved out before my house got hit. That happened the following January. It's simple enough. Direct hit, and you're done for, but near-misses can still bring the roof down on your head. Out here, bugger-all to fall on you. I was the first to move out. Plenty of others followed. See the old geezer weeding cabbage over there. That's Herman Bermann. Bloke planting carrots. That's Jürgen Bürgen. There's dozens more, men and women. I got nicknames for 'em all."

"There's safety in anonymity?"

"'S right. You got it. Buggers come asking questions. I don't know answers. I'll have to come up with one for you."

"I don't think that's needed anymore, do you? 'The buggers' won't come asking."

"Different lot of buggers. I've no idea who's looking for you, but you have or you wouldn't be wearing a dead man's shoes. So who are you? What's your name?"

"I am . . . Klaus Linz von Niegutt—"

"Well. I'd worked out you was posh."

"And until the day before yesterday I was a corporal-clerk in the Waffen-SS. Not so posh after all."

"Still . . . enough to get you shot."

"More than enough."

"Meaning?"

Klaus had already made his mind up. It required no further thought.

"I was in the bunker."

"What bunker?"

"The one under the Reich Chancellery."

"What? With Adolf?"

"Yes."

"You knew him?"

"Not quite. I had lunch with him several times. He could not bear to eat without an audience for his bon mots, but if he knew my name I'll eat these shoes."

Krankfuß pondered. Cracked four eggs into the frying pan.

"Best not tell Herman or Jürgen or anyone else. Entirely up to you, but . . ."

"Quite."

"Quite my arse, you posh bugger."

§218

If not infinite, Krankfuß's supply of eggs and somewhat stale black bread fed five. They were joined by Herman, Jürgen and a one-armed man Krankfuß called, with transparent irony, Fänger (Catcher).

"Who's this, then?"

Fänger was fortyish, the youngest of them all, bar Klaus himself, and the loss of his arm had likely as not kept him out of the *Volkssturm*. Klaus wondered which battle of the last six years had cost him an arm, but didn't ask.

Krankfuß answered Fänger.

"This is Schickimicki."

Inventive. A reference to the ridiculous brown brogues. If he had to have a nickname it made sense, and the rhyme was pleasing. "He's one of us now. So don't you go pulling your surly bugger 'I did my bit' act and asking questions what don't need answers."

"Suit yourself."

Klaus wondered about the "one of us" but didn't ask.

"We're getting low on tinned stuff," Fänger said.

"I gave sauerkraut and beans to the old women over yonder," Krankfuß replied. "We got enough."

"We *had* enough . . . before."

"Before what?"

"Before the peace broke out. You're older'n me. You must remember 1918. The stab in the back. Things get worse in peace, not better."

This was, Klaus knew, unarguable. His father had said the same thing many times.

"I got a raid planned," Krankfuß said far too simply.

Klaus wondered about the "raid" and asked.

"Well . . . we don't live off what we grow . . . couldn't live off what we grow, not at this time of year . . . so you might say we supplement our rations."

"Ah . . . You steal?"

"Not to put too fine a point on it . . . we raid Wehrmacht warehouses. The army got canned field rations stacked in the millions. We could starve to death before they whack it out, so we take it. We hit a couple of warehouses in Babelsberg last February—in the middle of a bombing raid. Great cover, and the horse don't scare easy. The place was stuffed: tins, hats by the thousand . . . and skis, pile upon pile of skis. What bleedin' use are skis in Berlin? But, there was lotsa grub too. We just loaded up Seraphine and brought back as much tinned stuff as she could carry. That's where I got my cigars, Dutch cigars—only a couple of dozen, but the best. And we got wine—mind you, I never had a taste for that sort of toff thing."

"What about the guards?"

"Got sent to the front last Christmas. Ever since then it's been *Volkssturm*. Blokes my age. All you have to do is say boo. Anyways, next one is up by the stadium. You in or out?"

Discretion being the better part of valour, Klaus dearly wished to say "out," but how much valour might discretion now require?

"In," he said.

§219

The warehouse was unguarded. Locked but unguarded. Chances were if the Russians had got there to find *Volkssturm* they'd have rounded them up as combatants and raided the warehouse themselves.

Herman sliced through the lock with bolt cutters and they loaded up with sauerkraut in five-litre jars, canned sausages by the gross, box upon box of rye biscuits, beans . . . peas . . . turnips and carrots "good as new if you scraped the mould off." The potatoes were old and a bit shrivelled but they took them anyway. There was no coffee, and no cigars.

"Bugger," was all Krankfuß had to say.

They lived off this for weeks. Until the allotment blossomed. The Russians never came near them, seemed reluctant to travel more than three metres from their tanks.

"Perhaps they don't like getting their boots dirty," Krankfuß said.

"Well," Klaus replied, "they got them dirty enough crossing Poland."

"Don't mention Poland. It's where Fänger lost his arm in '42."

"I was in Poland, but that was '39. Never set eyes on a Russian."

"So you wasn't always a chocolate soldier? All the same, don't mention it, don't let on you was ever there. It's his personal property. Barbarossa had one purpose: to chop off his arm. Poland had one purpose: to bury it."

"Might that not have been the sole purpose of the entire war?"

"Yep. The Second British War is better known on this allotment as the Battle of Fänger's Arm. And old Ma Krause wot you gave the carrots to . . . sole purpose of the entire war was to kill three out of her four sons. You got your own purpose?"

"No," said Klaus. "I don't think I have."

§220

A few days later, a Russian in baggy combat drabs was picking his way along the narrow path between the allotments and Großereichenweg.

"I knew it couldn't last," said Krankfuß. "Here comes bloody Ivan."

Bloody Ivan was short, Asiatic, with wide cheekbones, almond eyes and remarkably bowed legs. At his waist he had a handgun in a button-flap holster. He made no move to draw the gun. Plonked himself on a tree stump next to Klaus.

"Доброе утро. Получилось опять прекрасно."

Good morning. Turned out nice again.

Krankfuß replied, "No, no . . . Ivan . . . sprechen Sie, sprechen Sie!"

Klaus turned to Krankfuß. "Do you want to handle this or shall I?"

"Oh, you do it. I'm curious to hear your Russian."

"Доброе утро, товарищ. Чем мы можем вам помогать?"

Good morning, comrade. How can we help you?

"Яйца. Ходят слухи, что у вас яйца. Имеете яйца на продажу?"

"He wants to know if we have any eggs to spare."

"What?"

"Eggs. He'd like some eggs."

"What? I'm supposed to tell him I have eggs so he can nick 'em?"

"He's offering to pay."

"What? A Russki offering to pay for something?"

"Apparently."

"What with? I ain't taking no Reichsmarks. Ain't even good for wipin' yer arse."

This was almost true. Klaus could not remember when either of them had last had recourse to cash. Everything that was not theft was barter.

"My friend is happy to trade with you."

"Хорошо. Очень хорошо."

Good. Very good.

Bloody Ivan reached into a deep pocket on his thigh, no doubt designed to hold several magazines for his pistol, and pulled out four packets of American cigarettes. Camel and Lucky Strike.

"Сорок сигарет за яйцо. OK?"

Forty an egg. OK?

"Forty? Forty snout? For forty snout he can buy my false teeth."

Krankfuß snatched the cigarettes before the Russian changed his mind and took two speckly, shitty eggs out of the long grass.

"Fried or scrambled?" Klaus asked.

"Что?"

"We were just about to have breakfast. Would you care to join us? There is bacon too. And fried bread, although the bread is rather old."

Bloody Ivan reached into the matching pocket on his other leg, pulled out a knife and fork and half a dozen thin slices of dark brown pumpernickel.

"Хлеб. Да."

Bread. Yes.

Krankfuß cooked and muttered.

"Inviting a fucking Russian to breakfast . . ."

The Russian smiled, or was he grinning?

"The war is over," Klaus replied.

"Sez you."

"And I sez again, the war is over."

Attempts at conversation produced little more than simple *das* and *niet*s.

All the same the grin never faded.

Breakfast with the Cheshire Cat.

Klaus managed to get a name.

"Я – Люб из Новосибирска."

I am Lub from Novosibirsk.

And to establish that he was part of a tank crew stationed a few doors down from the house:

"У нас баранина, курица есть, картошка есть, мы получили посылки из дома. А чего у нас нет? Яиц вообще нет."

We got lamb, we got chicken, we got spuds, we got packages from home. What ain't we got? We ain't got eggs.

But about himself and the long, hard road to Berlin he would say nothing.

"Прошло. История."

Over now. History.

Wiping his lips on his sleeve, he stood up.

"Спасибо. Спасибо."

Thank you. Thank you.

And then to Krankfuß in fractured German, "Vor is offer. Tank you. Vor is offer."

And Krankfuß said, "Does that make it official?"

§221

"Tell me about the Fabians."

"Decent enough folk. Didn't shove it in your face."

"Shove what?"

"Being Jewish."

"Hardly necessary with a yellow star stitched to one's jacket."

"I mean before that. Long before. The twenties. They're the only family ever lived there, moved in the day it was finished. And these houses weren't cheap—not that you'd know it now. I got one as my dad had been a foreman on the construction crew. Mate's rates. I was the odd one out here, not the Fabians, 'cos I worked in a brewery and shovelled horse shit and all the other buggers had office jobs. Wore suits to work—Homburgs, not flat caps—gloves without holes in 'em—and didn't smell of horseshit. David, old Fabian, he was a professor of some sort . . . arithmetic or some such. The son, young Samuel, he was one too, professor of this and that."

"And they were rounded up when?"

"Prof and Missis, never. He died in '36, and she followed him the year after. Like she couldn't live without him. That was when Samuel moved back in, with his young wife—Maria."

"Maria?"

"Yep. You got it. Catholic kid. Saved Samuel's bacon—for a while at least. Her uncle was a Berlin nob, something big in the Prussian police, paid-up Nazi, answered directly to Goering. Samuel kept his college job. Didn't have to wear his yellow star at work. Lots o' little perks, and one big perk. He got to live. But then Maria got pneumonia, spring of '44, and died. Two weeks later you lot came for Samuel. I thought they'd reassign the house, but day after that another night raid hit, left the place pretty much as it is now. There used to be a sign on the front door, reading 'Reich Property—Eintritt Verboten' and lots of scary Hakenkreuz stamps. Maybe it was that kept the looters out. Till now."

"Yes. I suppose I'm the looter."

§222

Klaus continued to live in one room, ate with Krankfuß and his pals, helped with the cooking, much to the surprise of the women on the allotment, washed in rainwater, shaved with a sharpened kitchen knife, crapped in a hole in the ground and returned "home" to sleep and to read.

Fabian had most of the works of Thomas Mann on his shelves. As a teenager Klaus had struggled with *Buddenbrooks* and *The Magic Mountain*, failing to finish either. Now he fared better with the novellas, *Tonio Kröger* and *Death in Venice*. He read *Death in Venice* three times.

He still wore the clothes he had taken from the body of the hanged man. The upstairs closet was full of jackets and suits that had once belonged to Samuel Fabian, a man pretty much his own size, but he took none of them. An unconsidered superstition at the back of his mind or merely caution along the lines that looking good—they were smart, expensive clothes—was a way to attract unwanted attention? As he was, a raggedy man, if he met a Russian squad in the street—and they were camped out everywhere like gypsies—they were likely as not to offer him a slice of roast lamb or a bowl of kasha or to try to buy eggs and not bother with questions. He was just one more defeated German.

Knowing the contents of Fabian's study, knowing the contents of his cupboards and his closets, Klaus felt he almost knew the man. It was an illusion.

§223

July 2, 1945

Samuel Fabian had vanished. So many had vanished without trace. Samuel had left traces aplenty—chiefly the contents of his desk drawer.

Dozens, no hundreds of pages of scribbled equations that would only make sense to a fellow mathematician and served to make Klaus regret that his formal education had stopped when it had, the first draft of an unfinished book on Pierre de Fermat, and an expired identity card for a German Jew:

A 002031
Valid until 5 Nov 1943
Fabian
Samuel Israel
Born 2 May 1912
Birthplace Charlottenburg, Berlin
Occupation Universitätsprofessor

All in the *Sütterlinschrift* script he'd learnt at school—at once elegant and sinister. Klaus wasn't sure quite when all Jews had been required to add Sarah or Israel to their names, presumably when the yellow star had been imposed in 1941.

Over the handwritten entry was a faint *J* for *Jude* in brown ink. Whichever clerk had wielded the stamp had messed up, had not hit the ink pad quite hard enough the first time and so had slapped another, darker *J* on the opposite page, thereby adding to the obscuration of Samuel Fabian. Two utterly smudged thumbprints, a couple of Reich eagles, a postage stamp and the fact that his photograph had been attached not with glue but with a couple of pop rivets, one of which had emerged under his right eye, and the process was complete: this Samuel Fabian could be any Samuel Fabian, this Samuel Fabian could be Klaus Linz von Niegutt. As cliché had it, his own mother wouldn't know him.

§224

On July 2, American forces finally entered Berlin. They waited two days for a formal announcement and contrived a patriotic coincidence. On that day the British 7th Armoured Division, better known as the Desert Rats, entered Berlin, and made their announcement by hoisting a Union Jack in front of Germany's war memorial in the Tiergarten on the sixth. Atop the Brandenburg Gate would have made a better photo opportunity, but that wasn't theirs, it was Russia's. Berlin was now in sectors—Americans to the south, British to the west, Russians to the east. A week or so later Winston Churchill visited the remains of Hitler's bunker, now in the Russian sector.

The French arrived too, but nobody cared.

The Russians disappeared from the avenues of Eichkamp overnight. Krankfuß and Klaus never saw Lub from Novosibirsk again.

§225

The Glienicke Bridge

July 12, 1945

A single pedestrian path had been rigged across the collapsed bridge. All rope and planks like something out of a circus or a Tarzan film. Two American GIs stood guard at the Berlin end, a captain and a private, desultorily checking papers at what must be one of the world's newest frontiers.

Klaus showed the captain his Fabian ID.

"The bridge isn't open to Germans."

"Then to whom is it open?"

"To the guys who won the war."

"So? Who were you checking just now?"

"Three French and an Englishman, not that it's any—"

"I need to get to the other side."

"Why? This says you're from Char . . . Char . . ."

"Charlottenburg. I wasn't born in Potsdam, but I grew up in Potsdam."

The captain looked at the Fabian ID.

"What does the *J* stand for?"

"Jiminy Cricket."

"Oh . . . a wise guy."

"Very much so. You don't speak German, do you? I am a university professor. It says so right there. Or I used to be."

"Well, we all used to be something else. I played trumpet in a jazz band until 1942—yet here I am listening to you blow your horn."

"The *J* stands for Jew."

"You're a Jew?"

"You think anyone would pretend to be a Jew?"

"Not what I meant. More like . . . how come you're here? How did you survive?"

"After Egypt, after Babylon . . . you think Berlin could be a problem?"

"I only just got here. How should I know?"

"I survived. I stand here as living proof of my own survival. Can I cross now?"

"That's up to him."

The captain pointed to the far end of the wooden bridge, where a Red Army soldier stood on the Brandenburg side, staring back at them. The captain beckoned. The soldier walked towards them.

"This guy wants to cross."

"Что?"

The captain turned to Klaus.

"He doesn't speak English. And I don't speak Russian. He probably doesn't know what I just said."

"Permit me," Klaus said. "Я хочу посетить дом моих родителей. Это примерно в двух километрах от конца моста."

I wish to visit the home of my parents. It's about two kilometres from the end of the bridge.

The Russian shrugged.

"Документы."

Papers.

Klaus showed him the identity card. It surely meant nothing to him, a mess of a photo and words he couldn't read in an arcane script.

"OK," . . . in the universal language.

Klaus stuffed Samuel Fabian's papers back in his pocket. Followed the Russian across the plank bridge.

"You coming back?" the American yelled after him.

"Of course," Klaus replied. "They're Russians. They'll kick me out in a couple of hours. My own personal pogrom. Just you wait and see."

§226

The old street was lined with Russian tanks where once it had been lined with plane trees—tanks parked up in the sun and silence, peeling bark now peeling paint. Only the snoring of a man sleeping in a hammock slung between two tanks and the occasional rapid burst of summer birdsong broke the silence.

The houses looked to have fared better than Berlin, but the street was still strewn with rubble. The Russians had been in possession of Potsdam for over two months and had cleared just enough debris to allow them to park tanks.

The gates and one gatepost at his parents' house were missing. There was no soldier posted outside, so Klaus walked down the drive towards the villa on the lakeside waiting to be stopped. A half-track vehicle sporting a huge machine gun turret was parked across what had once been his mother's rose garden, its silver star glinting in the sun.

He'd rehearsed the next conversation a dozen times in many a variation. Be certain who you are, and once uttered stick to the lie. He didn't need much, merely to know, and if the Russians didn't know then to get away without suspicion. And if he got away, what? To forget?

"Was möchten Sie?"

A tall man in glasses, very short-cropped hair, sleeves rolled up, a pencil in his hand, a crest Klaus did not recognise on the shoulder and on the chest his name—di Mucci.

"Могу я вам помогать?"

Klaus realised he had hesitated too long, too late realising that the silver star on the tank was not a red star. This man wasn't Russian, he was American.

"Yes," Klaus said,

"You prefer English?"

"I'm fine with English."

"So, for the third time, how can I help you?"

"I used to work here."

"Aha."

"I was . . . the old count's secretary."

"Count?"

"Count von Niegutt. This is . . . was his family home."

One raised eyebrow, the door opened wide.

"Why don't you come inside and tell me more? I have real coffee. When did you last taste real coffee?"

Di Mucci led Klaus back to the kitchen, where once his mother's cook, Gerda, had ruled if not with a rod of iron then with a hefty wooden spoon to rap thieving little fingers. He had not been in the room in the best part of a year, his curiosity was not feigned.

Di Mucci filled an Italian moka pot and set it on the hob.

"Stanley di Mucci," he said. "New Jersey. Major, US Army Intelligence, and you?"

Be certain who you are, and once uttered stick to the lie.

"Samuel Fabian, Berliner. No rank to speak of."

"Papers?"

Damn, he'd forgotten that the ID stated Fabian's occupation, but di Mucci just glanced at it and handed it back. Perhaps he didn't know how to "read" a German ID, yet the *J* loomed large and ominous.

They sat opposite one another, a sheaf of papers di Mucci had been working on slewed across the deal table.

"Ask away."

"I am curious . . . no, worried . . . about the family . . . and I suppose the fact that you're here means they are not."

"Correct. The house has been empty for months. I'm stationed here courtesy of the Russians. My unit and half a dozen others arrived here last week. No one had bothered to tell us the bridge was down. So much for intelligence. The Russians assigned me this house while we wait for a pontoon bridge or some such. We're stuck here when we should be in the American sector of Berlin. Place called Schöneberg. You know it?"

"I knew it. Much of Berlin is unknowable now."

"Point taken."

Di Mucci poured two black, pungent espressos into Dresden china coffee cans. Red roses on a blue background, rimmed in gold. Klaus's grandmother had designed them. Di Mucci knocked his back Italian-style, in a single gulp whilst still scalding. Klaus cradled his, an old familiar object he might never see again, sipped and waited.

"So, I was passing the time leafing through the family papers. The von Niegutts left a lot behind."

Klaus steered him back to the point.

"I had heard the countess and her daughter were still here."

Di Mucci shook his head.

"Like I said, no one here. Been empty for months."

"Dead?"

"Herr Fabian, the fact that there's anyone left alive on this planet amazes me, but to say they're dead is just to guess."

"Are there still neighbours, might I ask?"

The head shook again.

"Nope. The Red Army commandeered every house in this part of Potsdam."

"Just threw people out?"

"Yep."

And now he steered Klaus back to his subject.

"I hadn't noticed the old guy was a count . . ."

"In Nazi Germany, or Weimar for that matter, it's the sort of title you'd only use when asking for a bank loan or trying to dodge creditors. You could stave off your tailor far more easily if you stuck a 'Graf' in front of your name."

Di Mucci laughed softly.

"They weren't real aristocrats?"

"Oh yes, very real. Impoverished aristocrats."

Di Mucci waved a hand in the air, inviting Klaus to assess the room, the house, everything.

"Does this look like poverty to you?"

Klaus did not even pretend to look around.

"Everything is relative."

Di Mucci shrugged this off.

"However . . . however, it appears he died a while back . . . The man that interests me—professionally, that is—would be his . . . son."

§227

It was a slight mental adjustment to think of himself in the third person, one or two degrees on whatever spectrum of identity.

Di Mucci showed him letters from Oberschütze von Niegutt, posted from the Eastern Front, and from Unterscharführer von Niegutt in the Reich Chancellery.

"We have von Niegutt's letters. I wish we had a photo—but we haven't. I guess the family took what mattered when they left—and that was photo albums, not dishes. He was in the SS. Did you know him?"

"Oh yes. I knew the boy."

"Boy?"

"Wars are fought by boys. Would you not agree?"

"I'm twenty-seven."

"And I'm thirty-three. The boy was twenty if that when he was drafted."

"You remember it?"

"No. I was long gone by then. However, your curiosity baffles me. This is . . . how to say . . . ancient history."

"No. It's not. Bullets have stopped flying, bombs stopped falling . . . but the war goes on."

"I had been led to believe otherwise. So . . . you're hunting Nazis."

"I am."

"Von Niegutt wasn't a Nazi. No one in the family was a Nazi."

"You're saying they were *good* Germans?"

This gave Klaus pause for thought. How much did di Mucci know? Was there a single note of irony in what he was saying? Could he hear the italics?

"Such a strange concept," Klaus said. "I'm sure it will run and run. A lifetime's preoccupation. The quest for the good German."

§228

By what remained of the gate, di Mucci asked one last question—the one Klaus had expected all along.

"You're Jewish?"

"Either that or my parents lied to me."

"So . . . so . . . how . . ."

"How did I survive?"

Be certain who you are, and once uttered stick to the lie.

"A Christian wife was an advantage, and when that . . . ceased . . . I went on the run. I hid. I have always depended on the kindness of strangers."

"Good Germans?"

"As I said, a concept that will run."

§229

Crossing the rope bridge he met the US Army captain again.

"So, you got your pogrom?"

"Not funny."

"You said it first."

"It wasn't funny then either."

§230

He followed the same trail the horse had led him along in May. It was a long walk back to Eichkamp—pleasant enough, a woodland walk in July, no bombs, no shells, just birds singing and the crunch of his own feet on twigs and stones—but Klaus had one big imponderable to ponder. Were his immediate family dead? Which led to . . . should he, could he make contact with his sisters in the USA, Sweden or Switzerland, which led to . . . should he break cover at all? In the light of di Mucci's rather lackadaisical enquiries—which may have been anything but lackadaisical—should Klaus von Niegutt disappear for good?

When he got to Krankfuß's allotment, Krankfuß was balanced on his bent foot and was plying a large fork with the other, lifting potatoes.

"They've flowered. That means they're ready."

"I'll take your word for it."

"I've a bucketful of Bismarcks—imagine that, you get to run a country, create a country even, and the buggers what come after name a spud after you. The missis takes a masher to you, adds a nob of butter, sticks in a few bangers and bang goes yer dignity. Remember that Nazi slogan from a few years back? 'We are the people of the potato.' What a load of bollocks."

Wir sind das Volk der Kartoffel.

Klaus did remember. Certain potatoes, like certain books . . . like certain races, had been banned.

"Kohlrabi too," Krankfuß said, easing his weight back onto his good foot. "I'll stick a few in a sack for you. Old Greta wrung a chicken earlier. You can have the legs off that. You can have all the fun of cooking for yourself tonight. The *Amis* put the power back on while you were out."

"Really? I wonder who they'll bill."

"Won't be anyone named Fabian, you can be sure of that. They're gone for good."

Which was just what Klaus had been thinking about the von Niegutts.

§231

A light had come on in the Fabian house. Why not? The power was restored and Klaus had had no idea which switch might be on or off, up or down. He'd tried none of them, there'd been no point until now.

The light was coming from the study. As he stood in the doorway, the man sitting at the desk turned around. "And who might you be?" he asked.

"Does it matter? I have potatoes."

§232

"Glad to hear it. So we won't starve? Meanwhile, who's been sleeping in my bed? Who's been eating my porridge?"

"At least I didn't break your chair, Papa Bear."

"Touché."

"I'm Klaus."

"And I'm Sam."

"Samuel?"

"Samuel no longer. Call me Sam."

He stood up. Moved further into the light. A man of roughly his own height and build but older, a face more "lived-in," and Klaus noticed for the first time that he was wearing *Konzentrationslager* striped pyjamas—the uniform of Dachau and Auschwitz *Häftlinge*.

Who else could it be? Samuel/Sam Fabian, back not from the dead but from *Nacht und Nebel*.

"As you're wearing my shoes, might I conclude those are your boots in my closet?"

"Yes."

"So, you're SS?"

"You know boots from boots?"

"Been kicked by them enough times."

Klaus set down the sack.

"It's late. You must be hungry, Professor Fabian. I also have kohlrabi and two chicken legs. I'll cook dinner and then we can talk."

"Or I could just throw you out now."

"No, Professor. If you were going to do that I think you'd have already done it. You are, dare I say, as intrigued as I am."

"Have you been into the cellar?"

"I didn't know we had a cellar."

"We? No matter. You haven't been down there. Good. Then perhaps some of my wine and beer has survived Nazis, air raids, Russians and you. The meal sounds better already."

§233

Sam blew the dust off a small bottle of schnapps and two tiny crystal glasses, which he set aside. They began with chicken and mash and four litre bottles of Engelhardt beer, poured into tall, slender glasses.

Bottle One

"A present from Krankfuß?"

"You know him?"

"He's still out there. Living on his allotment. The food came from him. He's lived feral for a couple of years."

"I think we may all be considered feral now. The post-Nazi condition. Still, Krankfuß was ever the survivor."

"I think I may owe my survival to him. Get up early enough and he'll give us breakfast. His hens are laying, and one of the old women has a side of pig, so he gets ham and bacon."

"An off-ration rural idyll in the midst of total destruction? How delightfully absurd."

He held up his glass to clink.

"L'chaim. To life? Another absurdity. Let me start again. I am Dr Sam Fabian, late of the Humboldt University of Berlin. L'chaim."

Klaus responded.

"I am Unterscharführer Graf Klaus Gerhard Ludwig Linz von Niegutt, late of *Leibstandarte SS Adolf Hitler. L'chaim.*"

"What a fucking mouthful."

Sam sipped at his beer, engineered a necessary pause.

"You know, Graf von Niegutt. I think it's time you told me everything."

Bottle Two

"The Russians are looking for you."

"By name?"

"Oh yes—they are trying to trace anyone who was there when Hitler died. They seem particularly concerned about Bormann and Axmann, somewhat about Kempka and less so about you. All the same . . ."

"Why?"

"They are sceptical about his death."

"Or pretend they are."

"That does seem more likely. Did you see the body?"

"Yes."

"The face?"

"No."

"So it could have been anyone?"

"No, it couldn't. I didn't need to see the face. His right arm fell free of the blanket Günsche had wrapped him in. I recognised the hand. Hitler was right-handed—signed lives away with his right hand—but it would not obey him anymore. For weeks before his death it twitched and jerked with a life of its own—it was difficult not to stare. It was like watching a body at war with itself. I'd know that hand anywhere."

"You're certain?"

"Oh yes. Hitler is dead. Bormann is dead too, by the way. He didn't get more than a couple of kilometres from the bunker. And this time I saw the face."

"Where?"

"Quite close to the Lehrter Bahnhof. Unless the Russians are digging for him right now, he's under the pile of rubble that almost buried me."

Bottle Three

"Why did you not flee?" Klaus asked. "There must have been opportunities open to you as an educated man. One of my sisters got out as early as 1933."

"Yet you did not."

"I was a child when the Nazis came to power."

"Of course. Why? Why did I not leave? It is like boiling a frog. You put off and put off until you believe your own lie, that it will never happen. After '39 leaving was impossible. After '41 the lie became harder and harder to believe. I saw Jews from Eichkamp transported from Grunewald station . . . hundreds, perhaps more than a thousand . . . some of them people I had known all my life. The date is burnt into my memory: October 18. Every day I lived here after that was on borrowed time, borrowed from my wife's family. I was in what was called a 'privileged mixed marriage.' I saw the risk and urged her to go. Instead she died, the privilege ended and at last the frog boiled.

"This was early 1944. They were so keen to get rid of me that they didn't bother to confiscate my house, ask me to list my assets or even pay the two hundred Reichsmarks for my own train fare to Auschwitz. Imagine, a free train ride from Hitler. Cattle class, return tickets temporarily unavailable. Hence we have beer and you have shoes. If it had been '41 or '42, the Nazis would have stolen everything. In Auschwitz I saw piles of shoes, piles of spectacles . . . the list might go on and on . . . and I realised at last what the Nazis really were: corporate rag-and-bone men."

Bottle Four

"Did you know?"

"Krankfuß asked me the same question weeks ago, and I give you the same answer I gave him. Any German who says they didn't know lacks either imagination or intelligence or both. It could be said that the overwhelming desire of Germans was *not* to know. An impossible delusion, yet on a national scale."

"In which case my intelligence did not fail me, but my imagination did. I knew there were no new cities in the East—but when I got to the East what I saw, what I experienced, was beyond any imagining. But . . . but . . . all this is dodging the issue. In capital letters, you KNEW."

"Of course. I have not been out of Berlin since 1940. I have seen nothing of what you have seen. And from last January till May I lived underground. The bunker shielded me from British bombs and Russian artillery. It could not shield me from knowledge. I decoded messages from both fronts, I sent messages from Hitler, I manned the switchboard and overheard conversations between him and his generals. When numbers were low I even had lunch with him, as he could never be without an audience. And when no one else was available I was press-ganged into drinking looted champagne with Fegelein, who had all the discretion of a town crier. Yes, I knew."

"And what did you do?"

"I waited till the frog had boiled."

Schnapps I

"I learnt in the East a lesson any Jew must learn, or for that matter any Gentile."

"That there is no god."

"On the contrary, that there is a god, a very real god, a malign god. Vengeance is mine, saith the lord. The god of Job."

"That's not in the book of Job, it's in the New Testament, Romans or perhaps Philippians."

"Suddenly he's a scholar. Oy gevalt."

Klaus grinned at the Yiddisher parody.

Sam laughed out loud at his grinning.

"I was raised a lapsing Lutheran," Klaus said. "Which is to say a lazy atheist. As with most atheists, the head and the heart compete, and I had longed to be able to believe in something. It is hard to believe in nothing."

"Very well, believe in this: 'The Lord, whose name is Jealous, is a jealous God,' blah blah blah . . . 'lest the anger of the Lord thy God be kindled against thee, and destroy thee from off the face of the earth,' et cetera . . . et cetera. Jealous god, angry god, malign god . . . damn near succeeded this time."

Schnapps II

"You need to pick a new spot to sleep."

"Eh?"

"I'd like my study back. It's neat. It's clean. It's mine."

"It's neat. It's clean. I've kept it neat and clean."

"Such ingratitude. Look, why not make up a bed under this table. It's solid chestnut. Seven centimetres thick. My great-grandfather made it. It will hold up against any rubble that might fall from above."

"This is Berlin, where would we find rubble?"

"Not funny. Not funny at all."

§234

Breakfast at the Café Krankfuß

Krankfuß was preparing bacon and eggs.

His first words on seeing Sam Fabian were "So, you're back, are you?"
And scarce a flicker of further curiosity.

§235

August 1945

Out on the allotments—a rolling sea of plenty, green-in-brown, late potatoes wilting, marrow and pumpkin beginning to swell, tomatoes so heavy they required a gardener's improvised scaffolding, a waft of home-grown white-blossomed tobacco—from somewhere Krankfuß produced a bike.

"Ta-da!"

A green, scratched, old-but-clean, functional, well-oiled English Raleigh with Sturmey-Archer three-speed gears, plump tyres and rear rack.

"What did this cost?"

"A dozen eggs, five kilos of potatoes and a crate of ale. More than a pig, less than a cow. No matter. It's not as if you'll ever pay me back. When you're gone, you're gone. Speakin' o' which—gone where?"

"I'm not sure. And you?"

"Me? I'm not going anywhere. Certainly not going back."

"Back? Your house is less than two hundred metres away."

"Might as well be ten thousand. Not going back. I'm staying put. I'll live on this allotment, in me shack, forever . . . or until the next load of nutters gets us bombed to bollocks. Same thing, really. I've found me . . . wotsername . . . Elysian Fields . . . me Elysian allotment. If this is what 'Elysian' means."

His hand swept an arc across the view, taking in the bounty of his labours, the bobbing heads of vegetables in the hazy sun and warm breeze of an August morning, under the silent sky.

"It does," Klaus replied.

§236

Klaus wheeled the bike back to Großereichenweg.

Sam said, "Hmm . . . do you have a destination in mind?"

"No . . . just west."

"Awfully big place, west."

"I'll cross into the Soviet Zone, and just keep pedalling until . . ."

"You're out of the Soviet Zone?"

"Of course."

"But you have no papers, surely?"

Klaus hesitated to say something he knew he should have said some time ago.

"I have your identity card from a few years back."

"Ah . . . were you going to tell me?"

"When I had to."

"Well, it will be useless to you. Come into my—so sorry—*our* study."

They sat opposite each other, not even at arm's length, all but touching.

Klaus handed Sam the identity card.

Sam glanced at it, then threw it down on the desk

"Why did you not go west sooner?"

"You might say I fell at the first hurdle. I went down to the bridge. I fell in with a large crowd—it seemed as if half of Berlin was on the move. Donkeys, horses, wagons, bicycles, prams. I found myself stepping over the things they dropped . . . cutlery, more often than not, children's toys, family photographs, hats, plates, pans, dishes . . . and twice I helped drag bodies to the side of the road as old women expired under the strain of this ad hoc exodus. I was stopped by the Russians, but that merely cost me my watch, and I arrived at Glienicke to find there was no bridge anymore. If it had been intact I might have carried on to Potsdam and from Potsdam . . . Who knows? But . . . the crowd dispersed and I sat in the dust and looked out over the Havel. I must have slept. When I awoke the crowd had dwindled to half a dozen dreamers like myself, gazing towards Potsdam. And the relief was quietly overwhelming. To be alone . . . to be alone at that moment was everything.

"Later that day I ended up here, I met Krankfuß, and I put off heading west, again and again. I decided that the way to avoid being herded, herded by anyone . . . Russians, Americans, British . . . it didn't matter . . . was to wait . . . let Flüchtlings go where Flüchtlings go. On Krankfuß's allotment it was as though I had slipped through a hole in time and space. No one knew me, no one came looking for me. Even when the Russians came looking it was just one lone tank driver in search of fresh eggs every so often. You might say that I hid in plain sight. It was strange, it was beautiful, I was content. It was, as you yourself said, a rural idyll in the midst of total destruction. And then . . . I met you. And another layer appeared in the Chinese box."

"I think perhaps matryoshka might have been the better image. But . . . but now?"

"I have a bike."

"So I see."

"I shall take the backroads westward, the rough ones, the forest trails."

"Why now?"

"They're all here. The city is in sectors. If we're not organised already, they—that is, the British, the Americans and the Russians—will organise us any minute . . . ration cards, identity cards, this thing that's called a *Persilschein* . . . God knows why . . ."

"It washes away the Nazi past. Cleaner than clean, whiter than white."

"And I have no wish to be organised or, for that matter, whitewashed. Ever again. Let Nobody be my name."

For a moment or two Sam seemed to weigh up the man sat opposite him, picked up the ID card and opened it.

"Well, Count Nobody, have you used my identity card? Have you been Sam Fabian?"

"Just the once. The day we met. I had crossed into Potsdam and back. Neither the Russians nor the Americans even raised an eyebrow."

Sam looked at the photo of himself taken more than three years ago.

"Yes, it's more you than me. I am become someone else. You are welcome to him. But . . . it's a hundred kilometres and more to the British zone. Even on the backroads you'll have to pass a dozen trigger-happy, stupid Ivans on patrol, some of whom may be far from stupid. Believe me, I know Russians. You'll need more than this."

He tossed the card down on the desk.

"I think I understand your wish to be nobody, but it's in your best interests if you go on being me."

"Don't *you* want to be you?"

"No. I'd rather be you."

§237

"You'll need these."

Sam unfolded four sheets of paper, heavily stamped in both black and red, a hammer and sickle in the top left corner. Rifkin had given them to him along with his wages. Klaus leafed through them, clause upon clause in Russian—quite comprehensible.

"It would appear to be both an *Ausweis* and a *Reisepasse*."

"It is. Now look at the signatures on the last page."

Georgy Zhukov
Konstantin Rokossovsky
Aleksandr Vadis

"Impressive. Zhukov, Rokossovsky of course—but Vadis? Who is Vadis?"

"He's the man who's looking for you. He's the general in charge of Smersh in Germany. Smersh is . . ."

"Oh, I know what Smersh is. I should be flattered. He's not been head of Smersh for long or I'd have come across the name."

"You should be flattered. They think you're more important than you ever were. However, what matters is that the photograph flatters no one. Could be me, could be you, could be a Rorschach test."

Klaus was not at all sure that he agreed. Some sort of developing chemical had run and dribbled, but a face so streaked bore scrutiny. It was a chance Sam was urging upon him and one worth taking.

Probably.

"Any Ivan who can read will quake in his boots at those signatures."

"And any Ivan who cannot read?"

Sam shrugged. "You hesitate."

"I do. It seems impossible. Absurd even."

"In the feral world isn't everything absurd or impossible? Why, I tell myself six impossible things before breakfast. But . . . I'll challenge you."

"For what?"

"For the Russian guarantee, for the right to be me."

"We flip a coin?"

"So unsubtle. No, an old Chinese game. Rock, Paper, Scissors. You know it?"

"Yes, I had younger sisters to amuse when I was a boy."

"Best of three, then."

Sam's paper wrapped Klaus's rock.

Klaus's scissors cut Sam's paper.

Then Sam's rock blunted Klaus's scissors.

"Ah . . . you remain Sam Fabian."

"That wasn't the wager. I won. Hence, the papers are in my gift, and I give them to you. In the hope they are not the gift of Nessus."

Klaus picked up the papers once more.

"You know, this really is absurd."

"So you said. I heard you the first time."

§238

Breakfast at the Café Krankfuß

"Why are you still wearing your prison stripes, Professor?"

"I thought perhaps there was a point to make."

"Well, they're just rags now—"

"They were just rags eight months ago when the Russians found me."

"—and the arse is hanging out, so come winter yer bollocks'll freeze. You two look like a pair of scarecrows. I'd've thought the Russkis could have found you some better togs."

"They did offer."

Klaus said, "Whatever the point, Sam, I think you've made it."

"Really, Graf von Niegutt? I doubt I shall ever be able to do that. However . . ."

§239

Again, the following day, breakfast at the café Krankfuß, as ever over an open fire.

Sam appeared in shirt and trousers from his wardrobe, dusty but devoid of moth holes. He carried a suitcase, a pre-war relic with stickers, all those triangles and circles, from hotels in Vienna, Paris, Milan and Bologna.

He opened the case and threw his Auschwitz uniform into the flames. And when the flames were high he reached into the suitcase and threw Klaus's jack boots onto the fire.

"'Ere!" Krankfuß said. "Them's my size!"

Sam ignored this and spoke to Klaus.

"It seems I will walk a mile in your shoes. I'd far rather that were merely metaphor."

He picked up the suitcase, about to throw it on the fire, but stopped.

"No, you keep the suitcase. You'll need it. It should fit neatly onto the back of your new bike. Herr Zobb is right. Scarecrows, indeed."

$240

August 13
A Fine, Sunny Monday

On what Klaus had assumed would be their last day together, and they had lived under the same broken roof for five weeks, he and Sam went through the wardrobe, feeling the bedroom floor shift beneath their feet with every step.

"Don't take too long choosing," Sam said, "or we'll end up in the dining room."

Klaus chose a black two-piece, two-button suit, pretty much identical to one he'd once owned in Potsdam, and swapped the brown brogues for plain black beetle-crushers.

Sam, despite seven months of regular meals, was still underweight, and the best-fitting suit, or least ill-fitting, was not ideal.

"Stripes again. From broad stripe to pinstripe. Will I ever be free of stripes?"

Klaus next picked a white cotton shirt. As he slipped one arm though, Sam said, "Not so fast. We don't want to get blood on it."

"Blood?"

"Follow me."

In Sam's study, both men shirtless, the mass of scars on Sam's torso contrasting vividly with the pale, hairless skin of Klaus's, Sam held up his left arm.

"Know what this is?"

$$\Delta\text{-}155515$$

"As I said a while back—I knew."

"You will not be able to pass as a survivor of Auschwitz without one. Of course, you could pass for a Jew without it, any old Jew—a Jew more fortunate than I was. You imitate my accent and speech pattern rather well, after all. But something tells me that is not enough. Passing as a survivor is part of your plan."

"I'm not sure I have a plan."

"You kid yourself. In or out?"

"In. And . . ."

"And what?"

"I already have one tattoo."

Just beneath the pit of his left arm was a blood group tattoo, so small a person with poor eyesight might mistake it for a blemish.

Sam put on his glasses and peered.

"ABn. Tell me, Graf von Niegutt, ever been wounded?"

"Eastern Front. Bullet to my left thigh."

"Blood transfusion?"

"Alas, yes."

"Well, I doubt they found a match. AB negative doesn't sit around like a barrel of beer waiting for a customer. It's rare."

"I didn't know that."

"No matter. Almost any other type would suffice. As with so much of the Nazi race theory, their idea of blood was nonsensical. Rare does not mean superior. You must get Krankfuß to touch the tip of one of his American cigarettes to it. The less you bleed, the better. However, right now, a little bloodshed is inevitable."

§241

Klaus had learnt to write with a pen like this, a simple shaft, with a nib as fine as a wren's beak, nib dipped into a well of black ink made up from powder—for all Klaus knew it could have been soot—and dispensed weekly by a bad-tempered schoolmaster—to whom blots were sacrilege—from something that resembled a small watering can.

It did not take long.

Sam seemed remarkably skilful.

Ten minutes of pinpricks.

"That hurt."

"Welcome to my world."

"The feral world?"

"Whatever. A gift from Pelikan. And now the bad news. You must wait a week. Firstly because I have known sepsis to set in—those branded rather than tattooed would scream at the pain, but the process was sterile. This isn't. A week to let it heal, safely. Then, you may notice it start to fade. They tend to turn purple. It would look more authentic if it did."

"We should have done this sooner."

Sam shrugged.

"Did I know you were pretending to be me? Did I know you were buying a bike? We have each been too vague about the what-next of our pact. All I knew, all I know is your 'West.'"

"And I know even less of yours. Palestine, perhaps?"

A pause.

A tidying away of the tool kit of identity. Ink and blood and blotting paper.

"Palestine? On reflection . . . no."

"Why's that?"

"Never had a taste for milk and honey."

"Why are you doing this?"

"You mean why are *we* doing this?"

"You first."

"Who knows? Perhaps I shall be able to put a spanner in the works of the rewriting of history—a process happening as we speak."

"A little too cerebral. Let me ask again. Why are *you* doing this?"

"I thought the world had taken its best shot at me, in order to show me the worst. Perhaps I judge too soon, and the worst is yet to come. This seems a good way to find out. And you?"

"I wish simply to . . . live."

"Good luck with that."

§242

On the last day Sam handed Klaus a small package.

"A parting gift?"

"A gift and a question. The last of many."

"Of course."

"Bormann? You're certain?"

"As I said, I saw his face, I smelt the cyanide."

"Noted."

"An important detail? Can the death of that fat pig of a man matter that much? If he'd lived, the Allies would most certainly have hanged him."

"Who knows, who knows? The dead may well have their uses."

Klaus opened his present.

A Russian watch and a bundle of English five-pound notes.

§243

August 22
A Warm Wednesday
Quite Early One Morning

On a dusty, deserted road somewhere between Kurnau and Tülau, close to the new border between East and West, Klaus, having passed no one and nothing since first light, saw something coming towards him. A young woman on a bicycle, a bicycle seemingly identical to his own.

She braked too hard and sent a cloud of white dust into the air, stuck out her right foot to steady the bike and said, "Snap!"

"You're going the wrong way," Klaus said.

"That all depends on what you think is the right way. I am a Berliner. I'm going home."

"I am a Berliner too. I'm leaving home."

Boldly—she did not look to be more than sixteen or seventeen—she stuck out her hand for him to shake.

"Christina Hélène von Raeder Burkhardt. Known as Nell."

"Sam," Klaus said. "Known as Sam."

He would have to get used to saying that.

Cabrera
Bormann
Von Niegutt
Fabian
Heller
Job
&
God

§244

Tel Aviv

September 1962

In 1960 a Mossad team of no more than a dozen agents snatched Adolf Eichmann from his home on the outskirts of Buenos Aires and transported him to Israel to face trial. Eichmann's escape had been successful in that he had evaded capture for fifteen years, but his life in anonymity, as Ricardo Klement, had not. He had tried various forms of agriculture, had even bred rabbits, but by May 1960 his life had improved—he was a department head at Mercedes Benz and had built his own house on Garibaldi Street.

Each evening he would return home on the same bus. On the evening of May 11, Mossad were waiting, and the fact that Eichmann was not on the bus was merely the first thing that went wrong. Eichmann caught a later bus, resisted arrest and fought back.

On the twelfth a "diplomatic" El Al flight had been arranged to spirit him away. If they made it as far as Dakar in West Africa, where they could refuel, then they would fly back to Tel Aviv.

The plane was delayed a week, a week in which Eichmann had to be restrained, sedated, concealed. It was May 20 before the team and their prisoner reached Israel. The only thing to be said for this planning catastrophe was that by the time Eichmann landed in Israel no one had any doubt as to who he was.

The following year Eichmann stood trial in Jerusalem—bespectacled, black-suited, unrepentant in his bullet-proof glass booth. He denied nothing, was hanged on May 31, 1962, and his ashes were scattered at sea.

In August Mossad commander Yitzhak Berg sent for one of the agents who had assisted in the arrest—Samuel "Sam" Fabian, a German, perhaps in his late thirties or early forties, who had arrived in Palestine from a DP camp in Bolzano, Italy, in 1946, joined Haganah, fought in the Arab war following partition and served Israel loyally since 1950 as an agent of Mossad.

"We have another," Berg said.

"Do we need another?" Fabian asked.

Berg had long since grown used to the sheer contrariness of Fabian and ignored this.

"It's Martin Bormann."

"Bormann's dead. Even Germany thinks he's dead. When was it, '54? '55? An official declaration from Bonn."

"I no more believe that than you do. We're going back to Argentina."

"Another tip-off?"

"What else? This time you're in charge."

"I'm flattered. Can I just shoot him?"

"No. We want him alive. He's a much bigger fish than Eichmann, so . . ."

"So a much bigger trial."

"I hear sarcasm."

"The trial was spectacular. For the first time since the war we held centre stage, but it was a huge drain on resources and I doubt our masters have any taste for a repeat. It almost went pear-shaped. We came close to being arrested by the Argentinians more times than I can count."

"Which is why I want you to get him into Paraguay on day one. If our source is correct, Bormann is in San Ignacio in the north, right on the border. A six-hour drive from Asunción. A plane from Asunción and in less than thirty-six hours Bormann could be here."

"If the Paraguayans don't catch us."

Berg paused, took a good look at Fabian.

"Sam, do not let me think I have made a mistake in choosing you. Stop kvetching and listen. This time—no, do not interrupt—this time we have bribed the right people."

"You mean we have bribed the right dictator?"

"At last. Thank you."

"And so we sup with the devil. General Stroessner is a torturer and a murderer. We are almost trading the one for the other."

"Stroessner has guaranteed no interference."

"If you let me shoot Bormann we wouldn't need Stroessner."

"For the last time, no. Bring him back alive.

§245

Finca Porco Loco
En el País de Uz
San Ignacio, Argentina

It was almost dusk. Quite possibly Cabrera's favourite time of day. He was just about to feed his chickens, one Rhode Island Red rooster and seven assorted hens, when the first man stepped out of the shrubbery between two clumps of yerba mate. Cabrera acknowledged him with a nod of the head and looked around. If there was one, there would be more. Five more appeared, none of them apparently armed, one by one, like actors assuming their places on stage.

Curtain up.

"Speak the speech, I pray you," Cabrera said in English.

"Domingo Diego Cabrera, formerly known as Martin Bormann, under the laws of Israel I arrest you for war crimes."

"Fine. Now what about the laws of Argentina?"

"Are you kidding?" Fabian said.

"Are you kidding? War crimes? Eichmann confessed to six million murders. How many are left for me? A dozen? Perhaps two dozen?"

"One will suffice," Fabian replied.

"Indeed," said Bormann. "May I have leave to pack?"

"No."

"Then at least let me feed my chickens."

§246

Jerusalem

Bormann had felt the needle go into his neck, then nothing else. They had patted him down for weapons—his habitual dress of rough linen shirt and pants had no pockets, and his feet were shod in dirty espadrilles. With no place for concealment he had assumed they would strip-search him, but he awoke in Jerusalem, in a cell with no windows, still in the clothes he had worn at the moment of his kidnapping.

Two guards stood one either side of the door.

Half an hour, tea and scrambled eggs later, Fabian appeared in his cell, accompanied by a portly man Bormann took to be a doctor.

Pulse, blood pressure, the stethoscope over his heart, the pinpoint light in his eyes.

"He's fine. Fine and filthy. He reeks of chicken shit."

When the doctor had gone, Bormann sat on the edge of the bed. Fabian pulled up a stool and stared at him.

"Plastic surgery?"

"No."

"Weight loss, then."

"Of course. After all, I had so much to lose."

"I fear the suit we have for you may not fit."

Bormann laughed softly.

"You snatch me from my home, drug me, fly me five thousand miles in a haze and you're worried the suit won't fit? Fabian, my cup runneth over that Israel should send me such a wag."

A third guard brought in a simple black two-piece suit. At least they had got his height right.

Fabian pointed at the only other door.

"You can shower and change in there. Some privacy."

"Privacy?"

"We're not monsters," Fabian said.

"Really? I am."

§247

It was a strange feeling. He could not remember when he had last worn a suit or shoes with laces—except that the shoes had lace holes, but no laces.

They took him down a short, well-lit corridor and into a room of shining porcelain and stainless steel, where a man in a white sleeveless smock, with hairy arms, stuck him in a dentist's chair.

"You will understand," Fabian said. "We have your dental records."

"They survived British bombs and Russian guns? In Berlin? Amazing."

Then the plate was in his mouth and no one spoke the more.

§248

It was the following morning before Fabian appeared again. Bormann had just breakfasted on brown toast and more eggs. Bacon would have been nice, but to ask would only provoke.

Fabian asked for the room. Took his seat on the stool again.

"Who are you?"

"You mean you don't know who you kidnapped?"

"You're not Martin Bormann."

"Ah . . . the teeth do not match?"

"You know damn well they don't."

"Perhaps I really am Domingo Diego Cabrera."

"If you were Cabrera you'd have protested in Argentina. And you would not have spoken to me in English and German. You're no more an Argentinian peasant than I am."

"Then perhaps I can have some shoelaces now?"

"You're German. One German to another, I know it. I know it in my bones."

"Ah . . . but am I . . . was I . . . a Nazi?"

"I'm waiting for you to tell me."

"Of course you are. But . . . what do my teeth tell you?"

Fabian was losing patience. "Bormann" could see that.

"OK. OK. You found nothing, no dental or medical record that would help, am I right?"

Fabian said nothing.

"So . . . I am . . . I am . . . Graf Klaus Linz von Niegutt, SS-Unterscharführer. Look me up. There'll be records. I might even be owed back pay. Don't let the title intimidate you, I'm not a snob . . . and besides, I was only a corporal, and you, I believe, are a colonel . . . more scrambled egg than I got on my plate this morning. Now, about the shoelaces . . ."

§249

If the guards had been told not to speak to von Niegutt, obedience had lapsed in the face of boredom by the third day. Fabian had not returned. They were as bored as he was. The night guards had it better, they could read while he slept, his eyes masked against perpetual light. The day guards could be tempted into chatting, tempted further when the one he knew as David produced a pocket chess set. Von Niegutt beat him in a long first game, then they taught Yonny how to play, both somewhat surprised that anyone could reach the age of thirty and not know.

Perhaps they were relieved that he wasn't Bormann—as he put it to them himself, "I am a Nazi-nobodnik."

On the sixth day Fabian reappeared.

"Put on your jacket."

"We going somewhere?"

Fabian produced a tie and shoelaces from his jacket pocket.

"A court appearance. We don't even leave the building."

"Am I to be charged?"

Fabian said nothing. Looked steadily on as von Niegutt used the reflection in his glasses to tie his tie.

"Shoelaces . . . tie . . . perhaps a mirror?"

"They're waiting. Please don't waste time."

Down the corridor, past the medical room, past a dozen closed doors and suddenly into a vast room bathed in sunlight from an overhead dome.

There was the glass booth. Empty.

There were the jury benches. Empty.

There were the public gallery and the press box. Empty.

Three judges, one woman flanked by two men, sat at the bench.

Fabian motioned von Niegutt to sit at a table, and then sat next to him looking more like his lawyer than his captor.

There was whispering.

The woman turned to each of her colleagues and back again, then she faced von Niegutt.

"Would you stand?"

Fabian stood with him.

"Please confirm your name and date of birth."

Von Niegutt coughed twice and spoke softly.

"I am Graf Klaus Gerhard Ludwig Linz von Niegutt, born August 3, 1917, citizen of Potsdam in the state of Brandenburg. I forget what country that's in now."

Nobody even smiled at that, although he could all but feel Fabian twitch with annoyance.

A pause, more whispers.

Then she looked back at him.

"No charges, case dismissed."

Von Niegutt looked at Fabian, but Fabian was looking at the floor.

"What do you mean, no charges? I was in the SS. I was with Adolf in the bunker! Dammit, I helped burn his body!"

"Graf von Niegutt, please . . ."

Von Niegutt stuck out his right arm in the Nazi salute: "Sieg heil!"

"Graf von Niegutt, you weren't even a party member!"

And then he began to sing. The tune was the German national anthem, "Deutschland Über Alles," but the words were English.

Saviour since of Zion's city
I through grace a member am,
Let the world deride or pity,
I will glory in your name.
Fading are the world's vain pleasures,
All their boasted pomp and show—

On the word "show" he rolled back his left sleeve all the way to the elbow and showed the court the six-digit tattoo in the soft flesh of the forearm, a few inches above the wrist.

Then he laughed, and laughed till he wept. And when he could weep no more, he slumped, and Fabian caught him.

$250

He must have slept several hours, he thought. David and Yonny had unlocked shutters to reveal a window and let in the fading light of early evening—as though he had in some way earned his dusk. His sense of the room changed. He was reminded of nights in the study in Eichkamp, the only room in which he had felt safe from the slowly collapsing house. Old neighbours lived on their allotments, in wooden shacks and tin huts. He stuck with the house, with its emotional pull and its quivering pool of memory, watching dusk, waiting on dawn. How often had he dreamt he was back in that room? A hundred, a thousand? In the dream he was not as he was then, in 1945, but as he had been ever since, ageing in a room that never changed—the fixed point to which his dreams returned. Time after time.

Two cups of tea and half an hour later Fabian reappeared, waved David and Yonny away and took to his stool again, less than two feet from "von Niegutt."

"Who are you?"

"Is that the only question you ever ask?"

"You're a Jew. A survivor of Auschwitz. What were you doing among the Nazis in South America? What is this masquerade?"

David and Yonny had left the teapot. "Von Niegutt" poured himself another cup and stared into it.

"Among the Nazis? Huh? OK. Since you ask. Who do you think tipped you off about Eichmann?"

Still he didn't look up.

"Who do you think tipped you off about 'Bormann'?"

Now he looked up at a speechless, baffled Fabian.

Fabian found words. Not many but perhaps enough.

"Why? I do not understand. Why?"

"Von Niegutt" sighed, breathed deeply.

"In 1944 the SS charged a friend of mine with something of nothing. I forget what, but this was Auschwitz, where everything is something. There was nothing so trivial it could be overlooked. So they stripped him naked, strung him up by his ankles and whipped him raw with the dried penises of bulls. By sunset he was nothing but meat. You could not see his face for blood. Then they herded us back inside and left him to die. But he didn't die. At roll call before dawn the next morning he was still hanging there, still breathing, still conscious, so half a dozen of them stood in a circle and pissed into his wounds. A bullet would have been merciful.

Skip forward a year or so. I am the guest of the Red Army. I have been fed and clothed, I am on my way to a bodily recovery—let us not talk of mind or spirit—and we entered a village somewhere near Katowice. The Germans have gone—well, most of them have gone—and Polish partisans have caught stragglers. I saw them strip a Waffen-SS man of his trousers. They left the tunic so anyone who came across him would know what he was and why. I say 'man'—a boy of eighteen or so, and not even a German. I know because he cried out in a language I did not recognise . . . Bulgarian or Romanian, I don't know.

"His cries for mercy went unheeded. The Poles had sharpened a fence post still standing in the ground long after some Soviet tank had driven through the wire. Then one of them, a man the size of an oak tree, picked him up and rammed him on the sharp end arsehole first. In all my time in Auschwitz I had not heard such screams. A bullet would have been merciful, but there was no bullet, no mercy. They left him there. I do not know how long it took the fence post to work its way through his guts and emerge through his chest. Our caravan of Häftlings had moved on by the time that happened.

"So you see."

"What do I see?"

"A world in which good can seem no better than evil. I thought in Auschwitz that the world had shown me its worst. I thought in Poland that the world had shown me its worst. Yet I knew it had not. I have been in search of the worst. And when I had found it, I raised chickens and the occasional goat."

"I don't understand."

"You will."

"Von Niegutt" cradled his tea and sipped at it.

Fabian seemed to drag himself back from Poland to the present.

"I am sorry to have to ask you this, but I need to see your tattoo. The court has asked me to do this. They wish to know the number. To . . . record the number."

"You first."

"What do you mean?"

"I've been here a week. You think your people don't talk to me? Colonel Fabian, I know more about you than you do about me. You were in Auschwitz too. So show me."

Fabian froze, then he shook his head no, then looked to the ceiling, perhaps to God, and pulled back the sleeve on his left arm, remembering the day it had been tattooed there in a DP camp in Fuchsundachs all those years ago.

"Hmmm," said "von Niegutt." "Sloppy. You do that yourself?"

Then he rolled up his left sleeve again and laid his forearm next to Fabian's.

The number on each was Δ-155515.

Fabian was still looking at God.

"Eyes down, Colonel Fabian."

Fabian looked.

"I . . . I don't understand . . . I don't understand."

The Real Fabian set down his teacup, took the Fake Fabian's head in his hands, noses all but touching, hot breath upon his face, and whispered, "Job 2:9."

"I . . . I'm not a bible scholar . . . I don't know the verse."

Real Fabian let Fake Fabian's head go, looked once to heaven and said just as softly, "Job 2:9. 'Curse God and die.'"

Then he picked up his cup in both hands and sipped his tea.

§

Stuff

Notting Hill: This is a novel. It would be a mistake to read it as history. I have compressed both time and place. In particular the pattern and incidence of West Indian migration is a fiction based quite loosely on fact. For example, the *Empire Windrush*, which docked in 1948 and has become emblematic of West Indian immigration to the UK over the best part of twenty years, carried 492 West Indians and, strangely, 76 Poles (that is another story), but between the end of the war and 1950 only five other ships carrying West Indian immigrants docked in England—a total of 1800 people. Nowhere near enough to feed the plot I had devised. The situation I describe in Notting Hill in the late 1940s is more typical of the late 1950s, but, again, the plot is a harsh mistress and I rolled time back ten years.

Otto Ohnherz: whilst clearly inspired by Peter Rachman is not a portrait of Rachman. The notion of "de-Stat and Shvartzer" is, of course, pure Rachman.

Jay Fabian: Jay Fabian is entirely fictional.

Bryce: is fictional; however, those who know their '60s history will be aware that Peter Rachman's girlfriend in the early '60s was Mandy Rice-Davies. Bryce isn't a sketch of Mandy. I pinched just two aspects of Mandy's life . . . being from South Wales . . . and the flat in Lowndes Square, in which Mandy lived in the 1990s, and on whose walls hung both a Picasso and a Kandinsky.
[A "footnote" à propos of not much—when Mandy died about ten years ago one of the English newspapers had a headline referring to her as "Profumo Temptress." She told me, and I have no reason to doubt her, that she never met John Profumo.]

Bormann: I had memory of a news item circa 1963 or thereabouts of Mossad arresting a man in South America on the assumption he was Bormann. It was very soon established that he wasn't. Nothing I've read in the time it's taken me to write this book supports that memory.

Gaggia: I bent time here and there. Gaggia coffee machines were not invented until 1947.

Pissarro: The painting of Lordship Lane station wasn't sold to a private individual in 1948; it was given that year by Samuel Courtauld to the institute which bears his name, where it remains. I've no idea what my fictional villain might have paid for it. About ten years ago Camille Pissarro's *Boulevard Montmartre, Matinée de Printemps* sold for just under twenty million pounds.

The Bridge across the Oder at Frankfurt did not reopen until after 1946. The Oderblick camp was real, as was the massacre of its inhabitants.

Mother Night and *The Man in the Glass Booth*, respectively written by Kurt Vonnegut and Robert Shaw. I read both these novels when they were relatively new, although in each case that would be some fifty-odd years ago. Not long after I began this book, memories of both began to surface. I re-read them, noticed the similarities and also enough differences to convince me to carry on.

I'd urge these novels on anyone who hasn't read them. Vonnegut long ago entered the literary pantheon but I suspect, forty-five years after his death, that Shaw the novelist is utterly eclipsed by Shaw the actor . . . *From Russia With Love* . . . *Jaws* . . . *The Sting* . . . it's a long list.

Why Write about Auschwitz (Again)?

When did I, child of the immediate post-war era, first hear of the Final Solution? (Note: I do not use the word "Holocaust," the Israeli writer Amos Oz talked me, and for all I know many a writer, out of using that term years ago . . . "It wasn't a phenomenon of nature, like a tornado or a flood." Indeed it wasn't, it was what man did to man. In addition, I had always been baffled by Hannah Arendt's shocked invention of the phrase "the banality of evil." What was she expecting of Eichmann, a tail and horns? Moreover, I can't remember not knowing, and that forced me back to my father . . . a natural storyteller, a yarn spinner with more than a kiss of blarney to him.

His war took him to Hamburg in 1945, where he was responsible for disarming the German stockpiles of bombs—this was a man who could dismantle a hand grenade blindfolded, I might add—but it was by no means his first visit. He was if anything a Deutschophile (don't reach for the OED, it ain't there), a regular visitor pre-war. I still have his last photo album. All the things that might interest a kid from a Lancashire cotton mill—beer and girls—except in the last photograph as he captured a street in Bavaria at first light, utterly deserted and lined with swastikas. He never went again as a civilian. Nonetheless, friendships persisted. His old pal Werner was unfortunate enough to be drafted into the Wehrmacht and finding himself on the Italian front in 1943 deserted and crossed the American lines into internment for the rest of the war and exile for the rest of his life. Back home in Bavaria his parents paid the price of his desertion. Dachau.

Sometime after the surrender, a letter reached my father in Hamburg. I've no idea how. Werner asked if he could find his parents. My father requested leave, surprisingly got it, and set off. Hamburg is nowhere near Bavaria, so the journey was south to Dachau across the American Zone, where he found Werner's parents alive if not actually well.

The implication of this journey did not hit me until years later. My father, who talked often about his war, had travelled the length of the Allied zones to a German concentration camp in the first weeks of peace. I have no single memory of him telling me what had gone on there, but given that the man would answer any question, buy you any book you might ask for, I have to conclude that this is why I have known about the German murder machine for as long as I can remember.

Aged seventeen or so I was surprised to find that I was an oddity in this respect.

Spring 1964 or '65. I had volunteered for a weekend filmmaking course at a country house in darkest Derbyshire—you may imagine what pretensions this imbued me with. After a day of shooting scripts by me that make Magical Mystery Tour look logical, we all sat down to watch what films the staff had brought for us.

La Jetée by Chris Marker. (I defy any writer to shuck off the influence of this film) and Alain Resnais's *Nuit et Bruillard*—the death camps in colour. Told me nowt I did not know, but told it in colour. Some of my fellow students wept. One turned to me and asked why she had never been told about this.

Well, one reason might be the willingness of any culture to accept and consider what had happened. Primo Levi was one of the first survivors of Auschwitz to write about it, in *Se questo è un uomo* in 1947. The book sold 1500 copies. Nobody wanted to know. Less than ten years later Resnais made his film—the French government tried to get it banned. Still nobody in power wanted to know . . . and, as Robert Littell remarked to me on a panel a few years ago, nobody thought they would be believed anyway. By the 1960s that had changed and a deeply disturbing book, *Treblinka* by Jean-François Steiner, became a bestseller.

Such is the operation of memory that when I came to watch *Nuit et Bruillard* again whilst writing *A Lily of the Field* I was surprised to find that it records, however briefly, the Ladies' Orchestra of Auschwitz. I had stored this memory, untapped for forty years and more.

Writing about Auschwitz, and I might add this novel depicts it for less than twenty-five pages, is asking to be shot down in flames. One American blogger described *A Lily of the Field* as delivering "Auschwitz attenuated, Los Alamos lite"—I thought about this—who wouldn't?—and then I googled all his other book reviews. He'd reviewed ten books in a fortnight and I stopped thinking about what he had said. I can't be arsed with skim-readers. Read seriously or watch reality TV. In the words of Prof. Brian Cox, "I don't want you! Switch to ITV!" But . . . better critics by far have mapped the shifting ground rules . . . Adorno's "Nach Auschwitz ein Gedicht zu schreiben ist barbarisch" (After Auschwitz to write, a poem is barbaric.) is often quoted, and in Adorno's further writing often qualified. George Steiner summed up succinctly why I wanted to write this book:

"We now know that a man can read Goethe or Rilke in the evening, that he can play Bach or Schubert, and go to his day's work at Auschwitz in the morning."

He can.

And it's still shocking.

In 2005, there was some remembrance of the liberation of Auschwitz by the Russians in January 1945—Primo Levi was among those so liberated. A neighbour, far younger than I, asked me, "How long do we have to keep going over this?"

I was tempted to say "as long as there's a single living survivor," but it would have been the wrong answer anyway. There is no right answer. And there have been poems after Auschwitz and doubtless poems about Auschwitz—and there is as Imre Kertész put it, just a couple of years before winning his Nobel prize, a "holocaust conformism, along with a holocaust sentimentalism, a holocaust canon and a system of holocaust taboos . . ." As I said earlier, expect to be shot down in flames.

Another Israeli writer, Michal Gavron, herself the child of an Auschwitz survivor, gave me another reason why we will "keep going over this," why writers will go on writing about Auschwitz . . . "How to go on living in a world that has turned into the enemy. With fear stamped into the blood . . . How to live within the world and outside it."

And in that last clause I think she just gave any thinking novelist a theme for a lifetime's work.

But here's another reason, another theme. Primo Levi again, somewhat towards the end of his life: "Everybody is somebody's Jew, and today the Palestinians are the Jews of the Israelis."

As apt now (2024) as it was when first uttered. Everybody is somebody's Jew.

Acknowledgements

Gordon Chaplin

Becky Brand

Zoë Sharp

Beatrix Schnippenkoetter

Peter Blackstock

Clare Drysdale

Clare Alexander

Mandy Rice-Davies

Barbara Eite

Marcia Hadley

Sarah Teale

Ann Alexander

Emily Burns

Alicia Burns

Elizabeth Cook

David Mackie

Amy St. Johnston

Ion Trewin

Mike Ripley

Giuliana Braconi

Nick Lockett

Pile Wonder

Bruce Kennedy

Patrizia Braconi

Ugo Mariotti

Gianluca Monaci

Nazareno Monaci
Tim Hailstone
Kevin O'Reilly
Ayo Onatade
Sarah Burkinshaw
Morgan Entrekin
Amy Hundley
Joaquim Fernandez
Nicola Bryant (& Nev)
Lewis Hancock
Justina Batchelor
Lesley Thorne
Deb Seager
Karen Duffy
Cathy Ace
Frances Renwick
Maggie Topkis
Jane Menelaus
Miriam Margolyes
Emanuele Paci
Valentina Memmi
Cosima Dannoritzer
Zuzanna Budziarek
Jerzy Kosinski
Max Bialystock
Aneta Malinowska
Magda Zarnecka
Dido & Tosca
Carole Teller
&
The Salmagundi Club NYC